FRACTURED TIME

BOOK 1 OF THE FRACTURED TIME TRILOGY

MICHAEL D'AMBROSIO

ISBN
978-1-958690-83-3 (Paperback)
978-1-958690-84-0 (eBook)
978-1-964982-18-2 (Hardcover)

TABLE OF CONTENTS

CHAPTER 1

STRANDED

Vesula was an alien planet with mountainous terrain, forests, and oceans, teeming with prehistoric and mythical creatures. On a distant mountain was an ominous castle. The overcast sky added to its sinister presence.

In the surrounding valleys, a vicious war waged beyond a wide moat surrounding the castle between hundreds of Drachma (troll-like creatures) in black leather, armor and axes, and shape-shifters in animal skins with primitive weapons. The orc-like creatures were controlled by the castle's owner, a wizard named Ruger, who delved in black magic and the shapeshifting tribes that were led by wise men, who sought to end Ruger's reign of terror.

Inside the castle, the walls, floor and ceiling consisted of ebony blocks of stone. Torches mounted on the wall in iron brackets illuminated the dreary room with the flickering light of the flames. One wall of a chamber on the upper floor of the castle was lined with pairs of iron rings (for securing prisoners) mounted shoulder high. In the middle of the room was a, wooden table. On the table was an ornate, silver chest.

Gorith and Pirocles, two apprentice wizards in hooded cloaks, dragged an elderly male prisoner in a torn, blood-stained robe into the chamber.

The prisoner was badly beaten with many cuts on his arms and chest. Pirocles carried a leather sack with him as well. The wizards secured the prisoner to two of the iron rings on the wall with leather straps.

Also appearing from another doorway in a dark cloak with a long scraggly beard was Ruger. Pirocles and Gorith respectfully genuflected before Ruger. Pirocles then handed over the sack to Ruger.

"So, you finally captured a guardian with a device," uttered Ruger sarcastically.

"There aren't many of them left and they rarely leave their confines," grumbled Pirocles.

Ruger removed a hi-tech device from the sack and studied it. It had two small screens and two keypads. Leather straps dangled from the device, designed to be worn on the back of the wrist. He approached the prisoner and yanked his hair. "What is this weapon?" he demanded to know.

"It's not a weapon," muttered the prisoner feebly. "It's for transportation."

Ruger stared at him with disdain and commented mockingly, "Is it now?" He placed his hands on the man's temples and closed his eyes. Pirocles and Gorith observed as the strain on Ruger's face indicated his intense concentration. The prisoner shuddered until Ruger removed his hands. He turned to his apprenticesand announced, "I have all I need from him."

Ruger strapped the device onto his left arm. The device startled him with three beeps and various illuminating lights. On the device, the first small screen displayed the planet Earth with a red dot where Philadelphia was located. The second small screen showed Vesula - an orange planet with two rings around it. It had a dot on it as well.

"Soon our enemies will be gone from this world and the whole planet will be ours to control!" declared Ruger.

"And that is just the beginning," added Pirocles.

Gorith was suspicious of the device and questioned Ruger, "Are you sure this isn't a trap, master?"

"Silence, you fool!" Ruger shouted at him. "Do not ever question me again or else!" He left the chamber by way of a dark stairwell.

Pirocles removed a short dagger from under his cloak and approached his captive. The prisoner struggled to raise his head and face Pirocles. "Looks like you lose, my friend," Pirocles taunted the man.

"It is you who has lost," the prisoner uttered, barely audible. "You are about to seal your own fate."

Incensed by the man's audacity, Pirocles slit the man's throat with the dagger. The prisoner's robe became soaked in blood. Soon, the man ceased breathing and died.

Gorith stepped in front of Pirocles, troubled by the man's words. Pirocles was unconcerned and nudged him aside as he approached the stairwell.

"What did he mean by that?" questioned Gorith.

Pirocles paused at the entrance. "Just a dying fool's last words," he answered with a snicker.

"I don't like this at all," complained Gorith. "What if it is a trap?"

"You worry too much. That's why I am Ruger's favorite student," replied Pirocles as he exited the chamber. Gorith grit his teeth and followed.

On the castle's rampart, Ruger stared down at the battlefield with the hi-tech device on his left arm. Gorith and Pirocles emerged atop the ramparts from a small, arched doorway. They watched the battle as well. Ruger aimed the device at the sky and pressed a button. The device made a series of beeps and the displays blinked. Ruger gazed down at the battlefield and laughed sadistically.

"The council will regret the day they turned their backs on me," Ruger bellowed. "Now, I will have my revenge!" Pirocles nodded to Gorith with a sinister grin. Gorith frowned and looked away uneasily.

A luminous cloud formed in the sky over the castle and grew. Lightning struck the cloud from several directions, fueling its growth.

The combatants on the field saw the display in the sky. The human shape-shifters ceased fighting and fled. The Drachma retreated inside the castle, also fearing what was happening overhead.

Ruger raised his arms in triumph. "My return to power has begun!" he announced confidently. All three wizards exited the rampart with Ruger leading the way.

— X —

Billy Brock waited patiently on the porch for the cab as rain fell steadily in the early morning darkness. In one hand, he held an eight-by-ten picture and in the other, his leather briefcase. A Yellow cab stopped in front of the house, catching his attention.

Billy stepped off the porch into the driveway and paused by a trashcan. He glanced at the picture of himself and his former fiancée one last time with a scowl. "Sayonara, bitch," he muttered under his breath. He lifted the lid and fired the picture into the trashcan. The sound of shattered glass in the can brought a contented smile to his face. Billy splashed through the puddles in the driveway and climbed inside the cab.

"What terminal sir?" asked the driver.

"C, please," he replied. Billy stared at the passing streetlights as the cab sped away. He looked younger than twenty-four with his wavy blonde hair, baby face and lean figure. Underneath his London Fog raincoat, he was dressed casually in a turtleneck sweater and corduroy pants for a business presentation in Philadelphia. Billy recalled his disastrous wedding a few weeks earlier. Charlene, his long-time girlfriend and fiancée, left the church just as the ceremony started without saying a word to anyone. He hadn't seen or heard from her since. Biting his lip in frustration, he realized it was just one of many problems in his life of late.

At the engineering firm where he worked, he was overwhelmed with extra duties of late. To make matters worse, his boss assigned a new software engineer to join him on this trip. The company never had more than one field engineer on staff and, with major cutbacks in the works, the writing appeared to be on the wall for him. *It's just a matter of time before they let me go. What the hell am I gonna do then?* fretted Billy.

His boss directed him to meet the engineer at the airport and to be cooperative, whatever that meant. He opened his briefcase and thumbed through the pages for the printed email. *What's this guy's name- Nichols? Yeah, that was it – P. Nichols formerly of CAE Corporation,* he callously recalled. Billy crumpled up the email and threw it on the floor of the cab.

There were few delays on the way to Logan International Airport at five-thirty in the morning. Traffic was fairly light and, with a gloomy weather forecast for the next few days, Billy was more than happy to get out of town. The rain grew more intense as the cab parked in front of the airport terminal. Billy got out and glanced up at the sky. Rain splashed off his face and streamed down his neck. Oddly, he didn't care. He had a strange feeling that it was going to be one of those days. Billy paid the driver and entered the terminal.

After passing through the security checkpoints and monitors, he continued down the crowded concourse to the gate and checked in at the counter. He picked up a newspaper and noticed two women sitting at the end of a row of seats. One of the women wore tight jeans and a sweater, standing at about five-foot ten-inches tall with long, dark hair. She carried a red satin jacket, embroidered with lettering for a rifle club tournament. Impressed, Billy figured she was about twenty-two.

The other woman had long, auburn hair in a ponytail, bell-bottom jeans, floral-patterned blouse and boots. She also had a satin jacket, which she carried over her arm. It was black with gold trim and lettering, from a martial arts tournament. She was tall and shapely, making her all the more alluring to him. The two were engaged in a spirited conversation as Billy ogled them.

The woman with the pony tail turned and her eyes met Billy's. She hesitated for a moment and then smiled at him. Billy blushed over the incident and retreated to a secluded seat.

"Flight 637 is now boarding zones 3 and 4 for Philadelphia," announced the stewardess from the podium. Billy got in line with his briefcase and newspaper in hand. He browsed about the seating area and wondered which one of the many faces could be Nichols. He'd surely find out soon.

The line moved quickly and, once on board, Billy removed his raincoat and stowed it in the overhead compartment. He sat down and placed his briefcase underneath the seat. The plane was only half full, and boarding was nearly complete. No one took the seat next to him and he pondered the possibility that Nichols would miss the flight.

A well-dressed African-American couple, Dr. Robert "Doc" and Maggie Smith, took their seats in front of Billy. The man was in his middle fifties, bald, somewhat muscular and wore a suit. The woman had thick, black, shoulder-length hair tied back in a ponytail. She wore a black, mid-length skirt and matching vest with a white blouse underneath. Billy glanced at the man and recalled seeing him before. He opened his newspaper to the Sports section and disregarded the thought.

"Flight 637 for Philadelphia; last call for boarding, all zones," the announcement came over the PA system once more. Penny Nichols hurried down the corridor to gate C-29. She stood about five feet-six inches tall and was petite with shoulder-length brunette hair. A young, male attendant closed the door to the jet way and returned to the counter. He noticed Penny rushing toward him and rolled his eyes.

"Wait, I'm coming!" Penny shouted. She stopped abruptly and presented her boarding pass to the attendant. "Please don't let me miss my flight. My boss will fire me," she pleaded.

The attendant picked up the phone. "I've got one more – seat 21B," he said passively. Penny leaned against the counter and listened anxiously. "Thanks, Captain. I'll send her back."

"Yeah, you made it – just barely," he said as he scanned her boarding pass.

"Thank you so much," said Penny excitedly.

The young man opened the door to the jet way. "You'd better hurry before the pilot changes his mind." Penny rushed down the jet way. Now that she made the flight, she pondered her boss's last words to her: Don't worry. Mr. Brock, is quite a character. You'll be fine with him.

This guy had better be something special, she thought bitterly. *Traveling wasn't part of my job description.* Penny hurried inside the plane and turned down the aisle. She felt uncomfortable as everyone glared at her for delaying the departure.

Billy was engrossed in the newspaper when Penny settled into her seat and opened her briefcase. He looked up and was captivated by her brown eyes. "Good morning, ma'am. Close one, huh?" he said politely.

"Good morning, sir. It sure was." She pretended to browse over her notes and summoned her courage. "You wouldn't happen to be Billy Brock, would you?"

"I certainly am," said Billy as he put down the paper. "You're not Miss Nichols, by chance, are you?"

"Why yes, I am. I'm the new software engineer from CAE Corporation. I'm here to assist you on your sales presentation."

"I don't mean to be rude but I really wasn't expecting a woman."

"Well, this is a business trip, so don't get the wrong idea," Penny mentioned abruptly.

Billy was embarrassed by her implication. "I'm good with that. I just wasn't aware they hired a female engineer; that's all," he said innocently.

"I want us to stay focused on this presentation. It's my first trip with the company and I don't want any problems, okay?" she continued.

Billy became annoyed with her interpretation of his civility. "I got it already – strictly business." Penny realized that her response didn't come out the way she intended by the tone of Billy's voice. She focused on her paperwork.

Billy looked out the window and watched the terminal fade from view as the 757 ascended into the rainy sky. He opened the newspaper and browsed at the front page. A picture on page two caught his attention. It was the man sitting in front of him – Dr. Robert Smith. Billy read the accompanying article.

A leading scientist in the field of physics, Dr. Smith discovered an energy source, believed to be the first real evidence to support the existence of portals in space. "Although it isn't clear what kind of portal this source could represent, it's an amazing first step in understanding the cosmos," says Smith. Several other renowned scientists have worked with Dr. Smith in an attempt to understand when and how this source appeared at the edge of our Solar System."

Wow! This guy's into some cool stuff, thought Billy.

Penny glanced at the paper and saw the article. "Can I borrow that for a moment, please?"

Billy pointed it at her and mumbled, "Have at it." Penny stowed her briefcase and took the paper from him. She scanned the article and flipped to the next page for the remainder of it.

"You should see these pictures, Maggie!" Doc said to his wife beside him. "I think we'll have an opportunity to explore this little speck of hope real soon."

Maggie leaned over the armrest and peered at the drawings on her husband's lap. "How so?" she asked.

"Joe Miller is working with NASA to see what kind of probe is available to gather data on the energy source for us. He expects to have an answer for me by the time we get to Philadelphia."

Maggie noticed a picture of a colleague of Doc's, Dr. Nikolai Athos, on top of a mountain with two other individuals. "Hey, there's your friend, Athos! What's he up to?"

Doc pointed at the picture's backdrop. "He's in the Appalachian Mountains, collecting seismic data. Eight years ago, he postulated a theory that ancient civilizations like the Incas, Mayans and Sumerians, didn't become extinct as many believed. He theorized that these civilizations might have somehow slipped into a time portal or alternate dimension; kind of a relocation. His theory wasn't accepted very well by the scientific world and they labeled him an 'eccentric'."

He flipped to another picture of Athos in front of a pyramid in Central America. "Back then, I believed in the existence of portals," he related, "but I never thought about the possibility of moving a whole civilization through one and the existence of parallel universes wasn't something I could accept based on any of the data he produced."

"So maybe there's something simpler to that theory like a tractor beam from an alien spaceship behind the disappearance of those civilizations," Maggie suggested.

"Now why would you say that?" he asked, curious.

"Imagine if someone up there could focus a tractor beam through a portal? They could pull us through it and maybe send us to another part of the universe."

"I doubt it. Can you imagine how much power it would take to execute something of that magnitude?" he scoffed. "Since we know very little about altered or 'fractured' time, Athos' theory sounds ludicrous. At this juncture, though, we can't discount it as the consequence of a portal either."

"Could it be a bad thing for us?" Maggie countered.

"I don't know. That little energy source might also be a doorway to another part of the universe. If so, then for whom, why and where?"

"This sounds fantastic, Doc! Imagine the possibilities."

"Yes," he replied. "And when we send the probe up, I hope to acquire enough data to provide some of the answers we're looking for."

Billy eavesdropped and was impressed with their conversation. Penny handed him his newspaper and stood up in the aisle by Doc and Maggie. Billy wondered what she was up to and listened intently.

"Excuse me. I'm Penny Nichols. I used to work with CAE," Penny said politely.

Maggie looked up and immediately recognized her. "Well, hello, Penny. It's good to see you."

Doc was pleasantly surprised and shook her hand. "Well, young lady, it's been a few years."

"You remember me, Dr. Smith!" she blurted. "I'm flattered."

"Sure, I do! You saved our Euripedes satellite project in Florida with your software program."

What the hell! She is a ringer, thought Billy frantically. *I'm doomed!*

"I never worked with anyone who knew software programming like you. We kicked butt together on that orbital thrust control issue," remarked Maggie.

"Yes, we did," Penny acknowledged.

"That software package you developed has carried the program for us. I could never thank you enough," said Doc gratefully.

"Thanks, Dr. Smith. Well, I just wanted to say hello."

Doc handed her his card. "Give me a call sometime. I could use your expertise on a new project."

"I sure will. It was nice seeing the two of you again."

"You, too, Penny."

"Take care and stay in touch," added Maggie. Penny sat down and retrieved her briefcase from under the seat.

Billy stewed as he considered the repercussions of Penny's affiliation with Dr. Smith. *No wonder they brought her in to replace me*, he thought. *She has contacts in the space program.*

Penny stowed the card and browsed over her notes. She reminded Billy of Charlene with her demeanor – bossy and arrogant. Billy recalled the time he spent with Charlene and tortured himself that their failed relationship was somehow his fault, but how?

Penny placed her hand on his arm and asked nicely, "Can we talk about this presentation, Billy?"

"What's the problem?" he countered.

Penny felt foolish for asking but persisted, "I really need to understand what you're proposing to these people."

"Here's how it works: We'll go in and I'll brief them on the system," he instructed her. "You'll give details on the software if they ask and that's it. There's nothing to it."

Penny tapped her foot and fought back the urge to snap at him. She counted to three and took a deep breath. "I was sent on this trip for a reason so there's obviously something to it," Penny reminded him.

"Maybe Epstein wanted to make sure you're capable of taking my place before he lets me go," Billy responded sarcastically.

Penny was baffled by his remark. "What are you talking about?"

"Come on, Penny, they only hired you because you're a woman and they're trying to save money."

Penny was insulted by Billy's remarks. She tried to keep her voice low and responded, "That's bull and you know it. I was hired because I'm good at my job."

"And, of course, they picked you to put me out of a job because you're the company's savior – the sure thing," Billy taunted.

Penny was appalled and hurt. "I don't believe that for one second. You're just paranoid."

"It doesn't matter what you believe," Billy responded tersely. He turned his head away from her and stared out the window.

Maggie overheard their squabble and stood up to rebuke Billy. Doc grabbed her arm and nodded for her to sit down. She reluctantly obeyed.

Penny covered her face with her hand to hide her tears. She wondered if taking this job was a mistake, especially since she was never good with office politics.

The plane started its descent but then shuddered violently. Everyone became alarmed. "What was that?" snapped Billy as the plane rocked again.

The cabin filled with the whispers of concerned passengers. Penny became frightened. "Something's wrong with the plane, Billy. We're gonna crash."

Billy saw the tears in her eyes and felt bad for her. "There's nothing wrong with the plane," he said calmly. "It's just a little turbulence."

Penny wiped her eyes with a tissue and felt embarrassed. "I'm sorry," she said. "I didn't mean to bother you."

"It's no problem," replied Billy. He stared out the window and watched the clouds change from gray to green pastel. The ocean below looked distorted and frothed.

Doc peered out his window uneasily. "This isn't ordinary turbulence. Something's happening to us!" he uttered to Maggie. She clutched his arm and gazed out the window, too.

Billy overheard Doc's remark and worried that this had something to do with his discovery. Two bells chimed from the speakers, followed by the captain's voice. "This is your Captain speaking. Please remain seated with your seatbelts on. We're experiencing rough turbulence which should dissipate shortly."

"See, there's nothing to worry about," whispered Billy.

He can be civil when he wants to, thought Penny as she glanced at him appreciatively.

— ✕ —

Inside a hot, steamy cavern, a grotesque alien witch stared with great concern into a boiling cauldron. She chanted an incantation and dropped small pieces of dried flesh into the pot. The witch, Diomedes, was part human and part alien, resembling a reptile with her thick tail reaching the ground and her ears pointed. She was over six-feet tall and had piercing, black eyes. Red mist formed over the cauldron, revealing the illusion of a young man with a sword. In the illusion, the man attacked Diomedes and beheaded her. He then pursued a cloaked wizard through a castle. Diomedes shrieked in anger.

Four cloaked wizards entered the cavern and stood before her. One of them, Ruger, was the wizard in the mist. When the mist cleared over the cauldron, the illusion vanished. "Ruger, you bumbling fool, you've started a chain of events that will lead to our destruction," Diomedes chided.

Ruger, the elder wizard, wiped sweat from his brow and looked befuddled by her accusation. "But how can that be?" he asked.

"A stranger will destroy both of us unless you stop him soon."

"Where is he now?" questioned Ruger, showing little concern.

"He's on his way here, thanks to your incompetence!"

"One man is not to be feared," Ruger declared confidently.

Diomedes pointed a crooked, bony finger at two of Ruger's companions. She uttered an incantations in an alien language. Blue smoke engulfed the two men. When it cleared, their faces were eerily similar to a beetle's head and their hands withered into leathery paws. They quivered and groaned feebly like farm animals.

Ruger was horrified but struggled to maintain his composure. "Silence!" he ordered the squealing wizards. The abominations promptly obeyed.

"What would you have me do, Diomedes?" he asked humbly.

"Can you control the device yet?"

Diomedes chest plates opened and two tentacles emerged, coiling around the two cursed wizards. The tentacles pulled the squealing creatures into the chest cavity and devoured them. Ruger was horrified.

"I need more time," he pleaded.

"Thanks to you, we don't have time. Find this stranger and kill him or you'll join your friends!"

"I will send the planet's own creatures after him immediately." He and his remaining companion Pirocles fled the cavern, Diomedes howled and retreated behind columns of flames.

Ruger hurried up the stone steps to his castle, followed by Pirocles. They entered the main chamber, lit well by torches along four walls. The chamber had several wooden doors along two of the walls. The wizards proceeded to a circular stone stairwell which rose through one of the castle's towers. When they reached the top, they entered the chamber with the ornate chest.

The chest was encrusted with rubies along the rim of the lid. Ruger approached the chest and opened it. He reached under his robe for a small sack.

"If we don't dispose of this man quickly, Diomedes will curse us, too," complained Pirocles.

"Don't you think I know that, you fool?" uttered Ruger. He sprinkled dust from the sack into the chest and watched as a plume of white smoke rose in the air. Within the smoke appeared an image of Billy and Penny exiting the plane. Ruger laughed at the image. "That young boy is no match for the creatures of Vesula. They'll be ready when he arrives."

Outside the castle, shape-shifter men in animal skins, armed with spears and lances, fought against Ruger's demonic minions. The hillside behind them was littered with corpses of both armies. Pirocles watched from high up in the tower and panicked. "The soldiers have driven the minions back inside the castle," warned Pirocles.

"I don't need these distractions right now. Summon more help," Ruger ordered him. Pirocles bowed and left the chamber. Ruger vanished into a transparent field against the stone wall.

He emerged inside a dark cave and uttered a brief incantation. Torches along the entire length of the cave suddenly burned brightly. The cave consisted of a clay floor and stone block walls with a soil ceiling enmeshed with the roots of trees. Ruger followed the cave to a flight of earthen stairs. He ascended them and emerged unharmed from a large fire in the middle of a massive cavern.

Hundreds of Neanderthals gathered in the cavern and were startled by his appearance. The creatures were ape-like in appearance with protruding jaws and long teeth. They warily approached him with crude weapons, poised to attack. Ruger pointed at one of the creatures and shouted a spell. The creature burst into flames. It shrieked and rolled about the floor in desperation until it burned to death. The other Neanderthals became frightened and backed away.

"You will bow to me now!" Ruger ordered defiantly.

One of the creatures raised its spear to attack. Ruger hissed and pointed his finger at the creature. It burst into flames, screaming in agony until its death as the other did. The remaining Neanderthals bowed obediently.

Ruger projected an illusion on the wall of Billy exiting the jet. He then displayed a Neanderthal attacking Billy and killing him. He entered the fire and descended the stairs to the cave below.

— ⧗ —

As the plane descended, Billy stared out the window in awe at majestic mountains and green forests. He was baffled by their presence on the east coast.

The plane shuddered again and lurched downward. Passengers panicked and cried. "Please remain seated. The captain is handling the situation," the stewardess announced sternly over the loudspeaker. The passengers reluctantly quieted down.

Billy saw the frightened look in Penny's eyes. "What's wrong?" he asked. "It's just turbulence."

"I'm scared, Billy! I don't want to die?" Billy reluctantly placed his arm around Penny's shoulders. "Thank you," she said appreciatively and nestled against him.

How could I be so cruel? I should be mad at Epstein, not her, Billy thought. He brushed Penny's bangs away from her eyes. "Don't worry. We'll be okay," he assured her.

"We're gonna crash," she fretted. "I just know it."

"It's only turbulence," Billy explained. "Haven't you ever flown before?"

"No, I don't travel much."

"Pretend it's a roller coaster," he suggested.

"I don't like roller coasters, either," Penny replied, embarrassed.

"Gee, you must not be much fun on a date," teased Billy.

Penny looked up at him sadly and nuzzled closer to him. "I don't date very often either," she said dejectedly. Billy was amused by her comment.

The cabin pressure in the plane decreased as it descended to a lower altitude. Penny felt safe in Billy's arms. She hooked his arm in hers and wondered if a friendship might work out between them.

The airport came into view and the plane circled for a landing. It shuddered again, despite the low altitude. Doc stared out his window with a grave expression. Maggie looked down at her lap with her hands clenched and prayed. The plane jolted again and the overhead racks opened, spilling pieces of luggage onto the floor. Many of the passengers were frightened and cried out in fear.

The airport and runway were wrecked as though a high-magnitude earthquake had struck. There was no sign of the surrounding city and suburbs which should have surrounded the airport. The plane touched down on the fragmented sections of cement and taxied to the terminal.

Billy placed his hand under Penny's chin and lifted her head. He looked into her eyes and felt a connection with her. "I told you everything would be alright," he said confidently.

Penny squeezed his arm affectionately. "Thank you so much for being patient. It means a lot to me."

Billy was touched that Penny appreciated his concern for her. "I'm sorry if I sounded like a jerk earlier," he explained apologetically. Penny smiled and released her hold on his arm. She was satisfied to be treated with a little dignity.

Billy peered out the window and was stunned by the terrible condition of the airport. The terminal was severely damaged and the south end disappeared into the ground. At the north end, the upper part of the tower had collapsed. The tarmac was an array of upheaved concrete sections.

Billy hid his concern from Penny as the plane taxied to a stop. Everyone on board breathed a collective sigh of relief as the plane's engines shut down and tensions eased. Most of the passengers in their anxiety failed to notice the damaged terminal. They scurried about the aisle, picking up their belongings.

Outside the plane, the low cloud ceiling was an eerie green hue. The wind gusted and lightning frequently flashed across the sky. The plane rocked again from a series of tremors and the remainder of the compartment doors popped open throughout the plane. Passengers stumbled about the aisle. An elderly man gashed his head open on the corner of one compartment door when he fell forward. "Someone help my husband, please! He's hurt," shouted his frantic wife. One of the stewardesses urgently pushed through the crowd and made her way down the aisle with a first aid kit.

Penny stood up but Billy grabbed her arm. "Stay here until we're sure it's safe to move," he instructed her. Penny obediently sat down and put her seatbelt back on. As if on cue, the landing gears collapsed and dropped the plane onto its belly. It tilted onto its left side as it slid off the tarmac and down a muddy slope. Passengers were tossed across seats and into the aisle.

Penny trembled and placed her arm around Billy's chest. When the tremors finally subsided, the plane was deathly silent.

"See what I mean," remarked Billy, "You never know what could happen."

"So, you think you have everything figured out, huh?" she remarked disappointedly.

"Almost. But I haven't figured you out yet," he kidded.

She forced a smile and quipped, "And you never will."

"Does anybody know what the hell is going on here?" exclaimed an irate passenger sarcastically. Billy heard fragments of sentences with "earthquake" and "demolished".

"We've crossed over, Maggie!" said Doc excitedly.

"What do you mean 'crossed over'?"

"You'll see when we get off the plane."

Penny looked up at Billy with a concerned expression, "Don't worry. I'll make sure you're okay while we figure out what's going on," he promised.

"Thank you, Billy. I'll try not to be a pest." She wiped her eyes again and looked down. "I didn't mean to get off on the wrong foot with you. I'm terrible at saying what I mean," she said humbly.

"Don't worry about it," he replied.

"Maybe we could have an early dinner together before we fly back tonight. I'd like to get to know you better," she suggested.

Gee, Epstein will kill me if I mess around with his new field engineer. Maybe I should, just to spite him, Billy thought and then responded, "I guess we could. I'll tell you a little about the company and the people in it."

"I'd really like that. We can keep it professional if you like," she offered.

"I'd prefer it that way," he explained. "I'm going through a bad time and relationships aren't my favorite topic right now." Penny grew more comfortable with Billy now that she knew why he reacted the way he did to her.

The plane rocked again, jarring everyone. Passengers screamed as the tumult engulfed them. Penny grabbed Billy's arm and held it tightly. Billy stared out the window in shock as part of the terminal crumbled. The tremors ceased and the plane became silent again.

The pilot, Captain Barnes, stumbled out of the cabin. "Can I have your attention everyone? There's been a major earthquake and the airport is badly damaged. We don't have communication with the tower so I don't have any information for you at this time. Assemble your things together and we'll deplane in an orderly fashion."

"Are we gonna be alright, Captain?" someone shouted from the back of the plane.

"I don't know. In fact, I don't even know where we are. It's obviously not Philadelphia."

Penny squeezed Billy's hand. "Don't worry. You're with me," he assured her. Many of the passengers ranted and babbled about their predicament. Penny felt safe as she clung to Billy. His confidence impressed her, as he seemed unaffected by the chaos around them.

Outside the plane, smoke spewed from one of the engines and the fragmented wing leaked fuel onto the wet soil. "I'll be right back. Don't move," Billy ordered.

"Where are you going?" Penny asked, concerned.

"Don't move," Billy reiterated as he stepped over her. He hurried up the aisle with his attention focused on the emergency exit. "Come back, Billy!" Penny called out.

Billy stopped at the emergency exit and recognized the two women sitting there as the girls from the airport with the fancy jackets. "Excuse me, ladies but it's time for us to get out of here," he announced. He took each girl by the arm and nudged them out of the way. When he attempted to unfasten the hatch door, it wouldn't budge.

The brunette pushed him aside. "Watch out, hero. This is how you do it," she explained. With ease, she unfastened the door and opened it, leaving Billy embarrassed by his ineptitude. Fortunately, two of the flight attendants arrived and assisted in evacuating the passengers through the open hatch. "Any more brilliant ideas," the brunette chided Billy.

"No, I think... Oh, never mind."

Both girls giggled at him. Red with embarrassment, Billy returned to his seat.

Billy took Penny by the hand and helped her into the aisle.

"So why you?" she asked. "Why did you have to be the one to open the door?"

"Because somebody had to do it," he answered. Penny found his remark strange. It wasn't the compassionate response she hoped for.

An elderly couple struggled to retrieve their luggage from the overhead compartment. Billy reached over them and pulled down their suitcases for them. They thanked him and filed up the aisle toward the emergency exit.

"That was nice of you," Penny commented.

Billy shrugged off her compliment. "No big deal."

The passengers exited the aircraft onto the soft, moss-covered soil. They struggled to keep their footing as the rain made traction perilous.

Billy and Penny were among the last to reach the exit. They looked past the captain and stewardesses at giant white cliffs in the distance. "Where's civilization around here?" asked Penny uneasily.

A blond-haired stewardess named Sabrina blurted, "This looks like the Andes Mountains in that movie about the plane crash and…"

"I think you should shut your yap, Sabrina, before you frighten the passengers," Captain Barnes interrupted and chastised her.

Sabrina glared at him. "Like they're not scared already," she replied sarcastically.

"Let's get off the plane first and then we can talk about it," suggested Billy.

The captain glanced at him with a sneer. "Don't tell me how to do my job, boy," he warned.

"Then do it already, won't you?"

Captain Barnes turned his attention from Billy. "Let's get whatever essential supplies we have off the plane now," he instructed the aircrew.

The flight attendants quickly rummaged through the cabinets at the front of the plane.

Billy and Penny exited the plane onto the moss-covered ground. "Will they send someone to pick us up? It's pretty wet out here," asked Penny.

Billy gazed at her as her hair blew in the wind. His impression of her was that, despite the front she put on earlier, she was innocent and caring. "I can see you don't get out much," he kidded.

"What was your first clue, smart guy?" she replied shyly. "You know, Billy, I was thinking…"

"Uh-oh. This could be trouble," kidded Billy.

"Let me finish. Maybe our boss set us up like a blind date," she suggested.

"I doubt it. Epstein is all about business."

"I heard that you were going through a tough time and the trip might do you good. I didn't think it was in reference to me, though."

"Is this like the Soprano's where you're supposed to whack me and dump my body in the swamp? That's one way to create an opening in the company."

Penny punched him in the arm. "That's not nice, Billy."

The rain fell steadily and the air had a biting chill to it. The overcast sky made for a gloomy atmosphere and fog rolled across the tarmac from the forests.

When the captain called for everyone's attention, the passengers anxiously gathered under large leafy trees away from the plane to hear what he had to say.

"Captain, what's happened to us?" asked an elderly man. Just as quickly, several others chimed in with questions and their voices grew louder.

"Please!" bellowed Captain Barnes. "Hold your questions for now."

"What can you tell us?" asked a young woman.

"We lost radio contact with the tower during our approach. Right now, I don't know any more than you do," answered Barnes.

Billy and Penny became disinterested in the captain's speech and gazed at the landscape around them. The treetops, some much higher than the others, covered the mountainsides like a lush, green carpet. Large, flying creatures glided over great white cliffs that rose into the sky like giant behemoths looking down at them.

Penny studied the ruined terminals. "Look at that, Billy. The terminals look like ships sunken in the mud."

"It's like they slid right into the ground," added Billy, worried. Penny shivered and folded her arms against her body for warmth.

"Captain, why don't we get everyone out of the rain first, then we can talk about this," suggested Billy.

"You got any ideas where to go, smart guy?" snapped Barnes.

Doc interceded and suggested, "Why don't we move them inside the terminal."

"That's better than standing out here in the rain," replied Billy. Barnes was skeptical and waited for other suggestions but none came.

Doc and Maggie approached the remaining section of "C" Terminal and slipped through a torn section of steel in the wall.

Penny inquired uneasily, "Do you think it's safe to go inside there?"

Billy led her by the hand and replied, "I think so. At least we can dry off for a while until we come up with a better idea."

Barnes finally relented. "Everyone into the terminal. We'll organize after everyone's had a chance to dry off," he instructed.

Doc and Maggie sat in a row of seats near one of the gates. Billy and Penny slid through the split section of steel wall and walked up the ramp to the gate area. Doc greeted them and invited them to sit down.

Billy was pleased to have a chance to meet Doc, especially after reading the newspaper article about him. "I'm Billy Brock," he said as they shook hands.

"I'm Dr. Robert Smith but Doc is fine. This is my wife, Maggie."

Maggie shook hands with Billy. "It's nice to meet you. I wondered how long they were all going to stand out there in the rain."

"Me, too. Thanks for the support back there."

"Someone had to make a decision. You did well," Doc complimented him.

The jet exploded in a fiery mass and rocked the terminal. A wave of heat spread across the tarmac and warmed the concourse briefly. Everyone scattered away from the crude entrance.

Penny clung to Billy as bright light from the flames flashed inside the terminal and flickered eerie shapes on the walls. "Gee, Penny, I hope you didn't leave anything important on the plane," Billy kidded.

"Always the funny one, aren't you?" she mentioned and then quipped, "I did leave my notes for the presentation under the seat, though."

"If I'm correct in my thinking, I don't believe we're going anywhere. We could be stuck here until we find out who is behind this," explained Doc.

"What do you mean by that?" asked Billy.

"I don't think this is a natural phenomenon. This was precipitated by someone or something."

"Then let's start looking for them," Billy urged.

"You don't understand, Billy. We're not on Earth." Maggie and Penny looked at Doc with shocked expressions.

"Then where are we?" inquired Billy.

"Look up at the sky," Doc instructed. "The answer is up there somewhere."

Billy placed his hands on his hips. "Well, that's just great. How the hell did that happen?"

"We'll talk about this later when I have a better understanding of things," replied Doc. He and Maggie left them to inspect the tarmac.

Many of the passengers were visibly upset, realizing that whatever possessions they left on the plane, were now gone. Outside the terminal, dark smoke billowed from the burning jet high into the sky, adding dismal gray to the green cloud cover.

CHAPTER 2

HIDDEN DANGERS

Billy and Penny exited the terminal and approached a large slab of concrete that was sheltered from the rain by a toppled jet way. "Where are we going?" asked Penny.

"I have to think of a way out of here," Billy replied. He sat on the concrete slab with his back to the forest while Penny stood in front of him with her hands on his knees. Billy removed his sweater and offered it to her. "Here, you need this more than I do."

As Penny put the sweater on, she ogled Billy's shoulders and chest under his t-shirt. She felt an air of confidence growing within her. *I think I'm gonna like this guy*, she thought to herself. "Thank you, Billy. You didn't have to do that," she said appreciatively.

Billy looked across at "B" and "A" terminals. They were all that remained of the airport and "A" terminal had two air traffic control towers located fairly close together; one being much newer than the other.

Penny noticed a fuzzy bush with bright red berries on it behind Billy. She picked one of the berries and studied it. "What do you think about this place, Billy?"

Billy looked distracted as he stared at the air traffic control towers. After a brief pause, he replied, "I don't think staying here is a good idea."

"What could be so bad?" Penny asked, curious about his concern.

"I'm not sure," he said hesitantly. "It's just a feeling I have."

Penny poked him in the side playfully and kidded. "Looks like you're stuck with me after all." Before he could respond, a Neanderthal peered out from the trees behind him. Penny saw the creature and panicked. "Billy, get away from there," she warned and retreated away from him.

The creature emerged from the trees with a wooden club in its hand. A protruding jaw and beady, black eyes highlighted its frightening face. Two long fangs jutting from the upper jaw. Its limbs were muscular and its hands and feet were similar to a human's but leathery.

Unaware of the threat, Billy looked naively at Penny. "What's wrong?"

Penny stared wide-eyed in horror and shouted, "Billy!"

Realizing the fear in her eyes, he instinctively leaped off the slab, fell to the ground and spun around. The creature struck at Billy's head with the club and missed. The club smashed against the slab, sending splinters of rotted wood through the air. Billy sidled away from the Neanderthal as it raised the remaining piece of wood over its head.

"Somebody please help us!" Penny screamed frantically.

Billy crouched in a defensive position. "Get away from here, now, Penny!"

"Run, Billy!" shouted Penny as she retreated further away from the creature. The Neanderthal quickly positioned itself between Billy and the terminal. Billy tried to dodge the creature to his left and then his right but couldn't get past it. The Neanderthal was agile and struck at him again, just narrowly missing his head. Billy tumbled across the tarmac and scurried to his feet.

"Somebody, please help us!" Penny shouted again. Doc and Maggie rushed from the terminal.

The creature forced Billy toward the trees, grunting in low guttural tones. "Come on, Hairball! Let's see what you got," taunted Billy.

Doc and Maggie arrived and were appalled by the sight of the Neanderthal. "It's an Australopithecine – a Neanderthal," exclaimed Doc. He attempted to distract it by waving his arms.

Billy retrieved a tree branch from the edge of the forest. He swung it at the Neanderthal several times and forced it backward. The creature growled and lunged at Billy. He danced around it several times but it cornered him against the jetway. "How about some of this, big boy?" taunted Billy again. He rushed at the Neanderthal and slammed the limb over the creature's head. The limb shattered, sending shards of wood over the creature's hairy body. Unaffected, the Neanderthal grabbed Billy by the neck. With one hand, it raised him up in the air. Billy gasped for air as his feet dangled helplessly.

Captain Barnes emerged from the terminal, armed with a pistol, and rushed toward them. "Get back, everyone!" he ordered.

The Neanderthal slammed Billy to the ground. He lay on his back and struggled to catch his breath. Captain Barnes aimed his pistol and fired three rounds at the creature. The first two rounds struck the creature's shoulder and chest. The third missed and shattered the bark of a tree. The Neanderthal staggered backward and retreated into the forest.

Penny helped Billy to his feet. "Oh, Billy! Are you alright?" she asked.

"I think so," Billy answered hoarsely as he massaged his throat. He extended his hand in friendship to Barnes and thanked him. The two men shook hands.

"I think we'd better stay together from now on in case there are more of those things out there," advised Barnes. The captain left them and returned to the concourse.

"I can't believe it!" Maggie exclaimed. "Did you see that thing?"

"Believe it and don't underestimate it. Neanderthals do have a degree of intelligence," Doc warned.

Billy walked to the terminal with one hand on his hip and the other on his throat. Penny, Doc and Maggie followed close behind. Penny felt sympathy for him as he hobbled ahead of her. "What were you thinking, Billy? That creature could have broken you in half," she chided.

He paused and looked back at her. "Believe it or not, I had a plan."

"You really don't want a piece of that creature. Trust me," warned Doc. "It could crush you."

"The next time me and that creature meet, it'll be a different story. I promise you that," replied Billy defiantly.

Penny laughed at him. "Billy, you are so funny."

"Yeah, I'm a barrel of laughs," he grumbled.

Penny placed her arm around his waist and helped him walk.

The rain slowed to a drizzle. The trees swayed gently as the winds calmed to a light breeze. The air grew noticeably warmer and the fog lifted. When Penny removed Billy's sweater, he couldn't help but notice her shape. He looked away to avoid eye contact as she folded the sweater over her arm. "Boy, what a change in temperature around here over the last hour," Penny complained.

"I can't believe how out of breath I am," Billy remarked as he labored.

"I suspect that there is a higher concentration of methane in the air to oxygen compared to what we have on Earth," Doc explained. "This will take some getting used to."

"What causes that?" Billy questioned him.

"With all the plants, trees and decomposition of creatures, there is likely to be elevated levels of methane."

"And that's all?" Billy inquired, quite interested in his new environment.

"No, there are other natural causes," Doc remarked.

"Can we change the subject? I see where this is going," requested Penny. They returned to the concourse in terminal "C" and sat near the entrance.

"Are you sure you're okay, Billy?" Maggie asked, concerned.

"I'll be alright. I'm just a little bruised right now."

"Please don't try to take on any more monsters around here. I was really worried about you," pleaded Penny.

Billy faced the trees and wiped tears from his eyes. "We'll see," he muttered. Penny crossed her arms and frowned at him.

Doc and Maggie were amused by their haggling. Maggie took a liking to Penny. Doc, on the other hand, preferred not to get involved in other people's concerns.

"So, Doc, what was the new project you were working on? I understand you had an interesting discovery," Penny inquired.

"My colleagues and I discovered an energy source on the edge of the Solar System that we believe is evidence of a portal. I fear that it might have some relevance to what happened to us. The timing is too ironic." Billy sat quietly in pain. He listened as Penny's curiosity inspired more questions.

"Do you have any idea what could have happened to us, Doc?" she asked.

"Yes and no. In simple terms, I think that part of the Earth's landmass, in this case, the airport, was transplanted onto another world. Since we've seen the Australopithecine, I figure it's entirely possible that some anomaly randomly placed pieces of the Earth here, perhaps from random intervals of time. For what reason, I have no idea."

"Or it's a completely different planet in a different phase of development," Maggie suggested.

"That could be, as well."

Billy's curiosity got the better of him. "But Doc, what if other prehistoric creatures are here as well?"

"I dread the thought of those possibilities."

"Is there a chance we could be stuck here forever?" asked Penny.

"I'm afraid so," Doc replied somberly and then he and Maggie left the concourse.

Captain Barnes barked orders at the men and paced about the concourse as if it was his own. His impatient and arrogant attitude didn't sit well with many of the passengers, particularly Billy. "Look at him. He thinks he owns the place," Billy uttered sarcastically.

"I don't trust that guy. There's something about him that bothers me," complained Penny.

"He'll have his day," responded Billy bitterly.

The corridor, which led from the gate to the other end of terminal "C", was dark and sloped downward into the ground. Billy studied it and pondered what resources were available in the shops below. "I need to see if there is a security center is down there. Wait here until I get back," he instructed Penny.

"No way! I'm going with you."

"It could be dangerous," he warned.

"And you think it's safer here?" Penny felt that if she was going to be stranded in a dangerous place, then Billy was the man she preferred to be stuck with. She gazed at him pleadingly.

Seeing her determination, Billy relented. "Okay, you win. Just give me a minute." Billy searched a podium near one of the damaged gates. He found two flashlights in the bottom drawer.

Penny looked down the dark corridor and wondered if she made a mistake. A chill ran down the back of her neck and she instinctively backed away. "Are you ready?" Billy asked and handed her a flashlight

"I guess so," Penny answered, unsure of herself. "What exactly are we looking for?"

"Anything we can use for protection."

Penny followed him down the dark corridor. The eerie silence frightened her and she held on to Billy's belt from behind. "Why is it that you feel compelled to handle everything, Billy?" she questioned him.

"I guess I don't trust anyone else to do what's best for me."

"Maybe you should start," she suggested.

Billy became annoyed with her persistent questions. "As you've already seen, we're going to need protection. Barnes has the only gun and I'm sure he doesn't have many bullets for it."

"So, what kind of weapons do you really expect to find in an airport terminal?" she inquired sarcastically.

"Well, Miss Know-it-all, I hope to find the Security Center and, with a little luck, see if I can get to the firearms. I'd also like to poke around some of the shops for knives, tools and maybe even some food."

Penny realized he was right and was embarrassed. "I'm sorry, Billy. I never thought of the Security Center."

They continued down the corridor, armed only with the flashlights. The corridor grew narrow in many spots and forced them to creep along in a single file. The air was thick with dust and Penny coughed several times. Much of the ceiling in that section of the corridor had collapsed from the weight of the soil. Bits of broken concrete and soil fell randomly and made a faint echo in the corridor. Penny jumped nervously each time pieces of debris hit the floor.

Billy rubbed the back of her neck gently. "Relax. There's nothing to worry about." When he brushed his hand across a low section of concrete, he duplicated the sounds by knocking loose pieces of dirt and stone to the ground. "See that," he said confidently.

"I see it, but I still don't like it," she complained.

Further down the corridor, the sounds of falling debris stopped and the silence became bone-chilling. Penny squeezed Billy's arm tighter for security. They spotted Wilson's Leather Shop that was partially blocked by mounds of debris.

"Wait out here. I'm going to pass some things out to you," instructed Billy.

"Please don't be long," pleaded Penny. "This place gives me the creeps."

"If you need me, just holler. I'll be there in a second." Billy squeezed through the wreckage and crawled inside the shop. He aimed his flashlight through the murky air ahead of him as he cleared the broken front gate. The crushed corpse of a young oriental woman startled him. Her eyes bulged as a large section of ceiling covered her lower torso and legs. Billy scrambled to his feet and nauseously backed away from the body.

When he regained his composure, he focused on the shop. Much of the store's inventory was covered or destroyed by the collapsed ceiling and rear wall. Billy found a bent rack with five leather knapsacks hanging from its hooks. He crammed four of the sacks into the fifth and passed them out through the rubble to Penny. He glanced again at the corpse and wondered if the young woman suffered before dying.

"Are you coming yet, Billy?" Penny called impatiently.

"Yeah, in a minute." Billy scanned the shop one more time and crawled out to the corridor. He took Penny by the hand, much to her relief, and led her through mounds of debris. They searched opposite sides of the corridor and descended further.

Billy craned past metal ductwork and peeked inside a Duty-Free shop. The shelves were empty and the floor was littered with broken bottles. The smell of liquor filled the air. He slid past the ductwork and entered the shop. A male corpse lay on floor nearby with a vacant look in its eyes. Billy never saw dead bodies before and the sight of these corpses didn't sit well with him.

Penny shined her light on broken cement and rebar across from the Duty-Free shop. There was a sign on the wall above it marked 'Security Center'.

"Billy, here it is!" she shouted excitedly.

Penny's scream startled Billy. He turned and banged his head on a piece of dangling conduit from the ceiling. "Ouch!" he groaned as he rubbed his head. "What is it, Penny?"

"It's the Security Center!" she repeated excitedly.

Billy emerged from the front of the Duty-Free shop and eyed the door. It was broken away from the hinges and the twisted doorframe bowed from the weight of the pressing soil above. An I-beam and a long section of ductwork partially obscured their access. "We're in business!" exclaimed Billy. Penny waited expectantly for some sign of appreciation from Billy like a hug or kiss but none came. She became frustrated and wondered what she'd have to do to gain his attention.

Billy tried to squeeze past the obstructions in front of the Security Center but it was impassible. He searched inside the adjacent news shop and found a broken wall in the rear corner. Penny reluctantly followed him and even considered returning to the concourse alone. "Wait out front. I won't be long," he said as he took the bags from her.

"I'm really scared, Billy."

Billy ignored her as he climbed over broken concrete and crawled through the wall.

"I can see this isn't going to work out," she muttered to herself. Shuffling sounds echoed from the lower regions of the corridor and Penny panicked. "Billy!" she called out. The shuffling sounds ceased. "Billy, get out here, now!"

Billy entered the rear of the security facility and spotted the weapons locker at the end of a dusty hallway. He heard Penny's call but disregarded it. When he crept closer to the locker, he discovered a long, steel beam lying across the front of it. One of the three doors was smashed cleanly off and lay on the floor.

Billy ducked under the beam and reached inside the locker. With the aid of his flashlight, he pulled out boxes of ammo and filled two sacks. He returned to the front door and pushed the sacks on top of the ductwork. "Penny, are you there?" he called out.

Penny was relieved to hear his voice. "Of course, I'm here. I heard something moving."

Billy pushed the heavy sacks out to where Penny could reach them. "Take these for me, will you?"

Penny struggled with the sacks. "Can we please go back now?"

"Just chill out," he muttered. "We'll be out of here soon."

Penny glanced in the direction of the shuffling sounds and shuddered. "Hurry up, Billy. I don't like this at all."

"Look, Penny, you wanted to come," he chastised her. "I'm doing the best I can."

Penny left the bags on the ductwork and hid behind a magazine rack. Billy returned to the locker with another empty sack. He retrieved six handguns and placed them inside the sack. When he returned to the front door and pushed the sack out, Penny was furious. "Billy, if you don't get out here right now, I'm leaving without you," she warned.

"Then go on back," he hollered angrily. "I told you this is important stuff."

"And I'm obviously not," she snapped back.

Billy realized that she wanted his affection but was annoyed that she kept telling him what he should do. He disregarded her threat and returned to the locker.

The shuffling sounds resumed and made a hollow echo in the corridor. Penny leaned through the opening in the wall. "Billy, something's coming. Please come out here, now!" she pleaded.

Billy heard her but worked methodically from his knees to pull the rifles from the locker. He maneuvered three of them under the beam and out of the cabinet. "Here I come, Penny," he hollered as he got to his feet.

Penny trembled as something crept closer. She searched the corridor with the flashlight but saw nothing through the dusty air.

Billy slid the rifles out over the ductwork. "Are you still there, Penny."

"Of course, I'm here, you ass! So is something else. Now can we please go?"

"One more trip and I'll be back."

"You idiot!" she cried. "There's something out here and its real close."

Billy paused near the locker and became impatient with her. "You're imagining things, Penny."

"Billy, you stupid son-of-a-bitch!" she cried out, tears streaming down her cheeks.

Billy aimed the flashlight inside the locker again. There was at least a dozen more rifles and a large quantity of ammunition. Then the ground quaked, followed by a low-pitched roar. A section of ceiling and the adjacent wall collapsed on and around the locker. Billy ducked under the beam for shelter but a piece of corrugated steel fell and grazed his head. He reeled from the hit and fell to the ground unconscious.

Penny tumbled to the ground over a fallen rack and dropped her flashlight. It extinguished and rolled a short distance away. "Billy, I need you!" she cried out.

The rumbling lasted about twenty seconds, but was enough to collapse more of the submerged terminal's ceilings and walls. Penny sobbed as she desperately felt the floor for the flashlight. When she found it, she was relieved that it illuminated. From her knees, she scanned the area with the light.

Three battered bodies were exposed from under an HVAC duct that shifted. Penny stared at the faces of the corpses and screamed. "Billy, why are you doing this to me?" she cried as she fell to her knees in despair. When she regained her composure and stood up, the corridor was eerily silent. Not even the shuffling sounds were heard. Tears streamed down her cheeks as she crawled through the debris to the opening in the wall. Panic set in when she found the hallway completely blocked and realized Billy could be dead. "Billy, please say something. Don't leave me like this," she sobbed. Feeling helpless, she fled the area.

Penny burst out of the dark corridor, teary-eyed, and searched the concourse. Everyone stood together, fearing more tremors. Doc and Maggie huddled near the narrow exit from the concourse.

"Doc Smith, where are you?" she cried.

"We're over here, Penny," Maggie answered.

Penny rushed to them. "You've got to help Billy."

"What's happened?" asked Doc, concerned.

"Billy's trapped in the Security Center," she blurted. "There was a tremor and then he didn't answer when I called." Doc took the flashlight from Penny and hurried across the concourse. "He went in through the news shop next door," Penny shouted.

Doc descended alone down the dark corridor. The flashlight dimmed as he followed the footprints on the dust-covered floor. He tapped it against his leg several times and it briefly brightened. When he located the door to the Security Center, he searched for a way in. In the rear of the news shop, he spotted three sacks and several rifles on top of the ductwork. Doc climbed through the hole in the wall and accessed the rear of the Security Center. "Billy, can you hear me?" he called. There were no sounds except for the small pieces of debris that occasionally fell to the floor.

Doc shoved chunks of metal and concrete out of the way and cleared a path to the locker. He shined his dimming flashlight ahead of him and located the top of the firearms locker. After squeezing around a bent section of corrugated steel, he struggled to move the beam that blocked the front of the locker.

Nearby, he found a piece of steel shelving on the ground and used it to pry the beam away from the locker. When he moved it away sufficiently, he found Billy lying motionless underneath. Blood seeped down his face from a cut on his forehead. "Billy, are you okay?" Doc hollered as he tried to rouse him.

Doc's light became dim again. He picked up Billy's flashlight and angrily threw his into the darkness. When he reached Billy, he was relieved to find him alive and only unconscious. Doc attempted to pull him from the locker without injuring him further. "Come on, Billy! You'll have to help me," he urged. He worked feverishly to free Billy from the wreckage. Finally, he dragged him over the debris and into the news shop. He wiped the blood from Billy's eyes with a handkerchief and examined him. As he checked Billy's pulse, Billy stirred.

"Oh, my head. What happened?"

"So, you're still alive," remarked Doc cynically.

"I think so."

"That's twice you almost got killed in less than a few hours," Doc complained.

"Where are we?"

"We're next to the Security Center. Penny sent me to find you."

"I guess I should have listened to her after all."

"Honestly, I think you're pushing your luck," Doc chastised. He saw the firearms stacked on the floor. "What's this all about?"

"I thought this would be a good idea if we had some protection."

Doc helped him to his feet. "Can you walk?"

"I think so."

"There are scared and desperate people back there. If the wrong person got their hands on a gun, it could lead to other problems."

"What do you think we should do?" Billy asked.

"Let's bring back four rifles, four pistols and a limited amount of ammunition? We can leave the rest for later."

Billy picked up two sacks containing the pistols and ammunition. He flexed his arms while holding the sacks and walked toward the corridor. Doc cradled four rifles in his arms. "Take it easy, Billy. We'll go slowly."

"No argument here."

The shuffling sounds returned and grew louder. Several grunts echoed from down the corridor. "I think it's the Neanderthals again. We'd better take cover," suggested Doc.

They retreated to the rear of the shop where Doc took a pistol from one of the sacks and filled a magazine with ten rounds. As soon as he loaded the pistol, he shined the flashlight toward the corridor. Three Neanderthals rushed at him. Doc fired the pistol until its magazine was exhausted. All three Neanderthals fell to the ground dead.

Billy loaded another magazine and handed it to Doc. He reloaded the pistol and waited but no more creatures appeared. "Let's get moving. There could be more of them," Doc suggested.

The two of them struggled with the rifles and sacks but heard nothing more from the Neanderthals. When they returned to the concourse, they placed the weapons discretely in a dark corner. "If you see Penny, tell her I'd like to see her," requested Billy.

"Of course. Now, please try to stay out of trouble."

The fading daylight left the terminal dim except for the glow of four small campfires in the concourse. Doc searched the terminal for Maggie and Penny but Captain Barnes intercepted him. "I heard shots. What happened?"

"Three Neanderthals ambushed us down in the corridor. We killed them."

"You found weapons?"

"Yeah, a few."

"Excellent. We'd better post two sentries in the corridor with a fire to keep an eye on things."

"I agree," replied Doc. "No telling how many more of those things are around." Barnes swore in frustration and then led six men outside the concourse.

Doc found Maggie and Penny near one of the campfires and approached them. "Oh, thank goodness you're back! We were so worried," exclaimed Maggie.

"Where's Billy now?" Penny asked.

"He's back in the corner – a little banged up but he'll be okay."

"Can I see him?"

"Sure. Be gentle with him, though. He's hurting." Penny hurried off.

Maggie kissed her husband on the cheek. "Thanks for helping him, Robert, even if he is a smartass."

"I have a feeling this won't be the last time we have to bail Mr. Brock out of trouble," muttered Doc.

"He's just a kid," Maggie reminded him.

"That's what I mean."

— X —

Billy was pleased when Penny approached. She threw her arms around him and hugged him. "Oh, you big jerk. I was so worried about you."

"What a pair we make?" Billy quipped.

"Please don't ever scare me like that again," Penny begged. "I was worried sick about you."

Billy still didn't understand what she meant. He explained, "I'm sorry but we really needed to get those weapons up here."

"There were dead people down there!" blurted Penny in frustration. "I was terrified."

"I know. I saw a few corpses, too," Billy admitted. "They weren't pretty."

Penny poked a finger in his face. "I mean it, Billy. What you did back there was stupid."

"I'm sorry, already! Can you just let it go?"

Maggie and Doc witnessed Penny's tantrum as they approached.

"I needed you and you wouldn't even answer me. You couldn't be any more inconsiderate than that if you tried."

"Look, Penny, I had to do this!"

"You promised to take care of me," she reminded him sarcastically. "Nice job."

"Come on, Penny. You have to understand," pleaded Billy.

"No wonder you got dumped." She stormed off like a spoiled child to another part of the concourse. Billy was stunned by her aberrant behavior. He also wondered how she knew that Charlene dumped him.

Doc and Maggie approached him. Doc commented, "Ouch. That one hurt."

"I'm sorry, Billy, but I think she really likes you," Maggie said giddily.

"She's got a funny way of showing it," he griped.

"How are you feeling?" asked Doc.

Billy felt the swollen lump with his hand. "I've got a splitting headache."

"Maggie, can you put a few butterflies (stitches) in him?" requested Doc.

Maggie shined the light on Billy's wound and examined it. "I'll have you fixed up in no time."

Billy rested his head on a seat cushion and waited patiently. Maggie opened a first aid box and set it next to Billy's head. Doc shined his flashlight on the wound as she placed three butterfly stitches across the gash on Billy's forehead. She admired her handiwork and said, "That should do it. Now, keep your hands away from it."

"Thanks, Maggie."

"Take it easy for a while. No unescorted trips," advised Doc.

"Believe me; I'll never do that again."

"Just take it easy for a while," Doc urged. He and Maggie left him to consider his predicament. Billy lay awake and wondered about Penny.

— ☓ —

Doc and Maggie sat alone as Doc contemplated what to do next. "Assuming our situation is permanent, are we going to stay here with these people or will we move on to someplace else?" inquired Maggie.

"Is there someplace in particular you have in mind, dear?" he responded.

"I don't know. Maybe there are others that were stranded here as well who can help us figure out what happened. I mean, maybe there is a way to undo this mess."

Doc placed his arm affectionately around his wife. "It'd be a tough trip whichever way we go. You've seen what the surrounding landscape is like."

"I know. Perhaps we can enlist some traveling companions," suggested Maggie.

"Like "

"Perhaps Billy and Penny would want to go."

"Perhaps," he replied, uncertain. "Billy seems ambitious and I'm sure we could use his help. He and Penny do make an interesting couple, so I doubt we'd be bored."

"Speaking of Penny, I think I'll check on her. I'll see you in a while."

"Be careful what you get yourself into."

Maggie assured him, "I know what I'm doing."

— ✕ —

Maggie saw Penny near the entrance to the concourse with tears in her eyes and approached her. "What's wrong?" she asked.

"I was afraid that I'd be alone if something happened to Billy. He's the only person I know and I think he cares about me even if he won't show it."

"If anything should happen to Billy, I'm your friend, too," Maggie told her. "I know it's not the same, but don't feel like you're alone out here."

"Do you think Billy will still talk to me after what I said?" Penny asked sheepishly.

"I think so but that was a cheap shot about being dumped."

"He needed to realize that he hurt me. Maybe, I should see if he learned his lesson." Penny walked away through the dimly lit concourse to find Billy. Maggie was amused by her reaction.

CHAPTER 3

THE CAVERN

Captain Barnes took four men with him and crossed the tarmac to the badly damaged control tower. He cautiously opened the glass door and entered the lobby. There were two sets of stairs with an entrance at the top of one stairwell and at the bottom of the other. He crept down the steps and pushed the door open slowly. Inside, the room was dark and eerily quiet with a rancid odor in the air. The room was a sign-in area for the controllers with a circular desk in the middle. "Give me a flashlight," he ordered and grabbed one from the man behind him. Barnes was keenly aware of the absence of survivors or corpses. "No wonder we didn't get a response during our approach to the airport," he uttered.

"Perhaps they were killed by debris when the upper tier collapsed," suggested Jerry Kraechyk, who was closest to him. Jerry looked like a younger version of Waylon Jennings with jeans, flannel shirt and ponytail.

"There's no debris in here, you idiot," Barnes snapped back.

"I meant outside. Perhaps they escaped before the tower was damaged," he replied sarcastically.

"There should still be some sign of the air traffic controllers around here – dead or alive," Barnes reiterated.

John Finch, a bronze-skinned man in his late forties, was an FBI agent. His wife and two daughters were killed a few weeks earlier in a brutal auto accident. The agency put him on paid leave for three weeks so he could clear his head. Finch didn't understand how that would make things better and, at this point, he really didn't care. "Maybe they fled to another location," suggested Finch.

Simon Berger, a younger fellow, was less rational about the situation and very edgy about it. "Maybe something around here ate them," he suggested.

"Shut up, you fool! You don't know what you're talking about," chastised Finch, fearing that one stupid comment like that could create havoc among the passengers. He shined his flashlight across the rear wall. The tables and file cabinets were smeared with blood. Even the walls were streaked. Finch touched one of the stains and rubbed the blood between his fingertips. "It's still wet," he remarked.

Simon panicked. "Of course, it's still wet! Something just killed them."

Finch grabbed Simon by the throat. They glared at each other threateningly until Barnes separated them. "Easy, girls. Save your strength for the real challenges."

"You barbarian," Simon groaned as he massaged his throat.

"See how long you survive out here, you little weasel," taunted Finch.

"That's enough!" shouted Barnes.

"What are we looking for anyway, Captain?" asked Simon in a raspy voice.

"A radio would be a good start. At least we could try to contact someone for help."

Jerry peered through another doorway with his flashlight. Inside the room were several radio sets and computerized panels. A few of the lights were illuminated on the panels, which indicated that a limited amount of battery backup power was still available. The back half of the room was an inclined slope of rock and gravel, a result of the collapsed wall. "In here, Captain!" Jerry shouted.

When Barnes entered the room, Jerry pointed to the radio sets. "There they are!" he announced excitedly.

Barnes pushed Jerry out of the way and reached for the nearest headset. A feeling of horror swept over him when he realized that the headset was attached to the head of an older man with curly gray locks. He regained his composure and focused on the radio again. "It looks like the radio still works."

Simon volunteered, "I can operate it. I just can't use that headset."

Finch grew more annoyed with the man's cowardice. He removed the head from the headset and threw it in the corner. "Any more problems, weasel?" he bellowed. Simon muttered something at Finch and seated himself. He manipulated the radio's controls as if he had prior experience.

Jerry shined his light in a hole near the collapsed wall and realized it was a tunnel. "Captain, check this out!"

The two men peered inside the dark opening. A pool of blood trailed inside the hole. Faint cries echoed from deep down the tunnel and unnerved them. "This place gives me the creeps," uttered Barnes as he retreated away from the tunnel.

"I'll keep an eye on it until we're ready to leave," Jerry offered and aimed his rifle at the hole.

Barnes returned to the radio and looked over Simon's shoulder. "Five more minutes and we're out of here."

A voice crackled from the radio, "This is Dr. Joseph Miller at the U.S. Naval Observatory. Please identify yourself and your location."

Barnes yanked the headset from Simon and placed it on his own head. "Dr. Miller, this is Captain Barnes, a commercial air pilot. We are located at the Philadelphia International Airport or what's left of it."

"How bad is your situation there?" inquired Dr. Miller.

"Pretty bad. We've encountered some dangerous creatures and we have very little to defend ourselves with. Can you help us?"

"We can't help ourselves. I'm sorry."

"Dr. Miller, what's going on? Is there anyone else we can contact?"

"We haven't had contact with anyone but you so we really don't know the extent of this anomaly."

"What can you tell us?" Barnes asked impatiently.

"We must learn to survive in this environment the best that we can. Good luck to you." The radio went silent.

"What a frigging moron? This ain't 'War of the Worlds'. It's a friggin' airport," shouted Barnes.

"What now, Captain?" asked Simon.

"Let's get the hell out of here!"

As Jerry glanced back at Barnes, a Neanderthal reached out of the tunnel and yanked the rifle from his hands. Jerry fell to the ground and cowered in fear as the creature stood over him. It raised the rifle over its head like a club and swung down at Jerry. Finch instinctively fired three shots at the creature. One shot penetrated its skull through an eye socket while the other two left gaping holes in the throat and cheek area. The Neanderthal struck the ground beside Jerry and died as it fell on top of him. Finch and Barnes pulled the dead creature off of him.

"I think I just crapped myself," Jerry uttered, while trembling.

"We can't let our guard down around these things! They're dangerous," warned Finch.

Barnes glared at Jerry. "And they're obviously a lot smarter than you. What the hell were you thinking?"

Jerry ignored him and picked up his rifle. He looked sullen over the incident and followed the others out of the room. They ascended up the stairs and exited the tower.

The rain stopped but the humidity covered the area like a wet blanket. Simon outran the group as they returned to "C" terminal. "That's right, you little shit, run away," mocked Finch.

"I guess he's had plenty of practice running. I've never seen a bigger chicken," commented Barnes.

When they returned to the terminal, the passengers and aircrew gathered about them. "We're staying put for the night. I want sentries and barriers erected immediately," ordered Barnes.

"You might want to build fires on the perimeter for a defense as well," suggested Finch.

"I want fires on the perimeter as well. Hop to it, people," echoed Barnes.

As everyone dispersed, Doc emerged from the terminal. "What's going on, Captain? Have you found something?"

"We contacted some guy from an observatory on one of the tower's backup radios."

Doc's eyes lit up with hope. "Who was it?"

"Dr. Miller, I think he said."

Doc couldn't believe his ears. "He may be able to help us!"

"No chance," replied Barnes, frustrated. "I spoke with him and he was useless."

"Tell me where the radio is and I'll go there myself," Doc requested. "This is very important."

"You can't go back there. Those creatures are all over the place," Barnes answered.

"But he could be our only hope!"

"If you really want to go back there by yourself, then it's on you," Barnes told him. "They're on the lower floor of the tower in the rear room."

Doc wasn't happy with Barnes' lack of support and trudged away. Finch sensed that Doc might know more than anyone else about their situation and pursued him. "Dr. Smith, can I have a minute of your time?"

"What can I do for you?"

"My name is Finch. I can take you to the radio inside the tower but it's dangerous. We'd be wise to find some means to protect ourselves. Those Neanderthals already have a tunnel inside."

"Weapons are not a problem," replied Doc confidently. Finch followed Doc inside the concourse.

— X —

Penny conversed with some of the women inside the concourse She spotted Doc and a stranger with flashlights near the corner where Billy slept. When she crept closer, she saw them rummage through Billy's sacks. Penny ducked behind a pillar and watched them. Doc handed Finch one of the rifles and three magazines. He loaded a pistol and placed two magazines in his pocket.

Billy heard the click when Finch loaded his rifle and awoke. "Hey, what's going on?" he asked.

"It's nothing, Billy. Mr. Finch and I are going to check on a radio in the control tower."

"The Neanderthals are still prowling the area nearby so we're taking some precautions," added Finch.

"I'll go too, just in case you need backup."

"Maybe you're not up to this yet," Doc suggested.

"I'll be fine."

Doc took another rifle and loaded it for Billy. "Here are three magazines. Do you know how to use one of these?"

Billy ran his hands over the rifle's components. "Not really, but I'm sure I can figure it out."

"I'll teach you on the way," offered Finch.

"Thanks, Mr. Finch. I appreciate this."

The three of them set out for the control tower. Strange noises from the forest kept them on their toes as they crossed the tarmac. Penny watched them from the terminal and wondered where they were going. She kept at a reasonable distance to the men for fear that they wouldn't appreciate her tagging along uninvited.

When the men entered the tower, Penny feared being alone. When she heard tree branches shake and snap, she was sure something lurked there.

Finch descended the stairs with his rifle pointed ahead of him. He held his flashlight against the side of the barrel and scanned the room from the bottom of the stairs. Everything appeared quiet, so he proceeded through the doorway into the rear room. The radio sets were undisturbed since their previous visit, but the tunnel made Finch uneasy. He kicked at the body of the dead Neanderthal for assurance. Billy kept watch behind them and backed down the stairs. He targeted the top of the stairs in case any of the Neanderthals followed.

When Doc saw the radios, he rushed to the closest one and donned the headset. He set his flashlight on the counter and familiarized himself with the controls. Finch took a defensive stance nearby and monitored the tunnel. Billy positioned himself next to Finch and maintained his focus on the doorway to the front room. He glanced back and saw the dead Neanderthal. "What happened to him, Mr. Finch?"

"He stuck his nose where it didn't belong, so I put him down."

"Nice."

"Hello, Joe Miller, are you there? This is Doc Smith. Come in, Joe. Do you read me?" Doc called excitedly into the microphone.

Billy glanced back at the hole and then at Finch. "So, they've been here, too, huh?"

"Yeah. They have one hell of an underground network."

Doc called repeatedly until a familiar voice crackled from the radio: "Doc Smith, is it really you?"

"Yes, it is, Joe. How are you, old buddy?"

"It's bad, Doc. It's worse than we ever thought possible."

"How do you know?"

"Satellite imagery. It seems that several areas were pulled from the Earth and dumped on this old rock."

"Your equipment is still operable?"

"For a short while."

"So, we can map out everything, right?" questioned Doc.

"Not exactly. We only have one satellite to work with. The others don't exist anymore, at least not here."

"So, what happened? Where are we?"

"We're on another world in a prehistoric environment. I suspect that there could be a hodgepodge of life from different time periods here, as well."

"Then we might have gotten caught in a time rift?" suggested Doc.

"I'm not sure. There are foreign elements here, too, that we're investigating. They could be alien or just undiscovered species from our history."

"Maggie and I would consider down with a few friends. Do you have room for us?"

"You really think you can make the trip here?" asked Joe.

"It's worth a try."

"Be careful, Bob. It's a dangerous new world."

"Are you still to the south of us?"

"Yes, we are. We're tracking your transmission as we speak. It seems that we're a little closer, too."

"Thanks, Joe. We'll see you as soon as we can." Doc turned off the radio and looked relieved.

"What do you think?" asked Finch.

Horrible screams from the tunnel interrupted them.

"What the hell was that?" yelled Billy.

"Guess," said Finch somberly. Doc aimed his flashlight into the tunnel but saw nothing.

"That tunnel must run at least a few hundred yards down," complained Finch.

"You think we should go down there?" inquired Billy.

"I think we need to plan for this in case there are more creatures than we're prepared to handle," recommended Finch.

"Maybe you're right," said Doc. "They must be somewhat intelligent if they're taking prisoners alive and selectively killing them."

"That's just wonderful – intelligent cavemen. There's an insurance commercial where the cavemen are intelligent but friendly?" Billy kidded.

"Can it, Billy. This is serious," chastised Doc.

"Sorry. I'm just trying to lighten up the mood around here."

"I've never known that Neanderthals were this aggressive," Doc commented. "It doesn't make sense."

"Could something drive them to behave this way?" asked Finch.

"I don't know. This isn't our world anymore and that puts us at a big disadvantage in regards to animal behavior."

Outside, the trees rustled and a limb snapped. Penny's heart beat faster until she thought it would explode. She rushed to the tower entrance but stumbled over broken pieces of concrete and then fell. Sobbing, she pulled the pumps (shoes) off her feet and threw them toward the trees. As she reached the doors of the control tower, she looked back. There was no sign of the Neanderthals. She paused to catch her breath inside the doorway and closed the door.

Three Neanderthals perched above the doors on top of the overhang. One of them leaped down and shoved the door open, striking Penny in the face and pinning her against the wall. Penny was terrified as blood streamed from her nose. "Billy, help me!" she cried.

One Neanderthal entered the lobby and grabbed Penny by the waist. She struggled but it tossed her over its shoulder and carried her into the forest. The other two creatures leaped down from the roof and followed.

"That's Penny's voice!" Billy exclaimed. Without a second of hesitation, he raced up the steps and out the doorway. He caught a glimpse of the

Neanderthals with Penny and pursued them. By the time he reached the trees, he lost sight of them.

Doc and Finch exited the tower and caught up with him. "Did you see where they went?" asked Doc.

"No, damn it!" he uttered and then hollered, "Penny, where are you?"

Finch and Doc searched through the trees. Billy stood on top of a rock and scanned the forest. "Penny!" he shouted.

"Quiet, Billy!" Finch ordered from a short distance away. Penny's faint cries could barely be heard.

Finch pressed through the bushes and spotted a tunnel beyond the trees. "They went down here, Billy!" Billy rushed past him and descended into the narrow cave.

"Looks like we're going in after all," Finch complained to Doc.

"I'm right behind you."

They entered the tunnel with weapons poised to fire and used their flashlights to guide them down the rocky path.

Billy gripped his flashlight against the barrel of his rifle and pursued Penny's screams. He followed the narrow tunnel as it zigged and zagged, while sloping steeply downward. The horrible screams haunted him as he pondered what dangers lay ahead. The rocky path leveled off and the reality of the surroundings kicked in. Sweat beaded on Billy's forehead in the chilly air, making him shiver. He felt as though he was on the edge of madness and questioned his sanity.

Billy took a deep breath and regained his composure. He approached a steep bend in the tunnel and saw the glow of firelight reflecting off the wall. Then he heard the loud thumping of feet on the ground and the echo of grunts with an occasional roar. The intensity of the sounds frightened him as he considered how many of the creatures could be down there.

Billy peered out from the tunnel and saw a large fire in the middle of a cavern. Along the walls were many other tunnels. The Neanderthals danced around the fire as if they were involved in some ritual. Their ominous heads had huge jaws, which protruded from their skulls.

Billy was startled by another scream. He watched one of the creatures drag a woman from a wooden pen. The woman cried out hysterically for help. Three other Neanderthals surrounded her. They savagely pulled her limbs from her torso and shredded the flesh from her body as her desperate cries for help ceased. Ferociously, they fought each other for each piece of the meat. Blood splattered on the creatures, much to their delight. They rubbed their hands in the warm, wet blood and lapped it from their leathery hands and arms.

Billy couldn't stand it anymore. He raised his rifle and fired twice. Two of the creatures fell to the ground dead. The other howled and retreated. He approached the fire and prayed that Penny wasn't the creatures' latest victim. His heart raced and a lump formed in his throat. This was just one more failure in his life that he'd have to live with if anything happened to her. This would be the nightmare that lasts forever.

Four Neanderthals pelted him with rocks. Moving toward the pen, he selected his targets and fired. Four of the creatures fell to the ground, briefly clearing a path for him. The others, sensing a quick death with each pop from Billy's gun, retreated from him.

Billy passed the woman's dismembered corpse on the way to the pen. He grew nauseous and gagged when he saw the horrified stare from the dead woman's eyes and her half-eaten body lying on the blood-stained cavern floor. Despite his relief knowing that it wasn't Penny, his hatred toward the Neanderthals grew. Another stone struck Billy in his shoulder.

"You sons of bitches! Now it's my turn!" He fired at the closest Neanderthal. His shot struck the creature's forehead and left a small crater. Blood and brains seeped from the wound as the creature fell to its knees. It stared at Billy with a strange gaze and then hit the ground with a thud. "How does that feel, huh?" Billy taunted the dead creature.

After shooting five more of the Neanderthals, he turned his attention to the wooden pen. The reflections from the lapping flames cast eerie shadows across the uneven ground. Billy became disoriented by the shadows and tripped. His rifle and flashlight flew from his hands and slid across the rocky ground. He tumbled hard on his stomach and found himself in the presence of a sickening stench.

When Billy retrieved the flashlight and rifle, he found the source of the smell. He lay next to a heap of human heads, with the brains removed through large holes in the back of the skulls. He trembled as he replaced the spent magazine in the rifle.

Two Neanderthals rushed at him with stone axes in their hands. Billy pointed the rifle at the nearest creature and fired into its chest. It staggered and fell to the ground. The second creature grabbed him and shoved him against the cavern wall, pinning his rifle against his chest. He pushed the end of the rifle under the Neanderthal's chin and pulled the trigger. The shot tore the creature's face off and it shrieked in pain. The noise deafened him as he pushed the Neanderthal away and fired again into its chest. The creature dropped to the ground in front of him.

Billy felt desperation taking over. He wiped pieces of flesh and blood from the creature's face off of him. Tears welled up in his eyes as he grew nauseous. His head throbbed from the gunshot blast and distracted him.

Finch took the flashlight from Doc and hurried down the tunnel. He nimbly jogged down the jagged path, while Doc struggled to keep up and stumbled continuously. They heard the echo of Billy's gunfire and saw the glow from the fire on the tunnel wall. "We're almost there," shouted Finch.

"I certainly hope so," replied Doc. "I'm too old for this shit."

Inside the pen, a dozen women pleaded for help when they saw Billy. He reached the gate and struggled to remove a large piece of wood that latched the gate shut. Three Neanderthals attacked from his blind side but one of the women warned, "Look out!"

Billy raised his rifle and fired at each one. They died instantly. He bashed the wooden latch with the butt of his rifle and finally removed it. "Everyone, calm down. We're getting out of here," he announced and entered the pen. "Penny, where are you?" he shouted.

"Over there in the corner. They just brought her in," replied a young woman.

Billy recognized Penny's limp body on the ground and was relieved. "Follow me," he ordered the women as he lifted Penny over his shoulder. When he attempted to leave the pen, more creatures blocked his path. The women panicked, adding to the chaos behind him. Billy laid Penny down and fired at the creatures. Four fell to the ground dead. Another rushed at Billy from his left.

"Look out!" shouted one of the women.

Billy took a baseball swing at the Neanderthal's head with the rifle and stunned it momentarily. He placed the end of the barrel against the creature's forehead and fired. Its head exploded, sending pieces of brain and shattered skull across the ground. Only the lower jaw was intact with the body as blood spewed from the arteries in the neck. The creature fell to the ground with a sickening thud. Billy removed the empty magazine and inserted the last one.

Doc and Finch entered the cavern. They saw Billy and the women surrounded by the Neanderthals. "Take out the biggest creatures first. When they fall, the smaller ones will run," instructed Finch. The two initiated selective firing.

"You're a hunter?" asked Doc.

Finch fired two rounds and replied, "No, FBI."

The sound of gunshots from the far side of the cave caught Billy's attention. He knew it had to be Finch. With renewed hope, he fired repeatedly at the creatures until he exhausted his ammo.

Doc and Finch fired at the creatures from the far side of the cave until the remaining Neanderthals retreated. The cavern floor was littered with the carcasses of dead creatures.

"Follow those men," Billy instructed the women. He lifted Penny over his shoulder and carried her across the cavern.

"Keep going and don't look back!" Doc shouted urgently and directed the women to the tunnel. They sobbed hysterically as they rushed past him.

Billy paused when he reached Doc. "Thanks. I really appreciate this."

"We'll talk later. Let's get the hell out of here." Doc saw the bloody, dismembered corpse near the fire and nearly vomited.

"Good eating, huh?" kidded Billy sarcastically.

"Shut up and move it!" Doc ordered and covered Billy's path, firing randomly at any creature that approached. Finch waited by the tunnel and directed the women up to the surface.

"Boy, am I glad to see you, Finchy!" Billy exclaimed.

"I'll bet you are. Keep moving." Doc and Finch fired repeatedly at the creatures.

"I'll cover you from here. That'll buy you time to get away," Finch informed him.

Doc understood the risk Finch was taking. "Don't be long. I'll cover you at the entrance."

"I'm counting on it." The two men shook hands and Doc hustled into the tunnel.

Finch took a defensive position at the mouth of the tunnel and shot three more of the creatures. The others retreated. Finch replaced the magazine in his rifle. He felt a short respite until the Neanderthals rushed at him again and pelted him with rocks. He hurried up the tunnel, while firing back into the darkness. The squeals of wounded creatures told him that his shots found their mark.

Doc exited the cave and saw the women huddled about in confusion. "Head for the terminal, all of you. Warn them that the Neanderthals may be coming," he instructed them. The women ran from the forest and crossed the tarmac.

Billy knelt on the ground with Penny in his arms. He looked rattled.

"Are you alright?" asked Doc.

"I guess so. Did you see how many of those things are down there?"

"I sure did. I never thought they congregated in such a large group. We used to believe they were tribal."

"And now?" questioned Billy.

"That's a whole friggin' nation of pissed off ape-men!" replied Doc sarcastically.

Billy cracked a brief smile. "That's the first time I've heard you say anything remotely funny."

"Don't get used to it. Now, get ready to cover Finch." Doc hid behind a tree and waited.

Billy set Penny down behind a clump of bushes. He knelt down and aimed his rifle at the cave's entrance. When he glanced back at Penny, he wondered why he felt so responsible for her safety and if she'd be all right after this. His thoughts were interrupted by loud grunts from the cave. "Are you ready, Billy? They're coming," warned Doc edgily.

Billy ejected the empty magazine from his rifle and searched his pockets for another. "No!" he shouted frantically.

Doc retrieved two magazines from his pants pocket. "Here, take these."

Finch burst into the daylight, followed closely by the ghastly creatures. Billy and Doc fired repeatedly at the creatures as quickly as they appeared. Finch reloaded his weapon behind a tree and returned fire as well. By the time the flow of creatures from the cave ceased, carcasses filled the mouth of the cave. "Let's get the hell out of here! I'm out of ammo," ordered Finch.

"Me, too," added Doc.

Billy handed his rifle to Doc. "Mine's empty, too."

Finch handed his rifle to Doc and helped Billy lift Penny off the ground. Each placed an arm under her thighs and another behind her back. They lifted her into a sitting position and hurried out of the forest.

— X —

Maggie stood on the tarmac with Captain Barnes and several other passengers in an intense discussion over duties. Captain Barnes saw the women approach them. "What the hell is going on, now?" he grumbled.

When the women arrived, Maggie grabbed one of them by the arm. "Where did you come from?"

"Some men rescued us from the cavern. They told us to warn you about the creatures in the cave. They're coming!"

"Must be the damned Neanderthals again," complained Barnes. "We have to do something about this."

Everyone moved inside the concourse. Three men stood at the entrance with rifles and kept watch.

Billy and Finch emerged from the trees, carrying Penny with Doc close behind.

Maggie hurried out to assist them. "What happened? Is Penny alright?"

"We don't know." Billy snapped.

"Take Penny inside the terminal and let Maggie care for her," instructed Doc. "After that, Billy, I need you to get every weapon and round of ammunition you can from the Security Center and get it up here fast!"

"Thanks for all your help, both of you," said Billy appreciatively.

"Just take care of our business in the Security Center and we'll call it even," urged Doc.

Maggie nudged Billy along and followed him to the isolated corner of the concourse. "Set her down right here and I'll see what I can do for her."

"Thanks, Maggie." Billy picked three volunteers and hurried down the dark corridor to the Security Center.

— X —

The fog lifted and the temperature rose dramatically, making the air thick and muggy. Added to this was the fact that the air was heavier due to a greater concentration of methane to oxygen than on Earth. This significantly fatigued everyone, although most of them had no idea why.

Finch assembled a group of men to set up a defense perimeter for the night. They arranged five woodpiles at regular intervals on the outer perimeter of the tarmac and three in a semicircle closer to the entrance of the terminal. Tree limbs and rocks were stacked as barriers between the outer and inner perimeters. Six armed men and women were posted behind the barriers.

— X —

Penny sat upright as Maggie held a wet rag against the back of her head. Doc knelt down next to her. "How are you feeling, young lady?"

Penny looked up groggily and groaned "I've been better."

"Do you remember what happened?" he asked.

"One of those horrible creatures took me into the woods. I don't remember anything else."

"Yes, well, I think you're safe now."

"How did you save me?" she questioned him.

"Billy deserves all the credit," answered Doc. "He went into the cavern alone to rescue you."

"Then what happened?" asked Maggie.

"Billy fought his way to the pen and freed the women. He found Penny and carried her out. We came in and had an old-fashioned turkey shoot with the creatures. Between the three of us, we took out quite a few of them."

"Where's Billy now?" Penny asked.

"He'll be back. He's getting some things for us."

"I've got to see him. He risked his life for me."

"You sit back down and rest. He'll come see you as soon as he returns." He gently rubbed Penny's shoulder and walked away.

Maggie dabbed the wet rag against the large bruise on the back of Penny's head again. "I'll make sure Billy comes right over when he returns. You take it easy and keep this rag in place."

Penny took the rag from Maggie and held it against the bruise. "Thanks, Maggie. You're a good friend."

"Anytime. Now get some rest." Maggie left Penny alone.

Penny leaned back and smiled. *Billy really does care about me. He just doesn't want me to know it yet,* she thought giddily.

Simon approached Penny with two cans of juice. He wore a T-shirt, shorts and sneakers with shoulder length dark hair. Penny saw him coming and wondered what was on his mind. "Hello. Who are you?" she asked.

"I'm Simon. What's your name?"

"Penny. Penny Nichols."

"Interesting name," Simon teased and offered her one of his cans.

"Why thank you, Simon." Penny accepted the can and popped the top. Simon held his drink out for a mock toast. Penny responded and tapped her can against his. "How about a toast to friendship?" he suggested.

"Are we friends?" asked Penny coyly.

"I'd like to be."

"Then friends we are." They sipped juice from their containers while gazing at each other.

"When you feel better, maybe we can talk some more."

"I'd like that, Simon." Simon got up and left in a spirited gait.

He is a cutey, but he's not the knight in shining armor like Billy is. Maybe I can use a little jealousy to adjust Mr. Brock's attitude, though, she thought playfully. Penny drank her juice and pondered her opportunity.

— X —

Doc joined Finch on the tarmac as he organized the men. "How are things going, Mr. Finch?"

"With the terminal at our back, we only need to defend three sides. We've established an outer perimeter on the tarmac for warning, an inner perimeter near the terminal for our primary defense, and the remainder of us can take up positions at the entrance if necessary."

"What about the corridor?" asked Doc.

"We're posting two men there as well." Then Finch cast a concerned look at Doc and asked, "How about those guns? Where are they?"

"They're on the way. I hope this is enough to get us through the night."

"I certainly hope so, too. It's all we can do right now."

Doc paused outside the terminal. His watch showed 5:00 and a scant blotch of sun peeked through the clouds. He wondered about the elapsed time and slow movement of the sun across the sky. Despite being late in the afternoon, the sun was still positioned high in the sky and not nearly close to setting. As he looked closer, it appeared as if there could be two suns very close to each other. He rubbed his eyes and dismissed it as an illusion.

Doc entered the terminal and crossed the concourse. The campfires were helpful in finding his way about without tripping over people or things. Maggie and Penny picked through the contents of a wrecked vendor's cart. Doc arrived and was disappointed to see Penny on her feet. "You should be lying down," Doc chastised her.

"Relax, Doc. We found some containers of juice and soda in a refrigerator. Would you like something?" Maggie offered.

"Do you happen to have a Gatorade?"

Penny pulled a plastic bottle of Gatorade from her sack. "I hope you like lime-flavored Gatorade. Catch!" She tossed the container to him but Doc clumsily fumbled it through his fingers and it bounced off Maggie's head. Maggie looked up at him inauspiciously. "Seriously, Robert, sometimes I wonder about you." She handed him the container of juice and made sure he held it securely in his hand before she let go. Doc chuckled meekly at her.

"Did Billy come back yet?" inquired Penny.

"No, but he should be soon. I really think you should take it easy for a while, but I can see that you and Billy are both as stubborn as they come."

Maggie and Penny laughed over Doc's comparison.

Billy and four men emerged from the corridor with eight sacks of ammo, a sack with ten pistols and eight rifles. Finch was elated when he saw them. "Perhaps we do have a fighting chance!" he exclaimed.

Billy saluted Finch. "I told you we wouldn't let you down."

"I see that." Finch looked at the firearms and ammo as if they were gold. He called a group of men together and distributed the guns with instructions where the men should post.

Two women approached the group of men and watched. Billy noticed and remembered them from the airport. He smiled sheepishly as he recalled his experience with them on the plane. Billy's thoughts were interrupted by a nudge from the fellow next to him. He looked up and saw Finch staring coldly at him. "Sorry, Finch. I guess I got distracted," Billy replied humbly.

Finch rolled his eyes at Billy while the girls stood by, eagerly listening. Billy peeked at them frequently while he listened to Finch's final instructions.

"I can't afford to use you if you can't focus," teased Finch. Billy's face reddened with embarrassment. Finch glanced at the two women and back at Billy. "They are a pair of lookers," he quipped as he walked away.

"I'm glad someone has a sense of humor around here," Billy muttered to himself.

Halfway from the terminal, the brunette intercepted him. "Hi, I'm Veronica, but you can call me Ronnie. Remember me on the plane?"

"How could I forget? You embarrassed me over that stupid hatch in front of everyone."

"Yeah, I guess I did," she replied meekly.

"I never opened one before. How was I supposed to know?"

"Well, I never opened one either. Look, I thought I'd make this easy for you since it looks like we're going to be stuck here together. How about we start over as friends?"

"As friends, huh?" Billy saw Ronnie's friend a short distance away with a coy smile on her face.

Ronnie noticed Billy's interest and motioned for her to join them. "This is Randy. We could tell right away at the airport that you were hot for her." Billy was speechless. This wasn't what he expected to hear from them.

"So, Billy, we finally meet," replied Randy.

Billy tried to play down their intimidation and extended his hand in friendship. "Hi, Randy. I really wasn't staring at you at ..."

"Don't grovel, Billy," Randy interjected. "It was what it was. Where's your girlfriend?"

"She isn't my girlfriend. We just met on the flight."

The two girls looked at each other and giggled. "That's a lame excuse. I heard you risked your life to save her from those creatures," teased Randy.

"I had to," admitted Billy. "I couldn't just let them take her."

"Uh-huh," replied the two girls in unison.

"Since we've been here, I've had nothing but grief from those damned Neanderthals. Cut me some slack."

"Maybe they're intimidated by your masculinity," Ronnie joked.

Billy turned to walk away until Ronnie grabbed his arm. "Wait a minute," she said. "We're only kidding around."

"What do you girls want?" he asked warily.

"It seems that you have a line on the action around here," she answered.

"Meaning what?" he wondered aloud.

"If you're going to find exciting things to do, we want in," She informed him.

Billy was baffled by her request. "I'm not looking for action, but it sure does seem to find me. Can't you find your own?"

"We're serious about this," Ronnie added.

"Why do you say that?"

"Oh, come on," chided Randy. "You scoped out our jackets at the airport to see what we were about."

"Was I that obvious?" asked Billy sheepishly.

"You could have come over and asked," suggested Randy.

"Alright, I guess I could use some help with my social skills."

"How about little Miss Muffet? What does she have to say about this?" asked Ronnie.

"Can we leave her out of this?" Billy requested. "She's a nice girl but she's a bit naive."

"Don't worry," Ronnie assured him. "Your secret's safe with us."

"We're watching you, Billy. Don't forget us," warned Randy. Giggling, the girls left him. Billy couldn't take his eyes off them as they walked away with a seductive sway in their hips.

Man-eaters, he thought to himself. *They're the most dangerous species.* Billy gazed at the white cliffs in the distance and pondered how his world changed so rapidly. This morning, he was in his own boring life. A few hours later, his world was gone, maybe forever.

Finch approached Billy and noticed he was absorbed in his thoughts. "Are you alright?" he asked.

"Yeah, I'm just venting a little."

Finch was a born leader with a sense of purpose. When he spoke, he naturally commanded people's attention. Billy could tell something bothered him, too. "How about you?"

"This is, without a doubt, the second longest day of my life," replied Finch. "The day I lost my family was the worst."

"I'm sorry. Do you want to talk about it?"

"Nah. Maybe some other time." Billy felt remorse for Finch as he watched him walk away. He returned to the terminal and sat in his secluded corner of the concourse.

— ⟨ —

Maggie lectured Penny inside the concourse about how she'd need to adapt to their new environment. She sensed that Penny grew weary of the conversation, so she changed the topic. "So, what's up with you and Billy? I don't mean to snoop, but it's not hard to tell that you have a thing for him." Penny blushed and looked away. "You don't have to tell me if you feel it's too personal. I just thought we might talk a little."

"I like him a lot but we just aren't in synch on anything," Penny revealed. "He's hiding his feelings from me, if he has any at all."

"Perhaps you've found the right person, but the timing isn't quite right."

"When do you know if the time is right?" Penny asked.

"You'll know. Don't rush things. They'll come to you."

"Thanks, Maggie. I needed to hear that."

"Anytime you want to talk, I'm here for you. I've had a lot of experience with these things and I don't think you can tell me anything I haven't heard before."

"Thanks, again. I think I'll go see if Billy's back yet."

"Good luck," said Maggie.

Penny waved and walked away. She used a flashlight to locate Billy in his corner and was disappointed to find him asleep. *What have I got to lose?* she thought. Penny lay next to him and considered how he risked his life to save her from the Neanderthals. *Oh, how I wish I could have seen him in action,* she pondered, then rested her head on his chest and slept.

— ✕ —

Ruger sat at the wooden table and stared at a plume of white smoke over his silver chest. Inside the plume was the image of the Neanderthals' carcasses scattered about the cave's entrance. "So, they have weapons," Ruger remarked sarcastically.

Pirocles entered the room. "Did they kill him?" he inquired.

"No, and I think I'll need to add another predator to the hunt." Ruger stared at Pirocles with a sinister leer and the two of them burst into devious laughter.

— ✕ —

The fires burned brightly on the inner and outer perimeters of the tarmac, displaying flickering traces of light against the night sky. The men grouped in pairs by each fire and watched for signs of danger. Finch marched with a rifle slung over his shoulder to the sunken end of the terminal and ascended its sloped roof. He stepped over broken pieces of aluminum, steel and concrete while circumventing large holes in the roof until he reached the highest section. From there, he had an ideal vantage point from which he could monitor the tarmac. *This one long day,* Finch thought to himself after glancing at his watch. He observed the fires on the outer perimeter. Curiosity got the better of him and he moved to the other side of the roof where he gazed out at the forest behind the terminal. Strange noises from unknown creatures lulled him into a daze.

When two moons emerged from behind the clouds, he could easily see miles of treetops across the vast expanse of forest. Clouds soon blocked the moonlight again and darkness engulfed the area. As Finch contemplated his plans for the next day, he felt the structure vibrate lightly at regular intervals. He stared into the darkness but saw nothing. A foul odor filled the air and made him nauseous.

Finch reminisced about the family he lost. At first, he couldn't understand why it had to happen to them. Now, it seemed as if they were the lucky ones. They would never survive the nightmare that his world had become. He looked into the night sky and promised them, "Someday, I'll be with you."

Finch dozed off for a few hours, against his better judgment. Again, he smelled a horrible odor that woke him and he winced. A huge, carnivorous reptile stood nearby and eyed him. Its body was similar to an Allosaurus but its snout was long like that of a crocodile with rows of sharp teeth. Finch couldn't help but notice that the warm stench came from his right like a rotten breeze. "Wow, something must have died upwind," he muttered.

The moonlight broke through the clouds again. Finch suddenly realized he was staring into the face of a monstrous reptile. Its huge powerful jaws shot out of the darkness and clamped down on him. He felt a second of pain throughout his body and then nothing. The creature swallowed him whole and trudged toward the low end of the terminal.

PREDATORS AND ALLIES

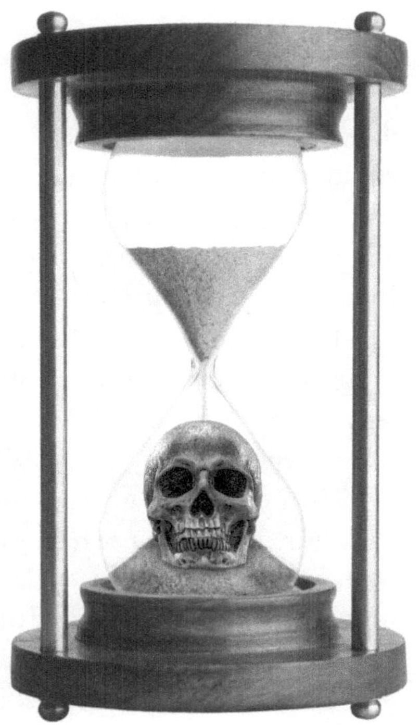

Jerry was on watch duty at the inner perimeter of fires when he felt vibrations in the ground. He saw a huge shape creeping toward them from the trees. "There's something out there!" he exclaimed. "It's coming this way!"

The men retreated toward the inner group of fires and waited anxiously until the dinosaur stepped onto the tarmac and was clearly defined by the firelight. It unleashed a deafening roar when it looked down at the men. "Fire at will!" ordered Jerry.

The men fired repeatedly but their rounds had no effect on the giant reptile. It thundered across the tarmac toward the fires, undaunted by the gunfire. They scattered in different directions with some running toward the fires, while others fled into the forest. The dinosaur rumbled after the men near the fires.

Doc exited the building and saw the men flee from the creature. Their screams beyond the fires were frightening. When the dinosaur rumbled toward the building, Doc and Jerry retreated inside and backed away from the entrance. The dinosaur rammed the wall with its head and rocked the terminal. Large pieces of debris fell from the ceiling and injured several people. Others scurried for safety in the dark corridor.

The creature tried repeatedly to penetrate the inner walls by ramming it but finally relented. It craned its head up through the length of broken glass windows and glared at everyone before storming off into the forest.

The steel beams and the corrugated walls were severely bent but held up. The narrow entrance by the ramp widened significantly as the left side buckled inward several feet. Jerry approached the broken windows and peered out. He saw no sign of the creature.

"I'm sure it'll be back," remarked Doc.

"Isn't there any good news, Doc?"

"Not yet." The two men watched as the fires still burned brightly in their semicircle pattern on the edge of the tarmac. "Have you seen Mr. Finch around?" inquired Doc.

"Last time I saw him, he was headed onto the roof."

"That's the direction the beast came from."

"Sure is. I hope he saw it coming."

"Let's get sentries posted again but keep them at the inner fires. We'll still need to keep the outer perimeter fires burning throughout the night so they'll occasionally have to go out there with wood."

"I'll take care of it," replied Jerry.

— ☒ —

Billy awoke later, unaware of the attack and enjoyed the serenity of his isolated corner. He found Penny nestled against his right side and slid his shoulder out from under her.

Penny stirred and awoke. "Hi, Billy," she said coyly.

"I'm glad you're here."

"Why?"

"So I can keep an eye on you. I told you I'd take care of you."

"Yes, you did. I wanted to thank you for saving me from the Neanderthals. No one else would have done that."

"Well, somebody had to do it."

Penny stared at him with a vexed look. "You keep saying that but I don't buy it." She placed her arm around Billy and kissed his cheek. She felt a desire to show her feelings for him but she recalled what Maggie said about timing.

Billy was surprised by her directness. "If you don't think I'm up to the job ..."

Penny placed her finger to Billy's lips. "I'm sure you're more than up to the job."

When Billy stood, she grew nervous and asked, "What's wrong?"

"Nothing."

"Billy, you're tuning me out again. Why?" Penny pressed for him to explain himself.

"Why don't we go for a walk?" he suggested as he helped her up.

"Where to?"

"You'll see. Come on."

"Only if you promise to pay attention to me."

Billy looked embarrassed by her request. "I promise."

Penny wondered what he had in mind as they stepped over sleeping bodies to reach the entrance. Outside the terminal, they overheard men talking about a monster. "This should be interesting," whispered Billy.

They took notice of the damaged wall and found Doc sitting on a folding chair. Doc gazed at the stars in the sky with his hands folded behind his head.

Billy and Penny approached him. "What happened to the terminal?" Billy asked.

"Sit down for a few moments, would you?" Billy and Penny sat on the ground next to him. "We have problems – big problems," remarked Doc somberly.

"How big?" asked Billy.

"As big as a large dinosaur different than any we know of. You didn't hear it?"

"I didn't hear a thing," answered Penny.

"Damn, I missed it!" complained Billy.

"Maggie and I are going to travel south to search for my colleague. The two of you are welcome to join us. Besides, I could use your help when we get there, Penny."

"My help?"

"Yes, my colleague's computers are still working and I know you can create a software program to analyze any data we collect that might explain what happened to us."

Penny was surprised by his request. "Are you sure your colleague is still out there?" she asked.

"Yes, I am. I spoke with him on the radio earlier. He was located at the observatory in Washington when this anomaly occurred."

"So, Washington was displaced here, too?" inquired Billy.

"Part of it was. It's likely that whatever caused us to be here was a random act that also affected at least one other part of the world. Maybe others."

"How long will the trip take?" inquired Billy.

"Two weeks, I think."

"Isn't it going to be dangerous?" asked Penny.

"You mean like this place?" replied Doc, grinning sarcastically.

Billy teased, "There you go again, Doc – another funny."

"Billy!"

"I know. I'm just trying to lighten the mood. I guess it really doesn't matter what we do since we're stuck here."

"I'd like to leave here as soon as possible since we're running out of defenses."

"Maybe we should try to find transportation?" suggested Billy.

"Like what?"

"Well, it was an airport. Maybe we can find a vehicle or a shuttle plane around here somewhere."

"Unfortunately, I think we'll be doing this trip on foot." Doc stood up and placed his hands in his pockets. He looked dejected as he scanned the tarmac once more. "I hate to bail on you but I think it's time to turn in. Good night, kids," he said somberly.

"Good night, Doc," said Penny.

"Don't let the bedbugs bite," teased Billy.

"Smart-ass!"

"See that. Doc does have a sense of humor," Billy kidded. Doc rolled his eyes at Billy and entered the terminal.

Penny leaned against Billy and put her arm around his waist. They looked up at the night sky. Two moons of different sizes broke through the clouds again and lit up most of the area. They were red and green, with the red one smaller than the green.

"After everything we've been through, it's a full moon or two. Isn't that the icing on the cake?" Billy noted.

Penny gazed into his eyes. "Uh-huh," she said coyly. When she leaned forward to kiss him, Billy looked away. Penny was embarrassed by his rejection.

Billy fumbled for the right words to politely diffuse her advances. "Why don't we go for a walk up on the roof?"

"We don't have to if you really don't want to," Penny replied, hoping he wasn't dodging the issue with her. "Besides, it could be dangerous."

Billy held out a pistol in one hand and three magazines in the other. "I'd like to talk about something important."

"I trust you, Mr. Brock, to keep me safe," Penny mentioned confidently.

"No problem." Billy placed the pistol in his pocket but kept his hand on it. He held Penny's hand with the other and they walked across the tarmac. They encountered two sentries on the perimeter. One was an older Hispanic man and the other, a young Asian man.

"Where are you going? It's dangerous out here," asked the Hispanic man.

"Up on the roof for some night time reconnaissance," answered Billy.

"I guess everyone's out for a walk tonight. Must be the full moons," quipped the Asian man.

Billy thought that was odd. "Who else have you seen out here?" he asked.

"Well, Barnes passed this way with a couple of the stewardesses. He was in a funny kind of mood."

"It seems Barnes is always in a funny kind of mood," Billy remarked.

"I'd be a little funny if I had two hotties like those stewardesses," the Hispanic man commented giddily.

"Well, I think he's a pig. I can't believe those girls would be so stupid," Penny responded sarcastically.

"Good luck, you two," the Hispanic man said. "I'd think twice about going out there if I were you."

Billy and Penny left them and scaled the sloped roof. From either side, they could look out over the forest and the tarmac. The landscape was beautiful under the moonlight. It appeared like a wonderland until the occasional roar from a large predator disturbed the serenity. Strange chirps and whistles from night creatures filled the air.

Billy sat comfortably with his back propped against a vent housing for the HVAC system. Penny sat between his legs and leaned back. "I need to get something off my chest," Billy informed her.

Penny slid sideways and faced him. "Am I going to like this?"

"I don't know. You'll understand me a lot better, though."

"I'm listening," she said and gave her full attention to him.

"It's like this - I'm going through a tough time. I was supposed to be married a few weeks ago. I dated a woman for seven years and she stood me up at the wedding with no word or clue as to why."

"I did overhear Epstein talking to his wife about it on the phone. After all, my cubicle was just outside his office," she confessed.

"So, what else have you heard about me?"

"You finish first," she insisted.

"Alright. Ever since I got engaged, Epstein has been up my tail to do all these extra things around the plant. I was losing my mind already and he dumped all this other crap on me at once."

"Did you ever wonder why?" Penny asked, knowing the real reason behind Billy's change of duties.

"I know why," Billy claimed. "Sales have been down and they already discussed cutbacks. I'm the easiest one to start with."

"And you think they brought me in to save a few bucks."

"Why wouldn't they? It's business."

"Well, since we're leveling with each other, I guess I should tell you the truth."

"About?" asked Billy, curious.

"About me and you."

"There was no 'me and you'."

"There is now. Epstein wanted to replace the general manager, Mark Larken, because he had no vision for the company. Since you were getting married, Epstein thought you'd be happy to get off the road and take Larken's spot. He admired you very much."

Billy was stunned. "Who told you that?" he demanded to know.

"Epstein. I was hired to take your place but not so they could fire you. You were getting promoted."

"Oh, shit! And all this time I thought ..."

"You thought I was out to get you."

"Well, you are, aren't you?" he asked playfully.

"That you'll have to find out for yourself," she teased.

"How about a hint?"

Penny placed her hand on his chin and pulled his mouth to hers. This was their magic moment and they were lost in a passionate kiss. Penny was pleased that he accepted her advance this time.

"Wow, that was nice," Billy responded, relieved.

"Do you think you can find a place in your heart for someone like me?" Penny asked.

"Be patient with me and I'll do my best."

"That's good enough for now," she said happily. Penny placed her hand behind Billy's neck and pulled him to her. She pressed herself against him and kissed him hungrily. Billy was overwhelmed by her passion and gave in to her desires. As the night wore on, they lay in each other's arms and enjoyed their budding love. Eventually, they slept, oblivious to the dangers around them.

— ⏳ —

The moonlight reflected off the surface of the water and illuminated much of the area. Barnes sat on a rock next to the stream. One stewardess, Marcy, cuddled up to him and kissed him. The second stewardess, Sabrina, stood by the edge of the stream and considered what she was about to do. "Why don't you come join us? I know you want to," Barnes suggested arrogantly to Sabrina.

"In a moment. I'm looking for something," she replied.

Four Neanderthals hid in the trees, watching them. Marcy unbuttoned Barnes' shirt and kept his attention focused on her. She lifted her blouse, exposing her lace bra. "Now that's what I'm talking about," remarked Barnes lustily.

Sabrina picked up a football-sized rock from the water and tiptoed behind Barnes. She bashed the back of his head with it. Barnes let out a brief moan and fell to the ground, clutching the back of his head with his hands. "Oh, you bitch!" he groaned.

"Now you know what I'm talking about, you ignorant asshole," Sabrina declared proudly. The two stewardesses high-fived each other.

Sabrina saw the Neanderthals emerge from the trees. "Come on, Marcy! The creatures are back!" One of the creatures struck Marcy in the back with a crude spear. She crumpled to the ground with a vague look in her eyes. When she looked down at the spear tip protruding from her chest, she started to cry but then gasped and fell to the ground dead.

Sabrina fled toward the tarmac but stumbled and fell to the ground. Another Neanderthal stood over her and cupped its leathery hand over her mouth. It lifted her off the ground by her head. Sabrina tried desperately to scream but the creature's powerful hand pressed tightly against her face and nose until she passed out. The Neanderthal tossed her over its shoulder and carried her into the trees.

Another Neanderthal grabbed Barnes by both arms and stood him up. The remaining two Neanderthals surrounded him. They studied his face for a moment and glanced at each other. The first one shook its head from side to side indicating a 'no'.

Barnes was dazed from the injury. "Screw you!" he shouted drunkenly and spit at the creature's face. The Neanderthal opened its mouth, revealing sharp, jagged teeth. Saliva dribbled from its mouth. It tore into his neck and gorged upon the tender flesh. The other creatures shoved their clawed hands into his abdomen and ripped out his entrails. Barnes eyes rolled back in his head and he gagged one last time before succumbing to death.

— ✕ —

Billy and Penny slept together against the side of the vent housing. Billy wore only his pants while Penny was dressed with her blouse unbuttoned. She felt the chilly morning breeze on her face and awoke from her slumber. When she looked out at the vast mountains, cliffs and forests, she accepted that this was her world now. The old world was likely gone forever. She then considered that this could be the beginning of something new and exciting with Billy.

Billy opened his eyes. The sunlight caused him to squint until his eyes adjusted to it. "Good morning, Penny. How are you feeling?" he asked.

Penny slid on top of his chest and kissed him passionately. "Wonderful. How about you?"

"Under the circumstances, I can't complain."

"I guess professionalism went out the window last night," she kidded.

"We could bring it back if you like."

"No, this was perfect," she replied, pleased.

When they stood up together, Billy placed his arm around Penny's waist. "You'll really do need to be patient with me. I'm not used to being with someone like you," he reminded her.

"Am I that bad?" she questioned him, curious.

"No, I am," said Billy sadly. "Charlene never gave me the time of day and I always accepted that."

Penny pressed her body against his and hugged him. "I'll give you all the time in the world if you want me to."

"Are we talking exclusive or are you just taking me for a test ride?" he kidded.

"I've never experienced a relationship with someone who actually cared about me and I'm afraid I might do something foolish. I want this to work and if I go too fast, just tell me. I'll back off."

Billy brushed her bangs from her eyes and smiled. "I don't feel like I could love a woman again after what happened. That's something I have to get over. I was really devastated by Charlene."

"I've never had anything good happen when it came to love either and I know we can make this work," Penny assured him.

"Well, we have lots of time. Let's be friends first, and then we'll see where things go. No commitments."

"I'd really like that. I'm not used to cooperation from the opposite sex."

Billy kissed her sensuously. "How's that for cooperation?"

"I like it. I have to tell you, though, if you were a test ride, I'd certainly be hooked." They laughed together.

Penny went to the edge of the roof and stared down at the tarmac. Billy walked to the other side of the roof and surveyed the land behind the terminal. He noticed a boot lying behind the HVAC unit. Suddenly, he realized that the leg was attached to it and it belonged to Finch. Billy kicked the leg toward the edge of the roof and knocked it over the side.

Penny saw him looking down over the side and came over to him. "Are you alright?" she asked worriedly.

"Yeah. I thought I saw something."

She noticed Billy's pale appearance. "You look like you've seen a ghost."

"It's nothing, really." Billy then noticed a jet hidden in the foliage. "Look out there, Penny. What do you see?"

She scanned the forest and saw the jet. "It looks like a jet. No, it's two jets!"

"There's something else to the right of the jets!" Billy pointed out.

"I see it. It's another plane – a smaller one!"

"Maybe this is our lucky day!" said Billy excitedly. "If it's a shuttle, we could fly with Doc and Maggie to the observatory."

"That would be awesome!"

"We should get back to Doc about this. He'll be excited."

Two fading moons, one green and the smaller one, red, were still visible in the sky. "Two moons – that's impressive," said Billy.

"We're definitely not on Earth anymore, are we?" asked Penny sadly.

"No, we sure aren't."

As soon as they stepped off the roof, they heard a woman's scream. "Now what?" Billy groaned. They rushed across the clearing toward the smoldering fires at the edge of the tarmac. Three dead men hung by their feet from the trees. They were without heads and their insides were gutted. A concerned crowd gathered a short distance away.

When Doc saw Billy and Penny, he pushed his way through the small crowd toward them. "When did this happen?" inquired Billy hastily.

"Just before sunrise. The Neanderthals took a lot of people."

"How did they get in without anyone noticing?"

"They came from the lower corridor down by the Security Center."

"The sentries?"

"They must have fallen asleep."

"So, these creatures organized an attack from within the terminal. Who would have thought?" complained Billy sarcastically.

"They're very intelligent and they use their network of tunnels efficiently. Worse yet, I don't think they're done with us."

"What's Barnes say about this?"

"He's dead," replied Doc.

"Can't say I'll miss him," said Billy coldly. "What happened?"

"We found him near the stream. I'd say he was struck in the head with a rock and then feasted on by our friends. His head was busted open pretty good and that was the recognizable part of him."

"So, the Neanderthals killed him?"

"Might have been the two stewardesses with him. Word is they really hated him."

"Serves him right. I guess the girls are dead, too."

"We only found the remains of one, although I'm sure the other is dead by now."

"Remember the planes, Billy! Tell him about the planes!" urged Penny enthusiastically.

"We saw two jets and possibly a commuter plane on the other side of the terminal. They were hidden in the trees. We'll check them out since it's not safe to stay here anymore."

"Penny, do you think you could stay with Maggie?" requested Doc. "She's really upset and I've got to help with some things out here."

"Go ahead, Penny. I'll catch up with you later," said Billy.

Penny and Doc returned to the terminal while Billy contemplated what to do about the aircraft. After seeing the headless corpses cut down from the tree, he decided to investigate the aircraft on his own.

Billy took the long walk around the terminal. When he rounded the last corner he had an eerie feeling that he was being followed. He found a branch with a sharp end. It felt rigid so he broke the smaller branches off to make a spear. As he waited behind a tree with his primitive spear, he heard branches snap nearby. His heart raced as he feared the Neanderthals were hunting him. Suddenly, Ronnie and Randy burst out of the trees and playfully pushed him backwards.

"Hello, Billy! Did you forget about us?" Ronnie questioned him.

Billy was annoyed with their startling arrival. "What the hell are you two doing out here?"

"What do you think?" asked Randy.

"With all the crazy stuff going on around here, you shouldn't wander out here unarmed."

Randy pulled out two pistols from the back of her jeans and displayed them to Billy. "I'm armed. How about you, Ronnie?"

"Of course, I'm armed." Ronnie took a knife from her boot and a pistol from the back of her jeans. She held them out for Billy to see. "See, Billy, you obviously don't know us too well."

Billy was amused and sat down on a log. He was attracted to the girls but leery of being mocked by them. "Okay, so what is it that you want from me today?" he inquired warily.

"I'm beginning to think that our boy really is naïve," Randy commented to Ronnie.

Ronnie shook her head disappointedly at Billy. "We told you not to be a stranger, didn't we?" Billy ignored them and started on his way again.

"Hey, wait for us!" shouted Randy.

Billy feigned disinterest, but the girls were a tough act to resist. "How did the two of you get your hands on those guns?" he questioned.

"The dead guys back there didn't need them anymore?" replied Ronnie.

"And why me? Why don't you look for your own adventures?"

"You started this at the airport. Don't tell me you forgot already," teased Randy.

"Alright, I get the point! So, what's your story?"

"Ronnie and I are marksmen or markswomen if you will. We hunt and do many other things that women don't normally do. For instance, I compete in martial arts competitions. I guess you could say it's a hobby of mine."

"Since high school, I've been infatuated with the designs of weapons from the earliest ages to our present day. I've actually created some of my own," explained Ronnie.

"Before drawing conclusions about us, you should know that we are very adventurous. We see our situation here as a challenge and aren't at all intimidated," declared Randy.

Billy was amused as the conversation progressed. "And let me guess, you find me to be a challenge."

"Hell, no! You don't stand a chance against either of us," kidded Randy.

"I don't disagree with that."

"We could be one heck of a team. You'll be surprised when you see what we can do," remarked Ronnie.

"What do the two of you need me for?" he asked.

"Do you think there's hope for him?" asked Randy, disappointed.

"He would make a nice toy," replied Ronnie playfully.

"Well girls, I'm flattered, but I don't know if I'm ready to be toyed with."

"Oh, not that kind of toy, Billy. I had something special in mind for you," Randy teased.

"Look, I don't have time for games right now. I have some urgent things to take care of." He walked away, but they followed, laughing and giggling along the way.

"You know, Billy, you need to lighten up," chastised Randy.

"Right now, I'm concerned about our survival."

The girls were entertained by Billy's conviction for helping out. "You're an interesting specimen, Billy. Don't ever change," teased Ronnie.

Billy refrained from further comment.

The girls followed him through the forest until they reached two 767 jets sitting on broken sections of tarmac among the trees. When they reached the hatch of the first jet, Billy pulled at the latch while Randy and Ronnie kept an eye on the trees behind them. The hatch opened with little difficulty.

"That's a big improvement from last time. Have you been practicing?" Ronnie pestered him. Billy laughed sarcastically as he peeked inside the jet.

It was dark except for sunlight shining through the windows. He and Ronnie entered the plane. Ronnie searched the rear section while Billy inspected the front. Randy remained at the hatch and kept watch.

"Everything looks fine back here," shouted Ronnie.

Billy exited the cockpit. "It's safe up here, too."

The ground shook, catching Randy's attention. The dinosaur's head emerged through the treetops a short distance from the planes. Randy spotted it immediately. "Uh, Billy, I think you'd better get over here fast!"

Billy felt the vibration through the aircraft. He hurried to the hatch and peered past Randy outside the plane. "I don't think that was on the list of activities for this morning," Randy remarked uneasily.

The reptile seemed to focus on them as if looking for someone. Randy backed inside the plane. "I think we'd better close the hatch, Billy!" she warned.

As the creature charged toward them, Billy patiently observed it. "I'll bet that's the same monster that attacked the terminal last night."

"Shut the damn door already!" shouted Randy. She finally nudged Billy out of the way and slammed the hatch shut herself. "What the hell, Billy? You want a date with that thing?"

"Why? Are you afraid of a little competition?" taunted Billy.

The dinosaur rammed the jet. The impact sent both of them sprawling across the floor. "I didn't know you like to play rough. I can do rough," Randy chided him.

"No, thanks. I'll pass." Billy scrambled to one of the windows and looked out. He couldn't believe the size of the creature.

Ronnie joined them from the rear of the plane. "What the hell was that?"

"The Crocosaurus is back," complained Billy.

Ronnie peeked out the window as the creature lowered its head and charged for a second time. The next impact knocked the plane back several feet. "So that's a Crocosaurus," she muttered.

"I don't know what it is. It looks like a T-Rex with a crocodile's head on it. That makes it a Crocosaurus."

"Do you know how much punishment this plane can sustain?" Randy inquired curiously.

"I don't know. I thought you two were the hunting experts!" answered Billy sarcastically.

"I said we were marksmen, not hunters," corrected Ronnie.

"So, what's your best guess, Ms. Marksman?"

The girls glanced at each other and shrugged their shoulders. "I have no idea," said Ronnie modestly.

"I never studied dinosaurs before," added Randy.

The dinosaur rammed the jet again. The three of them fell together to the floor. "I think a plane like this could withstand the impact of an elephant," suggested Randy.

"What's the difference between a dinosaur and an elephant?" questioned Billy, growing more concerned.

"A cubic foot of lizard has a different density than a cubic foot of mammal."

"Is that good or bad?"

"Hell, I don't know!" Randy replied, amused.

After several unsuccessful attempts, the dinosaur left the area. "This is probably its territory. I'm sure it'll be back," surmised Ronnie.

"Perhaps we should stay put for a while and see if it returns," suggested Randy. The three sat on the floor by the hatch, with their backs leaned against the center aisle seats.

"Now, Billy, tell the truth. Wasn't that a rush? Doesn't the thrill of danger turn you on?" asked Randy giddily.

"You girls are certifiable nutcases!"

"Come on, Billy. Tell the truth," Randy pressed him for an answer.

"Alright, it was a little exciting."

"I really enjoyed that. It was arousing," Randy said philosophically as she stared into his eyes, no doubt to torment him. Billy grew uncomfortable and looked away from her gaze.

"I could tell you were scared. I heard it in your voice," challenged Ronnie.

"No way! It takes a lot more than that to rattle me," replied Randy defensively.

Billy stood up and glared at them. "Am I the crazy one here?"

"Uh-huh," the girls replied in unison. Ronnie opened the hatch and scanned the area. She stepped outside and looked further but the dinosaur was gone.

"Don't you have enough manners to help a lady up?" Randy chastised Billy.

"Oh, so now you're a poor defenseless lady."

"Of course. At least right now I am."

Billy took her by the hand and helped her to her feet. They stared into each other's eyes for an awkward moment. "You want to say something," Randy asked.

"No, I don't think so," he warily replied. He wasn't sure what Randy was up to but he wasn't going to embarrass himself for either of the girls.

Ronnie peered inside the hatch and noticed how they looked at each other. "Looks like it's all clear. Come on out, you two."

Billy stepped outside the hatch and surveyed the damage to the plane. The side was wrinkled and mushroomed but it withstood the creature's attacks.

"Now what?" Ronnie asked.

"We should report back to the others. I think we proved that this is adequate shelter," declared Billy.

"But what if the creature comes back?"

"I'm sure you can design a weapon to slay the mighty beast."

"Look, the last time that monster attacked, Randy and I were guarding the corridor in case the Neanderthals came back. Neither of us saw it before."

"It's a shame you weren't guarding the corridor last night. More people would be alive today."

"Yeah, we heard," said Randy somberly.

"We did take out about a dozen of those Neanderthals. That should help thin the population," remarked Ronnie.

"Don't worry. There's plenty more where they came from."

"You're kidding?"

"Nope. Maybe even hundreds of them."

Ronnie and Randy glanced at each other uneasily. Their conversation was interrupted when they heard the dinosaur roar from the direction of the terminal.

"Damn it! The monster's going for the terminal!" Billy uttered.

"So, what do you expect us to do?" inquired Ronnie.

"What do you think? We have to help them!" Billy picked up his makeshift spear from the ground and raced off. The girls looked annoyed as they stood with their hands on their hips.

"He just doesn't understand teamwork, does he?" complained Ronnie.

"No, he doesn't." The girls left the plane and chased after Billy.

When Billy reached the tarmac, he saw the Crocosaurus crash against the wall where the ramp to the concourse was. The wall was broken wide open. He raced across the tarmac past several half-eaten corpses.

The dinosaur stuck its head through the opening in the wall, straining greedily to reach more prey. Billy maneuvered around the dinosaur's side to get its attention. He prodded it several times with the spear but to no avail.

Randy and Ronnie rushed up the sloped terminal roof. They approached the edge and looked down on the creature. "Let's give that lizard a little firepower," said Ronnie excitedly.

"I'm with you, sister." The girls drew their pistols and crept closer to the edge. They fired several shots at the dinosaur until it retracted its head from inside the terminal and roared at them.

As Billy waved his spear and taunted the monster, one of the girls' shots ricocheted off the cement near him. "Hey, watch it!" Billy shouted as he backed away defensively.

"Sorry," replied Ronnie.

Billy jabbed at the Crocosaurus' belly with his spear. When the creature finally noticed Billy, it snapped at him several times, forcing him against the wall. He defended himself valiantly with the spear but the third time the creature lunged at him, he stumbled and fell on his back. The dinosaur eyed Billy, as he lay helpless on the tarmac.

The girls fired at the creature's head. One of the shots struck the creature's eyelid and caused it severe pain. After clawing at the wound several times, it reared back and snapped at the girls. Ronnie and Randy tumbled away from the edge of the roof and scrambled to their feet.

The dinosaur barely missed Randy with its long jaws and massive head. It wasn't tall enough to reach over the ledge but its foul breath and a blob of sticky saliva doused Randy as she fell into a sitting position. She was terrified by the creature and disgusted with the foul smell from the saliva. "I guess you weren't scared that time either," chided Ronnie.

Randy wiped the gray goo from her face and arms. "No, I wasn't! Get that bastard!" she shouted angrily.

"Yeah, she was scared," Ronnie muttered to herself. The girls fired repeatedly and one of Randy's rounds struck the creature's left eye.

"I got it!" screamed Randy. "Take that, frog face!"

"I don't think so, Sweetheart. I fired that shot," challenged Ronnie.

"Let's go for the other eye. I bet I'll get that one, too."

The Crocosaurus writhed in pain and clawed at the damaged eye. Fluid seeped from the vacant hole and dotted the concrete below. It spun toward them and roared. The sound echoed through the forest and across the mountains. Large flocks of birds fled into the sky from the treetops.

Randy and Ronnie covered their ears and retreated sensing its anger. More gooey blobs of saliva splattered on the cement around them. The creature lurched forward and snapped again at the girls. They were ready this time and backed away. Randy fired three quick shots and reloaded her pistol. While the girls had the monster's attention, Billy crept closer to its belly. The dinosaur craned toward the edge of the terminal roof and reached for the girls.

Billy's spear wasn't sharp enough to penetrate the creature's tough hide, but he was determined to try anyway. He backed up to the terminal wall and raced forward, pointing the spear toward the dinosaur's underbelly. When the spear struck, it penetrated the thick skin only enough to irritate the creature. The Crocosaurus roared again and backed away from the terminal. Billy desperately clung to the spear, but couldn't free it from the creature's hide.

Ronnie fired her last rounds and holstered her guns. She picked up broken pieces of cement and hurled them down at the creature's head. Randy exhausted her ammo as well, and threw whatever debris she could pick up at the creature.

The Crocosaurus tried to rid itself of the spear and stumbled against the side of the terminal. Billy slammed into the wall and the spear broke loose. He felt pain shooting through his right shoulder from the collision and saw his spear six feet away. The Crocosaurus poised to pounce on him.

"We have to do something fast or Billy's dead!" exclaimed Randy.

Ronnie glanced over the edge of the roof and eyed the creature's position. "I know how to deal with this lizard!"

The Crocosaurus stooped over Billy, its head only about ten feet below the roof. Ronnie broke a four-foot-long piece of Unistrut off the HVAC housing.

"What the hell are you doing?" shouted Randy.

"I still think you were scared. Watch this." Ronnie leaped off the edge of the roof. Randy raced to the edge and looked down in horror.

Ronnie's leap was well timed as she landed on the creature's head. The steel piece of Unistrut embedded itself firmly into the top of the creature's skull. The Crocosaurus reeled backwards with Ronnie hanging on desperately to the Unistrut. It shook its head violently, but the wound proved lethal and quickly drained the lizard of its strength. Ronnie dangled from the creature's head with her legs draped over its upper lip. She struggled to pull herself up on top of the dinosaur's head.

Billy scrambled to his feet and picked up his spear. The dinosaur stumbled forward, forcing him to retreat. He tripped and fell on his back again. As he landed, he pointed the spear up and used the ground to brace it. The Crocosaurus stumbled toward Billy and fell with all its weight coming down on the spear. This time, the spear penetrated well into the creature's belly. Billy scurried out of the way of the wounded reptile.

The Crocosaurus roared in agony and spun toward the terminal. Again, it crashed into the wall and slid to the ground. Its huge body came to rest with a thud on the tarmac. When Billy approached, he heard the beating of the beast's heart as it slowed and then quit. The Crocosaurus had taken its last breath. He looked around but there was no sign of Ronnie.

Randy rushed down from the terminal roof. "Ronnie! Where are you, Ronnie?" she cried as tears streamed down her cheeks. "She's dead, Billy. That freaking monster crushed her." Billy tried to console her and was saddened as he hugged her. She cried on his shoulder.

"I don't know what I'll do without her. She was like my sister."

"We'll get through this," Billy assured her as he wiped tears from his eyes.

Penny and Doc rushed out to meet Billy on the tarmac. "Billy, thank God you and your friends came when you did!" exclaimed Doc.

Penny wrapped her arms around Billy and hugged him while Randy stood next to him. "I hope this is the last of these creatures. I think I crapped myself," Billy blurted.

"Unfortunately, I'm sure there are more of them and I'll bet they are territorial," replied Doc.

Billy stepped aside and pulled Randy to the forefront. "This is Randy. I don't think you've met."

Doc shook hands with her. "Hello, Randy."

"Hi, Doc," Randy said somberly. "Our friend, Ronnie, jumped off the roof and put a metal spike in the dinosaur's head. She must have fallen underneath it." She wiped the tears from her eyes and regained her composure.

"I'm sorry for your loss," Doc said sympathetically.

"I'm going to miss her a lot. We were close." Randy burst into tears again and hugged Billy. Penny glared at him with her arms folded but said nothing. She felt intimidated by both girls' attractiveness and knew she couldn't compete with them to keep Billy. Billy noticed her expression and sensed trouble.

Jerry arrived and looked at the dead dinosaur in awe. "The terminal's pretty much destroyed. We have to find someplace else to go before nightfall," he uttered despondently.

"Do you think there's a chance that we can safely make it to those planes?" Doc inquired.

"It can't be any worse than staying here," replied Billy.

Ronnie emerged from the trees, dirty and bruised. "Well, well. I guess you thought you'd gotten rid of me."

Randy was stunned. "Ronnie, we thought you were dead!" she blurted.

Ronnie crossed the tarmac toward them. "I leaped before the lizard hit the ground. Unfortunately, I rolled half-way down the hill." The girls hugged each other.

"Is there anything you won't do for attention?" Billy kidded.

"You'd be surprised," responded Ronnie, smiling.

Penny felt as though she lost Billy to the girls and stormed off. She couldn't believe how easily that Billy was swayed by them. He watched disappointedly as Penny returned to the terminal. He felt a spirit of camaraderie with Ronnie and Randy after their experience with the dinosaur, yet was frustrated by Penny's reaction to the situation.

"I guess your woman's on the warpath, huh?" commented Randy.

Billy shook his head and muttered. "It doesn't matter."

"Sure, it does. If you like, I could talk to her."

Billy sat down and stared at the ground. "No, it's not worth the trouble."

"Maybe you should talk to her. If she doesn't understand, she'll just have to move on," suggested Ronnie.

"If only it was that simple."

Doc examined the dinosaur and marveled at the precision with which Ronnie drove the uni-strut into its head. Billy stood next to him and gazed in awe at the size of the dinosaur.

"We're leaving tomorrow," Doc informed him. "It's gotten too dangerous here and I'm worried for Maggie's safety. You're welcome to come, along with anyone else that you care to bring."

"I'd like to talk to Penny first." Doc understood and left him to consider his options.

Billy, Ronnie and Randy sat on a log at the edge of the tarmac, staring at the dead dinosaur. "What are you thinking about, Billy?" asked Ronnie.

"I don't understand why Penny got upset."

"Maybe she loves you and she sees us as competition," suggested Ronnie.

"If that's the case, I don't think Penny's very good at competing like you are."

"Maybe you need to clear that up with her. We aren't her competition."

"I might as well face the music," relented Billy. "I'll see you in a while." He stood to leave.

"If you need any help, let us know," offered Randy.

"Thanks, girls," Billy muttered and walked away from them with his head down and his hands in his pockets.

"Hey, wait a minute! I have something of yours," exclaimed Ronnie. When Billy looked back, Ronnie removed a Beretta from the back of her jeans. "I found this on the tarmac. I believe it's yours."

Billy felt his pockets and realized it was his. "Thanks, Ronnie."

"I took the liberty of putting a full magazine in it for you."

Billy took the pistol from her and stowed it in the back pocket of his pants. "Thanks again, Ronnie."

— X —

Inside the terminal, Simon sat with his arm around Penny. She nestled against his shoulder. "I can't believe he betrayed my trust like that," she whimpered.

Simon kissed her forehead. "I'd never do that to you. I would be so happy to have a girl like you to take care of."

Billy approached and was shocked when he saw the two of them together. *Boy, that didn't take long*, he thought. Penny and Simon were surprised to see him.

"Am I interrupting something?" Billy asked sarcastically.

"What do you want, Billy?" Penny asked coldly.

"Can I talk to you alone?"

"When hell freezes over!" she shouted.

"What are you so upset about? I didn't do anything to hurt you."

"You're right, Billy, as always."

"I almost got eaten by a dinosaur out there. Let's talk about this."

"I never want to see you again!" she cried.

Billy tried hard to control his temper but felt betrayed once again by a woman. "Good because I'm done with your nonsense, too," he replied arrogantly.

"My nonsense! How about yours?"

"You think you know everything but you don't know a damn thing. I don't care if I never see you again." Billy marched away; his heart heavy with the consequences of their argument. Penny cried again on Simon's shoulder while he smiled smugly.

Billy went outside the terminal and sat alone under the toppled jetway. After some thought, he decided that he wouldn't make the trip with Doc. It hurt too much to be near Penny.

Randy and Ronnie have the right idea. I don't need a relationship. Perhaps just being friends should be enough to keep everybody happy, he considered.

Billy walked across the tarmac to the dinosaur's carcass to where Doc took notes on the creature. "The creature should give us food for about three days if we cut it up and smoke the meat," Doc remarked.

With no interest in the creature, Billy informed Doc, "I'm staying here. Things aren't going well with Penny and I think it's best for all of us."

"I understand," replied Doc. "I'm sorry that things didn't work out."

Billy trudged away toward the terminal where everyone congregated with their belongings. The girls felt sorry for him as he approached. "We're heading out to the planes, Billy. Are you coming?" asked Ronnie.

"I'll catch up. Get them out of here before our Neanderthal friends show up again."

Penny and Simon walked hand in hand away from the terminal. Billy noticed and became frustrated. "Life sucks and then you die. At least I know what's coming," he muttered.

Billy sat down on a log at the edge of the tarmac. His back ached and his shoulder throbbed with pain. "What the hell am I gonna do now?" he uttered to himself.

Ronnie stood a short distance away and watched him sympathetically as the first group of passengers migrated around the terminal and into the forest.

A large recluse spider, the size of a basketball, descended on a string of silk behind Billy's head. Its legs reached hungrily toward him. Billy turned his head slightly and trembled when he saw the spider from the corner of his eye. He slowly removed his pistol from his pants pocket and turned off the safety. He felt two of the spider's legs touch the side of his head and ear.

Ronnie couldn't see the spider but noticed Billy holding the pistol. She wondered what he was doing and approached him. Billy turned the pistol around and anticipated where the spider was positioned. "Oh, I'm gonna feel this for a long time," he fretted aloud.

From Ronnie's view, Billy pointed the gun at his face. "No, Billy!" she cried out. Billy pulled the trigger and shot the spider. It flew off his shoulder and struck a tree ten feet behind him. He dropped the pistol and fell to his knees. His head pounded from the blast as he covered his ears with both his hands.

Ronnie was relieved to see that he didn't shoot himself. She cradled him against her and comforted him. "Oh, Billy, what the hell were you thinking?" she said sadly. Billy looked up with tear-filled eyes and pointed to the tree.

Ronnie saw the wounded spider twitching on the ground and laughed. "You friggin' jackass! I thought you were going to kill yourself."

Billy looked at her innocently. "What did you say? I can't hear you."

Ronnie grabbed him by the collar and pulled him to his feet. "Let's go hero, before something else happens to you."

Billy stood up and doubled over in pain. "Give me a minute, will you? My head feels like it's going to explode."

Randy hurried over. "What the hell happened?"

"Our hero shot a spider off his shoulder," Ronnie explained.

"You dumb ass. Couldn't you come up with a better way than that to get rid of a little spider?"

Ronnie pointed to the still-twitching spider. "That's not such a little spider."

Randy walked over to it and stomped the life out of it. "Now it's a dead spider." The two girls escorted Billy away from the terminal. He slowly recovered his hearing and equilibrium.

— X —

Ruger and Pirocles gazed at the white smoke rising from his silver chest. He saw the image of the dead dinosaur on the tarmac and groaned in disgust. Another image formed of the spider, smashed to pieces on the ground. Ruger shrieked and pounded his fist against the table.

"What do we do now?" asked Pirocles, concerned.

"I'm not done with him yet. I swear I'll make sure he dies a horrible death."

"Why don't we just go there and kill him ourselves?"

Ruger pulled Pirocles by his sleeve to the window. He pointed down at the battle raging outside his castle. "How long do you think my army would last if I leave them now?"

"But, Ruger, I could empower them for you."

"I need to know what resources our enemies have before I risk leaving, even for a little while."

"I will find out," Pirocles offered and left the chamber. Ruger glared out the window at thirteen cloaked figures on top of the neighboring hillside. They stared back at him defiantly.

— X —

Once everyone was moved to the jets with their belongings, the men set about making the area defensible. The women performed domestic preparations and scavenged materials off the planes for use in the camp.

Ronnie and Randy rummaged through cabinets in one of the planes and took inventory of all the medical supplies. Billy limped inside the jet and took a seat by the girls.

Ronnie was surprised to see him. "Back so soon? We didn't think you'd be out to play for a while," she kidded. When Billy didn't respond, she felt pity for him. "Say something, Billy."

"I think I need to be alone until I get my head on straight."

Ronnie sat on Billy's lap and tried to console him. "You don't have to be alone. We're your friends." She held his head in her hands and kissed his forehead but he didn't respond. "Where do you think you're going to hide until you're ready to face your problems?"

Billy stared out the window. "I'm not hiding. I want to go to the top of those cliffs and see what lies beyond them."

"If you get your fool self killed after I just risked my life to save it, there isn't any place in heaven or hell where your soul can hide from me. I will come kick your ass," warned Ronnie.

"We care about you, Billy. There's nothing that can't be worked out," added Randy.

"I know, but I have to do this. I'm already coming off one piss-poor relationship and now I do the early death spiral in another. It's too painful for me."

Randy turned her back to him and became teary-eyed. She knew it was suicide to venture off alone and Billy knew that as well. Ronnie stood up and stared at him, speechless.

"When I come back, I'll be my old self again. I'll make it up to the two of you for putting up with me," he promised.

"If you come back. You know what you're risking," chastised Ronnie.

"I do." Billy hugged each of the girls and departed the plane.

"I hope he makes it back," whimpered Randy as she sadly watched him leave. Randy felt a certain attraction for Billy but was reluctant to share it.

Jerry observed the winged reptiles flying over the treetops when Billy approached him.

"What do you think of this place so far?" Billy asked.

"I'm still waiting for someone to pinch me or tell me that I'm on Candid Camera," answered Jerry.

"Yeah, this is hard to believe."

Jerry pointed at the large flying reptiles in the sky. "Did you ever see anything like them?"

"They look very similar to Pterodactyls except their beaks are shorter."

"This is absolutely astounding. These creatures could be distant cousins to the reptiles that once inhabited Earth."

"I've got something to tell you, Jerry."

"What's that, partner?"

"I'm going away for a few days to sort some things out."

"Do you know where to find a good pub that you're not telling me about?" he kidded.

Billy tried to force a smile but couldn't. "I need to figure some things out for myself. I'll be back when I have the answers." He hoped that Jerry would have some words of wisdom for him. Jerry was like the favorite uncle in a family, the way he cared about everybody and never acted selfishly. He was forty-five years old and very practical about things.

"Want some company?" Jerry offered.

"No. I have to do this myself. It's really important to me."

"When you return, I hope you decide to stay. These people need a leader or two to help them survive. Without one, they are like sheep in a slaughterhouse."

"How about you?" suggested Billy.

"You're young and have much to learn, but good leaders lead by example. You motivated everyone to get off the plane before it exploded. You found these planes for shelter. You saved Penny from the Neanderthals and you killed a big old dinosaur. That's a tough act to follow."

"But I didn't kill the dinosaur, Jerry."

Jerry laughed at him. "It doesn't matter. You had the courage to confront it and the end result was good. Now we even have food for a few days, which solved another pressing issue."

Billy realized that he did make a difference and was glad he confided in Jerry. Unfortunately, he had his own troubles to think about, let alone everyone else's.

"Think about it," pleaded Jerry.

Billy shook Jerry's hand. "I will. We'll see what happens when I return."

As Billy walked away from the two jets, Maggie intercepted him. She handed him a bag with six cans of juice and a few pieces of fruit. "Good luck, Billy. I'll miss you. I really hoped that things would work out for you and Penny."

"Thanks, Maggie. I did, too."

Maggie reluctantly walked away from him. Billy felt like a pariah for leaving his friends like this but his issues with Penny opened old wounds. Until he found closure, he would never have a normal relationship. He looked back hesitantly at the planes and wondered if he'd ever see any of his friends again. When he thought about Randy and Ronnie, his emotions jumbled and he grew more confused. They cared about him but in a strange sort of way – kind of like sisters.

— X —

Randy saw Penny with Simon by the fire and approached her. "Hi, Penny. Mind if I join you?"

Penny looked up at her with sad eyes. "What for?" she replied bitterly.

"I'd like to clear the air on a few things."

"I don't have to clear the air about anything. You can have Billy. I'm not interested in him anymore, alright!"

"Missy, you are so naïve. You don't have a clue about anything, do you?"

"Look, I'm leaving with Simon and I don't care what the three of you do. I'll be gone and you'll all be happy." Simon smiled arrogantly at Randy.

"Girl, you need to grow up fast. You're letting a good man slip out of your life and all you can do is feel pity for yourself."

"What do you mean by that?"

"Billy cares about you very much and he made that clear to us right from the beginning. We became friends because we're adventurous. It has nothing to do with love or sexual attraction. He's a rare man and you're tossing him away."

Penny became embarrassed. "Did he really say that?" she asked sheepishly.

"Why do you think I'm telling you this? You need to do something before it's too late."

Penny was stunned by Randy's revelation and was speechless. Randy's attraction to Billy wasn't going to be tarnished by Penny's misconceptions about their friendship. She was going to do right by Penny and Billy then let nature take its course. "You know, Penny, we could be friends. You don't have to resent us and we sure don't resent you."

"I appreciate your kindness, Randy but it's too late. I'm leaving tomorrow," Penny explained sadly.

"Things have a funny way of working out. Perhaps we'll meet again."

"I hope so." When Randy walked away, Penny was more confused than ever about what to do.

"Don't let them fool you," warned Simon. "I know they don't like me. They'll do anything to sabotage our relationship."

"Is it a relationship, Simon? I barely know you."

"You will, in time."

Penny was fretful over her situation. "I need some space right now, Simon. I hope you can understand that." Simon became annoyed and walked away. Penny walked sullenly to one of the jets and stepped through the open hatch. She took a seat inside the empty aircraft and reclined. All she could think about was Billy. She curled up in the seat and cried herself to sleep.

CHAPTER 5

KINGDOM OF THE SPIDERS

Billy walked at a brisk pace through the trees until he reached a swift, winding stream along the base of the cliffs. The water splashed noisily off the rocks before passing smoothly downstream. The stream grew wider and deeper with sandy banks on either side.

Billy knelt in the warm sand, cupped his hands in the water and sipped. It tasted good, not at all like he was used to. After a brief rest, he hiked further. Strange sounds surrounded him, both exciting and frightening. The distant roars of creatures like the Crocosaurus unnerved him. At times, he found himself talking to no one in particular and laughed over his tendency to do so. Further downstream, he sensed something in the air that made him edgy.

Billy ducked between two large tree trunks and squeezed into a rotten tree stump where he was well concealed. If someone or something was following, he would find out soon. The branches above him shook and five small creatures dropped to the ground. Billy watched curiously as the little critters walked erect. They were only a foot high and yellow in color.

They were hairless with pointed ears. His first impression of them was that they were a harmless species of penguin.

The creatures probed the grass and rocks until the snapping of branches sent them scurrying into the trees. A dappled pony trotted out of the forest and perched at the stream to drink. The little creatures emerged from the trees, squealing like angry chipmunks. They bared nasty little fangs and sharp claws as they circled the frightened pony.

When the pony attempted to flee, two of the creatures leaped at its front legs and gnawed rabidly on them. One by one, the others leapt upon the helpless pony until it stumbled and lay helpless in the sand. Billy was stunned with the precision that the creatures attacked. Within a few moments, they tore out the pony's entrails and devoured them. They feasted on its limbs in satanic fashion and reveled in its blood.

Billy was horrified as he watched. Sweat beaded on his forehead and he itched all over. With all the patience and self-control, he could muster, he remained motionless inside the tree stump. When the little creatures finished their meal, they vanished into the trees as quickly as they appeared.

Billy was relieved. He listened for the telltale sound of the trees before leaving the stump. He heard nothing but the wind. When he emerged from hiding, he inspected the bloody remains of the pony. He was awed by the carnage left by such innocent looking creatures.

Billy waded across the stream toward the cliffs. He hiked upstream for three more hours and then paused to rest. The wind whistled across the cliffs, creating an eerie sound like a voice calling to him. "Is someone out there?" shouted Billy. He waited but heard nothing.

"Ronnie! Randy! If that's you, I'm going to be really ticked off." Again, he heard nothing. Billy studied the cliffs and discovered a narrow crevice about a third the way up the face. The cliffs sloped steeply upward with a ledge cut into the side of the cliff. It led to the crevice like a welcome mat to him. There was no sign of danger so he hiked up the long, jagged trail to the crevice.

— X —

Ruger studied the image in the smoke over his silver chest and saw Billy scale the side of the cliff. He left the table and opened an old wooden cabinet in the corner with rickety doors. Inside were four shelves, each lined with masons' jars and boxes. He retrieved a brown box from the top shelf and returned to the table with it.

After glancing one more time at the image of Billy, he opened the box and eyed its contents. Inside the box were dozens of tiny spiders. Ruger raised his left arm and chanted a spell. He laughed sadistically as he dumped the spiders from the box into the silver chest. "Now, I'll put this pest out of his misery for good."

Ruger took a brown sack from under his cloak and sprinkled a small amount of dust from it into the box. He focused on the smoke as images formed of giant spiders swarming around trees and rocks, weaving their web everywhere.

"Now, it's time to end this war, once and for all," declared Ruger. Returning to the window, he pointed at the thirteen wizards on top of the adjacent hill and shouted an incantation. A bolt of lightning struck the hill and deflected back at his castle. A loud bang, followed by an explosion left a gaping hole in the side of one of the towers.

"Damn, you!" he shouted at his enemies as he fled to another chamber.

— X —

The early morning sun shone through the windows of the aircraft. Penny slept across seats in the aircraft with a blanket over her. When the light reached across the blanket and touched her face, she awoke, feeling tired and hungry. She grabbed a towel from the luggage compartment overhead and went to the stream to bathe. The air was chilly but the sun warmed her skin and gave her a sense of security that she was safe for now.

Penny searched the area around the stream to ensure that she was alone. She stripped down to her bra and panties and stepped into the stream. The water was crystal clear but chilly. She bathed quickly and dried herself off. As she sat on a large flat rock by the edge of the stream, she toweled off her hair and wondered if Doc's trip might be a mistake.

Simon approached and sat next to her on the rock. "Good morning, Penny. How are you feeling, today?"

"Alright, I guess."

"Is there anything I can do for you?"

"No, not really." Penny suddenly realized that she was scantily dressed and became embarrassed. "Can you give me some time alone to dress? We'll talk later."

Simon couldn't help ogling her. "Of course," he said reluctantly.

Penny modestly covered herself with the towel. "Thanks, Simon. I really do appreciate your patience."

"Perhaps it will be rewarded later," he hinted. Simon walked away with an air of arrogance that bothered her. She dressed and returned to the jet.

Jerry opened the cargo bay doors on one of the planes. He retrieved pieces of luggage from inside and stacked them on the ground. "Hi, Jerry. What are you up to?" Penny asked pleasantly while on her way back from the stream.

"Just doing a little clothes shopping." Jerry pointed to several bags stacked nearby and suggested, "Why don't you browse through those and see if you can find some things to take with you. I don't think the owners will need them anymore."

"I guess I could use a few things," she replied. Together, they pulled out pieces of luggage and sorted through them. Penny found some jeans and shirts in her size. "These will do."

Jerry removed more bags and set them neatly in front of the plane. Penny searched another suitcase and found a yellow dress. After holding it up and eying it for a moment, she decided that it would fit nicely. She hoped that someday there would be an occasion to wear it. She also took some socks, a pair of sneakers, and a jacket. "This should be plenty, Jerry. Thank you."

"You're welcome, Penny." Jerry stared at her pitifully but said nothing.

Penny sensed that he wanted to say something. "What's wrong?" she asked.

"I wish you and the good doctor would reconsider your trip. It's going to be really dangerous. At least you're safer here than out there in the wilderness."

"But it's dangerous here, too," she remarked.

"I know, but you have the shelter of the aircraft and friends."

Sadly, Penny explained, "I have to go, Jerry."

"But what if Billy comes back?"

"Billy and I are finished," she informed him. "Some things just weren't meant to be."

"Well, good luck. I hope you make it to wherever you're going."

"Thanks, Jerry."

They hugged briefly and she walked away.

— ✕ —

Doc and Maggie walked across the compound. Doc noticed the position of the sun in the early morning sky. "I figure that each day is thirty-one hours long instead of twenty-four," he estimated.

"This is going to take some getting used to. Between the atmosphere and the long days, I'm really tired," complained Maggie.

"We'll adapt to it like we always do, Sweetheart."

They stopped to observe the men working on wooden fences along the perimeter around the two large aircraft. Doc was impressed that the area around the planes was cleared of foliage already and the fences were partially erected. Nearby, the women set up facilities for cooking.

Five men, including Simon, joined Doc and discussed the details of the proposed trip to the observatory. Penny greeted them, sounding tired.

"It's time to leave, everyone. This is your last chance to change your mind," announced Doc. He studied each of their faces but no one replied. "Then let's get going, shall we?"

Simon stood beside Penny and held her hand. "Do you mind if I go, too?"

"It's your choice. I'm not very good company right now."

"Well, I'm your friend and I'm here to help."

"Alright, friend. Let's stop talking and start walking."

The group departed the camp and headed south.

— ✕ —

When Billy reached the crevice, he looked back at the fading daylight and wondered if he would ever see it again. After some hesitation, he entered the crevice armed with his pistol and a flashlight. A short distance later, he entered a huge cavern. The first thing he noticed was that the bottom was shaped like a large, white bowl and had an eerie glow to it. He inched along a narrow ledge and encountered long strands of white rope dangling along the walls. When he touched one of the ropes, it felt sticky but soft, like wet silk. He considered that large quantities of this material might make up the glowing, white aura below.

Stones and loose sediment trickled down the wall and fell to the cavern floor but there was no sound. Billy thought that was odd. He scanned the walls above him with his flashlight but saw nothing. When more stones and dirt fell around him, he became worried and hurried past the strands.

A twanging sound from above caught his attention. He again searched the wall above him with the flashlight. It was difficult to recognize anything on the black, rocky wall but Billy sensed something was up there. He sidled along the narrowing ledge until he reached a cave.

Billy ducked into the cave and backed away from the entrance. Small spots glistened in the darkness covering the cave's opening.

Billy became curious and approached it. Suddenly he realized he was looking into the eyes of a huge spider. Before he could retreat, a long hairy leg with barbs shot toward him and caught on his pants. The force of the limb knocked him down and dragged him toward the mouth of the cave. His pistol fell from his pants pocket on the ground behind him. Billy desperately clawed at the ground and clutched at a rock until his pants tore away from the spider's leg. He scurried to his feet and retrieved his pistol. The spider retracted its leg and disappeared from the entrance. Billy curled up against the wall in tears. After several minutes, he regained his composure and fled down the tunnel.

— **X** —

The animals were restless as darkness engulfed the forest. Strange noises and howls made everyone uneasy. Doc kept an aggressive pace as his group trekked through the forest. The warm, humid air brought beads of sweat across their brows.

A short, bald fellow named Ted complained, "How 'bout we call it a day, Doc? I'm beat." The other two men nodded in agreement.

"We've got all the time in the world to get there. What's the rush?" asked another man.

Doc was overzealous about reaching his colleague's observatory and realized the dangers of traveling through the forest at night. "Alright, let's find a place to camp for the night," he said reluctantly.

Ted noticed a remote spot at the base of the cliffs that could be defended easily. "How about we camp over there, Dr. Smith?"

Doc studied the area and agreed that it was adequate. When they reached the clearing, Ted and Jeff made a small fire while the others unpacked and set up camp for the night.

Simon sat with Penny and held her hand. "What's it going to take for you to open up to me?" he asked.

"What do you want from me, Simon?" Penny replied, frustrated with his persistence.

"I want to be your lover. I know I can make you happy."

"That's why I can't open up to you," she responded sarcastically. "This is all about you and your personal needs."

Simon grew frustrated. "Come on, Penny. That's not fair."

"Look, Simon, Billy wanted to know the real me and was content to take things slow. You want to bed me, wed me and shed me after knowing me less than a week. Find someone else." Penny got up and walked away from him.

"You're a real pain in the ass, Penny. You know that?"

Penny thought to herself, *Yeah, I am. That's the story of my life.* She lay down alone by the fire and cried herself to sleep.

— X —

Randy and Ronnie sat on rocks by the stream with their feet dangling in the water. Each carried a pistol and kept a wary eye on the forest around them. They were bored and couldn't wait for Billy to return. "At least when Billy was here, something exciting always happened," complained Randy.

"Yeah, things have been a little too quiet for my liking," Ronnie replied, disappointed.

"So, what do we do about it?"

"What if we follow Doc's group like an escort in case they get into trouble?"

"Good idea," Randy responded, feeling enthused. "It beats sitting around here." The girls gathered a few days' worth of supplies from the supply hut and set out in search of Doc's group. After four hours, they exited the forest and crossed a rolling field. Soon, they were on the fringes of another forest with huge trees. Nightfall descended and forced them to halt their progress.

"I guess we're going to rough it here tonight," complained Randy.

"Suck it up, you big crybaby," mocked Ronnie.

Randy nestled between two rocks and rested her head on her knapsack.

Ronnie studied the tree limbs above. "We should sleep up in the trees, you know. It'd be a lot safer."

"I'm good here. You go play Tarzan in the trees."

An insect, resembling a giant tic, rose from behind the rocks over Randy's head.

"Don't you ever…" Ronnie replied but stopped abruptly. She saw the insect and instinctively retrieved the knife from under her belt. The insect raised a sickle-shaped leg over Randy's head and green fluid dribbled from its jaws. Ronnie raised the knife behind her ear and aimed at the insect.

Randy heard the insect's clicking sound and saw the intense look on Ronnie's face. Drops of green fluid dropped onto her cheek. She was frozen with fear. "Do something, Ronnie!"

"Hold still."

Randy closed her eyes and trembled. Ronnie fired the knife at the insect's head and knocked it off the rocks. The knife stuck out of the insect's face from under its right eye.

Randy opened her eyes and looked behind the rock. "Oh, shit, Ronnie! You could have hit me."

"I said 'hold still'." Ronnie walked behind the rock and retrieved her knife from the dead insect. She wiped the insect's fluids from the blade with a broad leaf and stowed it under her belt.

Randy stood up and examined the dead insect. "Oh, that is so gross!" she uttered.

Ronnie climbed up a tree and nestled in between two branches. "You should reconsider my suggestion," she reminded Randy. "Good night."

Randy scurried up another tree and settled between two large branches as well.

— ⧗ —

Billy crawled on hands and knees across the rough stone ground until he tired and his back ached. The tunnel narrowed in many places and the ceiling became low. He lost hope that he would ever find his way back to the outside world. The flashlight grew dim as the batteries drained down. He paused at a split in the cave. It was eerily quiet except for the whistling of the wind. He stared at the two paths with his dim flashlight. The right path sloped steeply downward while the left path rose gradually and had a higher ceiling. He chose the left path where he could at least stand up and walk. The beam from his flashlight became barely noticeable. His head struck a rock, jutting down from the ceiling. He fell to the ground unconscious.

Billy awoke when he realized someone carried him through the tunnel. His head spun from the earlier collision and he felt nauseous. He saw a torch ahead of him and feared that his captors could be Neanderthals. He struggled but his arms were bound to his body by a blanket wrapped around him. A warm breeze swept into the tunnel and gave Billy hope as he realized it was fresh air. They emerged from the cave onto a plateau with four primitive huts and a campfire under an evening sky. Two of his captors set him down inside a bamboo hut. Billy slid out of the wool cloak that wrapped around his body. He sat against the wall of the hut and watched his captors.

"Who are you and where did you come from?" asked one of them.

Billy was relieved to hear a man speak in English to him. "I'm Billy Brock. I'm not from around here, if that's what you mean." The man pulled his cloak back and revealed a worn, bearded face.

"Who are you?" Billy asked.

"In time," answered the man. "Come with us."

Billy exited the hut and joined them. Eleven men sat in a circle around the fire and removed their hoods. All of them had worn appearances and seemed very secretive. Two of the men moved apart and made room for Billy to sit between them. "My name is John Murdoch of Suffolk, England," said the eldest of the men.

"I'm Billy Brock from Boston. Where did you sail from?"

"My men and I sailed from our homeland to the colonies but were caught in an unusual storm. We ran aground at the base of these cliffs."

"Is this all of your men?" asked Billy.

"Yes. Shortly after our arrival, creatures from the sea attacked us. Fighting was futile and we lost many. We found a cave that led us up to this plateau but we've been stuck here ever since."

Billy recalled the strange clouds and the intense storm his plane passed through and wondered if it was the same phenomenon that affected these men.

John continued, "The other day, we experienced a storm similar to that fateful day. We found nothing strange had come of it, until we found you in the tunnel."

"You mentioned 'colonies.' What year did you sail to the colonies?" asked Billy.

"November of 1746."

Billy was amazed at the thought of being stranded with 18th century Englishmen. "Would you believe that I'm from the year 2021?" The men stared at him and wondered how this could be possible.

Another man stepped forward. "My name is Seamus McCourt. Were others stranded here with you?"

"Yes, there were many. We are ill prepared for this environment, though, and many have already died."

"Is your camp better suited for survival compared to this isolated region?" asked John.

"It's hard to say. We've only been here a short while," answered Billy.

"We had another visitor from the future a few days after our arrival."

"From my future?" inquired Billy.

"I'm not sure. We lost several of our men to poisoning. He taught us many things about surviving here. One night, he left us to fulfill his mission."

"Have you encountered any dinosaurs up here?" Billy inquired.

"No, it's been relatively peaceful thus far. Why?"

Billy related the story of the Crocosaurus and the Neanderthals. The men were impressed with his successes against the creatures. "It sounds like you've already come a long way toward surviving in this world," commented John.

"Not far enough."

One of the men brought Billy some meat on a wooden dish and a mug of water. John and Seamus walked a short distance away and quietly discussed something that obviously involved Billy. A young man knelt in front of Billy. "Hi, Billy. My name is Wills. Are there any women with your group that might require the services of a man?"

"I think you could find one or two to your liking out of the bunch," Billy replied, amused by the question.

"That would be nice. It's been quite lonely around here."

"I'll bet it is."

John returned and explained to Billy. "We are limited to where we can go from up here. We've explored the tunnels in search of a way off this forsaken plateau but never found one. Perhaps we can help your people defend themselves if you can lead us out of here."

"So long as you can get me back to where you found me," responded Billy. "Do you mind if I ask you a question, though?"

"You may."

"Why the cloaks? Are you part of a religious cult or something?"

Seamus thought Billy's question was very funny and laughed heartily. "Nay, we're not of a cult. After the first few days, we developed rashes. Something in the air up here attacks the skin. Since we wore the cloaks for protection, the condition of our skin has gotten better," he related.

"Xerxes identified the germs and instructed us to wear the cloaks," added John.

Billy wondered about the stranger. "This Xerxes, did he say when he came from?"

"He claimed to have traveled here through a portal. He didn't say much about it except there were evil forces were at work and we're all in danger."

"The stranger spoke just like you. His English was very smooth," mentioned Seamus.

"Where did Xerxes go?"

"He left for the northern mountains," John responded. "He would not allow us to accompany him. All he said was that his mission was to destroy evil."

"So, when do we leave?" asked Billy.

"How about 1746?" replied Seamus cynically. The men laughed at his humor.

"We'll leave at the crack of dawn, if you don't mind," suggested John.

"That's fine with me."

The men left him and retired to their huts. Billy finished his meal and when the last torch flickered out, he fell asleep. Things were much quieter on the plateau. The only inhabitants were birds and small animals. Further up in the mountains were undoubtedly larger creatures, but that was a distance from their camp.

When morning came, Billy awakened to a warm breakfast. One of the men prepared a meal of poached eggs and bread. They also had hot tea, which was a pleasant surprise to Billy. "How did you make tea?" Billy asked.

The man pointed to a steaming spring in the rocks. "Hot water comes from the spring. Xerxes found these leaves growing nearby and instructed us to boil them in the water. It's surprisingly better than our regular tea blends back home."

The man poured the tea into a wooden mug and handed it to Billy. He sipped from it and nodded with approval. "This is definitely better than the tea I'm used to," Billy remarked. He finished his tea and walked to the edge of the plateau. He gazed at a vertical drop down the cliffs to the ocean below. To the north, he saw a fantastic chain of mountains, larger than any on Earth.

When the Englishmen stowed their cloaks, each revealed a coat of armor and donned a sword in a scabbard. Billy was impressed and realized they were special. "So, you weren't just sailors on the ship, you were also warriors, huh?"

"Not quite warriors, but we can fight," replied John.

"This is really cool: swordsmen from the seventeen hundreds!"

"We use guns as well, although ours are much more primitive than yours, I'm sure. We expected gunpowder to be a limited resource, so we've tried to conserve what little we have left," explained John. He reached under his armor and pulled out Billy's pistol. "I believe this is yours," he said as he handed it to him.

Billy was grateful and responded, "Thanks for everything. I'd never have found my way out of these caves if it weren't for you and your men."

"Our hopes grew when we found that you were civil and human."

"I may be human but civil – I don't know," kidded Billy. The Englishmen appreciated Billy's humor and laughed.

Four of the men lit torches and waited by the cave's entrance. "Well, boys, are we ready?" asked Billy.

John pointed to the cave and stepped back. "It's your show now."

"Then let's get out of here." Billy descended into the cave followed by the others.

After a long stretch of silence, John commented, "I take it that you have much on your mind, Billy. Is this why you travel the caves alone?"

"I'm afraid it does. If you can believe it, women are driving me crazy."

"I'm sorry to hear that. It sounds complicated."

"Oh, it is."

"What is the future like, Billy?" interrupted Wills.

"Where do you want me to start? You're about two hundred and seventy years behind." The men laughed.

"What am I missing that's so funny?" inquired Seamus.

"History, Seamus. Lots of history," quipped John.

"What became of the New World? Does Britannia still rule America?" Seamus asked excitedly.

Billy chose his words carefully so as to not offend his friends. "In the twenty-first century, Great Britain and the United States are very good allies. They worked together to win some very big wars as well as several smaller ones. Originally, the thirteen colonies broke away from Britain and formed the United States. They fought a very intense war, but the United States eventually succeeded. The thirteen colonies became states and grew to become fifty states that reached across the entire continent." The other men overheard them and clustered more closely together.

"Can you tell us what happened to the English monarchy after 1746?" asked Seamus. The group huddled even closer as Billy did his best to remember his history.

"The United States didn't conquer England. They only broke away. The Monarchy is alive and well."

The men cheered at the news. They recognized several of the names Billy mentioned in his stories and urged him to continue. Their history lesson passed the time pleasantly until the men tired. As they approached the cavern, Billy became edgy. "We'll have to get past a huge spider in the cavern before we can leave."

John laughed at him. "A spider, eh?"

"You'll see."

When they reached the entrance to the cavern, they found it blocked by a wall of silk. John rubbed some of the silk between his fingers and frowned. The silk had a sticky quality to it that made him uneasy. "How big of a spider are we talking about?"

"I was twelve feet away from the entrance when its leg reached in and snagged my pants. It must have been pretty big."

"Perhaps we can burn the web away from the entrance and maybe the rest of this thing's lair as well," suggested Seamus.

"No, we'd all choke to death from the smoke. Cut a hole in it," ordered John.

A tall broad-shouldered man with long, reddish hair stepped forward with his sword drawn and cut into the web. At first, it was difficult but once he started the cut, he was able to slice through it much more easily. After several strokes, the man pealed a section of the silk to the side.

"Be careful. We don't know if the spider's waiting on the other side," warned John.

"It's nothing we can't handle," replied the man confidently. He took the torch from Seamus and stowed his sword. As soon as he leaned through the opening, his body writhed violently. The webbed wall ripped away with the man's body and the passage to the cavern was open. The man's guttural screams sent chills down Billy's spine. The others were horrified as well.

"Let's go before it comes back!" exclaimed Billy.

The men followed Billy into the cavern and onto the ledge. Billy stumbled several times on rocks as he hurried. They nearly reached the cave when the ledge gave way. Billy tumbled first and fell helplessly. The remainder of the ledge gave way and the Englishmen fell, too. They screamed as they plummeted to the bottom of the cavern.

Billy landed on a giant web and became entangled in the sticky strands. He looked up fearfully as three torches fell around him and stuck to the web. The men landed near him and became stuck as well. The web shook several times as the men struggled to free themselves.

"It's like quicksand! I can't get loose," cried Billy.

"The more you struggle, the worse it gets. Don't move," ordered John.

— X —

Ruger opened the silver chest and peered inside. He chanted an incantation and watched as the white smoke arose. Pirocles entered the room. "There are enemy reinforcements approaching from the western regions. We need to do something to counter them!" he announced frantically.

"Not now, you fool. So long as these distractions exist, I cannot focus my powers on them."

An image formed, showing Billy and his English friends trapped in the web. "Excellent!" shouted Ruger. "Our problem is solved."

"Should we recall the Neanderthals?" Pirocles asked. "We could use their help."

"No, I want all of the humans killed before we summon them. There must be no chance of their interference in my plans. Now, I must see Diomedes and give her the good news."

"But the battle, Ruger? There are more armies coming!"

"I'll deal with them. My power will strengthen now that I'm rid of this distraction."

— X —

John pulled a knife from his boot and cut his legs free, leaving holes in the web. He saw the rocky floor of the cavern only six feet beneath him. He cut his arm free and dropped to the ground. One of the men screamed and the web shook wildly. The man disappeared in the clutches of the spider.

Seamus struggled frantically. "Please cut me loose, John!" he pleaded.

John methodically cut the web away from Seamus' arms. Seamus saw the dark shape of the spider swinging above them. "Please, John, hurry! It's coming again." John cut Seamus' legs free and lowered him to the ground. Another man screamed as the web shook crazily. His voice soon ended in a gurgling sound.

Billy panicked when he saw the shadow of the spider approaching him. "It's coming again!" John cut Billy loose and helped him to the ground.

Wills screamed as the giant spider closed in on him. Seamus realized that he couldn't free Wills in time and hid beneath him. He drew his sword and waited patiently.

"Seamus, help me! Don't leave me here!" cried Wills.

"I'm right here, Wills. I won't abandon you."

"Seamus, let's go! It's too late for him," ordered John. Seamus waved him off and held his position.

Billy watched Seamus and wondered what he was planning. Suddenly, he understood. He searched the ground and found a long, dead piece of wood. He kicked at the end and snapped a section off, leaving a sharp point on it. "Here, Seamus. Use this instead."

Seamus caught the spear-shaped branch from Billy and stowed his sword. He shoved the spear through the web into the spider's throat just as it descended on Wills. The spider emitted a shrill, high-pitched sound that echoed deafeningly throughout the cavern. Seamus cut the remaining silk from Wills' legs amid the dripping fluids and sagging web.

The spider struggled to free itself from the spear embedded in its neck. Its front legs desperately slapped at the spear but to no avail. Wills fell to the ground, visibly shaken. Billy and Seamus helped him away from the web to the wall of the cavern. The spider's body slid down the shaft of the spear and crashed through the web. Rocks smashed the ground around them as strands of web pulled away from the wall of the cavern.

The men felt sympathy for Wills as he fought back tears. "Are you alright?" asked Billy.

Wills trembled as he wiped the spider's fluids off of his face and chest. "Never been better," he replied sarcastically.

Wills patted Billy and Seamus on the back. "Thanks, guys. I thought I was a goner."

"You'd have done the same for me," replied Seamus.

"I let my men down," John muttered dejectedly.

"Forget it," replied Billy. "It worked out."

"Which way do we dare try now?"

Billy searched the cavern walls but it seemed hopeless as he couldn't see anything in the dark. "There's got to be a passage out of here. How else would a spider that size feed?" he complained.

"Maybe it didn't come from the outside," suggested John.

"What do you mean by that?"

"The web is still wet so it's recent. How does something that big get into a cavern like this without a big entrance?"

"Beats me. How?"

"I don't know. Perhaps it's black magic or something worse."

"It's not like we have a lot of options here, guys. How about we start looking for a way out?" suggested Wills.

"Relax, Wills. I'm sure you're upset right now but it's not helping."

"Upset! Who me? Why would that be?"

"Wills, I didn't have any choice," John replied, embarrassed by his decision to leave him. "You know as well as I do, we have to be smart to survive."

"If Billy didn't get me that spear, I don't know that I could have saved you," added Seamus.

"Well, I'm still shaking in my boots."

Billy rubbed Wills' shoulder. "You'll feel better once we get out of here."

"I'm gonna have nightmares for years over this," he grumbled.

"Just wait until you meet some of the other creatures. I promise, you'll forget all about this one."

Wills burst into laughter. "I like you, Billy. You're funny."

"Ah, it's just that twenty-first century humor. It'll get old."

They retrieved two torches from the web that still burned and searched for an exit. After circling halfway around the cavern, they felt a gentle breeze blowing through one of the tunnels. "That could be our way out!" exclaimed John.

Wills paused by a white mass next to the path. He poked at it with the tip of his sword. "Holy Father in heaven!" He turned and vomited against the wall.

Seamus examined the mass and recognized the remains of one of their comrades taken by the spider earlier. The body was covered in silk like a cocoon, and the face was contorted in a horrible shape. The throat was ripped open, but there was no blood. "Damn spider sucked him dry," commented Seamus somberly.

John made the sign of the cross over the corpse and said a short prayer. He cut through the web until he found the man's sword and scabbard. He removed it and turned to Billy. "Take this sword. I want you to wield it with pride. It belonged to a brave warrior."

Billy accepted the weapon and strapped it around his waist. "Thank you, John. I'll do my best."

"Let's go, men," ordered John.

They entered the tunnel and followed the draft. Billy unsheathed his new sword and admired the workmanship. The sword was no ordinary weapon. It was custom made for its previous owner by someone with exceptional skills. On the hilt was a skull with roses and rubies around it. He hoped that he could use the sword with even some of the skills that his warrior-friends had.

Wills noticed how much Billy admired it. "I'd be happy to teach you to wield the sword like a true warrior."

"Thank you, Wills. I gladly accept your offer."

As they proceeded through the webbed tunnel, Wills instructed Billy on basic exercises in sword technique. Billy practiced the techniques repeatedly until they reached a white wasteland. The trees were rotted and wrapped in web, covered with layers of silk so thick that daylight couldn't penetrate through. It looked like a ghostly underworld.

The men stopped for rest and a bite to eat. Billy sat alone on a stump and ate some of their wafer-like pieces of bread. As much as he enjoyed the company of the men, he found himself obsessed with Penny. Billy lowered his head in disappointment. He remembered that Doc was leaving and wondered if Randy and Ronnie, or Jerry, would go along, too. *Perhaps they're all gone. I may never see any of them again*, he thought to himself.

An eerie sensation filled the air around them like the tingling of electricity. The web above them rippled. "On your feet, men. The demons are about us!" exclaimed John.

"Something stirs above us, but I don't see anything," said Seamus.

The men formed a circle with their backs to each other and waited. Black spiders descended strands of glistening web from the white ceiling above. They looked remarkably like wolf spiders with thick furry legs and piercing, black eyes. "At least they're smaller than the last spider," quipped Seamus.

"I'm gonna put a hurting on these spiders like they never saw," Wills replied sarcastically.

"Don't underestimate them," warned John.

Billy drew his sword, as did the others, and prepared to do battle. When the first spider dropped within striking distance, Seamus struck with his sword and slit the belly open. White fluid spewed from its belly onto the ground. The other men slashed at the spiders in the same fashion.

Billy's first cut was awkward. He slit the spider's side open and hacked two of its leg off. The spider stood up and stalked him. Before he could strike again, the spider leaped at him. His next stroke found its mark across the spider's head and slashed it open. The wounded spider and Billy both tumbled to the ground. The spider lay dead on top of him. Its fluids seeped over his chest. "Son of a bitch! This thing smells," he muttered.

"Get back in the circle, now!" ordered John. Billy pushed the spider off and hurried back into formation.

"Keep your eyes on them and don't break the circle. That means you, too, Wills," warned John.

"Yeah, yeah. I know."

Billy saw another spider descend close by. He struck at the spider using the same technique that Seamus used. When he felt the smooth stroke of the sword slice the stomach open, he knew he grasped the proper technique. He sidestepped the white mess that oozed from the dead spider and stepped out from the circle toward another spider. Again, he struck successfully at the spider before it reached the ground.

"Get back, Billy! They're baiting you," ordered John.

Billy saw more of the spiders outside the strands. They spun their web from strand to strand and produced walls of silk that trapped the men in a small area. "They're trapping us!" Billy exclaimed.

John slew the last descending spider and observed the spiders' creation. "This is the devil's work. Spiders don't herd their prey like this," he uttered, growing fearful. John poked his sword into the silk wall and sifted it. "This stuff is damp and sticky. If we set a fire, it won't burn, but if we heat our sword tips, we could melt our way through it."

"I'll take care of that," volunteered Seamus. He took two flints and a small pouch of gunpowder from his pocket. He then found a long branch and tied a piece of cloth to the end of it. After rubbing the flints together repeatedly, he ignited the gunpowder into a small flame and extended the torch into the fire. The rag immediately caught fire. Billy was impressed with his efficiency.

"Not bad, eh?" remarked Seamus.

"Not bad at all," replied Billy.

"Are we ready, men?" John asked. They raised their swords in unison. "Here, here!"

John placed his sword in the flame until it glowed red. He inspected the glowing blade and announced, "I believe it's time to slay our devils." He slashed at the web and left a smoldering slit in the silk wall. He burned the area around the slits with his sword and widened the gap. More spiders descended on them as soon as they exited through the wall of web.

"Here they come again," warned Billy.

Their escape caught the spiders off-guard and gave them an opportunity to avoid another confrontation with them. As they fled, they heard rustling in the webbed ceiling above. "We have to keep moving or they'll cut us off," urged John.

They hurried down the hardened dirt path through the dead forest until the webbed world receded. When green shrubbery and live trees appeared beyond the silk strands, they slowed their pace.

Billy was happy to leave the dead world behind. "I hope I never see another spider again, as long as I live."

"Me neither," replied John.

The tension eased among the men.

— ⏳ —

Morning came with cooler temperatures and less humidity. Everyone in Doc's group sat around a campfire and ate from the fruit and canned goods they brought. Doc and Maggie stood by the edge of the clearing and waited. The others sensed their eagerness.

"Let's go, everyone. We have a lot of territory to cover," urged Doc.

They marched until noontime and stopped to rest at the top of a hill. From there, they saw the cliffs to the right and dense forests to the left. Their path took them along a stream, which split the two. Doc thought it wise to avoid the trees as much as possible. When he focused on a layer of white haze in the distance, Maggie noticed. "What is it, dear?" she asked.

"I'm not sure. It could be a thermal layer or just some early morning mist."

They continued further until the forest grew silent. It was an eerie silence. Doc searched for an alternate route but opted to stay on the original path. When they came upon silk strands dangling from the trees, everyone grew uneasy. The quantity of strands increased as they proceeded further. "This looks like spider's web but it would take one big spider or a whole lot of little ones to make this much silk," commented Doc.

Maggie shuddered at the thought. "I don't look forward to an encounter with any spider that makes this much silk. Perhaps we should go back"

"It's not much further before we're out of the forest. I can see the mountains from here."

"I certainly hope you're right, Honey."

The men kept their rifles ready and scanned the area warily. Penny and Maggie stayed in the middle of the group for protection. Ted stopped and investigated a white lump of silk near a tree. He poked at the webbing with his rifle and uncovered the disfigured head of a deer. "Holy shit!" he exclaimed. "I don't like this, Dr. Smith. I think we should go back." Two other men were frightened and agreed with him.

"There's no point in arguing, so do as you wish," replied Doc.

"I'm going back with them. It's your decision now what happens with our friendship," Simon informed Penny.

"I think you made that decision for yourself. Good luck, Simon."

Three men, including Simon, departed with one of the rifles. Doc's group kept the other two. "Are you sure we shouldn't go back with them?" asked Maggie uneasily.

Doc grew irritated. "Yes, I am. Now please don't ask me again." He allowed his group to rest until the men returned in a panic.

"Doc, we've been cut off!" Ted exclaimed.

"What do you mean?"

"The entire path is blocked by a thick wall of silk! There's no way around it," ranted Simon.

Doc trembled as he thought about the trap they stumbled into. "It seems that there's no other choice but to go forward. I suggest we all remain vigilant since we don't know what we're up against."

Everyone was tense as they proceeded deeper into the webbed world. They entered a clearing surrounded by dead trees, draped in silk. The naked, white trees wavered from the weight of the silk like ghosts dancing in the distance. Four spiders the size of cows emerged from behind the trees and stalked them.

"Spiders!" shouted Simon frantically. Maggie and Penny screamed at the sight of them.

"Everyone, get in a circle and remain calm," ordered Doc.

"That's easy for you to say!" stammered Simon. The spiders herded them together, observing them eerily.

"They appear to be looking for Someone!" exclaimed Maggie.

"That's nonsense," uttered Doc.

— X —

Randy and Ronnie reached the edge of the webbed forest. "That's strange. The tracks go right through this wall of silk," said Ronnie.

"You happen to notice how quiet it is out here?" inquired Randy.

"Uh-huh and I don't like it."

They were startled by screams from beyond the webbed wall. "That was Maggie and Penny! We've got to do something," exclaimed Randy.

"Like what? Look how thick this stuff is."

The girls poked and pulled at the web with their rifles but to no avail. "We've got to find a way through or they're dead!" exclaimed Randy.

They searched until they found a narrow opening in the silk wall. Ronnie stepped through first and entered a white cavern of silk. Randy followed behind her and gazed in amazement at the webbed world. "It's beautiful in a sick sort of way, isn't it?"

Ronnie was horrified as she scanned the area. "If there's one thing in the world I hate, it's spiders."

A twenty-five-foot-high spider approached from behind Randy. Ronnie nearly fainted from fright. Her face became ashen and her mouth was agape. Randy's back was to the spider but the look on Ronnie's face worried her. "What's wrong with you?"

When Ronnie pointed at the spider, Randy turned and was mortified. The women rushed into a smaller webbed tunnel. "Still like spiders?" chided Ronnie.

"That's not a spider. That's a monster!"

They raced down the white tunnel but the spider closed on them. It slowed considerably when it hunched down to fit through the tunnel. The girls paused behind one of the silk-covered trees and waited nervously. Ronnie hyperventilated and became pale.

"Are you alright?" asked Randy.

"What do you think?"

Randy fired three shots at the spider's head. The bullets stunned it but had no lasting effect. They retreated until there was no place left to go. Ronnie trembled and watched helplessly. Randy struck at the spider with the rifle and snapped its front leg with a loud crunching sound. The spider shrieked and knocked Randy to the ground with one of its legs.

Ronnie fired three shots at the spider's head. It swatted her with its leg into the webbed wall. She struggled to free herself but to no avail. The spider craned its head over her.

"Do something, Randy!"

Randy scrambled to her feet and raced at the spider. "Oh, no you don't!" she shouted and leaped on the spider's leg. It moved awkwardly in circles while trying to shake Randy off. Fatigue soon slowed the huge arachnid. Randy took her pistol from the back of her jeans while clinging to the spider's leg. She aimed at the head and fired randomly, but the bullets again had no effect on it. Ronnie sobbed as she struggled to free herself from the sticky wall.

— ⏳ —

Billy and the Englishmen rested at the stream when Randy's gunshots sounded faintly and caught Billy's attention. "I heard gunfire!"

"There's no one out here but us fools," replied John.

Two more shots rang out and startled the Englishmen. "My apologies, Billy. I hear them now."

"I guess this means we're going back in there," complained Wills.

"Do we have to?" groaned Seamus.

"Yes, we do. To arms, men," ordered John.

They drew their swords and rushed back into the white forest. When they reached a clearing, three of the Englishmen dropped back to cover the rear. "The shots came from this direction," said Billy.

Wills, Seamus and John followed Billy down the tunnel. They entered one of the webbed chambers and saw the spider reeling crazily with Randy clinging to its leg.

"You've got to be kidding me!" Billy uttered cynically. He drew his sword and rushed to their aid.

"Billy, please help us!" pleaded Ronnie.

"What the hell are you girls doing here?" he shouted as he cut the web away from Ronnie's arms and legs.

"What does it look like we're doing?" shouted Randy breathlessly.

"Thank you so much, Billy," said Ronnie humbly.

"Forget it. Let's get Randy off of 'hairball' and get the hell out of here."

The spider finally shook Randy from its leg. She tumbled across the ground and lay in front of them. She picked up her pistol off the ground and scurried to her feet. "That son of a bitch is gonna die!"

"How about if I help?" suggested Billy.

"I thought you'd never ask."

The spider seemed energized by Billy's presence and stalked him. When Billy moved to his left, the spider remained focused him. He struck at the spider's rear leg with his sword and shattered it. The spider squealed an ear-piercing shriek and struck at him with another leg. Billy dove out of the way and scrambled to his feet. "Why the hell is it chasing me?" he shouted. The spider lunged again at him, but he tumbled forward, underneath its head. He shoved his spear up into the spider's underbelly and quickly crawled out by its left side legs.

John and Seamus drew their swords and crept to the spider's right side. They hacked at the rear legs, while Wills distracted the spider from the front. It stumbled to the ground but still struck at them with its remaining four legs.

When Billy charged at the spider from the side, it raised the rear of its body and sprayed wet silk at him. He fell to the ground, frantically trying to free himself from the silk. One of the Englishmen, Titus, rushed at the spider's head and pierced it with his sword. The spider raised one of its front legs and drove it down into Titus' chest, killing him instantly.

John charged at the spider and drove his sword into the side of its head. Its squeal faded into a hiss, then silence. He backed away and stood somberly over Titus' body. Ronnie and Seamus cut away the strands of silk from Billy's body.

"That spider was more interested in you than us," remarked Randy.

"Yeah, what the hell's up with that?" complained Billy.

John, Seamus and Wills knelt around Titus' corpse. After a brief prayer, John removed Titus' sword and scabbard from his waist. He handed it to Wills. "Take care of this, would you?"

"I'd be honored. He was a good man." The men made the sign of the cross and approached Billy.

Ronnie hugged Billy. "I mean it. I really owe you for this," she said humbly. "I'm terrified of spiders."

"You saved my ass already. It's the least I can do."

Randy limped over to them, bruised and dirty. "I hope that's it for the spiders. I've had enough, too," she complained.

"Where are your other men, John?" inquired Billy.

"They're covering us from the rear. We'd best find them."

They hastened down the webbed tunnel and found three of John's men; Stefan, Nigel and Krill, battling several of the smaller spiders. John drew his sword and rushed into the fray.

"I guess we should get in there, too," Billy suggested to Seamus.

"Yeah, I'm afraid so."

Billy and Seamus charged at the spiders and battled tenaciously. Ronnie and Randy were helpless to assist them with only a rifle and their pistols to fight with. Another spider, twenty-feet high, entered the webbed chamber and stalked them.

Billy ordered, "Let's get out of here! I don't want any part of this one."

They raced into another tunnel. The webbed surroundings receded, but the spider still pursued them. Its legs worked in a mechanized motion like a giant robot. The face was more horrifying than anything they had ever seen. Its large, beady eyes were pitch black. The head had two very powerful jaws that worked sideways, followed by a smaller mouth within that quivered and emitted strange squeaks as if it were communicating with the other spiders.

John spotted an opening in the webbed wall. "Through here, everyone!" he called.

Billy covered the rear while the others hurried through the wall. They entered into a separate tunnel that led to they found another opening. "This place is a frigging labyrinth," he complained.

"Let's try this way," suggested Ronnie. She leaped through the slit and collided with Doc Smith on the other side. "Oh, shit! My heart!" she exclaimed.

Also standing there were Penny, Maggie, Simon and two men from camp. Ronnie panted heavily and paced in a circle with her hand on her chest. Randy and the Englishmen passed through the wall and stared at them in disbelief.

"What the hell are you doing here, Doc? You scared the living daylights out of me," Ronnie questioned him, while breathless.

"Funny, I was going to ask you the same thing."

Billy emerged through the wall and burst into laughter when he saw them. Penny was elated to see Billy arrive in time to save her once again. He winked at her with a smile and she hugged him. "I can't believe you came for us!" she said excitedly. Suddenly Penny gagged and backed away from him. "Oh, what's that awful smell?" she blurted, nauseous.

Billy took his shirt off and tossed it away. "Spider guts. They do smell pretty bad."

Simon glared briefly at Penny and fled down another tunnel. Two other men followed him. At that moment, four smaller spiders appeared. "Oh, no. They're back again," grumbled Randy.

"Swords out, men!" ordered John.

"Billy, wait!" called Penny.

Billy and the Englishmen charged at the spiders. They hacked and cut at them until they crippled or killed them. Billy took a quick count of everyone. He noticed Doc's three companions were missing, including Simon. "Where are the other men?" he asked.

"They were just here," replied Doc.

"I guess they're on their own now." He took Penny's hand and led his friends back through the webbed tunnels. When they exited the last tunnel into the white forest, they noticed three shapes covered in silk against the trees. The contorted faces of Simon and the other two men shone through the web with horrible stares frozen on their faces.

"So much for them. They should have stayed with us," remarked Billy sarcastically.

Penny pushed the web away from one of the faces and recognized Simon. "I'll never be a pain in your ass again, will I, Simon?" she whispered coldly.

Billy noticed that She showed little remorse for Simon and felt optimistic about their relationship. Her cold-heartedness made him realize that she wasn't the naïve girl he thought she might be. "I've had enough of this place for one lifetime," he declared.

"I second that. I've had enough spiders as well," replied Ronnie. They passed through another tunnel but found it blocked by a silk wall.

"Looks like we'll have to burn our way out. Got a light?" Billy asked Seamus.

"I most certainly do." Seamus fabricated a torch from dead wood and dried silk. He ignited it with the flints and, after several attempts, set the web on fire. Billy and John heated their sword tips in the flames and sliced a large opening through the web.

Billy waited as everyone hurried through the slit. When he finally ducked through, he found everyone paralyzed with fear. He looked up and saw another giant spider perched over them. "Anybody know the number of a good exterminator?" he asked sarcastically. No one responded as they retreated from the spider.

"How can we stop this one? It's monstrous!" exclaimed Doc in a panic.

"Ronnie. Randy. You're the big game hunters. Don't you have any ideas how to kill this thing?" challenged Billy.

Ronnie's voice quivered, "It's too big to kill."

Billy stepped to the right of the spider. Randy noticed that it instinctively crept toward Billy. "What the hell kind of cologne are you wearing, Billy? These creatures go after you every time!"

Billy raised his sword in defense. "Maybe it's the smell of spider entrails."

"Something else is going on here," she shouted, growing more suspicious.

Ronnie and Wills moved away from Billy and followed Randy. The other Englishmen spread out to the left of the spider and distracted it. Each time it lunged for Billy, they hacked at the legs. Billy leaped left and right to avoid each challenge by the spider.

"Hey, Ronnie, I owe you for the lizard," Randy announced and then took Titus' sword from Wills.

"What are you doing?" asked Wills.

"I need to borrow this for a little while."

"Oh, this ought to be real good," uttered Ronnie. Randy approached one of the trees and climbed in between the strands of silk.

"She's insane!" muttered Ronnie.

The spider lunged at Billy but he tumbled to his right. It knocked Billy down and pinned him to the ground with its leg. Billy struck at the leg with his sword but couldn't muster enough strength to damage it. Four smaller spiders approached from the rear, cutting off any chance of escape.

"Krill, Nigel, Stefan and Wills: take care of the small spiders," ordered John.

The men left and then John stood alone in front of the big spider. While it focused on Billy, John rushed at it and pierced its head with his sword. The spider shrieked and lifted its leg off of Billy. "I've had enough Arachnamania for one day. It's time to finish this!" Billy exclaimed and staggered toward the spider.

"Billy, what the hell…?"

"I know what I'm doing, John."

Billy crept closer and raised his sword defensively, waiting for the right moment. Seamus lit another torch and distracted the spider from the right side. When the spider swung one of its legs at Billy, his sword slammed against it and snapped it with a loud, crunching sound. The broken portion of the leg struck him and sent him sprawling to the ground. The spider let out a high-pitched whine as its broken leg dangled from its body. It stabbed at Billy with one of its front legs. He dodged the leg sideways and struck at it with his sword. The sword cut into the leg and stuck. The spider pulled its leg back and ripped the sword from Billy's hands.

"Billy!" shouted Seamus, who then threw the torch to him. Billy caught it and waved it in the spider's face. The spider retreated and crouched again. Seamus rushed at it from the side. The spider was off balance when he chopped at its left front leg. It broke with the same snapping sound and fell harmlessly to the ground. The head of the creature was low to the ground now, without the support of the two front legs.

Penny and Maggie trembled in fear as they watched the battle. All Penny's earlier fears were nothing compared to what she felt now. The two women held each other tightly and sobbed.

Billy shoved the torch into the spider's eyes. The spider lurched and spewed white liquid from its mouth onto Billy's face. His eyes were covered with the fluid and he was blinded. He fell on his back, but jabbed wildly with the torch in the direction of the spider. The spider's head hovered close to Billy, just out of the reach of his torch. It maneuvered to his left away from the torch. "Come on, you hairy bastard!" bellowed Billy. The spider lowered its head near his chest and opened its jaws for the kill.

Randy swung down from a strand of silk overhead. She released and dropped twenty feet onto the spider. As she landed, she buried her sword into its head, pinning it to the ground. "Well, Ronnie, I'm one up on you now," she proudly announced as she jumped off the spider.

"Was that necessary?" Ronnie challenged with an attitude.

"Of course. It was the only viable option."

Billy could see well enough to know that the spider's head was about a foot from his face. He shuddered as he noticed the two swords through its head, not far from his shoulder. "Do you think you could have waited just a little longer, Randy?" he complained.

"My timing had to be perfect."

"Why me, Lord?" Billy uttered in pain.

John reached down and pulled the swords out of the spider's head. Seamus and Wills helped Billy to his feet. Seamus wiped the liquid from Billy's face with his shirt.

"Can we please get the hell out of here, now?" pleaded Ronnie.

"What's your hurry?" Randy teased.

"You are such a bitch," Ronnie complained as she searched for more spiders.

"And a damn good one at that!" Randy replied.

The men laughed at them and then exited of the webbed world. When they reached the stream, Penny put her arm around Billy's waist. "I'm going to take care of you from now on. You'll see," she promised.

"Um, I don't think..."

Penny put her finger across his lips. "I don't want to hear it. Just relax and let me take care of you."

Doc informed Billy, "I want to examine your eyes more closely once you've rinsed them with water."

"I'll be fine," replied Billy.

"I'll be the judge of that."

The three of them knelt down by the edge of the stream. Penny took a tee shirt out of her knapsack and soaked it in the water. She dabbed Billy's eyes until his vision cleared. "See, Billy. You're in good hands, now." Billy grimaced, much to her chagrin.

Doc examined his eyes and concluded, "It's nothing permanent. I think you'll be fine."

"Thanks, Doc."

"I'd better check on your friends, now." Doc tended to John and Nigel. John had a laceration on his forehead and brow. Seamus held a wet rag against the wound for him. Wills wrapped Nigel's hand with a rag. "What happened here?" inquired Doc.

"One of those spiders got a bite on my hand. Fortunately, it got my sword through its head before it could do any real damage," explained Nigel.

"That's going to need tending to as soon as we get back to the camp. The last thing you need is an infection from a spider bite."

"Are you a doctor?"

"Not quite, but close enough."

Doc approached John and asked, "Are you okay?"

"I'll live."

Doc examined the injury and suggested, "You could use a stitch or two."

"What do you mean?" asked John.

Doc placed two butterfly stitches across John's forehead and one in his brow. "He doesn't understand some of our lingo. He's not from our time," explained Billy.

"What are you talking about?"

"It's a long story."

Doc placed a bandage around John's head. "You'll be fine by tomorrow. Now we can get out of here."

"Thank you, Doc."

"You can thank me by keeping Billy out of trouble."

Everyone laughed except for Billy. He frowned and walked away. The group left the stream and hiked through the woods.

— ⧗ —

Ruger stood before Diomedes in her fiery cavern and trembled. "There's no way he survived the spiders! I saw them trap him," he explained, growing frantic.

Diomedes summoned him closer to her cauldron. "Look in here," she ordered.

Ruger warily leaned over the cauldron and stared into the red mist. He saw Billy and several others at the stream. "I don't understand it! He should be dead."

Diomedes shoved Ruger's head into the cauldron and held it there. He struggled to free himself from her leathery, clawed hand. When she finally let him up, he gasped for air. His face was severely scalded and he groaned in pain. "Take care of him – now!" warned Diomedes. "Next time, I won't be as lenient."

Ruger fell to his knees and crawled away from her.

— ⧗ —

Penny clutched Billy's arm tightly and waited for her opportunity to speak with him about their relationship. Billy paused ahead of the group and placed his hands on his hips. Everyone stopped behind him.

"Before we go any further, I have to know something," he announced. "How is it that all of you wound up in the same place? Every time I turned around, someone else showed up."

"Believe me, we didn't plan it this way," answered Maggie.

"I wanted this trip so I could find myself."

Penny kissed him on the cheek and reminded him, "You did and you found us, too."

"She does have a point," replied John.

"Don't take her side. She's complicated enough without getting any encouragement."

"Sorry, friend." Everyone laughed at their remarks.

"Young lady, you have got to tell me where you learned to execute your moves. You were outstanding," Seamus complimented Randy. The two of them walked ahead of the others and talked.

Penny and Billy lagged behind the group. "I am so glad to see you, Billy. I'm sorry for all the grief I caused you and it won't happen again. I promise."

"Penny, this isn't the way to build a relationship. I've known you for less than a week and I feel like my heart just went through the cheese grater again. I think we need to slow down and build our relationship the right way."

"Don't you want me back?"

"There you go again. I like you a lot, but I can't handle this hot and cold attitude of yours. Now, let's start over with a nice conversation. Let's talk about us and get to know each other better." He kissed her forehead. "We'll be fine. Trust me," he said confidently.

"I'm sorry," she said humbly. "You're right about this."

Everyone listened eagerly as John educated Doc on English history. Adding to the mystery was the tale of Xerxes, which left Doc baffled.

"So, how did you get into this picture?" Billy asked the girls.

"We were bored," answered Randy.

"If we stuck together, things would have been much simpler," complained Ronnie.

"I'm one up on you now. I'd like to see you top that move!" challenged Randy.

"But my dinosaur was alive and well when I jumped on it. Your spider was already wounded," countered Randy.

"Are they always like this?" John asked Billy.

"I'm afraid so." Billy's group camped for the night in the same location used by Doc's group the previous night. Billy sat across from Doc in front of the fire. Penny nestled against him and slept in his arms, while Doc stared dejectedly at the flames.

"Will you try again?" asked Billy.

"I really don't know how. This experience proved to me that we don't make the rules in this world."

"I told you before; I know a way to get you there safely."

"Don't screw with me, Billy. I'm not in the mood."

Maggie interrupted them and hugged Billy. "Thank you so much for saving us. I thought we were done for," she said appreciatively.

"I'm glad we were able to help. I really hope we never have to face spiders again. My eyes are killing me."

"Don't worry, Billy. It's just an anesthetic that the spider used for self-defense," Doc assured him.

"Self-defense! That thing was going to kill me. I'm the one who needed self-defense." They chuckled together.

"Would you mind if we discussed the trip later? I would like to hear your idea when we have more time to analyze it."

"Not at all, Doc." Billy stared past Doc at the dark forest. He looked uncomfortable and pained.

"Is something bothering you?" asked Doc, curious.

"Yeah, there is. Randy pointed out a few times that the spiders seemed to key on me. Even the Neanderthals were focused on me."

"You're getting paranoid," Doc explained. "I'm sure it's just a coincidence."

"You don't think there's any way they could do that, do you?" asked Billy.

"There is no scientific rational I know of that would make it possible."

Billy looked relieved. "I didn't think so. I just needed to hear it from someone I trust."

"Thanks, Billy. I appreciate the compliment. Good night."

"Good night."

Doc and Maggie moved to the other side of the fire. They lay on the ground and slept together. The Englishmen and the girls joined Billy by the fire. Ronnie and Randy intrigued the English warriors, who never met women with warrior-like qualities before. Meanwhile, John took a subtle interest in Ronnie. They sat together but focused their attention on the others. Seamus was enamored with Randy who thrived on the attention.

"So how did you really contrive that remarkable feat, Randy?" queried Seamus.

"As I said, it just came natural."

"She copied it from a move I did recently," said Ronnie.

"And what, pray tell, did you leap onto?" asked John.

"A dinosaur." The men laughed heartily at her response.

"You didn't really jump on a dinosaur, did you?"

"I most certainly did. I drove a metal spike right into its skull and rode it to the ground. The men turned to Randy for her response.

"Yup, we all saw it," she assured them.

"The two of you are extraordinary women."

"Thank you, John," replied Ronnie. They made eye contact and gazed at each other for an instant.

"I think it's time for me to get some sleep," said John as he stood up.

"Yeah, me, too. It's been a long day," added Seamus.

The two men moved a short distance away. John slept soundly while Seamus sat on a log and stared at the stars in the sky. Randy winked at Ronnie. "That could be our cue," she whispered.

"Don't be such a slut," Ronnie scolded. Randy giggled and joined Seamus.

Ronnie glanced over at Billy. "Good night, Billy. Thanks again."

"Anytime, Ronnie." Ronnie moved to an empty area by the face of the cliffs and slept alone.

Later, Penny awoke and sat up next to Billy. "Hi," she said tiredly.

"Hi, Penny. Did I wake you?"

"No, I had a nightmare."

"Maybe I can help you relax."

"And how would you do that?"

"Why don't you tell me some things about yourself? I'd like to know about you and what you like."

"Why?"

Billy put an arm around her. "Because I like to know a woman before I fall in love with her."

Penny smiled coyly. "What makes you think I want to fall in love?"

"Well, if you don't, I won't waste your time."

Billy stood up as if he would leave. Penny grabbed him by his arm and ordered, "You sit right down here, Mr. Brock." She nestled against him and everything seemed right again.

"Why do you feel the need to lose your temper when things don't go your way?" inquired Billy curiously.

"I'm used to getting screwed over, and I expect that it's going to happen again," she revealed sadly.

"By who?" he inquired, curious.

"By everyone. I know people don't think much of me, especially here."

"That's not true. You have to make an effort to get to know people first before you judge them, especially Ronnie and Randy."

"Maybe you're right." Penny saw Randy watching them from a short distance away. Randy winked and gave her approval with a thumbs-up. Penny blushed and looked down at the ground.

"I know how hard it is to trust a person after your heart's been broken," explained Billy. "I'm still not right from my experience."

"I wasn't aware that you were hurting so bad."

"Uh-huh, but then you hurt me, too. I never expected that from you."

"I realized that afterward and it tore me up. Can you give me another chance?"

Billy looked up at the starry sky. "I suppose so, but you're on probation, young lady."

"I'll be good, I promise." She cuddled against him and closed her eyes. The two of them drifted off to sleep, content that their relationship was finally going somewhere.

Everyone rotated watch over the camp at regular intervals and the night remained uneventful until just before dawn. Wills stood watch at the edge of the clearing and heard branches snap nearby. He listened more alertly as something trudged through the mud. He shook John and alerted him.

Billy awoke and overheard them. "Don't chase it. It could be a trap," he warned.

"Do you know the intruder?" asked John.

Billy sat up and laid Penny down on her side. "It's a Neanderthal. They're a dangerous lot and we've already had several run-ins with them."

"What are these creatures like?

"They're big and ugly. They fight very well and are quite strong. They're like a bunch of angry gorillas."

"I'll take it out. We can't risk it bringing back others."

"If you insist," replied Billy.

As John disappeared in the trees, Billy and Wills waited anxiously.

"Are these things carnivorous?" Wills asked Billy.

"It's horrible what they will do to a human. They're worse than any animal."

"There he is," Wills whispered as John slipped through the trees.

Billy strained to see through the shadows created by the moonlight. He saw the brief glisten of light off John's knife and heard a thud.

"I got it," announced John as he emerged from the trees and stowed his knife.

Billy was impressed. "Boy that was slick," he remarked.

"He's got a knack for surprising people," replied Wills.

Billy lay down next to Penny and kissed her cheek. "I like this much better than fighting," he confessed.

"There's more where that came from if you're good."

"But what if I'm bad?" he kidded.

Penny blushed and nuzzled against his shoulder. "We'll see," she said coyly. "What's going on?"

"John killed a Neanderthal in the trees. It was spying on us."

"Oh, no!" she blurted.

"He thinks that we should move on in case there are more of them."

Penny quickly packed her things into her knapsack. "I'm ready to go when you are," she announced.

"Boy, that was quick."

"I don't ever want to see another one of those things again."

John and Seamus stood by them, waiting to move on. "Were there any more creatures out there?" asked Doc.

"I couldn't tell. We need to get moving though, just in case."

The sun peeked over the mountains and the sky brightened. Billy's group resumed their trip back to the camp. "How far is it to your encampment?" asked John.

Doc looked at his watch and replied, "I think about another three hours and we'll be there."

"John claims that their visitor arrived through a portal and knew something about a huge catastrophe," explained Billy.

"If only we could find him to ask him," replied Doc.

"Maybe he can help us return to our world," suggested Billy.

"Perhaps, but how about your plan to get to the observatory? Do you want to elaborate on that?"

"A few days ago, when we discovered the planes, we also spotted a small commuter plane sitting a few hundred yards beyond the other planes. All we need is a runway and you could be shuttling back and forth, soon enough."

"We could carve a path in the forest to pull the plane onto the tarmac," suggested Penny.

"We don't know if it has fuel in it and the tarmac's a mess. We couldn't take off without risking an accident," reminded Doc.

"We could find another runway," said Billy confidently.

"And where would you find this runway?"

"Did you see the tops of the buildings over the mountain? Where there's a city, there are streets."

"That's a long way off, though," Doc commented.

"I thought about investigating the city anyway. All we need is a stretch of road that's intact."

Doc realized the potential in Billy's idea.

When they entered a field of tall grass at the edge of the forest, Penny noticed something unusual in the foliage. She looked closer and saw an odd shape between two large flowering plants. "Hey, look at this, everybody!" she shouted.

A look of horror swept across Doc's face. "Back away from it, Penny. Back away very slowly," he warned urgently.

John sensed his concern. "Let's go, everyone. Move to the clearing at the top of the hill," he instructed. Penny was surprised by Doc's concern but retreated to Billy's side.

"What's wrong?" asked Billy.

"Go, quickly! There's no time to waste," ordered Doc.

As they hurried through tall grass to the hilltop, they heard rustling in the grass around them. Near the top of the hill, they heard a scream. One of John's men disappeared behind them.

"Everyone, form a circle with your weapons drawn!" shouted John. They waited for several minutes, but nothing happened.

"What kind of creatures are we talking about?" Billy inquired.

"They look like a species of raptors."

"Oh, shit!" he complained. "I know that ain't good."

Before another word was spoken, the sound of gunfire erupted from the camp on the other side of the hill. "It's always something around here," Billy uttered, frustrated.

The creatures stayed hidden, while pursuing them. When they reached the edge of the tarmac, they were mortified to see an army of Neanderthals attacking the camp from all directions.

"Look at them all!" exclaimed Billy.

The area between the hill and the planes was cleared of trees and bushes, giving them a clear view of the camp. Barriers of rocks and branches bordered about half the perimeter around the planes. Doc, Ronnie and Randy drew their pistols and fired at the Neanderthals.

"Follow me!" ordered John. The Englishmen and Billy attacked the Neanderthals from behind and cleared a path through the wave of creatures. Carcasses of both humans and Neanderthals littered the area near the two aircraft.

Jerry emerged from behind one of the barriers. As he fired shots at the Neanderthals, he saw Billy's group enter the camp. "Billy, you're back!" he exclaimed.

Billy fired two shots and killed a Neanderthal. "I sure am."

Jerry fired a shot and killed another. "I hope you have a plan for this mess," he commented.

"I believe I do. Get everyone inside the planes and close the hatches."

Jerry was dumbfounded by Billy's order. Seventeen raptors about the height of a man rushed out of the trees and attacked the Neanderthals. The creatures ran like wingless birds on two legs. They had razor sharp claws and curled, pointed teeth.

"Damn, Billy! You did it again," Jerry remarked from the hatch.

"Just get inside. Nobody comes out until I say so. Understand?" ordered Billy.

"I'll make sure." Jerry promptly closed the hatch.

"John, send your men inside the other plane. I'm going up on the roof of the building to watch the battle. I'll let you know when it's clear." John ordered his men into the plane but he remained with Billy.

"John, you don't have to come. I'll let you know when it's safe," said Billy.

"I'm coming with you. You need someone to watch your back."

"Then let's get up there before those creatures come looking for dessert." The two of them rushed through the trees to the end of the terminal. They killed four Neanderthals with their swords along the way and ascended the sloped roof. When they reached the top, they perched behind the HVAC unit and watched the massacre.

Outside the barriers, four raptors remained and feasted on the last of the Neanderthals. When they finished, the creatures vanished into the trees. Billy sat down and leaned against the HVAC unit. "You know, John, it seems like we're fighting one battle after another. Some days you just don't want to fight anymore."

"I'm surprised at you, Billy. Every day is supposed to be a battle and every day you win is a good day."

Billy stood up and turned away from the battle scene. "Oh, shit!" he uttered as a young raptor stormed at him. It crashed into him and nearly knocked him off the roof. Billy clutched the raptor's throat and one of its claws but it slashed his chest repeatedly with its free claw.

John drew his sword and pierced the raptor's side. Despite the wound, it turned on him with amazing speed. John retreated but it lunged at him. He instinctively pointed his sword at the creature and deflected the raptor's momentum away from him with a quick sidestep.

The creature writhed in agony when the sword penetrated deep into its chest. It swiped its razor claws across John's arm and tumbled to the ground. "Damn you, demon!" John screamed as he dropped his sword and clutched his arm. Angrily, he kicked the dying creature off the roof.

Billy got to his knees briefly. His shirt was wet with blood and his flesh had been torn from his shoulder to his abdomen. He looked down at his wounds and teetered. "I think I'm screwed, John."

John helped Billy to his feet and together they staggered down the sloped roof. When they reached the hatch of the nearest plane, Jerry opened the door and rushed out.

"Billy needs help," muttered John weakly.

Penny and Doc exited the plane and were stunned by the sight of Billy covered in blood.

"Oh, Billy!" cried Penny.

"This looks really bad!" exclaimed Doc. They helped John and Billy into the plane.

Maggie ordered everyone inside the plane, "Give us some room, quickly."

"We need to pile up the corpses. They have to be burnt before they attract scavengers," announced Jerry. The men and women heeded Jerry's instructions and exited the plane.

Doc laid Billy across the seats and examined him. He peeled back the shredded shirt and cleaned the wounds with a rag soaked in isopropyl alcohol.

"Can you fix him?" asked John.

Doc looked at John's arm. "Don't worry about him. I think you need some fixing, too. That arm's a mess."

"Maggie, take care of Mr. Murdoch. I'll holler if I need you." Maggie escorted John a short distance away. She cleaned and stitched his arm.

Penny was in tears as she watched from the hatch. Randy tried to comfort her. "He'll be all right. Doc will have him fixed up in no time," she said, uncertain herself if Billy would survive.

Penny rested her head on Randy's shoulder. "Look at him. He's all torn up," she blurted.

"Let's go out and get some air," suggested Randy.

The girls encountered Ronnie on her way from the other jet. She was visibly upset. "I thought we were a team. What the hell's he trying to prove?" she shouted at them.

"I don't think he expected anything to happen," Randy replied. "Cut him some slack,"

Ronnie felt guilty for not fighting the giant spider, and now she allowed two of her companions to be injured while she was secure inside the plane. "This won't happen again, I guarantee you," she bellowed.

"I know it won't," said Randy in agreement. We're gonna talk about it when Billy's able."

Ronnie peered inside the jet and watched Doc clean Billy's wounds. "How bad is he, Doc?" she inquired.

"He's lost a lot of blood and there's no way to replenish it." Doc stitched the gashes and bandaged the wounds. The gashes were long and jagged so the stitching did little to neaten the wound. Small blotches of blood formed on the bandages. Billy regained consciousness but was very weak.

"Perhaps I went into the wrong field. I spend more time here as a doctor than a scientist," kidded Doc.

Billy forced a smile. "How bad is it?" he asked weakly.

"I think you'll live. I sewed you up the best I could but it's going to take some time to heal."

"Thanks, Doc."

Doc called outside to Penny, "You can see him now if you like."

Penny hurried inside the plane. "Is he alright?" she asked anxiously.

"We don't want him up for at least a few weeks. Hopefully he'll be able to replenish some of his blood. Please, be gentle with him."

"Thanks Doc." Penny knelt on the floor beside Billy and rested her head on his legs. John felt sorry for her as he watched from several rows away.

Maggie placed the last stitch in John's arm. "Take it easy for a while until the arm heals," she instructed him and helped him to his feet.

"Thank you, Mrs. Smith."

"Please, call me Maggie."

"Thanks, Maggie."

As John exited the hatch, Ronnie intercepted him. "Are you okay, John?" she asked with a note of concern in her voice.

"Yes, I am. It's just a scratch."

"How about Billy?"

"Sounds like he's got a fighting chance."

Ronnie looked relieved. "I hear that you have some interesting battle skills. Could we discuss them?"

John was surprised by her request. "We can talk now if you like."

"Let's go sit on the patio. I've got a bunch of questions for you."

They walked under a bamboo patio and sat on seats removed from one of the jets.

"I see you don't waste words."

"Time is precious in my book. Can you teach me to use a sword?" Ronnie requested.

"If you're serious, I'd be happy too."

"Can you make me a sword of my own as well?"

"You don't waste time either, young lady," John quipped. "Swords take considerable time to make, but I'll ask Nigel to make one for you. Billy's sword belonged to one of my men. Randy, more or less, inherited Titus' sword."

"I appreciate your help. I think you'd be surprised what I can tell you about weapons. I've actually designed some of my own."

"I see you are full of surprises like your friend, Randy. Give me a few days for my arm to heal and we'll get into some sword techniques."

"I'm looking forward to it."

— X —

Seamus watched as Jerry instructed the men working on the barriers around the planes. He approached Jerry and introduced himself.

"I've been watching you and your men work for a while."

"What do you think so far?" asked Jerry.

"Those barriers aren't bad but they won't last. The weight of the cement on the soft soil will cause them to eventually lean and fall. Also, the height will be considerably limited because of the weight."

Jerry was already frustrated by the progress on the barriers and Seamus' remarks didn't help. "Do you have any better ideas, Mr. McCourt?"

"I designed many of our fortifications in the old country. Is this going to be a permanent settlement?"

"I don't see us going any place else, so I'd say yeah, it's permanent."

Seamus picked up a stick and drew a line in the dirt. "The cliff base provides one wall of natural defense. There is a large stream not far from here. We can dig a moat and use the stream to fill it. The concrete slabs will make a good foundation for a wall of dirt approximately six feet thick and fifteen feet high. The soil that we remove from the moat can be used to build up the walls. These walls will be durable and will harden with time. Then, I believe we can make a drawbridge from material taken from your flying machines."

Randy joined them and teased, "Aren't we the busy bees today?"

"Listen and learn, young lady," chided Seamus.

"Yes, teacher," Randy answered playfully.

Seamus pointed at the wing of one of the aircraft. "That material can be removed, can it not?" he inquired.

"I suppose so," responded Jerry.

"We can create cutouts on top of the walls for turrets. A turret is a protected cubicle for us to fire at any attacker outside the walls without exposing ourselves to injury. Individual stations should be built within the confines for armament, supplies and food. We'll bring fresh water from the stream into the fortification by placing a small dam further upstream. It will raise the water level high enough that it will flow through an artificial channel we develop to an opening in the wall."

Jerry was impressed with Seamus' plan. "I like it. Unfortunately, it's going to be a lot of work."

"Your temporary barriers will be critical during the construction of the permanent walls. That should buy us some time and protection as well."

"When the men stop for dinner, we'll assemble and discuss your plan," Jerry announced. "Perhaps you can make a model of what we intend to build so they'll understand."

"I'll see what I can come up with."

— X —

John lectured Ronnie on tactics of war used by his people in comparison to her techniques and ideas. He was impressed with Ronnie's knowledge as he learned more about her experience with weapons. "How long did it take for you to learn so much about the art of battle?" Ronnie asked.

"My whole life has been a learning experience. A warrior must continuously learn new ways to adapt and survive." The discussion shifted to strategies used in English warfare, much to Ronnie's delight. She knew she could get an edge on Randy through John's experience. John, meanwhile, felt a special bond develop between them. "I can teach you many things, but skill doesn't happen overnight," he informed her. "Nigel can show you how to make weapons from raw metal, but to make them out here in the wilderness will take patience and creativity," he cautioned.

"Where's Nigel now?"

John flexed his wounded arm and grimaced. "Relax young lady. I'll arrange it with Nigel."

"I'm sorry, John. I'm just so excited."

"That's enough for one day. I need to rest now."

Ronnie hugged him delicately and thanked him for his help.

— X —

Three weeks passed without any crises at the compound. Billy and Penny spent many hours together during that time and grew closer each day. Seamus and Randy hunted each morning, then assisted Jerry with the fortification during the afternoon. John instructed Ronnie on the art of sword fighting. They practiced with bamboo sticks for hours each day. Meanwhile, Doc surveyed the area and took notes on the wildlife. Maggie taught the women how to make clothes and prepare food in their new environment. They discovered many new creatures in the mountains and forests but none as formidable as those they already faced.

Further downstream was a large lake, which served as a watering hole for the larger animals. The lake proved to be their food source. The artificial water channel that Seamus suggested, worked quite well. A few of the men made a warm water shower from a tank removed from the aircraft. There were eleven women and nine men left, excluding Billy's group of friends. All of them seemed to respect Billy for his valor thus far, making him uncomfortable with the possibility of being their leader.

Billy stared out the window of the plane. His wounds healed sufficiently and he was ready to get on his feet. He strapped on his sword and stepped out of the plane. A short distance away, he found Doc writing notes in a notebook.

"Hey, Doc!" shouted Billy.

"It's good to see you up and about, Billy. What's on your mind?"

"I think we should talk about that plane trip."

"I don't know, Billy. There's a lot of 'ifs' to deal with right now."

"Well, that small commuter plane is still sitting on the other side of the camp about a hundred yards or so from here. I think it's worth a shot."

"How do we get it into the air? I can't fly and we certainly don't have a runway to take off from. Besides, how would we move the plane to a suitable location, even if we had one?"

"Have you asked any of the men if they can fly?"

"No, not yet."

"I'll see what remains of the city. There could be a road surface intact that's long enough to use for a runway."

"I still don't see how we'll get the plane there, even if you do find a suitable surface."

"Trust me. We'll make it work."

Doc was amused by Billy's enthusiasm. "I know you're anxious to get out again, Billy, but I think you should be careful. Wounds like yours take time to heal."

"Believe me, I understand."

CHAPTER 6

THE CITY

Billy spotted Randy and Ronnie stringing a homemade bow near one of the barriers. "Hey, girls, what's going on?" he called to them.

"Well, if it isn't wonder boy," Ronnie teased.

Billy laughed at the barb. "How about joining me on a road trip?"

"You mean you want us to join you? I never thought we'd get an invitation to hang out with you again," kidded Randy.

Billy felt embarrassed. Since he and Penny made up, most of his time was spent with her. "I sincerely apologize for that," he responded humbly.

"So, we're buds again?"

"Yeah, we're buds. I'll be back for you in an hour." They high-fived each other. Billy left them and sought out the Englishmen.

Outside the barriers, the men cleaned and gutted four boars they recently caught. Billy approached them and marveled at their catch.

"It's good to see you up and about," said John, surprised.

"Yes, I was going crazy inside that aircraft. I see you've been busy."

"We'll be eating well, tonight."

Billy placed his hands on his hips and complained, "Well that sucks!"

"Why? You don't like pig?"

"No, it's not that. I wanted you boys to join me on a field trip."

"Hmm, I guess I could stand to lose a few pounds. I'll go with you." John looked to his men for their responses.

"I'll pass this time. Stefan and I are roasting the pig," answered Seamus.

"I'll join you," responded Nigel.

"I'd like to see something a little more interesting than this place. I'll go too," said Krill.

"Oh, you will see some interesting stuff," said Billy. "I can assure you of that."

"When do we leave?"

"I'll meet you in an hour, right here."

"See you then," said John.

Billy returned to the plane and grabbed his knapsack. He paused in front of the makeshift food hut for some goods. The hut was a distribution point for foods like fruits, vegetables, juices, water and canned consumables. Other items, like meat, were cooked for the group over an open fire. Two men were responsible for smoking the meat and maintaining it.

Billy filled his canteen with water and took two apples and a banana. The elderly woman who managed the hut asked curiously, "Are you going somewhere, Mr. Brock?"

"As a matter of fact, I am."

"I saw the knapsack and figured as much. Good luck."

"Thank you, ma'am."

Billy left the hut and approached Penny by the water trough. She was surprised to see Billy with the knapsack over his shoulder and his sword strapped around his waist. "Were you going to leave and not say anything to me?" she asked, curious.

"I was getting around to that. I didn't know if I'd have enough company to make a trip today."

"Where are you going?"

"Into the city. We should be back by late tomorrow."

"Any particular reason?"

"Just a 'look and see' mission."

"Mr. Brock, you make sure you come back in one piece. I'll be waiting," Penny remarked and kissed his cheek.

"I'll be fine. Don't worry." Billy kissed her again and walked away.

The Englishmen and the girls waited outside the compound. They witnessed Billy's farewell kiss and were amused. "I see the lovebirds are getting along for a change. How about that?" Ronnie commented.

"Yes, but when the cat's away, the mouse can play," joked Randy.

"I'm not used to Penny being cooperative. I like it," said Billy, pleased.

"Don't get used to it. It's likely the calm before the storm," suggested John with a rare sense of humor.

Everyone laughed, including Billy, as they walked into the woods. During their conversations, Billy learned a lot about the Englishmen and their lives in the old world. They shared a desire for adventure as did Billy and the girls.

By late afternoon they reached the top of the mountain. Fog rolled into the valley below them, casting an eerie presence. Thunder echoed ahead of an impending storm. They quickened their pace down the mountainside.

"What exactly are we looking for?" inquired Ronnie.

"If this is, in fact, the remains of Philadelphia, then there's a train that shuttled from the airport to the city. I'd like to find some remnants of its tracks."

"Why is that so important?"

"We need a passable route to the city so we can move the plane. I figure that we'll need a wagon or flatbed of some kind to carry it."

"Do you really think this plan of yours will work?"

"Of course, I do. If the main road is intact, it's a piece of cake."

"I'm only on this trip for one reason," declared Randy.

"And that is?" questioned Billy.

"Shopping!"

"It'll be more like looting," he teased.

"No, it's shopping. Looting is when you break in and steal from someone. There's no one here to steal from so it's shopping."

"What a warped sense of humor you have?"

Darkness closed in as they descended below the layer of fog to the base of the mountain. Thunder rumbled around them and lightning flashed in the distance. The faint outline of several buildings appeared in the flashes of light.

"I see the buildings out there! We're not far," exclaimed Randy. Another flash of lightning lit up the sky.

"I see them, too. If we hurry, we can reach them before the rain starts," said Billy.

The wind picked up considerably and bowed the treetops. The rain fell lightly at first and then gradually grew heavier.

— ⧗ —

Ruger and Pirocles watched the images of Billy and his friends as they approached the city.

"What do you have in mind this time?" inquired Pirocles.

"We'll have to pull the minions from the battle lines."

"But, Ruger, that means …"

"I know what it means, you fool!"

"Can't we send the Neanderthals?"

"The Neanderthals have been reduced to a useless tribe of heathens."

"Can the minions hold the line if we pull some of them?"

"I don't know, but we must get that boy soon before it's too late."

"Then we'd best take care of this quickly," advised Pirocles.

— ⧗ —

When they emerged from the woods, they came upon a bridge over a wide river. It was a four-lane concrete structure with sidewalks on both sides and railing. They crossed the bridge and searched the area ahead.

"Let's head for the Post Office. We can stay there for the night," shouted Billy above the gusting winds.

"So long as it's dry, I really don't care," Ronnie uttered as she held her hair from whipping her face.

They hurried across the field and ascended the steps to the landing in front of the Post Office. Billy pushed the glass door open and peered inside. Ronnie and Randy nearly knocked him through the doorway. "What the hell, girls?" chastised Billy.

"Well, get out of the way! We're getting soaked," complained Randy. The Englishmen hurried in behind them.

The wind increased to gale force and the rain became torrential. Wills struggled to push the door closed. "Ahem! I could use a little help here." Billy grabbed the crash bar and helped him pull the door closed.

"That's one hell of a storm out there," complained Wills.

"We won't be going far if it stays like this," replied Billy.

John picked up two wooden chairs and carried them to the center of the hall. He smashed them on the floor and stacked the wood in a small pile. Ronnie found a wool coat lying across a counter and brought it over. She ripped it into shreds and handed the strips to John.

John struck his flints and started a small fire in the middle of the floor. He took four of the wooden legs and tied a shred of cloth to each one. After several tries, John's torch burned brightly and he scanned the area. The flames cast, eerie shadows up and down the massive hall. There were customer service windows at several counters on the right side and a number of wooden doors on the left.

"Ronnie and Randy, why don't you search the upstairs?" suggested Billy.

"We've got it covered," answered Ronnie. She and Randy turned on their flashlights and went up the stairs.

"Nigel and Krill, you search the offices on this floor," ordered Billy. "Look for anything useful,"

Wills and John remained behind and tended to the fire. Billy peered out the door and watched the rain drive against the glass. He was amazed by the storm's fury.

— X —

Ronnie and Randy entered a break room on the second floor. They scanned the area with their flashlights and found a refrigerator and a microwave near one wall. Along another wall were vending machines with drinks and snacks.

Ronnie examined the contents of the refrigerator while Randy inspected the candy machine. "Hey, Ronnie, got any change?"

"Nope," she replied, while rifling through lockers and drawers.

"Oh, well." Randy drew her pistol and smashed the glass on the vending machine with the butt of the gun.

Ronnie was startled and jumped back. She drew her pistol and glared at Randy. "What the hell was that all about?"

"I'm hungry." Randy dumped a box of coffee filters on the counter and filled the box with snacks from the machine.

Ronnie opened the refrigerator and found several lunch bags with sandwiches in them. "Hey, Randy, the refrigerator is still cool. These sandwiches might be okay to eat."

"I'll pass. I've got Oreos."

Ronnie threw the lunch bags and boxes on the counter next to Randy. "What's this?" asked Randy.

"Pack it up. We'll take it downstairs."

"What do I look like, a mule?"

"Not yet, but you will soon if you eat all that junk food."

"Ooh, you bitch!" Randy then bashed the lock on the soda machine door with the butt of her pistol until she broke it open.

Ronnie went to the next room and discovered the body of a dead Postmaster on top of a desk with a primitive spear embedded in his chest. "What in the hell happened in here?" Ronnie muttered to herself.

Randy entered the room and took notice of the spear. "Looks like something you'd make, Ronnie."

Ronnie became annoyed with her. "Don't you have Oreos to eat?"

Randy opened a packet of cookies. "I sure do. Want some?"

"No, thank you." Ronnie shined the light on the floor and found a pistol under the desk.

"I guess he tried to defend himself from someone."

"Or something," added Randy.

"We'd better make sure these rooms are clear," Ronnie warned her. Randy kicked over a table and startled Ronnie. "Do you have to make so much damn noise?" Ronnie sniped.

"No, I don't have to."

"Oh, you're a pain in the ass tonight."

"Why thank you," Randy replied, pleased to get under Ronnie's skin. Ronnie swore under her breath at her. "Let's get out of here already. That guy gives me the creeps," complained Randy. The girls finished their sweep of the second and third floors uneventfully.

Nigel and Krill searched the last of the offices on the main floor but found nothing of value. They returned to the main hall. Ronnie and Randy descended the stairs to the hall. Ronnie carried the spear while Randy carried the brown box containing drinks and snacks.

"What the hell was all that racket up there?" questioned Billy sarcastically.

"Ask Randy," Ronnie replied, irritated.

Billy shined his light on Randy and she innocently dropped the box on the floor.

"Well?" inquired Billy.

Randy held up the bag of Oreos. "I was hungry and didn't have any change."

"So, you busted up the machine?"

"Yeah. What else was I going to do?"

Billy noticed Ronnie's spear. "What's that for?"

"I took it out of the Postmaster. It seems that someone or something didn't like the service."

"Do we have an agenda for tomorrow?" asked John.

"As a matter of fact, we do," replied Billy. "We'll split up into two groups: one group will go to the train station to look for the tracks that lead to the airport; the rest of us will search the nearby buildings for medical supplies, survivors and anything else of importance."

"Maybe we can establish a better residence here than in your aircraft," suggested John.

"We'll consider that, too."

"This building would make for an ideal fortification. It's very defensible," commented Krill.

"Let's see what else is out here first before we make any decisions," advised Billy.

"I'll search for the tracks. I've been to Philadelphia before and I know the train station," said Ronnie.

"Wills and I will accompany Ronnie," added John.

"That's fine. I'll take the other misfits," replied Billy.

"Who are you calling a misfit?" asked Randy defensively as she chewed on another Oreo.

"You, cookie queen."

"I'll fix you later, Brock."

"Any questions?" Billy asked. No one answered. "That's it, then. Sleep tight everyone."

They lay across the floor and slept despite the booming sounds of thunder and the flashes of lightning. Later in the night, John opened his eyes and saw someone or something outside the glass door. He sat up and noticed during a flash of lightening that Billy was missing as well. When another flash lit up the hallway, John spotted Billy creeping along the wall toward the door. He drew his sword and crept along the opposite wall. When they met at the door, Billy pointed outside and opened the door. He stepped out onto the landing and turned on his flashlight. Whatever was there disappeared into the rainy night.

Billy returned to the bench and slept. John remained with the blade of his sword propped against the bottom of the door. If anyone or anything opened it, the sword would scrape against the floor and awaken him. The remainder of the night, however, was without incident.

— ⧗ —

Billy awoke and joined John by the door. They stared disappointedly at the heavy rain. "Any more interruptions during the night?" asked Billy.

"No, none at all."

"I don't think we're alone out here. We'd best be careful," warned Billy.

"I have that same feeling."

Randy got up and joined them. She looked like a crazy woman with her long, auburn hair tussled about wildly. She peered out the door and frowned. "Well, it looks like another crappy day in the land of Oz."

Billy straightened her hair over her shoulders. "It sure is."

Randy was pleased with the attention Billy gave her. "Thanks, Billy. You really are a gentleman. It doesn't make up for last night's comments, though." Billy smiled at her with a degree of satisfaction.

"I guess we'll get a good soaking today," complained John.

"I can find something to help with the rain," said Randy confidently. She left them and ascended the stairs.

Ronnie awoke and meandered over to the men. "Good morning. You guys look a little intense for this early in the morning."

"Good morning, Ronnie. You look nice," said John politely.

"Why thank you, John," she replied coyly while blushing.

Randy returned, carrying plastic trash bags over her arm. "Look what I found!"

"You are the best, Randy," teased Billy. "I don't care what Ronnie says about you."

"Stuff it, Brock," warned Ronnie. Billy was pleased to elicit sarcasm from Ronnie.

The other men awakened and joined them. They ate fruit and bread from their supplies for breakfast. "You know, John, this bread isn't half bad. How did you boys come across it?" inquired Randy.

"It grows up on the plateau."

"We may have to go back for more."

"No, Randy, I don't think we want to do that," replied John. Randy thought better of it and dropped the subject.

"When and where do you want to meet?" asked Ronnie.

"How about here in four hours?" suggested Billy.

"That works for me."

"If either group fails to return on time, the others will immediately head back to camp for help," instructed Billy.

"We're out of here. Good luck, everyone," announced Ronnie.

"Be careful. We're not alone out here," reiterated Billy.

"You, too. None of us wants to carry you back in pieces. Penny will have a fit." Ronnie, John and Wills tore holes in the plastic bags and slid into them. "Not exactly fashionable but it'll work," remarked Ronnie.

Ronnie, John and Seamus exited the Post Office. They crossed a small hill covered with shrubs and small bushes. A flat stretch of field separated them from the train station. A dense strip of trees lined the left side of the building, partitioning it from the river. The ground was laced with patches of clay which made for a slippery surface. As they approached the station, John noticed movement in the trees. He held his hand up for silence and stared intently. Four, sabertoothed tigers moved through the trees parallel to them. "Stay close. We have company," warned John.

They walked with a sense of urgency to the far side of the building away from the trees. When they were within twenty yards of the doors, John shouted, "Run!"

The four tigers burst out of the trees and raced toward them. Wills yanked the door open and leaped in with Ronnie right behind him. John lunged through the doorway but was jerked down from behind. One of the tigers clamped its mouth onto John's leg and shook him repeatedly. It tried to pull him outside the door but John held on to the doorjamb. The other three tigers shoved rabidly at each other to get at John as well.

Ronnie drew her pistol and fired two shots into the tiger's head. The tiger tugged once more and dropped. Ronnie pulled John inside the door and Wills slammed it shut. The three remaining tigers threw themselves against the thick glass door relentlessly.

John lay motionless on the ground, still stunned from the attack. "We should get away from the door. If they can't see us, they might go away," suggested Wills.

"Good idea," said Ronnie. She held John in her arms and looked concerned. "Are you alright, John?"

"Yeah, I think so. My leg may be a foot longer, though."

Ronnie and Wills helped John to his feet and escorted him around the corner to a bench. Ronnie removed his boot and inspected his leg. He had four gashes in his calf. "I'll be fine," John assured her.

"No, you won't. I'll fix you up." She tore the sleeve off her shirt and wrapped the cuts on his leg. She was teary-eyed as she bandaged his leg. John was surprised. "What's wrong, Ronnie? You're crying."

She looked up at him and sobbed. "I was afraid you were a goner. That tiger shook you like a rag doll."

He put a hand on her cheek. "I didn't realize you cared so much."

"I guess I am too." She helped him to his feet and held him by his arm. John hobbled a few steps.

"I can make it," he assured her. Ronnie hugged him and surprised him with her affection. It seemed so unlike her. "Now, now, young lady. I'm fine," he said and placed his arm around her shoulder.

She wiped the tears from her eyes. "I'm okay. I was just a little worried about you." John kissed her on the forehead.

"Can't the two of you wait to get a room? Those tigers are trying to get in and you're playing courtship," complained Wills.

John enjoyed a rare tender moment. "Shut up, Wills, you fool," he kidded.

Ronnie felt sympathy for Wills. "When we get back, I'll make sure I introduce you to some nice ladies." Wills pretended to ignore her offer out of manly pride, but his attitude improved significantly.

They descended the stairwell to the train platforms and scanned the area with their flashlights. They saw numerous rail cars lined up in the darkness. "It's a big change from our horse and carriage," John quipped.

The trio entered the nearest car and sat down. The sound of breaking glass from upstairs echoed through the platform and startled them. "The tigers are coming! How do we close these doors?" exclaimed Seamus.

"Grab a handle and pull!" ordered Ronnie.

Wills hurried to the rear door and yanked it shut. "Are we safe in here?" he asked.

"I think so," replied Ronnie, unconvinced. She tugged at the front door but it wouldn't budge. John grabbed a hold and helped pull but it still wouldn't move.

"Pull harder!" shouted Ronnie frantically. They struggled with the door until it finally budged. It was nearly closed when three tigers galloped toward them and crashed into it. Their combined weight rocked the rail car and knocked them to the ground.

The door was ajar by a few inches and the tigers clawed rabidly at the opening. Ronnie was awed by the long pairs of fangs that protruded from the tigers' jaws. They added to the fearsome image of the tigers. Their albino fur gave them a ghostly appearance. "I think one of those would make a nice trophy," she remarked cynically.

"You've got to be kidding," groaned Wills.

One of the tigers hooked its fang inside the door and yanked at it. The door quivered and budged.

"You're going to have to earn this trophy," John commented.

"What trophy is that, John – you or the tiger?" she teased.

"I see you keep your sense of humor well under pressure." Ronnie giggled at his remark.

Wills approached the door and studied it. He drew his sword and pointed the blade toward the gap. He kept the hilt close to his body and focused on the opening. The tiger turned its head while tugging on the door and exposed its throat. Wills lurched forward and pushed hard on the hilt. When the blade penetrated the tiger's throat, it gurgled and spewed blood from its mouth.

Ronnie peered out the window and saw the tiger collapse on the platform. A pool of blood formed on the ground from its wound. The remaining two tigers continued their assault on the door. Wills returned to his initial stance and waited patiently. The tigers clawed at the door and rammed it repeatedly with their heads. One of the tigers wedged its paw inside the door and pulled. Wills darted forward again with his sword and, once more, the blade found its mark. The tiger staggered and fell to the ground next to the other. Blood oozed freely from the gaping wound. The last tiger was already wounded when it crashed through the glass door upstairs. It ceased its attack and hobbled away in obvious pain.

Ronnie approached the rear door of the car and slowly pushed it open. There was no sign of the tiger. "I think it's safe, now."

John and Wills followed Ronnie onto the platform with their swords poised to attack. They stopped briefly to examine the dead tigers. Ronnie studied the tiger from end to end with her flashlight. She grabbed the fang of one tiger and pulled open its mouth. "This one would look good over my fireplace," she kidded.

"I think they look fine right where they are," commented Wills.

Ronnie noticed pamphlets on a nearby table with details on the trains' destinations, platforms, and times of departure. On the back of the pamphlet was a map showing the train route to the airport. "Do you want to go on, John, or should we go back to the Post Office?" asked Ronnie.

"I can go further if you like. My leg isn't too bad."

Ronnie looked at her watch. "We have some time left. Why don't we double back and find the others?"

"I think I like that idea," said Wills.

— ⧗ —

Billy, Randy and the two Englishmen proceeded down Market Street, surveying the empty buildings. "I think this street could be the perfect runway for a small shuttle plane to take off," declared Billy.

"It certainly looks long enough," replied Randy. They grimaced as the rain fell harder and the wind gusted.

"Why don't we get out of the rain and talk about this?" suggested Krill.

"Yes, I'm getting soggy under this bag," groaned Nigel.

"My hair's a mess," complained Randy.

"Then it's unanimous," Billy announced. "Let's find someplace dry."

Randy noticed a pub on the next corner. "I see just the place!" she exclaimed.

Billy saw it, too. "I second that motion." When they reached the entrance of the pub, Billy peered through the glass to make sure it was safe inside. "Looks like Happy Hour! I've got first round," he announced.

Billy pushed open the door and stepped inside. After surveying the area one more time, he walked behind the bar and mixed rum and cola in a tall glass for himself. Randy sat down on one of the stools and browsed at the selection of liquors. Billy leaned across the bar and asked, "Can I get you something, Sweetheart?"

"I believe I'll have a Vodka Tonic," answered Randy.

"One Vodka Tonic coming up."

Nigel and Krill sat at one of the round tables. Billy returned with a drink for Randy and suggested to the Englishmen, "I'm sure you gentlemen are in the market for an old-fashioned beer."

"That would be most excellent," replied Krill.

Billy took out two bottles of Guinness Stout from the warm refrigerator and opened them. He set them on the table in front of the men. Nigel and Krill were thrilled.

Two hours later, the four of them were feeling tipsy. Billy and Randy joked and grew frisky toward each other. Nigel and Krill reminisced about old days and good times.

At noon, the rain finally stopped. One of the suns even appeared once or twice through the clouds. Seven of Ruger's minions galloped down the street on green dragons. They wore black leather uniforms and carried primitive weapons. The dragons had big heads with long snake-like tongues, darting out periodically. When the dragons opened their mouths, they revealed sharp, jagged teeth. Bony stumps protruded from each side of their torsos that were wings at one time.

Nigel peered out the window and was horrified. "What in bloody hell?"

The others rushed to the window to see what caught his eye. Billy saw the creatures and urgently pushed everyone toward the back of the pub. "We've got to hide fast. I don't think we're in a position to fight with them."

"Nor the condition," kidded Randy giddily.

Billy located the stairway to the basement. "Get down there and don't move until I tell you." Nigel and Krill hurried downstairs.

Randy paused at the top of the steps. "Aren't you coming?" she asked as she grew concerned.

"Not yet. I want to see what they're up to."

"Come down with me now. I don't want you to get hurt." The two stared into each other's eyes and felt something between them.

"Get down there. I promise I'll be down shortly." Randy reluctantly left him. Billy watched the minions through the glass. One of them stopped at the window and stared inside the pub. A feeling of horror came over Billy when the minion took notice of their glasses and bottles on top of the bar and table. It dismounted from its dragon and entered the pub.

Randy knelt behind empty beer cases, waiting for Billy. He tiptoed down the steps into the darkness. As he felt his way toward the front of the basement, Randy reached up and grabbed him by the belt. He fell awkwardly to the floor. "Gee, Billy, I see you've fallen for me," she whispered playfully.

"You think," he murmured. He felt a rush of excitement swim through his body as he lay against her, face to face. He started to get up, but paused. Randy sensed his hesitation and slid into a comfortable position.

"Where are Nigel and Krill?" whispered Billy.

"They're up front. Don't worry about them." Billy could feel Randy's breath on his lips.

More minions entered the pub and shuffled across the floor. "This isn't fair," complained Billy.

"Who said life was fair?" said Randy as she toyed with his hair. They heard several grunts and then the door to the basement creaked open.

"Damn it! Some things just weren't meant to be," he complained.

"Why do you say that?"

"Could there ever be, you know – us?"

"Maybe. Maybe not."

Billy snapped, frustrated with her games, "It couldn't be a simple 'yes' or 'no', could it?"

"Of course not, at least not right now."

Billy heard a squeak from the top step as one of the minions stepped onto the stairs. He looked disappointedly at Randy. "So be it," he muttered dejectedly. Billy got up off the floor and reached for his sword. As he slid it from its scabbard, his heart raced with anxiety. He hid near the steps and waited for the minion.

I'm really getting to like that fool, thought Randy.

The steps creaked again as the minion cautiously descended the stairs. Billy crept closer, still hidden in the darkness. When the minion reached the floor, Billy struck at its head with his sword. The minion's neck bones cracked and the head hit the floor with a thud. The dim light from upstairs shone on two kegs which wobbled when the headless body fell against them. Billy dove at the empty kegs and wrapped his arms around one of them. Unfortunately, the second one fell on its side. He tensed and waited anxiously but heard nothing from upstairs. Billy breathed a sigh of relief and stepped softly up the stairs.

Randy felt her way past stacked beer cases to the ramp up front. When she reached Krill and Nigel, she whispered, "Billy went upstairs. We have to help him."

"Let's wait and see what he's up to first," suggested Nigel.

"I won't just sit here and let him get hurt again." Randy left them and returned to the steps.

Billy peeked around the corner and saw two minions standing guard in front of the glass window. Another minion searched the rear of the pub. He heard the thumping of the fifth minion ascending the stairs to the second floor. He spotted the last one behind the bar. It ran its paw across the moisture on the counter from their glasses and snarled.

Billy knew it was onto them and had to act quickly while he still had the element of surprise on his side. Instinctively, he rushed at the two minions in front of the window and slammed into them. All three of them crashed through the glass and tumbled onto the wet sidewalk. Billy scrambled to his feet first and drew his sword. Before the two minions could get to their feet, he drove his sword into the first one's chest. The other drew a short, curled dagger and poised to attack him. He carefully stalked the minion until the others stormed out of the pub and surrounded him. "Oh, that plan went to hell in a hurry," he groaned.

Randy emerged from the pub with a steak knife in her hand. She surprised the minions and stabbed the nearest one in the back. The hurricane doors swung open and slammed against the sidewalk. Krill and Nigel emerged from the basement and attacked two more of the minions.

Billy took advantage of the distraction his friends provided and lunged at the closest minion. He struck once at its shoulder then drove his sword through its chest. Before falling to the ground, the wounded minion swung its club and caught Billy in the jaw. He sprawled across the ground in pain. Nigel and Krill quickly disposed of three more minions with their swords. Randy jumped on the remaining minion from behind and slit its throat with her knife.

Billy got up slowly, holding his jaw. "Son of a bitch! That hurt."

Randy examined his jaw and kissed it. "You'll be fine," she teased.

"Gee, thanks for the sympathy."

Seven dragons rounded the corner and galloped toward them. Foamy saliva dribbled from their mouths, accompanied by low-pitched growls. "Here we go again!" groaned Billy.

Krill noticed a bank across the street. "There's a solid building, Billy. We can barricade the door from inside."

"Let's go then!"

The dragons pursued them to the bank's entrance. Once inside, Krill slammed the door shut behind them. The dragons rammed the door and relentlessly clawed at it. Nigel pushed desks and file cabinets in front of the door for extra support.

Billy was light-headed from his injury and sat down on the floor. He leaned against the wall and hid his face in his hands. "Is there anything I can do for you, Billy?" Randy asked sympathetically.

"No, I think you did enough."

Randy realized that she hurt him with her earlier remark. "Billy, I…"

"Maybe you can check upstairs for an escape route? I don't think we're leaving the way we came in."

Randy placed her hand on his cheek. "I'm sorry. I'll see what I can do."

Billy was aware that the girls never took things too seriously. He forced a smile and asked, "Why are you sorry?"

"I was afraid you took my remarks the wrong way."

Billy grimaced and covered his jaw again. Randy reluctantly left him and searched the rear of the bank.

— ☒ —

Ronnie, John and Wills marched north along Market Street toward the taller buildings in the heart of the city. Ronnie felt bad for John as he hobbled. She saw several vehicles parked on the side street and decided to procure one. "Don't go away, boys, I'll be right back." The two Englishmen wondered what she was up to and waited.

Ronnie checked each vehicle on the street until she found an Expedition with its doors unlocked. She reached under the steering wheel and fished for the ignition wires. When she crossed the wires to the ignition, the engine roared to life. She slid into the driver seat and sped toward the men. After skidding to a stop, she opened the passenger door. "Hop in, boys! We're going for a ride," she yelled excitedly.

"Nice carriage," remarked John.

"You know, I always wanted one of these and I've got to say, the price is right!"

John and Wills marveled at the vehicle as they climbed into the back seat. Ronnie popped open the glove compartment and found several CDs. "We're saved! We have tunes, boys!"

"Tunes?" echoed John and Wills.

"Yeah, tunes. How about some Guns and Roses' 'Welcome to the Jungle'? Isn't that appropriate?" The men had no idea what she was talking about. Ronnie inserted the CD into the stereo and turned the volume up. "Hold on tight!" she warned. The vehicle raced up and down the streets, slipping and sliding from time to time on the wet surface.

— ☒ —

Randy returned to the front of the bank. "I checked everywhere. There's no easy way out of here without a ladder or a long rope," she informed him disappointedly and then opened several of the bank tellers' drawers. Billy was shocked as she greedily stuffed wads of bills in her pockets. He frowned at her until she acknowledged him. "What's the matter?" she asked.

"I see old habits die hard."

"They're not old habits!" Randy responded defensively. "It's just in case we ever do go back to our world and I have to pay bills again. A woman needs security."

"You are a work in progress, Randy."

"Why thank you," she said and resumed raiding the tills.

— ⅄ —

Ronnie sang the words to the song as she whisked around a corner. Suddenly, she saw the dragons in front of the bank and slammed on the brakes. John and Wills groaned as they leaned forward against the seats. "It looks like someone's inside the building. Maybe it's Billy and the others," suggested John.

Ronnie revved the motor. "Let's find out." John and Wills looked nervously at each other.

Ronnie sped toward the dragons at a high rate of speed. Grinning deviously, she turned up the volume on the music and honked the horn repeatedly. The dragons were startled and scattered at the sight of the noisy Expedition racing toward them. Ronnie spun the vehicle around and chased them again. The dragons scurried away from the bank. After Ronnie's third pass, the dragons fled down the side street. She pulled the vehicle around to the front door of the bank and honked the horn.

Billy stood by the door with Krill and Nigel. They listened as the clawing sounds were replaced by the sound of the horn. "Help me move the desk. Someone's out there," ordered Billy.

They shoved the desks out of the way and opened the door. Billy peeked out and saw the Expedition with Ronnie in the driver's seat. Ronnie turned off the music, much to the relief of John and Wills. She saw Billy at the door. "Hey, slacker! Do you want a ride or not?"

"Hell, yeah! Took you long enough." Billy opened the door and ran to the truck. Nigel, Krill and Randy followed closely behind.

"Girl, am I glad to see you," Randy announced, relieved. The girls high-fived each other.

"Where to next, people? We've got a full tank of gas and plenty of time," said Ronnie.

Billy jumped back out of the vehicle. "Someone give me a hand. I want a closer look at these things."

"Are you out of your mind?" chided Randy.

"This will only take a minute."

"You've already had your minute," joked Randy.

"And that's all you're gonna get from me," Billy shot back.

"What, pray tell, are they babbling about?" asked John.

"You really don't want to know, do you?" Ronnie answered calmly.

"I sense that this is but another strange custom from your time?"

"You ain't seen nothing yet, John," she remarked cynically.

Billy and Krill collected the corpse and dragged it toward the vehicle. "This thing reeks," complained Krill.

Billy looked away from the creature nauseously and took a fresh breath. "Phew! You're not kidding." He and Krill were utterly repulsed by the horrible face on the creature. "Oh, geez, that's one ugly son-of-a-bitch!" said Billy.

"What are we doing with it?" asked Krill.

"Doc, our scientist, should look at this thing. He's probably into this kind of stuff," suggested Billy.

"Better him than me," Krill replied, disgusted. They lifted the corpse onto the roof of the Expedition and tied it down. Krill climbed into the back seat with John and Nigel. Billy climbed in the front seat with the girls.

"Let's get this thing back to Doc, ASAP," ordered Billy. "You know how to get to the tracks, right, Ronnie?"

"Of course, I do."

They raced away from the bank and drove toward the train station.

CHAPTER 7

URBAN FEARS

When the Expedition approached a hospital on one of the secondary streets, a gray-haired nurse rushed out of the heavily damaged building, waving her arms frantically. Ronnie slammed on the brakes and nearly struck her. The woman was hysterical and babbled incoherently. "What the hell's wrong with you? You could have been killed," Ronnie scolded her.

"The creatures – they came and took many of our people away. Only eight of us are left. Can you help us?"

"Who are the others?"

"Nurses and two doctors." The woman noticed the carcass on the roof and screamed.

"Shut up already! The damned thing is dead," Ronnie chastised.

"What should we do about them?" Randy asked Billy.

"We could use some doctors and nurses at the compound, especially with my luck."

"How are we going to get them back?" Ronnie reluctantly asked.

"You found one vehicle. Can you can find another?"

"I guess I could."

"Get your companions together along with any supplies you can carry," Billy instructed the nurse.

"Will you take us with you?"

"Absolutely. We'll get you a vehicle." Billy and Ronnie left the Expedition and searched the side street. Ronnie eyed a van as the most practical vehicle. She opened the door and ducked under the dash. In a few seconds, the motor roared to life.

Billy was amazed at how easily Ronnie hotwired the vehicle. He climbed in the passenger side and stared at her as she drove the vehicle away. "What's wrong with you?" she asked indignantly.

"You're pretty good at stealing vehicles."

"Keep it up and I'll steal your heart."

"Too late. It's been stolen, wrecked and broken one too many times."

Ronnie was surprised by his openness and stopped the van. "I'm sorry, Billy. I didn't mean that."

"It's alright. I just went through this with Randy. I'll get over it."

"Neither Randy nor I ever mean to hurt you. We're friends."

"I'm realizing that a true relationship can't be had and I'm fine with it."

"What about Penny?" she asked.

"It won't last and I'm learning to adjust to that. Next week, something else will be a problem for us."

"You know, Billy, I think we have a lot more in common than I thought possible. They say misery loves company." The two chuckled and high-fived.

When they returned with the van, the medical people waited on the sidewalk with their supplies. Billy opened the side door and jumped out. "Load 'em up and we'll get rolling."

The strangers loaded the supplies into the van and squeezed inside. Randy and the Englishmen waited impatiently as Billy and Ronnie climbed into the Expedition.

"Are you sure this new route of yours is going to work, Billy?" asked Randy.

"It better. We have a lot riding on it."

Ronnie punched the accelerator and the vehicle sped off toward the train station. She looked in the mirror regularly and checked that the van stayed close behind them. They drove through the city past wrecked vehicles and debris until Ronnie saw the tracks coming up on the left. "Get ready, everyone. It's going to get bumpy," she warned.

The Expedition veered off the road and onto the tracks. It bounced crazily until they reached the last set of rails. The van kept pace with some difficulty but never lagged too far behind. "I'm surprised they're keeping up," Ronnie remarked.

"I think they're happy to get the hell out of there," replied Billy.

The tracks disappeared into the foliage after a half mile just before the mountains but they followed a natural path that was passable. John pointed to the right. "Isn't that the mountain we crossed going into the city?"

"It sure is. We need to get over to the right somehow," mentioned Randy.

"Let me worry about that," Ronnie responded. She maintained a wary eye and kept the Expedition moving at a brisk pace. Both vehicles continued their course without incident.

"How are your matchmaking skills? Can we hook John's friends up?" Ronnie asked Randy.

Randy looked back at the men and giggled. "It might be a little tough with this lot, but I think we can help. I do have someone special in mind for Wills."

Wills eye lit up with hope. "That would be great!"

"I'd be satisfied so long as we have more of that beer. It was quite good," Krill mentioned.

"Yes, if I can't have a good woman, a good beer is perfectly acceptable," added Nigel.

"A good beer will never break your heart," kidded Billy.

"See if you boys can make love to a good beer," Ronnie joked.

"But Billy's right," Nigel replied.

"Watch what you say around these girls," warned Billy. "They never let you forget it."

"Billy, I'm hurt. How could you even think that?" replied Ronnie in mock surprise.

Billy laughed and then confessed, "Well, boys, there's something I have to tell you. That beer was from the land of Eire. It's Guinness."

"As I said before, a good beer is perfectly acceptable," reiterated Nigel.

"What a relief? I was afraid you guys would take exception to it."

"Under the circumstances, we're perfectly content with the beer."

The Expedition wound its way around trees and boulders until it reached a wide stream. "What do you think?" asked Ronnie.

Billy thought for a moment. "I think that's the stream that leads to the dam. Head downstream."

"Downstream it is."

Billy leaned out the window and studied the stream. "The water's getting deeper so we must be close. It'll be coming up any second. There it is!"

Ronnie cut the wheel to the left and pulled the vehicle out of the sand onto solid ground. She passed a group of trees and saw the compound straight ahead.

"Well, there it is. Good call, Billy."

Billy was pleased with himself. "So, I was right. We can move the plane to the city and use the main street for a runway."

"It looks like we have a lot of work to do just to get it out of the forest, though," said Randy.

"Yes, but this was our biggest obstacle. Now we know it's doable."

— X —

Pirocles trembled and retreated from Ruger when he slammed his fist against the table. "Did the minions fail?" he asked.

"Yes, they failed!" Ruger screamed.

"We can't afford to send more, can we?"

"Pull them back inside the castle and raise the drawbridge."

"But Ruger …"

"Do it! We have to finish this now."

"Maybe Diomedes can help."

"I can't go to her with news of another failure. She'll curse me forever." he looked down at the battlefield from his window high atop the castle. "He'll pay dearly for interfering with my plans," he swore bitterly.

— X —

Seamus and Jerry were surprised to see two vehicles speeding toward them. They waved and yelled excitedly. Doc and Maggie watched from the gate and saw the creature tied to the top of the Expedition. "I wonder what kind of trouble Billy's gotten into this time," Doc quipped.

"I hope that's a stuffed animal on the roof because it sure looks scary," Maggie commented. They slowly meandered out toward their friends. The vehicles parked and everyone got out.

"We picked up some new friends from the hospital – doctors and nurses with supplies," announced Ronnie.

"Excellent. Let's find them a place to sleep and give them a tour of the compound," said Doc.

"I'll take care of them."

Doc looked at the creature on the roof and was concerned. "What in the world is that thing, Billy?"

"I thought you'd find it interesting." Billy nodded to Krill and Nigel. They took the dead creature down from the roof and laid it on the ground.

"Where did you find it?"

"A half dozen of them showed up in town on dragons. They're not very friendly," explained Billy. Doc cracked a smile.

Their conversation was briefly interrupted when Penny arrived and stood next to Billy. She wore the yellow dress that she saved for a special occasion. Billy was amazed at how lovely she looked. When she put her arms around him and attempted to kiss him, he pushed her away and covered his jaw. "What's wrong, Billy?" she asked.

"Oh, I had a little accident."

"Billy got popped in the jaw by a troll," Ronnie interjected playfully.

"I can't let you out of my sight for five minutes without you getting hurt."

"Yeah, it seems that way."

"When you get cleaned up, I have a hug and a kiss for you."

"That'll work. Give me a few minutes." Penny smiled at him and walked away. Billy cast a quick glance at Ronnie and Randy. He knew what their sordid minds were thinking.

Randy related the story about the tigers and minions to Jerry and Seamus. Others gathered to hear the tale as well. "I really wish I could have brought back some drink for this evening. It was unfortunate that we were interrupted at such a bad time," complained Krill.

Nigel pulled a bottle of Scotch Whiskey from under his cloak. "Maybe you didn't remember, but I sure did," he proclaimed proudly.

Krill's smile reappeared. "Let's drink my friends!" urged Nigel in a celebratory tone.

— X —

Billy met Penny at the rear of the encampment. Behind them were several thatched huts that lined the face of the cliff. She led him by the hand inside one of them. Billy was impressed with the interior of the hut. "This looks like one of the huts on 'Gilligan's Island," he joked.

Penny lay back on the bed and pulled him on top of her. "This is more like it," Billy crooned.

"I thought you'd say that." After several minutes of playful kissing and caressing, Penny asked, "What do you think?"

"I think you're beautiful."

Penny unbuttoned his shirt. "No, I mean the hut."

"You want to know about it now?"

Penny kissed his chest and neck, then answered, "Yes, silly. I want to know what you think. This is going to be our home."

Billy was taken aback by her statement and was speechless. Penny sensed his apprehension and grew impatient. Billy browsed around the hut and saw furniture pieces that were salvaged from the terminal. Some of Penny's clothes were stacked neatly on a table at the end of the bed. In the corner, he saw a quilt rolled neatly on top of a plastic wrap. "This is nice but you said 'our home'?"

"Yes, I did. Jerry and some of the men helped construct it for us as a present. They're really grateful for all that you've done for them." Penny slid out of her dress and nestled up to Billy. He kissed her passionately.

"So, you and I have our own little place all to ourselves."

"Uh-huh and I was thinking that maybe we could start a family. I've accepted the fact that we're not going home."

Billy was startled by her remark. He pulled away from her and lay on his back. Penny rolled on her side and faced him. "If we're going to live together, I want us to be happy," she explained.

"Uh, starting a family isn't what I had in mind right now. I told you before; we need to build our relationship. We don't know for sure if our situation is permanent yet."

Penny became annoyed with him. "If you want to have a relationship with me, I need a commitment, Billy," she said adamantly.

"Why the sudden rush?"

"Because, you and I both know that we're stuck here. I care about you a whole lot and I want us to consummate our relationship."

"Penny, this isn't a good idea. As much as I want you, this is the wrong way to do it."

Penny got up and put her dress back on. "Then you need to take some time and reconsider your decision. Don't take too long, though, because I may not be here when you do."

Billy became flustered with her and sighed. "Penny, you're approaching this the wrong way," he explained.

Penny stood facing the wall and said dejectedly, "Please, just leave me alone and don't come back until you've made up your mind."

"Why, just for once, can't things be easy?" uttered Billy and he left the hut. When he returned to the campfire, Maggie and Doc knew by his expression that things turned out badly.

"I was afraid of this," said Maggie.

"I'd better discuss our other problem with Billy."

Billy stood by, listening to the conversations near the fire. Doc approached him and suggested, "You might want to come with me."

"Where to?"

"Something about your dead friend you need to see."

They walked over to one of the barriers where the corpse lay on the ground with a sheet wrapped around it. "How much do you know about these creatures?" asked Doc.

"Not a whole lot. They showed up and we fought with them." Doc held up the dead creature's arm up for Billy to see. "What about it?" asked Billy curiously.

"See the device on its arm; it's a transmitter of some sort."

"No kidding."

"Did you hear these things communicate at all?"

"Not really."

"Well, we have a big problem. This transmitter could lead others to us. Do you know how many more of them there were?"

"Only six that we saw. They're all dead"

"We have to get rid of it as soon as possible," Doc advised him.

"I'll take care of it right away," he said somberly.

Doc unstrapped the transmitter from the creature's arm and handed it to Billy.

"You understand the implications of this, don't you?"

"Of course, I do, Doc. What else have you learned about this thing?"

"Its body has some similarities to that of a man, but the skeletal system is quite different."

"Is it alien like extra-terrestrial alien or just unusual alien?"

"I don't know. These things must be intelligent, though, if they carry transmitters."

"Either that or they have a higher breed of intelligence controlling them like slaves," suggested Billy.

"Possibly. Be very careful around them."

"You're telling me! One of them almost broke my jaw."

"Anything else I should know about?"

"I did find a strip of roadway long enough to use for a runway."

"Take care of the transmitter first and then we'll talk about the runway."

Billy looked at the transmitter and at Doc. "I'll see you when I get back," he replied.

"Good luck, Billy." Billy waved and meandered away.

The sun vanished behind the mountains and Billy's friends sang cheerfully around the campfire. Billy secretly took the Expedition and drove away from the compound. He had difficulty seeing in the dark, even with the headlights on in the dense forest. On several occasions he thought he saw creatures in the trees but dismissed it as his imagination. He felt fatigued so he pulled out a CD from the glove compartment and inserted it into the stereo. Van Halen's "Running with the Devil" blared from the speakers. Billy felt renewed enthusiasm and drove faster. He thought better of going through the city in case more of the minions waited for him, so he took the new route through the mountain pass to the train station. It was a bumpy ride, and driving through the tunnel on the tracks was tricky with very little clearance on either side to maneuver the vehicle.

When he arrived inside the train station, he parked next to one of the train platforms and stepped out. He strapped on his sword and turned on his flashlight. As he approached the steps, he heard a peculiar sound, like the shuffling of slippers on the cement from a dark corner of the platform. On his right, he saw two tiger carcasses lying in large puddles of blood.

I guess they didn't exaggerate about the tigers, thought Billy. He ascended the steps and approached the broken glass door. The shuffling sound grew louder and Billy's heart beat faster. He ducked around the corner and waited. A few moments later, a large tiger staggered in front of him. Billy was terrified but the tiger appeared ill and held its ground. He noticed a piece of glass embedded in the tiger's flank and another in its right front leg. The tiger was in pain and its eyes seemed to plead for help.

Billy stood motionless for several minutes until the tiger lay down on the floor. It was a magnificent creature with two long fangs protruding from its upper jaw. Its albino coat was thick but shorthaired. The bloodstains soiled the tiger's beautiful coat. He mustered his courage and approached the tiger. For some insane reason he gently tugged on the glass shard in the tiger's leg. The tiger flinched but remained passive. He carefully manipulated the shard from the animal's leg. It was difficult at first, but the shard slid out with a slurping sound. The animal moaned briefly and panted heavily.

Billy tore off his T-shirt and ripped it into pieces. He tied one piece gently around the animal's leg. Next, he attempted to remove the large glass shard from the tiger's flank. This proved to be more difficult and took some time. After several manipulations of the shard, it slid free. The tiger growled softly, baring its long fangs. Billy was sure that the animal would attack him any minute and shuddered. Sweat dripped off his forehead from anxiety and exhaustion. He took the last piece of cloth and wrapped the animal's flank. The tiger stood up and hobbled several feet. It lay down again and slept. Billy leaned back against the wall. He was exhausted and didn't care what happened next.

— ⧗ —

Ronnie joined the men in their merriment by the campfire. She took a swig of Scotch and listened to their stories until she noticed that Billy was missing. "Has anybody seen Billy?"

"He went back into the city to take care of something," replied Doc.

Ronnie raced to the gate and saw that her Expedition was gone. "Where's my truck? I'll kill him!" she shouted.

Doc placed his hand on her shoulder and tried to calm her down. "We found a transmitter on the dead creature's arm. Billy had to get rid of it."

"I don't care. He had no business leaving without telling me."

"I didn't know he was going alone, but the transmitter had to go back for all our sakes."

"Wait until I get my hands around his neck. He's gonna wish he was dead."

Randy overheard and became concerned. "He won't last out there at night alone. We have to do something?" she fretted.

"We can't do anything tonight. Let's wait until morning and see if he returns," said Doc calmly.

"But it could be too late by then."

"Randy's right," said Ronnie.

"And what if you don't find him? Worse, what if you get killed looking for him?" Doc pointed out. Ronnie paced back and forth, unsure of what to do.

Penny and Maggie heard the argument and emerged from their huts. "What's happened?" asked Maggie.

"Billy left for the city alone in Ronnie's truck. She's a little upset," answered Doc.

"So, Billy went out alone, again," said Penny sadly.

"I'm sure he'll be fine," replied Maggie.

Penny became teary-eyed. "I don't care. It's his life," she said dejectedly.

"Come on, Penny. It's not like he had a choice."

"It doesn't matter." Penny returned to her hut. Maggie considered following her but thought better of it.

— X —

Billy was surprised when he woke up inside the train station. Everything that happened yesterday seemed like a distant dream. He looked at his watch and remembered the black transmitter. The saber-toothed tiger slept nearby so Billy stepped quietly. He almost reached the door when the tiger hopped up and limped after him. Billy put his hand on the hilt of his sword but the tiger showed no interested in him whatsoever. He strolled down one of the corridors and entered a deli. The tiger trotted after him.

On the countertop, he found a loaf of raisin bread, a tub of butter and some assorted muffins. The tiger watched him curiously. Billy picked up a muffin and rolled it toward the tiger. "It's never too late to be housebroken," he suggested to the tiger.

The tiger sniffed the muffin and, with one lap of its tongue, swallowed it whole. Billy rolled another muffin to the tiger and watched as the tiger engulfed it. He fed the tiger until the muffins were gone. "What a brute you are, my friend. That's it! I'll call you Brutus." When the tiger stood up, Billy saw the gender of the big cat and decided, "Yes, Brutus it is."

Billy opened the refrigerator and inspected its contents. Immediately, the smell of sour milk filled his nostrils and he turned away. He found seven containers of juice on the top shelf and removed them. On the bottom shelf, he found a container of bacon and sausage. When he removed the lid, he heaved from the odor. Brutus smelled the bad meat but wasn't deterred. He approached Billy with his eyes glued to the meat. Billy set the container on the ground by the side of the refrigerator and the tiger greedily ate the meat. He didn't see anything else in the deli that interested him so he packed a bag of juices and left the shop.

Brutus followed from a short distance behind as Billy exited the train station and walked into the warm sun. Billy and the tiger headed north up the street toward the tall buildings. After seven blocks, Brutus sensed something and became agitated. Billy didn't see anything, but he knew that if Brutus was worried, he should be, too.

When they reached the pub, Brutus would go no further. Billy was worried when Brutus hobbled back toward the train station. The tiger had given him some reassurance and, despite being nervous around it, Billy was growing accustomed to having it nearby. He removed the transmitter and tossed it across the street into a wrecked vehicle.

Billy then entered an office building in search of a vantage point to watch for the minions. Inside the lobby, the silence was bone chilling and made him nervous. The stairs were badly damaged and filled with debris but Billy ascended them to the upper levels. When he exited on the ninth floor, he passed a receptionist's desk and came across several offices. Only one of the office doors was closed. Billy tried the door but it was locked. He struck at the knob with his sword and watched contentedly as it fell to the ground in pieces. When he barged into the room, something struck him in the head and knocked him to the ground.

Four people stood around him when he awoke. They talked but Billy couldn't hear them. He thought it was weird that they looked blurry like angels in the faint light from their flashlights. His head throbbed and he couldn't move. After several attempts to get up, he realized that someone was holding him down. His vision cleared and his hearing returned.

"I'm so sorry. I'm really sorry. I thought you were one of those things," a young man stammered.

Billy was confused. He looked at the other faces and saw three females; two young girls and a middle-aged woman. "You have to lie still," one of the girls emphasized.

Billy felt the back of his head and his hand was covered with blood. His hair was wet and matted. "What did you do to me?" he asked feebly.

The blond-haired girl, Melanie, placed a wet rag against the wound on Billy's head. An older woman, Helen, entered the room with a first aid box and placed a square bandage on Billy's head. He cringed when he looked at her face. The woman reminded him of an old crone. She had a growth on her chin and a wrinkly face. Her attire wasn't much better. She wore a long skirt, well below the knees and a thick sweater.

When Billy sat up, he saw a longneck, brass lamp lying on the floor that was bent severely. He assumed that was the attempted murder weapon. "What is wrong with you people? You could have killed me," Billy screamed at them.

"I'm really sorry, sir. I thought you were one of the soldiers," apologized Ben, who was only nineteen.

"You had no business coming up here! Now they'll find us," exclaimed Helen.

"What the hell are you talking about?" Billy asked sarcastically.

"Demon soldiers came and took everyone prisoner."

"And you couldn't tell the difference between me and one of them?"

"No, sir," answered Ben. "I swung before I saw your face."

Faye, an attractive, middle-aged woman, introduced everyone to break the tension. Billy reluctantly shook Ben's hand while Helen glared and said nothing. Melanie, at seventeen, was blonde-haired, blue eyed, and petite. Tanya, at eighteen, was dark-skinned, tall and thin with long hair, tied back by a yellow ribbon. Both were dressed professionally in pants suits.

"If you're smart, you'll leave here before they find us," advised Helen

"I'll leave when I'm damn well ready," Billy declared.

"I'm sorry I had to restrain you, but I don't think you realized how badly you were bleeding," said Tanya sorrowfully.

"How long have I been here?"

"About eight hours," she answered sheepishly.

"About eight hours too long," taunted Helen.

"You should know that we're just trying to defend ourselves. Those things are ruthless," said Faye defensively. Billy struggled to get off the floor and into a chair. He looked Faye over as he regained his faculties. Faye, who at thirty-seven, was shapely in her black skirt and tan blouse. She wore her dirty blond hair in a bun, much like a librarian does. "How much do you know about these soldiers?" asked Billy.

"Only that they come in large groups every few days to search for prisoners."

"Weren't you here when the soldiers invaded the city?" inquired Ben.

"No, I was at the airport. I didn't know about the soldiers until yesterday."

"How did you get away from them?" asked Tanya.

"I killed them."

"So, you brought them back here!" screamed Helen. "We can't leave the building to look for food for two days now. Those things are all over the place and they're probably looking for you."

"Get a hold of yourself. You don't know that for sure," chastised Faye.

Billy went to the window and looked down at the darkened street. "Don't stand near the window," warned Faye.

"Why not? They can't see me in the dark."

"At night, giant insects fly around the buildings. We think they have a nest on the roof."

Billy was amused. "I haven't seen any of these flying bugs yet."

Helen stormed across the room and inadvertently stood in front of the window. "You treat this like it's some kind of joke! We're all going to die," she shouted at him.

One of the glass panes shattered and startled them. A giant insect resembling a dragonfly speared Helen with two of its legs and pinned her against a cubicle. It chewed her head off and retreated into the night sky with her body dangling beneath it. Everyone retreated to the doorway.

"What the hell was that?" Billy exclaimed.

"We told you," said Faye somberly. "You didn't listen."

"I'm sorry about Helen," Billy replied humbly.

"No sweat. She was a pain in the ass to all of us."

"It's still a horrible way to die."

"Please, tell me you can get us out of here," pleaded Faye. "We've been living in fear ever since this nightmare started."

They heard footsteps in the lower stairwell. "The soldiers are coming again," fretted Melanie.

"I'll check it out," said Ben. He descended the stairs.

"I'm terrified of this place. Can't you do something, Billy?" Melanie pleaded, while bursting into tears.

"We'll figure something out," promised Billy.

"What do we do if the soldiers come back?" asked Tanya.

"Too late. They're coming," said Ben, returning fearful.

"How many?" asked Billy.

"About a dozen."

"Let's go up to the roof?"

"No way! The insects are up there," exclaimed Ben.

"Well, the soldiers are down there," quipped Billy cynically. "Pick one."

"What do we do?" questioned Faye, panicked.

Billy thought for a moment and then answered, "Maybe I can bait them into a trap."

"How would you do that?" asked Tanya.

"It's simple. We could lead them upstairs to the insects."

They looked confused by Billy's plan but followed him up the stairwell. The stairs worsened as they climbed higher. Several sections were damaged precariously with large sections missing. There were gaping holes to the floors below which made the trip precarious.

Ben waited at the fifteenth floor and monitored the minions' progress on the lower floors. The others reached the thirty-first floor and paused for a rest. The girls panted heavily from the climb.

"Where's an elevator when you need one?" complained Billy.

Melanie chuckled much to the chagrin of the others. "I thought it was cute," she said coyly.

"Thanks, Mel," replied Billy appreciatively. He and Faye looked out from the stairwell at the surrounding area. The roof was missing and office furniture was piled against the walls.

"It looks like they cleared out the middle of the floor for some reason," remarked Faye.

"Maybe there's a nest up here," suggested Melanie once more.

"That's got to be it, Mel!" exclaimed Billy.

"What's so good about that?" Faye asked.

"All we have to do is kill the queen."

"Uh-uh. We're not hunting any queen bugs," Melanie stated. Ben hurried up the stairs and burst into the office. "They're searching each floor. It'll take some time before they get up here, though."

"Good. That gives us time to find the queen."

Ben looked at the girls expectantly. "He's kidding, right?" They shook their heads 'no'.

"Listen to me if you want to live," Billy ordered. "Who has a cigarette lighter?" Melanie and Tanya both produced cigarette lighters. "Aren't you girls a little young to smoke? Cigarettes will kill you," scolded Billy.

"So will giant insects," retorted Tanya.

"Okay, you've got a point."

"We're not that young, either," Melanie protested.

Billy took the lighters from them. "I need one person to go with me. Any volunteers?" No one offered.

"Fine, I'll do this alone." Billy turned to leave but Faye grabbed his arm.

"I'll go, too," she said reluctantly.

"If the soldiers get within sight, throw as much debris as you can down the stairwell to stall them," Billy instructed Ben and the girls.

"What if you don't come back?" asked Ben.

"Shut up! You're going to jinx them," groaned Melanie.

"Of course, we're coming back," said Billy confidently.

"But there's always that chance."

"Save it, Ben. They're coming back." Billy appreciated Melanie's support for him. He and Faye left the stairwell and followed the open hallway.

"I want you to start a fire every twenty feet," Billy instructed her as he handed her the lighters.

"Why twenty feet?"

"So, we have room to run when the fires spread." Billy sensed Faye's fear and felt compassion for her. "Don't worry. I'll get you out of here."

"I'm trusting you with my life. Please don't let me down," she pleaded.

"You can count on me. Now light those fires."

Faye opened file cabinet drawers and removed the files. She piled them along the wall. Billy crept around the corner and peered into the vacant offices. The moonlight illuminated the entire floor, exposing everything in detail. Billy crossed the open floor and paused by a large meeting room. He stood on top of a file cabinet and peeked over the wall. There was no sign of the insects. He jumped down off the cabinet and entered the room through the doorway. Inside, he found half-eaten bodies strewn about. Suddenly, he recognized Helen's remains by the shredded sweater clinging to her bloodstained skeleton. He felt ill and left the room.

Faye flicked the lighters repeatedly but they failed to light each time. The queen dragonfly descended into the meeting room that Billy just vacated. It was bloated with two spear-like legs folded near its head and a treacherous mouth armed with razor sharp teeth. Two red bulbous eyes accented the furry head. The dragonfly leaned over the wall and looked down at Faye. Saliva streamed from its mouth and slid down the wall near her. She was oblivious to the creature and focused on burning the paper.

Billy turned the corner and saw the insect's long forelegs hovering over her. "Faye! Look out!" He instinctively dove into Faye and knocked her clear as the insect's legs slammed into the floor where she just stood.

"I couldn't light the fires," sobbed Faye.

"Forget the fires! Let's get out of here."

When the queen dragonfly shrieked, the other dragonflies suddenly circled overhead. They buzzed wildly and crashed into the glass windows of the building on different floors. Inside the stairwell, the dragonflies hunted the minions and devoured them.

Billy took Faye by the hand and led her to the stairwell. The wall exploded in front of them and the queen dragonfly emerged, cutting them off.

"We're trapped!" cried Faye.

"No, we're not!" Billy grabbed a folding chair and pulled her to the elevator. He drew his sword and pried the elevator doors open. The two of them stepped inside and struggled to push the doors closed. Billy set the folding chair in the corner and instructed Faye, "I'll lift you up but you'll have to pull yourself through."

"What about you?"

"I'll be right behind you." Billy pushed the corner ceiling tile open and lifted Faye up to the access hatch. She crawled through and sat on top of the elevator. The queen dragonfly hammered relentlessly at the elevator until the doors bent inward from the impact of her powerful legs.

Billy handed his sword up to Faye and grabbed the lip of the hatch. With help from Faye, he hoisted himself up. The queen crashed through the elevator doors and lunged at Billy's legs. Before he could pull them through, the dragonfly caught one of his legs in her mouth. Billy screamed as he tried to pull himself up. "Get my sword!" he cried in pain.

Faye grabbed the sword and held it out to Billy. "Stick its eye. Hurry!"

"But Billy ..."

"Stick the damn sword in its eye, now!" Billy fought back the tears as he held onto cables tightly. His leg burned with pain from the acidic saliva in the dragonfly's mouth. It tugged at him and he slid down through the hatch. Billy looked desperately at Faye. "Use the sword, Faye. Use it now or else." Faye leaned over the hatch but was terrified of the dragonfly. "I can't hold on any longer, Faye!" Billy pleaded.

Faye reached down and shoved the sword into the eye of the queen. It shrieked and released its hold on Billy. He pulled himself out of the hatch and rolled away. Blood streamed from several gashes on his leg and much of the skin was chafed off.

"Oh, God, it hurts," sobbed Billy.

"What can I do, Billy?"

Billy struggled to his knees and saw a service ladder leading up to the pulleys. "We've got to get up the ladder," he said as he fought back his tears. Faye took his arm and lifted him to his feet. Billy stowed his sword and pushed Faye toward the ladder.

"You first," he ordered.

"But your leg."

"Get up there now or we're both dead!" he shouted at her.

Faye reluctantly climbed up to the small service landing by the pulleys. Billy pulled himself up one rung at a time to the top. When he reached the landing, he braced himself against the pulley mounts and watched the queen rip parts of the ceiling from the elevator.

"It's coming through the elevator, Billy!" Faye fretted. "We're trapped!"

Billy drew his sword and stuck it under one of the elevator cables at the pulley. He pried back with all his strength using the pulley for leverage. The cable snapped and whipped down the shaft. The elevator lurched from the weight of the dragonfly and staggered it. Billy stuck his sword under the second cable and pried hard on it. The queen burst through the elevator ceiling and stabbed at Billy with its foreleg. Faye pulled Billy out of the way as the queen struck the steel plate in front of him.

"Thanks, I owe you for that," said Billy gratefully.

"Just finish that thing off and we'll call it even."

The queen pushed through the top of the elevator again and crept closer. Billy stuck his sword under the third of the four cables and pried back on it. The cable broke and whipped off the queen's head. She was stunned briefly.

The elevator groaned and squealed as the lone cable strained under her weight. Billy pried desperately against the cable with his sword. The dragonfly caught Billy across the arm with its leg and knocked him down. Blood streamed from the laceration but he held onto his sword and applied continued pressure to the cable. He yanked harder on the sword and finally severed it.

The elevator squealed loudly as the cable flew down the shaft. A loud roar filled the air as the queen and the elevator plummeted thirty-one stories to the bottom of the shaft. Several seconds passed and then a loud crash rocked the building.

The dragonflies sensed the death of their queen and took flight into the night sky like a dark cloud in front of the two moons. Billy laughed cynically and fell on his back. After resting for a few minutes, he got up and pulled himself to the ladder. Faye helped him down the ladder and out of the elevator shaft.

Ben, Tanya and Melanie waited anxiously for them in the stairwell. "What did you do, Billy? All the dragonflies have gone," asked Ben.

"I killed the queen."

"The drones killed all the soldiers."

Billy pointed to a couch in the pile of debris. "Can you pull that out for me? I need to sit down." Melanie and Tanya helped Ben pull the couch to the middle of the floor.

"Thank you," Billy replied, exhausted. He sat down and breathed a sigh of relief.

"I told you I wouldn't fail you," he said to Faye proudly.

Faye sat next to him and kissed his cheek. "I knew you wouldn't," she admitted coyly.

Ben suggested to the girls, "Let's go downstairs for the evening. I'm sure they'll join us later."

Melanie watched Faye with disdain. "But, we ..."

Ben grabbed her by the arm and interrupted, "Let's go. Leave them some privacy." The three of them went to the floor below.

Billy looked up at the stars and remarked, "It's a beautiful night."

"Now it is," said Faye. "But you need serious attention."

"What did you have in mind?"

"I'll find a first aid kit. I'm no doctor but I'll see what I can do." Faye left him alone on the roof for a short period. Billy felt delirious and slept from exhaustion.

— ❖ —

Ruger stood with his hands clenched against the side of the oak table. White smoke arose from the box and spread slowly. An image formed of Billy cutting the elevator cables, followed by the dragonfly falling with the elevator to its death.

Ruger screamed and threw the silver chest against the wall. He snarled like a mad dog as he flipped over the heavy wooden table. Pirocles entered the room. "What is wrong, Ruger?" he asked.

"Is the castle secure?" shouted Ruger.

"Yes, it is."

"Gather all of the minions from the south wall! This has to end now!"

"But Ruger …"

"Do it now!" Sensing urgency, Pirocles hurried from the room.

— X —

When Billy awoke the next morning, he felt the heat from sunlight across his body. He lay on the couch and wore only his boxers. Faye knelt on the floor next to him and gazed at him. "How are you feeling?" she asked.

"Wow. What a night?" Billy recalled the battle last night. When he stretched, he felt pain in his arm and leg.

"It was that good, huh?" kidded Faye.

"Maybe in my dreams."

"I cleaned your leg and arm with antiseptic. You'll have to change the bandages a few times a day until it heals."

"Thanks so much. I couldn't have done this without you."

"I could say the same thing about you," she replied coyly.

Billy hobbled to the edge of the roof and scanned the streets. Faye eyed him from the couch and wondered if he had any interest in her. An army of seventy minions marched down the street. They were divided into five groups, led by tall creatures in cloaks. "Oh, no. Here we go again," groaned Billy.

They watched as the minions searched the surrounding buildings. Billy knew that there was no way to escape if they stayed on the roof but considered the possibility of escaping from the basement. Faye looked upset as she followed Billy back to the stairwell. "What can we do?" she asked.

"Let's get the others. We'll try the elevator shaft."

Faye was bewildered again by Billy's plan but followed him down the stairs to the floor below. They found Ben, Melanie and Tanya asleep on posh furniture in the office of a law firm. Faye shook each of them and ordered, "Get up! We have to move fast!"

"What's going on?" asked Ben groggily.

"More soldiers are coming."

"We're going down to the second floor to another elevator shaft. If that doesn't work, look for a heating duct," explained Billy.

"What good is that?" inquired Melanie.

"We need to get to the basement to escape."

When they descended the stairs to the second floor, Billy rushed from the stairwell and looked out the nearest window. The soldiers entered the adjacent building. He returned to the elevator across the hall and used his sword to pry the doors open.

The elevator was stopped on the third floor and the shaft was clear. Inside the shaft was a service ladder mounted on the wall for service personnel to perform elevator inspections. Billy ordered everyone down the ladder.

At the base of the shaft was a service hatch. Billy opened the hatch and peered into a maintenance shop with benches and several propane tanks on a rack in the corner. The room was filled with an acrid smell from the dead dragonfly in the adjacent shaft. Billy searched with his flashlight and found a metal plate in the floor. "There it is!" he exclaimed.

Still baffled, everyone remained hopeful. Faye placed her hand on Billy's cheek affectionately and remarked, "You are special, aren't you?"

"I try," he responded, unconvinced. After removing the bolts which secured the plate, Billy drew his sword and pried the plate up from the floor. Faye pointed the flashlight at the sword. "Where in the world did you get that? It's beautiful," she queried.

Billy held the hilt out for her to see. "I inherited it from an Englishman who died in battle recently." He took the flashlight from Faye and pointed it down the hole. They saw a steel ladder with eight rungs. At the bottom was a main storm drain.

"Follow the storm drain to the train station. Inside the station, next to one of the platforms, is a beige Expedition," Billy instructed. "If I haven't made it back by evening, take it and follow the trail until you come to a stream. That stream leads to my camp. You'll be safe there." He gave Ben the flashlight and turned his attention to Faye.

"You're not coming with us, are you?" she inquired sadly.

"No, I have to put the plate back down."

Ben went down the ladder first, followed by Tanya and Melanie. Faye hugged him and sobbed. "I know I'll never see you again."

"Sure, you will," he said confidently.

"Take care of yourself, Billy."

"I'll be fine. I always am."

Faye kissed him on the cheek and pulled away. "I still don't understand why you have to stay. So, what if they chase us?" she argued.

"Faye, I have to do this. It's the only way out."

When she reached the bottom of the ladder, she looked up with tears on her cheeks. She blew a kiss to him and lowered her head. Billy placed the plate over the hole and installed the bolts. He pushed a large toolbox on top of it and searched the area. Tears streamed down his cheeks as he realized he might never see Faye again. There was something about her that appealed to him – something that Penny would never understand.

"Why do I keep doing this to myself? It isn't fair," he groaned. Billy wiped the tears from his eyes and noticed seven propane cylinders. His eyes lit up and he placed the cylinders next to a gas valve. He used a wrench to remove the cap off the valve allowing the gas to flow freely. He then ignited one of the torches and set it at the opposite end of the shop. *That should keep them off my trail for a while*, he thought.

Billy busted open one of the HVAC ducts with his sword and crawled inside. He pushed himself up to the first floor but his path was blocked by a modulator. He tried frantically to rip it loose but to no avail. "Oh, you've got to be kidding me," he complained. "After all I've been through, I get to die like this."

The minions swarmed down the ladder and searched the shop area next to the shaft. One of them stuck its head inside the duct and looked up at Billy. It hissed and crawled inside the duct. "I am so screwed," Billy muttered.

A large flash and an explosion muted his thoughts briefly. He was rocked and tossed about. There was a period of silence as the duct flew through the air with Billy inside it. He was jarred when the duct bounced off the street and rolled a short distance before coming to rest. Billy crawled out of the duct and rolled on his back. He stared dizzily at the sky and moaned, "Son-of-a-bitch! That wasn't what I had in mind."

The building erupted into flames as explosions from the basement of the building rocked the street. Every minion inside was incinerated. The remaining minions were spread out among four buildings, leaving only five to patrol the street. They were preoccupied with the explosion. Billy rushed toward the five minions at the end of the street. He attacked the nearest one and mortally wounded it with one stroke of his sword. Billy kept the other four minions in front of him and jabbed repeatedly at them. After the fourth lunge, he wounded another. It fell to the ground, clutching at its torn throat.

— X —

Underneath the street, Ben led the girls through the dark storm drain. They reached the first intersection where sunlight shone through a grate from the street above. They felt the explosion and were knocked to the ground. Ben handed Faye the flashlight and climbed up onto a large pipe. From there, he watched Billy fight the minions in the street. He climbed down from the pipe. "Have a look, Faye," he said somberly.

Ben helped Faye onto the pipe. She watched sadly through the grate as another of the minions fell to the ground. With only two minions preventing Billy's escape, Faye saw more coming and cried, "Run, Billy! Run!"

Billy couldn't hear her and slew another of the minions. He attempted to run but one of the soldiers threw a boomerang at him. The boomerang had white cord attached to it and tangled around his legs. He stumbled and fell to the ground. Tears trickled down Faye's cheeks as she watched Billy struggle.

Billy stood up with his legs tied together and fought the soldiers. They could have killed him but they toyed with him instead in a ritual of slow torture. Three of them got too close and Billy severed their arms and claws off. The others grew more wary of him and kept their distance. More soldiers joined the melee and swarmed on Billy. Faye nearly fainted as she watched Billy's body disappear under the wave of creatures.

The minions formed a circle while two of them held Billy's bloody, beaten body up by his arms. He opened his swollen eyes and saw one of the wizards before him. Gorith wore pointed studs on his gloves, sleeves, shoulders and knees. He also wore a black cloak.

Gorith punched Billy in the side of the head with the studded portion of his glove. The pain in Billy's head was excruciating as blood trickled from the fresh gash over his left ear. He warned Gorith, "One more time and I'll …"

"You'll what?" Gorith said arrogantly.

"What do you want from me?"

"Who are you?"

Billy held his head up proudly. "I'm Billy Brock from the planet Earth. The question is: What do you want with me?"

Gorith took him by the scruff of his neck and stared into his eyes with a sinister smile "I am Gorith. I serve Ruger and we are sworn to kill you."

"Why me?"

"Because it has been deemed that you shall die. By your very presence here, you are a threat to us."

Billy was stumped and responded hoarsely, "I don't know anyone here. How can I be a threat to them?"

"It doesn't matter. My orders are to kill you."

Billy knew this was the end. He kicked at Gorith and shouted, "Screw you, you mutant piece of shit!"

Gorith punched Billy in the face and dazed him while holding him by the throat with the other glove. The grip on Billy's throat became tighter. As he gasped for air, his legs shook and spasmed but he continued to struggle.

— ⋈ —

Faye trembled and nearly fell from the pipe until Ben helped her down.

"Is it over?" he asked.

"Yes, it is."

The women cried and Ben looked down sadly in a moment of silence. "He did so much for us," said Faye.

"He was like a knight in shining armor. I wish I had someone like him," blubbered Melanie.

"You didn't even know him," chided Ben.

"Shut up! Like you know everything."

"That's enough!" ordered Faye.

They continued through the dark sewer to the train station until it ended in a collapsed pile of dirt and rubble. Ben searched for a way up to the street, but there was none to be found. He climbed up the embankment of rubble and dug through the rocks and debris. "Come on. We're not stopping now!" he shouted.

The girls watched Ben work pitifully and had no hope of escape since Billy was captured. Ben pulled more rocks out of the way until a ray of light shone through. "I can see daylight!" he exclaimed. He clawed madly at the opening until it was wide enough for him to squeeze through to the street's surface. "Come on, already," he urged them.

The girls crawled through the narrow opening to the street above. They became excited when they realized they were a block from the station with no minions in sight. Ben entered the tunnel at the train station first and followed the tracks. He reached the platform and saw the tigers' carcasses by one of the rail cars. Faye, Melanie and Tanya waited in the tunnel for Ben to return.

Ben shined his flashlight around the platform and saw nothing of consequence. "Come on, girls. I think it's safe." Ben eyed the carcasses and noticed the wounds in the tigers' throats. "Looks like Billy's been here."

Faye wiped tears from her eyes and replied sadly, "I wish he still was."

Melanie glared at her and wiped the tears from her own eyes. She was attracted to Billy and felt that Faye took advantage of the opportunity to keep Billy's attention from her.

Tanya spotted the top of the Expedition parked three platforms over. "Look, there's the vehicle!" she exclaimed. They hurried to the Expedition and climbed in. Ben was baffled as he realized there weren't any keys in it. "Hot wire it, stupid! The wires are already hanging down," Melanie mocked him from the back seat.

Ben glared at her and then put the two wires together. "Ouch!" he yelled as he was shocked. Faye offered to do it but Ben was determined. The second time he crossed the wires, the vehicle started up. "See," he said. "I can do it."

"Great, Ben! Now can you just get us out of here?" pleaded Tanya.

Ben put the vehicle in reverse and backed down the tracks as quickly as he could. The Expedition bounced wildly over the railroad ties. "My freakin' braces are falling out. Slow down," complained Tanya.

Ben almost lost control of the vehicle several times and had no choice but to slow down until he exited the tunnel. He turned the vehicle around and followed the trail. They drove in silence until they reached the stream. "Now where?" asked Ben.

Faye spotted tire tracks in the soft soil. "Follow the tracks downstream. They should take us to Billy's camp."

Jerry and another man guarded the north wall. They basked in the warm sun and gazed at flying reptiles, gliding over the treetops. The Expedition emerged from the forest and raced toward their compound. "Hey, Billy's back!" Jerry shouted. He left his partner on the wall and rushed to greet him.

Ronnie and Randy heard Jerry and exited their hut. "Now I can kick that boy's lily-white ass. Next time he'll ask permission to borrow my truck," declared Ronnie.

Penny heard them but remained in her hut. She was extremely bitter about being rejected by Billy. Maggie peered inside the hut and asked, "Don't you want to see if he's alright?"

"No, I'm not interested." Maggie realized it was useless to pursue the issue any further. She left Penny and joined the others.

The Expedition stopped and four strangers got out. Everyone stared in surprise at them.

"Where's Billy? How did you get his vehicle?" Jerry questioned them.

"Billy's dead," Ben answered sadly. A grim silence fell over the group. Faye stood in the background with tears streaming down her cheeks.

Randy couldn't believe the news. "I told you we should have gone after him," she cried out.

Ronnie put a hand on her shoulder. "Billy knew the risk he was taking," she said.

"But he was our friend."

"Look, Randy, he was a good warrior. We had a lot of fun and any one of us could have died any number of times. Give him that respect."

Randy couldn't bear it. Neither could Ronnie, but she hid her emotions. Randy sobbed and returned to her hut.

Jerry led the strangers inside the camp for food and drink. They sat around the fire and listened as Ben related the events that occurred. Doc was interested in Gorith and what kind of creature he was.

Penny overheard talk from the men that Billy was killed by an alien creature and suddenly felt alone. She went outside and found Faye standing alone.

"Excuse me. Did you see what happened to Billy?" she asked Faye.

"Yes, I did. He saved our lives, but was captured by the soldiers. One of their leaders killed him."

Penny held back the tears. "So, he's really dead?" Faye nodded and burst into tears. "We can go inside and talk if it helps," offered Penny. Faye followed her inside her hut. Penny gave her a drink of water and sat down with her.

Faye related the details of Billy's brave deeds. When she finished the story, she said sadly, "You know, Billy was the kind of guy that every woman dreams of. He's like the shining knight that appears in your dreams but disappears when you wake up. That quickly, he's gone."

Penny knew what she meant and wondered what had she done. Perhaps Billy would still be alive if it wasn't for her. "That's the problem with Billy – that quickly, he's gone," she explained, feeling depressed

Faye sensed her deep sorrow, and wondered if Billy meant more to Penny than she knew. "Were the two of you close?" she inquired.

Penny wasn't sure how to answer. After some thought, she replied, "We could have been, but never quite got around to it." Penny could only think of how they both lost the same shining knight. It seemed like such a cruel thing to endure, but she brought this grief on by herself. She had Billy and drove him away.

Penny changed the subject and offered, "I know you must be exhausted. You can sleep here if you like. Tomorrow, we'll talk some more."

Faye thanked her. She was drained emotionally and soon was fast asleep. Penny wasn't so lucky. She cried for half of the night until she slept out of sheer exhaustion. At least there was someone else with whom she could share her grief.

— ⧗ —

Billy felt the last gasp of air leave his body and fell to the ground. *Is this what death feels like?* he pondered as he lay motionless. He suddenly became cognizant of growling and shrill screams around him. He struggled to his knees in a daze and searched for the cause of the chaos. Four saber-toothed tigers, led by Brutus, attacked the minions. Gorith focused on the tigers and mumbled part of an incantation but Brutus leaped on top of him and ripped his throat out before he could finish.

Billy saw his sword lying on the ground nearby and reached for it. His legs were weak and he struggled to stand up. He cut away the cords from his legs and prepared to do battle. More tigers joined the battle and quickly depleted the army of minions. Billy felt a renewed surge of energy at the sight of the tigers and attacked the minions nearest him. The tigers' assault took its toll and left minion carcasses all over the street. The remainder of the minions, about a dozen of them, fled to the north.

Billy fell to his knees, thankful for his unexpected saviors. The tigers dispersed as quickly as they had come, except for Brutus. The tiger sauntered over to Billy, still wearing the bandages.

Billy untied the cloth from Brutus' leg and flank. He was pleased that it healed sufficiently and left the make-shift bandages off. Billy patted the tiger's head before it raced off after the other tigers. Not knowing where else to go, Billy hobbled to the pub. He craved a strong drink and some much needed sleep. His body ached badly, his head throbbed and his vision was blurred from his injuries.

When he entered the pub, he found the place just the way he left it, somewhat of a mess. He took a bottle of rum from under the counter and a can of cola from the cabinet. It didn't matter that it was warm, it would be the best drink he ever had. When he finished the drink, he leaned back in the chair and dozed off.

— ☒ —

Ruger glared into the white smoke as it rose from the silver chest. The side of the box was dented and one of the hinges was broken on the lid. Pirocles watched apprehensively from the doorway. The image in the smoke showed dead minions in the street, including Gorith. Billy stood over them with a tiger by his side and walked away. The smoke cleared.

"How can this be? What will it take to stop this boy?" uttered Ruger, in a fit of rage.

"Perhaps we can seal the castle with a spell and go after him ourselves," suggested Pirocles.

"We have no choice. I'm sure Diomedes is aware that we've failed thus far and her patience is limited. What is left of our army?"

"We have three hundred stranded in the north region. They're cut off from us."

"What do we have here, you fool?" shouted Ruger.

"About sixty minions."

"We'll settle this once and for all." Pirocles followed Ruger out of the chamber and down the spiral steps.

CHAPTER 8

BATTLE FOR THE CITY

B illy slouched uncomfortably in the wooden chair with his feet up on the table and was fast asleep. Four men entered the pub armed with guns and pulled up chairs next to him. Billy opened his eyes and stared at the strangers. Nothing surprised him at this point.

"Nice work out there, son. I don't know how you pulled that off with the tigers and everything, but it was impressive," remarked the oldest man of the bunch.

"Who are you gentlemen?" Billy asked, curious.

"We were policemen in the Old World. Now we're like everyone else, just trying to survive. I'm Sam McDermott. My partners here are Martin Smythe, Brent Jones and Norman Conrad."

"We've been planning to get rid of those pests since this whole mess started. You came along and did it in short fashion," remarked Norman. He extended his hand to Billy in a gesture of appreciation. Billy shook hands with each of the men.

"Mind if we join you for a drink?" asked Brent.

Billy pointed to the counter. "Open bar. Help yourself."

Sam was a stereotypical police officer; big and burly, thin-haired and rugged looking. He was in his late forties. Martin was short with dark hair and a mustache. He looked like a weightlifter and was built like a small fireplug; rock solid. He was younger and about twenty-eight. Norman had short blond hair and was as tall as Sam, but in significantly better shape. He looked to be about thirty-five and tough. Brent was the youngster of the bunch. He had very dark skin and a shaved head. He was about twenty-four years old and solid like a linebacker. Together, they looked like a rough bunch. "I guess you're wondering what we want," Sam started the conversation.

"In a roundabout way, yes."

"Those things are part of a bigger contingency. None of us are safe until they're all destroyed. You've accelerated our plans quite a bit and made us aware of some oversights, including the big ugly thing that nearly killed you." Sam got up and poured some rum in a glass. He sipped it straight. "Care for one?" he asked Billy.

Billy stared at his empty glass. "Why not? Rum and cola will do."

Sam poured a warm can of cola into Billy's glass followed by a healthy hit of rum. "We plan to track the rodents that escaped and see just how big the rest of their army is. Would you care to join us?"

"I guess there won't be any peace until we finish this," complained Billy. "When do we go?"

"How about sunrise? I'm sure they won't get far between now and then," suggested Sam.

"After a good night's sleep, I think I'll be up to the job."

Sam shook Billy's hand again. "It's good to have you on the team, son."

Brent pulled a package out of his knapsack and tossed it on the table. "What's this?" asked Billy.

"A hoagie from your new friends. We have a generator to keep our refrigerator running, so it's still fresh," explained Sam. The men got up and walked to the door.

Billy stood up and thanked them.

"You can stay with us at the station if you like or we can come by for you in the morning," offered Sam.

Billy considered the offer but replied, "I think I need a night alone to recover. Thanks anyway." Sam waved and exited behind the others.

Billy ate the sandwich and had another drink. He placed his feet up on the table and slept. The night passed without incident and the streets remained quiet. Billy dreamed about going home but the vision of another wizard like Gorith, kept appearing in his mind. "Leave me alone, damn you!" Billy shouted in his sleep.

Ruger laughed hysterically at him and said, "We will meet again."

Billy was petrified with fear. He felt suffocated and finally, as if a spell were lifted, screamed loudly. He fell out of the chair and awoke. It was just a nightmare, but he was covered with sweat and shivered.

Outside, the street was illuminated from the moons' rays as if it were almost daylight, confusing Billy even more. He ran into the street and looked up at the sky. There were two moons shining bright and the sky was clear. He couldn't go back to sleep, so he sat on a bench by the street. His mind cleared, and for the first time, he understood his problems.

Ruger was in his head now so he had to finish this business no matter how far it went or how long it took. He still didn't understand why this wizard was after him but maybe it had something to do with his presence there. He noticed a shooting star in the sky and thought of Penny. He wondered if they would ever see eye to eye on anything.

— ⏳ —

Randy, John, Nigel and Krill sat around the fire in the middle of the compound. "Billy was more than a friend. He was special. He cared about people and would do anything for anyone. We can't just let this go," whimpered Randy.

"What do you want to do about it?" asked Krill.

"I want to hunt down every one of those bastards and kill them. I won't stop until Billy's death is avenged!"

John stared at her, surprised by the fire and the fury in her words. "If you feel so strongly about it, I will join you."

"Thanks, John. You realize that this is to the death. I won't stop until they've paid for what they did to him."

"To the death, we will avenge Billy," he swore and placed his sword across his heart.

Krill and Nigel looked at them in disbelief. "Are the two of you insane? Think about what you're saying," said Krill.

"I have to and I will do this," replied Randy.

"Well, you can't go without us! We're coming, too," said Nigel arrogantly.

Ronnie heard the shouting and joined them. "What's all the commotion about?" she asked.

After Randy explained their intentions to her, she replied, "I'm in."

"You're not obligated to go, Ronnie. This is personal for me."

"I understand and I'm in. No one kills one of my friends and gets away with it."

"Wow, they have some serious attitude, these girls," whispered Seamus to John.

"Those are kind words."

"I heard that!" exclaimed Randy.

"Have you and Ronnie always been like this?" John, wondering how much more to the girls' audacity there was.

"What do you mean by that?"

"Never mind. It's not important."

— ⓧ —

Doc worked with Jerry and Seamus to alter the van and transport the shuttle plane into the city. Given that they now had a route into the city, he felt that it was a good time to execute Billy's plan. He discussed the idea in depth with Seamus, who believed that they could rig the van to perform such a mission. The three men modified the van into a flatbed truck by removing the body from it. They worked through the night relentlessly under torchlight.

— ⓧ —

Sam and his men returned to the pub at sunrise, carrying bags and boxes. They dropped their things on the floor and made themselves at home. He took a bottle of vodka off the shelf and mixed himself a Bloody Mary. The other men shared a bottle of Scotch and a pitcher of water. They seemed eager for the conflict ahead.

Billy stared at the bags and boxes on the floor and queried, "Are you guys moving in? There's plenty of room upstairs."

"I like your sense of humor," replied Sam.

"What is all this stuff?"

"We brought some presents for our alien friends," answered Norman.

"Why don't you show Billy some of our surprises?" Sam suggested to his men.

Brent opened one box and took out a grenade launcher. "This is for crowd control, the old-fashioned way," he explained. Martin opened another box and held up a plastic-covered block. "That's C-4 – a real attention-getter if you know what I mean," he joked.

Billy was impressed. "You guys really are ready for war, I see"

"There's a lot more where that came from," added Norman.

"Then let's go kick some alien ass."

They had only traveled a few blocks from the pub when Sam motioned for them to stop. He retrieved binoculars from his bag and scanned the mountainside at the end of the street. Marching toward them was Ruger's army of minions. There were sixty of them with Ruger and three other cloaked wizards walking among them.

"Sweet Jesus! Will you look at that?" uttered Sam. He passed the binoculars to Brent.

Brent looked briefly through the binoculars. His jaw dropped in awe and he nearly turned white from the sight of the oncoming army. Billy anxiously reached for the binoculars and looked through them. "It looks like we won't have to go far to find them, will we?" he commented cynically.

"Jones. Conrad. Take the grenade launchers and position yourselves on the rooftops of those two buildings. Don't fire until I give you a signal," ordered Sam. The two men took separate paths and disappeared.

"Take position on the left corner with the .22 minigun and the bag of incendiaries. Wait for the second signal," Sam instructed Martin. Martin hurried across the street and hid behind a delivery truck.

"What's left for us?" asked Billy.

"We have mop-up duty. Whatever comes through is ours."

"You're serious about this whole thing, aren't you?"

"Absolutely. Aren't you?"

"Of course, I am. I'm just getting in the mood."

Sam opened a crate containing hand grenades. "These are to thin the heard," he explained. "When the others run out of ammo, they'll join us for the finale."

"I can see you're the kind of guy who likes to be the life of the party," kidded Billy.

Sam nodded in appreciation of the compliment and lit a large cigar. He placed the binoculars up to his eyes and watched the oncoming army.

Billy sat down on the curb. He pretended to admire the weather and the surroundings. *I wonder if anyone will ever know what happened here, today,* he thought.

"Get ready, boy! The fun is going to start in about five seconds," Sam alerted him.

Billy strolled over as Sam fired a shot. Whistling sounds filled the air, followed by several explosions as Norman and Brent laid down a cross fire of grenades and gunfire at the flanks of the oncoming army. A loud boom shook the area. "Jonesy loves his C-4," quipped Sam.

"I see that," replied Billy, amused.

The wall of smoke hid the minions' casualties, but the pattern of gunfire forced them to the middle of the road. "Just like we planned," proclaimed Sam proudly. He raised his gun when the minion army was in sight a half of a block away from them and fired a second shot.

Martin opened fire with the minigun and took out a significant section of the right flank.

— ⧗ —

The Expedition and the makeshift flatbed arrived at the end of Market Street. Everyone helped to unstrap and roll the plane off the back of the truck. It was awkward at first, but the shuttle plane, a small -100 model, slid down the home-made ramp onto the ground smoothly.

When the pilot was satisfied that the plane was ready for flight, they gave their last farewells.

The sound of a gunshot in the distance caught Randy's attention. "I heard gunfire!" she exclaimed.

Suddenly, an enormous amount of gunfire erupted followed by several explosions that caught their attention. "It sounds like a war is breaking out!" yelled Ronnie excitedly.

"But between whom?" Doc wondered aloud.

"Let's go find out. I thought only Billy could start something this big," kidded Randy. She and Ronnie ran to the flatbed, followed by the three Englishmen. Ronnie got in behind the wheel and started the truck. They raced down the street toward the fracas.

"I think we should wait to see what's going on. I'd hate to fly into their line of fire during takeoff," suggested Doc to his pilot. The man agreed and they waited patiently.

— X —

"How's your pitching arm, son?" inquired Sam.

"As good as ever," boasted Billy.

He tossed Billy a grenade and instructed him, "Pull the pin while holding the latch in. When you release it, you had better be throwing in three seconds or else it's game over. Understand?"

"No problem." Billy examined the grenade and the latch.

Thirty minions emerged from the smoke and charged at them. "Start throwing!" shouted Sam. Billy pulled the pin and held the latch as Sam instructed. Sam threw two grenades and took out a group of minions. Billy aimed for the right side and heaved as hard as he could. He was amused when the grenade exploded, dropping a handful of the attackers. He reached into the box and took out more grenades. He and Sam threw them until the box was empty.

Ten minions and two wizards, Ruger and Pirocles, remained. They closed in on Billy and Sam, from about thirty feet away. Gunfire from Sam's men ceased and it was eerily quiet. Billy drew his sword and prepared to fight. Sam was out of ammo and drew his club.

As the truck approached the end of the street, Randy noticed two men. "Looks like we're here just in time to save their asses from those creatures."

"Are you blind? It's Billy!" Ronnie yelled excitedly

"I knew he couldn't be dead!" Randy exclaimed giddily.

Billy slew the first two minions but was forced to retreat from the others. The remaining minions circled the two of them. Billy slew one minion with his sword but another slashed his arm with a spear. Three more minions surrounded Sam. He fought furiously with his nightstick and kept them away.

Ruger and Pirocles approached Billy. They glared at him with glowing red eyes and focused their magic on him. Billy sensed a cold feeling in his soul from those dark empty eyes. As with Gorith, he couldn't muster the strength to fight them. He felt his heart pound rapidly until it nearly exploded. His thoughts blurred and his breathing became irregular.

"Now, we'll be rid of you, once and for all," declared Ruger. The two wizards raised their arms and chanted an incantation. A flash, followed by a stream of fire darted toward Billy. Out of desperation, he held up his sword like a mirror toward them and was knocked to the ground. The flash deflected from the sword sent a swirling column of fire at the wizards. They screamed in pain as the fire engulfed them.

Billy was stunned but relieved when their influence over him faded. He fretted how he was fortunate enough to protect himself from their magic. Just as one minion was about to deliver Sam a deadly blow with its lance, Billy rushed to his aid. He struck at the minion's head from behind with his sword. After the sickening sound of cracking bone, he watched as its head separated from its body. Yellow fluid oozed from the headless body. The other two minions backed away from him.

Billy helped Sam to his feet, while keeping a wary eye on his attackers. He searched for the wizards but there was no sign of them. Sam pointed to the side street on the left. "Here they come again, Billy. I think the party's over." Twenty-five minions rushed at them.

"We're taking as many of them down with us as we can," Billy declared. Sam bled profusely from wounds on his arm, shoulder and the side of his head. He tugged at Billy's arm. "Save yourself. Get out of here now," he urged.

"No way!" Billy couldn't abandon his comrade. For all he knew, they were fighting for the future of mankind. He attacked the two minions on his left. In his rage, he found renewed strength and courage. The minion swung its club at Billy but he blocked it and buried his sword into its chest. He then spun its body into the other minion, while pushing his sword into the second minion. Both minions fell to the ground mortally wounded. He pulled his sword from the minion bodies and turned to face the next wave of attackers.

From the opposite side of the street, Brutus appeared and raced to Billy's side. "Brutus, am I glad to see you!" Billy exclaimed elatedly.

The tiger snarled in the direction of the minions. Billy heard the sound of a honking horn and then a truck skidded to a stop just behind him.

Sam stared in disbelief at Billy's reinforcements. "You have got to be the luckiest son-of-a-bitch I ever met," he uttered weakly.

"Sometimes it seems that way," replied Billy, smiling.

Ronnie, Randy and the Englishmen charged into battle against the minions. Billy and Brutus attacked as well. After some nifty swordplay, Nigel and Krill killed four minions. Randy and Ronnie fought like demons possessed: shooting and swinging, cutting and hacking at every minion they encountered. The number of attackers dwindled to ten.

Ronnie ducked in time to avoid a mace, but was engaged in hand-to-hand combat with the wielder of the weapon. Randy attempted to help her but was tackled by one of the wounded minions. Billy was intercepted by two more minions. He fought them for a lengthy time before he could dispose of them. John came to Ronnie's aid and drove his sword into the minion's back.

As Ronnie turned to thank him, the last minion swung its club and struck the side of John's head. He dropped to the ground with a dazed look in his eyes. Ronnie fired four shots into the minion's head. She grabbed its club and pounded it unmercifully, swearing with every swing.

Randy rushed to her side and grabbed her. "Stop it, Ronnie! It's over. It's all over."

Ronnie knelt down and coddled John in her arms. She cried and cursed the minions for injuring him. John had a deep gash on the side of his head, but was still coherent. "Oh, John!" she cried.

John winced and covered the wound on his head with his hand. "I've got a splitting headache," he complained.

"What the hell are you doing here? You're supposed to be dead!" Randy shouted at Billy.

"I thought you missed me?"

"Ronnie's going to kick your ass for taking her truck. And then you had the nerve to give it to those strangers. You are in deep trouble, boy."

Billy remembered the three youngsters and Faye. "They made it back to camp okay?" he asked humbly.

"Yes, they did."

"What went on between you and that woman, Faye?" she questioned him suspiciously.

Billy had a pained look on his face. "What did she say? Did she talk to Penny?"

"I don't think it was the words that told the story. She said she saw one of those goofy-looking monkeys choke you to death! Is that true?"

"Yeah, kind of. But there's no way that I'm ready to leave this world and let the two of you have all the fun. Besides, wasn't it you that taught me about the thrill of danger?"

"Oh, no," groaned Randy.

"That's right. You've created a monster."

Ronnie helped John to his feet. "I'm okay," he assured her.

Nigel and Krill limped to the truck. Nigel's arm was broken and Krill's leg was cut. Billy's arm was gashed but, other than fatigue, he was okay. Sam hobbled over and hugged Billy.

"Why don't you come back with us? You could use a little first aid and we have some doctors," suggested Billy.

"I'll be alright. I'll just have to lay low for a little while."

"Thanks for everything, Sam."

"Anytime. I'm going back to the station and look for my boys. We'll be in touch."

"Don't forget us, Sam."

"I won't. I do have one question for you."

"What's that?"

"How the hell do you keep getting away with this stuff? I mean, every time you're in trouble, tigers come; people come. It's particularly uncanny the timing they all have."

"I guess I'm just lucky." Sam patted Billy's arm and limped away.

Brutus approached Billy and growled fiercely while looking down the side street. Billy stroked the tiger's head. "What's wrong, boy?" When Billy looked, he saw Ruger and Pirocles staring at him. Their robes were burnt and their faces charred from the fire.

"What do you want from us?" Billy screamed.

"Your life! Wherever you go on this planet, we will be waiting to kill you," warned Ruger.

"Not if I kill you first. Let's finish this now!" Ruger and Pirocles vanished in a puff of smoke.

"What just happened?" Ronnie asked sarcastically.

"I'm not sure. I guess all those creatures really were after me."

Randy hooked her arm in his. "Come on, Billy, I need a drink. This place is too weird for me."

"I think we have to stop at the plane first. They're waiting for us," John reminded them.

"Yeah, that's right. And Billy's got to clean up a few loose ends," Randy tormented him.

"I guess I have to deal with this," whimpered Billy.

They climbed onto the truck and rode back to the plane. When the flatbed approached the plane, Billy asked, "Is Penny leaving on the plane?"

"Uh-huh, and so is Faye," answered Randy giddily. Billy felt a chill run down his spine. He didn't foresee dealing with both girls at the same time.

"This could be ugly," he uttered.

Randy was amused by his reaction. "Is there anything you want to talk about before we get there?" she asked.

"No, I've done enough for one lifetime."

When the truck rolled to a stop, Doc rushed to the vehicle and was stunned when he saw Billy. "How did you …? What happened?"

"I see you took me up on my idea," Billy mentioned proudly.

"Yes, and it turned out to be brilliant."

"How long will you be gone for, Doc?"

"There's a chance we won't be coming back."

"I see."

Billy saw Penny and Faye standing near the plane. He hopped off the flatbed. "Excuse me, but there's something I have to do."

Billy walked over to the girls and wondered how bad a scene it was going to become. Doc pondered how Billy would handle both women at one time. Billy was always a constant source of entertainment to him when it came to women.

Faye stared at Billy as if she saw a ghost. "I watched that creature kill you!" she stammered.

"I might have died for all I know," he quipped.

"We all thought you were dead," said Penny, still surprised by his appearance.

"I want to apologize for hurting the both of you through my selfishness."

Billy reached his hands out and held Faye's. "I realize what I put you through by staying behind in the building. I didn't mean to hurt you like that. I'm sorry," he said humbly. "Can we still be friends?"

"I owe you my life. Of course, we can still be friends. I am so glad that you're alive. I'm going with them but I hope we see each other again sometime." She kissed him on the cheek and boarded the plane. There was a certain quality about Faye that Billy found arousing.

Billy then turned to Penny and took both of her hands in his. "Penny, many things have happened to me since I last saw you. After being so close to death, I realize that life is precious and that I need to put the past behind me. If we have the chance, I'd like to try again with you."

A tear streamed down Penny's cheek. She placed her hand on Billy's cheek. "I'd like that. I know I expected too much from you but it was a sign of my love for you. When you walked away from me, a part of me died" She hugged him and whispered into his ear, "I'll always love you for what you did for me." She kissed Billy on the cheek and boarded the plane.

Doc shook Billy's hand. "You're a better man than me," he kidded. "Good luck to you."

"Thanks, Doc. You, too."

Maggie emerged from the plane and hugged Billy. "I'm gonna miss you. I hope things work out for you. You're a good man," she cried and then boarded the plane, followed by Doc. Billy watched sadly as the hatch closed. Maggie, Penny and Faye each waved to him from a window.

Billy was teary-eyed as the plane took off and disappeared from sight. He wiped his eyes and returned to the others. The Englishmen shook his hand and welcomed him back. Ronnie and Randy each hugged him and teased about his 'death'.

"What took you all so long?" chided Billy.

"Next time, let us know when you're going out," chastised Randy.

"And think about getting your own vehicle as well," warned Ronnie.

— ☓ —

Ruger appeared before Diomedes in the steamy cavern. "This man has many allies. I underestimated him. He is also cunning. My powers have been severely hampered as have Pirocles' due to his treachery," he admitted.

Diomedes lashed out at Ruger and slammed him against the wall of her cave. "I told you I'm losing patience with you," she warned.

"Please, Diomedes, give me another chance. I have many more ways of destroying this man," he pleaded from his knees.

"One day, he will find his way to your castle and he will kill all of us. Consider that before you blunder again, you fool."

"Yes, Diomedes." Ruger hurried from back his castle.

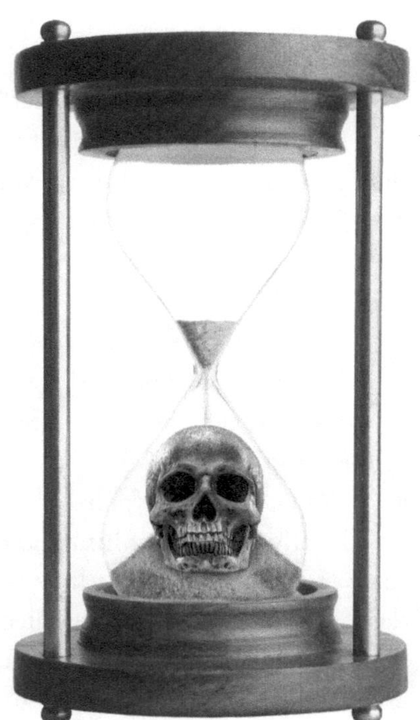

CHAPTER 9

A NEW HOME

Two weeks passed and Billy's wounds healed. He sat down on the edge of the bed one evening and noticed two shadows outside the hut. "Come on in, girls" he called out to them, knowing he was asking for trouble.

Randy rushed in and jumped on Billy. She tickled him and grabbed him in a headlock. They tumbled to the floor, laughing like little kids.

Ronnie carried a six-pack of cola and a bottle of rum. She sat on the edge of the bed and poured the rum into one of the cans. "Any time you children are done playing, we can celebrate the immaculate return," she announced.

Billy grabbed Randy's hands. "That's enough. It hurts when I laugh," he groaned.

"You felt fine when you fell on top of me in the pub, didn't you?" challenged Randy.

"You'll never let me forget that, will you?" complained Billy.

"Nope." Randy got up and sat on the edge of the bed.

"Why don't you clear the air with Billy about your feelings?" Ronnie suggested.

"Randy has feelings for me?" inquired Billy with mock surprise.

Randy pulled Billy up off the floor by his hand. "Yes and no. Yes, I like you a lot, but no, I don't want a relationship with you."

"What the heck kind of logic is that?"

Ronnie opened another cola and poured rum into it. She handed the can to Billy.

"You might need this," she advised.

"It's simple," explained Randy. "I like you a lot as a friend and that's as good as it gets. Someone dear to me died a few years ago and I haven't gotten over him yet."

"You could have fooled me."

Randy frowned at him and continued, "That day in the pub – it was nice to be treated like a lady by you. What happened in the basement later was nice, too. I appreciated your sincerity. My problem is that you and I are too much alike to be involved. I don't think we could ever have a serious relationship."

"Well, suppose I want to try?"

"Then you'll have to hope that Penny comes back."

Billy chuckled and laid flat on his back. "So, I guess I'm on my own," he complained. "What's your excuse?" he asked Ronnie.

Ronnie looked surprised. "What excuse? I'm not involved in this."

"Oh, come on, Ronnie. I see the way you look at me."

Ronnie laughed hysterically at him. Billy enjoyed the relaxed noncompetitive state that they were in. "I kind of like John but he seems apprehensive around me," she admitted candidly.

"Can you blame him?" teased Billy.

"I behave like a classy lady, don't I?"

Billy and Randy both looked at each other and nodded together. "Sure!" they replied in unison, giddily.

"I see the way you look at John. I know how bad you want him," Randy teased.

"Stop it. He's just a friend."

Billy sensed that this was a sore spot for Ronnie. "Don't be mad, Ronnie. If you do have a thing for John, we're happy for you," he said compassionately. Ronnie looked away from them and was silent.

"Ronnie had a very bad experience in school. She hasn't been with a man since," explained Randy.

"Do you want to talk about it?" asked Billy.

"Not really. All you need to know is that I was hurt by someone I cared very much about. Details don't matter."

"And she's had a hard spot for men ever since," added Randy.

"What do you girls do about dating?" he asked, baffled by their excuses.

"We took up hobbies like shooting, archery, mountain climbing, and martial arts. There's a bunch of things we've tried," answered Randy.

Billy was impressed. "So, the both of you are living in the fast lane to forget about bad pieces of your life?"

"That's exactly what it is," said Ronnie. "You've become a good friend, almost like a brother to us. We can kid with you, harass you, and you understand us."

Billy felt good that the girls thought of him like this. "I'm really flattered that you shared this with me."

Randy opened a cola and poured rum in it. "How about a toast?" she suggested, feeling good that their feelings were out in the open.

Billy held his can up and asked, "To what?"

"To our destiny! We're going to take this world by storm and we'll make it our own," proclaimed Ronnie.

The girls held their cans up to Billy's and tapped them. The three of them yelled cheerfully, "To our world!" They each chugged a portion of their drinks.

"And when do we start taking this crappy world by storm?" Billy inquired, wondering.

"How about tomorrow?" suggested Ronnie.

"And what's first on our agenda?" questioned Billy.

"We need a better place to stay. This place is like the slums of Jurassic Park," complained Randy.

"And where do you girls propose we go?"

"I like the Post Office, myself," said Ronnie.

"The Post Office, huh?" pondered Billy.

"Yes. The night we stayed there, I studied its structure. It's the perfect fortress."

"I see you've given this some thought."

"Do you have a better idea?" asked Randy.

"Not really. I do like the idea of the Post Office."

"Then the Post Office it is," she replied enthusiastically.

"I do need to get some sleep if you girls are done with me."

"I'm done with you for now. I could have a change of heart, though," kidded Randy.

"Bring it on. I'm ready."

"You two are like little kids. Good night," said Ronnie.

"Good night, Ronnie," said Billy and Randy in unison.

When Ronnie left the hut, Randy gave Billy a quick kiss on the lips and whispered, "Another time, another place, just like you said." She smiled at him and left the hut. *What I'd give for one night with her*, Billy thought as he finished his drink.

Billy awoke the next morning, feeling better about things. He took a towel from an open suitcase in the corner and exited the hut. The two suns shone brightly and a cool breeze made for a pleasant morning. Both were much lower in their orbit than previously which made for the cooler temperatures. Billy approached the partially enclosed hut with two shower stalls and met the girls.

Ronnie and Randy wore dripping wet shorts and T-shirts. They wrapped shirts around their wet heads to cover their hair. The T-shirts revealed much more than Billy was prepared for, leaving him quite aroused. "Now look, girls, this is asking too much," he kidded.

"What's the matter, Billy? Never seen real women before?" Randy inquired.

"Sure, he has. Well, on second thought, maybe not," teased Ronnie.

"If you aren't selling, you shouldn't be advertising," Billy fired back.

"Maybe we're looking for a qualified buyer," Randy teased.

"Okay girls, enough games. Are we still going to the Post Office or not?"

"Right after breakfast," answered Randy.

"That's all I needed to know." Billy tossed the towel over the door and stepped into the makeshift shower stall. He stripped down to his Scooby-Doo boxers and tossed his clothes over the stall door. As he sang to himself, he kept a wary eye out for the girls to try some sort of prank.

Randy hid by the entrance to the stall. She opened a bottle of shampoo and reached over the stall door. Billy looked up and saw the bottle in her hand. He grabbed her wrist and pushed the door open. "Help me, Ronnie!" Randy shouted playfully.

Billy pulled Randy into the stall and closed the door. "That's how people get hurt. I'm leaving," warned Ronnie.

Billy and Randy wrestled with the bottle over both their heads. They stumbled backwards against the wall and slid to the floor. Their arms tangled together and they found themselves face-to-face. The shampoo poured from the bottle over both of them. They laughed hysterically. "See what you started," Billy teased.

Randy stared into his eyes seductively. "You mean what you started." They lay on the floor and kissed passionately.

"Are you sure you want to do this?" Billy asked.

"What do you think?"

"Oh, boy. I guess I won't get out of this one," moaned Billy.

"Shut up, you big baby." Randy rolled on top of Billy and kissed him again.

— ⧖ —

Ronnie sat at the makeshift table in front of the jet and ate a banana. She was miffed at Randy's behavior with Billy. John approached from behind and placed his hands on her shoulders. He gently massaged her muscles up to her neck. She looked relieved. "John, you're an angel. That feels great."

"How are you doing today?"

"I don't know. I have good days and bad days."

John sat next to her and noticed the bowl of fruit on the table. "Mind if I join you?"

"Not at all."

John nervously picked up an apple and bit into it. "Is something wrong?" Ronnie asked.

"Actually no. I did want to talk to you about something, though."

"Well, I'm right here."

John held her hand and gazed into her eyes. "Lately, we seem to have drifted apart. I just wanted to…" Billy and Randy giggled as he chased her to the table.

"Maybe we'll wait for another time, John," said Ronnie disappointedly.

"Yes. Perhaps later."

Billy and Randy sat down across from them. "We aren't interrupting anything, are we?" asked Randy.

"No, not at all. You two children just keep on playing," remarked Ronnie bitterly.

"We'll stop, mommy. Don't be mad," teased Billy.

Ronnie reached across the table and grabbed Billy's ear. "Ouch!" he groaned.

"You're pushing your luck," she warned and let go of him. John noticed the tension in Ronnie's voice.

Randy took a banana from the bowl. She stared at Billy and peeled it slowly. Ronnie took notice and became angry. She pulled the banana away from Randy and slammed it on the table. "That's enough!" she shouted. "Let's go before I change my mind."

John wondered what set Ronnie off this way. He looked at each of them for an explanation but none came.

Billy struggled to keep a straight face but burst into laughter. Randy stared at Ronnie in disbelief. "What is wrong with you today? You're miserable," she said.

"You know what's wrong! You're doing this on purpose."

"I think we should get moving," Billy suggested when he realized they interrupted something important.

"Good idea," replied John. He and Billy got up from the table.

"Why don't I fetch Seamus?" John suggested to Billy and left them.

The girls walked with Billy across the yard to the supply hut. "I know what you need, Ronnie," Billy mentioned innocently.

"And what would that be, jerk?" snapped Ronnie.

Billy grabbed her by the waist and tickled her. They fell to the floor, laughing. Ronnie tried to speak but Billy wouldn't stop poking her side. She grabbed his left arm and twisted it. Randy enjoyed watching them. Billy rolled her over twice but Ronnie wound up on top each time.

When they were face to face with each other, Ronnie leaned close to Billy's face like she would kiss him but she bit his nose instead. "Ouch, that hurt!"

"You might get away with that act around Randy but it won't work with me," Ronnie chastised. She got up and walked away. Billy sat up, holding his nose gingerly.

"Ronnie's sure got a chip on her shoulder, doesn't she?" Randy remarked as she helped Billy to his feet.

"Yeah, you're not kidding."

Billy and Randy joined Ronnie, John and Seamus at the gate. "Everyone have a weapon of choice?" asked John.

"I sure do," Billy answered as he patted the hilt of his sword.

Randy drew her Glock and placed a hand on the hilt of her sword. "Me, too," she added. Seamus nodded to John, indicating he was ready.

"I have John to protect me," Ronnie replied.

"Ooh!" teased Randy.

"That's enough, girls. We're going outside the walls and it's dangerous," John scolded them.

"We can handle it. It's nothing new," declared Ronnie confidently. John rolled his eyes at the men.

The gate to the compound consisted of a wing from one of the jets and several cables from the fuselage. Four men raised and lowered the gate for passage to and from the compound. A thick earthen wall and an exterior moat surrounded their compound. The gate was lowered when the five of them approached it. When lowered fully, the wing acted as a bridge for them to cross the moat.

The Expedition and the flatbed were parked outside the compound because the wing wasn't strong enough to support a vehicle's weight. Ronnie unlocked the door to the Expedition and climbed in. John climbed in the passenger side front seat while Randy sat in the back between Seamus and Billy.

"I like this. I get to sit between two handsome men," quipped Randy.

"Can it, already," retorted Ronnie.

"Come on, Ronnie. We're only trying to have some fun," Billy responded, concerned.

"Well don't." Ronnie started the truck and drove away from the compound.

"If that's what you really want. Let's call a truce," suggested Randy. She reached her hand over the seat and waited.

"Fine, a truce," Ronnie muttered and reluctantly shook her hand.

The Expedition bounced along the trail at a decent speed. "Do you expect any of your friends to show up, Billy?" inquired John.

"I hope there aren't any left. Sam wants to make sure they're all gone after he's had time to recover."

"His buddies never came back?" asked Ronnie.

"No. He's hoping that they're hiding out someplace."

"Maybe we'll look for them after we relocate to the Post Office."

"That would be a nice gesture. They're brave men."

"Do you have any idea why those creatures are after you?" John asked.

"I was kind of wondering that myself."

"Were you messing with any of their women? You sure know how to bring out the worst in them," taunted Randy.

"Gee, you are so funny."

When the Expedition pulled up in front of the Post Office, Billy got out first and walked to the entrance. John and Ronnie got out and promptly searched the area around them.

"Don't go in there by yourself," John warned Billy.

"I'll be fine," Billy replied confidently and then entered the Post Office alone.

"He'll never learn," John complained to Ronnie.

"If you only knew the half of it."

When Billy ascended the stairs, two minions waited at the top for him. "Not again!" he groaned. "Don't you guys have a day job?" Billy drew his sword and retreated down the stairs. He turned to run, but two more minions waited at the bottom. "Here we go again," he uttered, realizing this was a bad idea.

He rushed up the stairs and dueled with the minions. They were much more tenacious than the others he faced thus far. "John! Ronnie! Randy!" Billy urgently called out. The two minions at the bottom climbed the stairs toward him. "Anybody! Help!"

Billy pierced one of the minions in the chest with his sword and then shoved it down the stairs into the others. He battled fiercely with the remaining minion at the top and forced it onto the second floor.

The minion cut Billy's arm with a short thrust. He struck back at the minion three times and slashed its face. It retaliated with another jab and caught Billy's shoulder. His arm weakened as it bled, but he continued to duel with the minion. Billy deflected a thrust and rammed into the minion, using his shoulder. The two of them tumbled to the floor near the top of the steps.

The two minions ascended the stairs again and approached Billy from behind. As Billy dueled with the minion on the second floor, it smashed his hand with the broad side of the blade. "You stupid son of a bitch!" shouted Billy angrily.

Billy deflected the next jab from the minion and punched it in the mouth. He pulled the sword out of the minion's paw and beat on its head with the hilt. He grabbed it by both arms and threw it down the steps at the other two again. The minions tumbled down the stairs for the second time. Incensed, the minion rushed up the stairs toward him.

Billy wiped the blood from his hand against his pants and shouted, "You're gonna wish you left while you had the chance." He relentlessly struck at the minion with his sword and forced it down the hall.

Outside, John strapped on his sword as Ronnie placed a full magazine in her pistol. She looked back inside the vehicle. Seamus and Randy sat in the back seat, acting suspicious.

"What are you two up to?" asked Ronnie.

"We're talking," Randy replied innocently.

"It seems you're having a lot of these discussions lately."

"Don't be jealous, Ronnie."

"Watch yourselves. We're going inside."

"Yes, momma," quipped Randy. Seamus and Randy giggled.

Ronnie and John entered the Post Office and heard swords clanking. "I knew it. I just knew it," complained John. They hurried to the stairs and saw two minions.

Billy cut the throat of the minion in the hall and kicked it in the chest. The minion tumbled down the stairs into the others and knocked them down once again. "Take that, you rotten bastards!" he shouted.

John and Ronnie danced away from the falling minions. Ronnie fired a round into each one's head. Billy looked relieved to see them and descended the stairs.

"I told you not to go in by yourself," John reprimanded him.

Billy walked past them and commented, "You win. I was wrong."

"You're missing the point, Billy."

"No, I got the point. Actually, I got it a few times." Billy stopped and raised his arm to display his wounds.

"That's why you should have listened to us. Then you wouldn't have been injured." Billy grew annoyed with John. He left them and dragged the dead minions outside the building.

Ronnie and John went up to the second floor and searched it thoroughly. "I think I want a room at the end of the hall. It'll be quieter down there," said Ronnie.

"Would you mind if I took one across from you?"

"Of course not. I'd like that."

From the car, Randy noticed Billy with the minion corpse. "Not again!"

"What's wrong?" asked Seamus.

"Billy's got one of those creatures."

"So?"

"So, it must have been inside. What if there are more?"

"Alright. Let's go check it out." They exited the vehicle and walked toward the entrance. Immediately, they noticed the blood on Billy's shirt.

"Billy, are you alright?" asked Randy, concerned by his wounds.

Billy waited patiently for them to come over. "Just cleaning out a few rodents in the house."

Randy looked at Billy's wounds and asked again, "Are you sure you're okay?"

"Yeah, I'm fine." Billy left them and dragged the corpse to the edge of the forest.

"Something's bothering him," said Randy.

"I got that impression, too," replied Seamus.

Billy walked past them on his way inside the Post Office.

"What's wrong, Billy?" asked Randy.

"Nothing. I'm fine."

"You don't look fine."

Billy entered the Post Office and dragged another corpse outside.

Randy and Seamus watched, curious. "Where are John and Ronnie?" Seamus inquired, wondering what happened.

"Upstairs, I guess."

"We'll help you with those."

"Thanks."

Randy and Seamus went inside. Each grabbed a corpse and dragged it out to the forest. Seamus stepped in front of Billy and blocked his path. "Look, Billy, we're all friends. If something's bothering you, we can talk about it."

"Come on, Billy. After all we've been through…" urged Randy.

Billy blurted out angrily, "I don't like being preached to. I feel like I'm being tag-teamed, two-against-one, by Ronnie and John. I'm always the one who's wrong."

"Sometimes tension affects people in different ways," suggested Seamus.

"Why are they tense with me?" asked Billy.

Randy chuckled. "I know why?"

"Well, enlighten me."

"Ronnie has it bad for John. Until they resolve things, it's going to be rough."

"How hard could it be? If they like each other, then do something!"

"We're talking about Ronnie. Just getting a date is a big deal in her life."

Billy realized Ronnie's sensitivity and said regretfully, "Maybe I should have given them some space this morning."

"Maybe we all should have."

"Thanks, Randy. Thanks, Seamus. I appreciate your help."

Seamus rubbed Billy's head playfully. "We're a team now. There's gonna be good days and bad days, but we're always a team."

Billy felt camaraderie with Randy and Seamus. "I like the way you put that, Seamus. Well spoken."

As they entered the Post Office, Randy questioned Billy, "Did Ronnie and John pick one room or two?"

"Randy, that's naughty," replied Seamus.

"I know," she replied coyly.

Billy shook his head at them in disbelief and then ascended the stairs alone. He walked halfway down the hall and took a room on the right with a good view of the field out front. Ironically, this was what he thought he wanted all along – to be alone.

Randy and Seamus returned with the first aid kit. "Sit down, hero, before you bleed to death," ordered Randy. "I'm not the best at this so don't mock my handy-work."

Billy touched Seamus' arm with his left hand as Randy bandaged his right hand. "Seamus, I can't tell you how much the sword techniques you boys taught me have saved my butt. Thanks so much."

"Don't thank me. Thank Nigel."

"I'm just worried that there are soldiers out there that are better than what we've faced so far. I mean, maybe these are the scrubs."

"Maybe, they fight in a mob mentality. If enough of them show up, they're bound to win," suggested Randy.

"They do seem persistent but I do fear for you, Billy. Whatever the reason, this wizard really has it in for you," remarked Seamus.

"They claim that I will destroy them," revealed Billy. "If they keep pissing me off, you bet I'm gonna destroy them."

Randy bandaged his wounds and smacked him on the back of his head. "See if you can stay out of trouble for just a little while," she suggested. "You lost quite a bit of blood."

"Thanks, so much, Randy." They helped him to his feet and left the room.

— X —

After a few weeks, Billy recovered sufficiently from his wounds and grew impatient, staring at the office furniture in his room. He moved the furniture out, one piece at a time, into an unused room down the hallway. Randy and Seamus entered and were surprised to see the room empty already. "You really want new furniture that bad, huh?" inquired Randy.

"Yeah, if I'm going to be the lonely bachelor here, I might as well have a bachelor's pad to dream in."

"If Penny doesn't want you, I'm sure several of those ladies at the compound would be interested," suggested Seamus.

"I need a date, not a grandmother," complained Billy.

"Faye was no spring chicken, you know," joked Randy.

Billy was stunned by her remark. "What do you know about Faye?" he asked, wondering what they knew.

"I know that you made quite an impression on her and I'm sure it wasn't just your charm."

"Tell me the truth. Did she say anything about us?"

"Why? Are you feeling guilty?"

Billy was embarrassed. "Just forget it," he grumbled.

Randy inspected Billy's wounds under the bandages. The stitches were effective but ugly and the wounds were still wet. "You really ought to take it easy for a while. No woman wants a beat-up clunker for her man," advised Randy.

"It seems that women don't want a perfectly healthy one either," Billy replied sadly.

"Penny told me about your wedding. Perhaps it was better that way."

"How could it be better?"

"Maybe the two of you would have grown to hate each other over time."

Billy lowered his head. "It wasn't supposed to be that way."

"It never is. My fiancée died and I never had a chance to say goodbye."

Billy was stunned by her revelation. "I'm so sorry, Randy."

"Well, I guess we all have something in common."

The next morning, Billy awoke on a pile of jackets from the closet. Daylight filled the room through two windows. *I'm gonna' have to do something about furniture today. I'm not sleeping one more night on the floor*, he thought. Billy dressed and strapped on his sword. When he looked out the window at the sky, he noticed that the two suns were much more visible today than before. They shared a nearly parallel orbit. During this time of year, they didn't overlap as before and moved further apart each day. "Multiple moons, multiple suns. Multiple headaches. What am I to do?" he uttered.

Billy went downstairs into the main hall, but no one was there and the doors weren't barricaded. He grabbed a can of lemonade from a knapsack on the table and exited the building. There was no one outside either and the vehicles were gone as well.

"I guess I'm not good enough for them anymore. Maybe I should just leave," he muttered to himself. Billy moped across the field toward the forest.

The Expedition crossed over the bridge and parked in front of the Post Office. Wills, Nigel and Krill emerged from the vehicle along with three women. Ronnie stayed behind the wheel and waited.

The flatbed truck appeared next with Ben, Tanya and Melanie riding on the back. Inside the cab were Randy, John and Seamus. Randy noticed Billy walking across the field. She got out of the truck and approached Ronnie's vehicle. Seamus waited inside the flatbed truck while the others entered the Post Office, carrying whatever belongings they possessed.

Randy leaned on the driver's door and asked Ronnie, "Did you say anything to Billy about moving everyone into the Post Office today?"

"No. Why should he care?"

"Did you tell him that we were leaving?"

"No. What are you getting at?"

"Ronnie, he's our friend. You just don't forget about him."

"It's not a big deal, Randy."

"Yes, it is. Look over there." Randy pointed across the field. They watched Billy enter the forest alone.

"Where the hell is he going now?" complained Ronnie.

"Why should he tell you? Why would you care?" Randy stormed back to the flatbed truck. She climbed inside and slammed the door.

"Is something wrong?" asked Seamus.

"Yeah, Ronnie's being a bitch." Randy started the truck and drove across the field. "Let's see what Billy's up to," she said.

"Does he have a habit of disappearing like this?"

"He's lonely. We left him here alone this morning with no word about what we were doing or where we were going?"

Billy hiked into an unexplored part of the forest. He heard strange noises but none of the threatening variety. Randy pulled up behind him and hollered, "Hey, where ya' going?"

"Just walking."

Randy parked the truck and got out. "We'll walk with you."

"You don't have to do that."

"Sure, we do." Randy and Seamus walked next to Billy.

"Where are we going?" asked Randy.

"I want to check out the area beyond the train station."

"Looking for anything in particular?" asked Seamus.

"No, just wondering what's out there."

— 𝚡 —

Ronnie slammed the dashboard of the Expedition with her fist. "Damn it!" she shouted.

"What's wrong?" asked John.

"Everything is so complicated anymore."

"Like what?"

"It doesn't matter."

"It must be Billy, again."

"What was your first clue?" Ronnie started the engine and drove across the field. John gazed at her and smiled.

"What's the matter?" she asked defensively.

"I was just noticing how beautiful you are," said John.

"Stop it. You're embarrassing me."

"I just want you to know that I'd like to be more than your friend if you're interested. I know I certainly am."

Ronnie stopped the truck. "I think I would like that, John. You'll just have to go slow with me," she explained, surprised by his interest in her.

"That shouldn't be a problem. We have all the time in the world."

"I wondered how long it was going to take you to bring this up."

"I was afraid you'd hit me," he admitted. Ronnie giggled and drove forward. "Is that what's been eating you?" asked John.

"Of course, it was!" she exclaimed and nestled against him. John put his arm around her shoulders.

Ronnie saw the empty flatbed up ahead. "I don't see them anywhere," she mentioned, curious.

"I'm sure they didn't go far."

Ronnie drove past the flatbed. From a clearing, she spotted them halfway up a steep embankment and honked the horn several times.

"I'm not ready to go back," Billy informed them.

"I'll let them know what we're doing," volunteered Seamus.

Billy and Randy climbed to the top of the embankment. "Are you feeling this way because of me?" inquired Randy.

"No, of course not. I know where we stand."

"I never wanted to come between you and Penny. I do like you a lot and we do have some naughty fun together, don't we?"

"Oh, yes. And we'll get along just like we always do."

"And how is that?"

Billy tickled Randy's sides. She fell to her knees and cried, "Stop it. Seamus is going to think there's something wrong with us."

Billy helped her to her feet. "Too late. He already knows." The two of them laughed.

When Seamus returned, they hiked up the steep, bushy slope to a clearing at the top. Far below them on the other side was a beautiful lake surrounded by a white, sandy beach. Water fell from the mountainside high above and splashed into the lake below. Around the base of the falls were several large, flat rocks.

"Will you look at that?" Billy uttered in awe.

"I've never seen anything so beautiful," Randy remarked.

"Shall we check it out?"

When Randy looked back, she saw John and Ronnie waiting at the bottom of the hill.

"Not today. Tomorrow would be better," she suggested. Randy and Seamus started back down the slope.

Billy gazed at the lake and found the beach very tempting. "Come on, Billy. We're not leaving you here," said Randy. "You know what always happens when you're left alone."

Billy reluctantly descended the slope behind them.

— 𝕏 —

Ruger stared at the smoke over the silver chest. He saw Billy, Randy and Seamus on top of the hill, overlooking the lake. Ruger waved his hand over the smoke and the face of a snake appeared. "I have just the fate for them. They won't escape this time," he muttered and laughed heinously.

— 𝕏 —

John and Ronnie leaned together against the Expedition. John held Ronnie's hands affectionately and gazed into her eyes. "Really, why'd it take you so long," she asked shyly.

"I was afraid you'd turn me down. Are you okay with this?"

"I am now."

John pulled her close to him and kissed her briefly. She closed her eyes and waited for more. John kissed her again passionately. He ran his fingers through her dark hair and squeezed her tightly. Ronnie melted like butter in his arms.

Billy, Randy and Seamus rambled out of the trees. They saw the couple kissing. Randy grabbed both men by the arms and turned them around. "We'll come back later," she announced, surprised by what they saw.

Ronnie and John noticed their three friends walking back into the forest. She called to them, "Hey, where're you guys going?"

Randy saw that they still clung to each other and replied, "We've got a few more things to check out if you need some privacy."

"We can continue this later if you like," suggested John.

"That would be perfect," replied Ronnie.

"Come on back. We've had enough fun out here for one day," shouted John.

Ronnie and John entered the Expedition. Ronnie started the engine and hollered, "Are you guys coming or what?"

Randy arrived first. "The flatbed isn't far. We'll walk."

"Then we'll see you back at camp." Ronnie waved to them and drove off.

"Well, that's an improvement," Randy remarked, still stunned.

"Perhaps they've spoken their peace," suggested Seamus.

"Is that what you call it?" asked Billy, grinning. The three of them laughed as they returned to the flatbed truck.

When the vehicles returned to the Post Office, Ronnie and John stayed inside the Expedition and talked. The others went inside the Post Office. The other Englishmen and their new ladies prepared a simple lunch from the scraps that they gathered earlier. They laid out the food on the table for everyone and enjoyed a peaceful meal.

"Ah, just in time for lunch. You guys are great!" Billy exclaimed.

"Nay, it was the women who were great," replied Nigel.

After lunch, Billy sat on the front steps of the Post Office. He admired the green, lush forests that surrounded them on three sides. Randy and Seamus exited the building and sat next to him.

"What are you up to this afternoon, Billy?" asked Randy.

"I was thinking that I'd like to find some new furniture. There are buildings that need looting."

"Now you're talking."

"Ah, the simple things in life – furniture," kidded Seamus.

"It's the complicated things that eat you alive," said Randy playfully.

"Please don't eat me," teased Seamus.

Randy growled in Seamus' ear. She took both men by their hands and led them to the flatbed.

Ronnie and John watched the flatbed truck drive away toward the city.

"I wonder what they're up to," pondered Ronnie.

"Don't worry about them. We have much to do."

"Like what, John?"

John kissed her briefly. "I hope I'm not being rude, am I?" he asked.

"So, what if you were? Kiss me, you fool." The two held each other tightly and kissed in the afternoon sun.

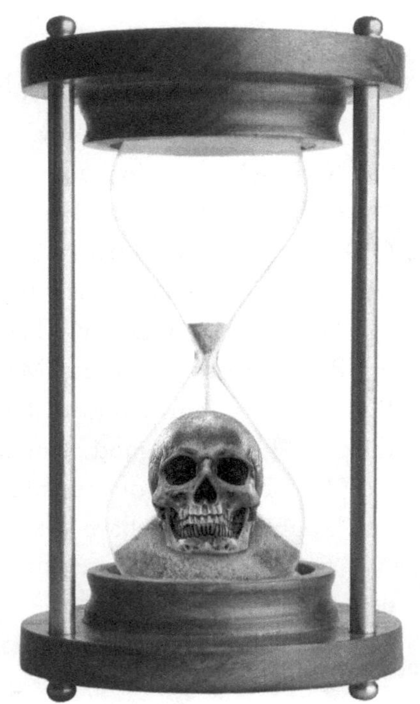

C H A P T E R   1 0

LAKE OF HORRORS

Three days later, Billy's room was furnished. He admired his sheer, burgundy red curtains with black drapes tied off to the side. *It looks a little gothic, but I like it.* He sat on his king-size bed and marveled at the funky black and white zebra-striped area rug. *Now all I need is a woman to share it with.*

Randy popped her head in the door. "Hey, Billy, what are you doing?"

"Enter into my realm of darkness, oh mistress of the night."

"Ooh! This is so cool."

"What's up?" asked Billy.

"I was thinking that we could check out the lake today."

"I'd love to."

"Come on. Seamus is waiting downstairs."

Billy grabbed a knapsack and followed her down to the main hall. Tanya and Melanie saw Billy and rushed over. "Hi, Billy. Where ya' going?" asked Melanie.

"Hi, girls. Out for a little field trip."

"Can we come?"

Billy looked at Randy for approval. "Why not?" she replied.

"If you have a swimsuit, you might want to bring it," Billy recommended.

"Sorry. We don't have any," said Melanie, disappointed.

"Oh, well. Come on, anyway."

Seamus waited at the flatbed truck. Randy and Billy exited the Post Office, followed by the two girls. Seamus was amused when he saw the girls.

"I see you have some new friends, Billy."

"Yeah, pretty ones, too." The girls blushed at his compliment.

Billy helped Tanya and Melanie onto the back of the truck while Randy and Seamus climbed into the cab. Billy enjoyed sitting between the girls. They were good company for him.

"We heard some of your stories," mentioned Tanya.

"Sounds like you have lots of fun," added Melanie.

"Every place I go, something crazy happens. It's hardly fun, though," he replied.

"Why did Penny leave?" asked Melanie.

Billy was surprised by her question and wondered why the interest. "She's got issues to get over," he answered.

"That's interesting."

"But then, so do I," continued Billy.

As the flatbed rumbled across the field, the two girls moved closer to Billy. They sat with their backs to the cab. "If you were my boyfriend, I'd be here with you," said Melanie coyly.

Billy was flattered but both girls seemed young. "How old are you, Melanie?"

"I'm nineteen."

Billy was surprised. Tanya noticed his expression and added, "I'm eighteen."

"Wow. I didn't realize..." he started.

Melanie interjected, "We're adults. You don't have to worry."

"I'm sorry, girls. You're both very attractive, but I was preoccupied with other things when we met."

"So, where are we going?" asked Tanya.

"There's a beautiful lake on the other side of the mountain. It's got a beach and everything." The girls were thrilled.

When Melanie nestled her head against Billy's shoulder, he became uncomfortable and thought, *Oh, no. This isn't gonna work.*

— 𝕏 —

Ronnie and John sat on the front steps of the Post Office. "Where'd Randy and Seamus go to?" John inquired, wondering.

"I heard they were taking a field trip to a lake they found last week."

"It's a nice day for it. Feel like joining them?"

"I'd love to."

John took Ronnie's hand and escorted her to the Expedition.

— 𝕏 —

When the flatbed came to a stop at the bottom of the embankment, Randy and Seamus hopped out of the cab. Randy looked at the back bed and immediately sensed Melanie's attraction to Billy. She winked at Billy and his face reddened.

Billy appreciated that Randy didn't add to his problems by adding her two cents. He hopped off and helped the girls down off the truck. Together, they hiked up the steep slope. Randy and Seamus reached the top ahead of Billy and the girls. They peered down at the crystal-clear water. "I've never seen water so clear," remarked Randy.

"Neither have I," replied Seamus.

Billy, Melanie and Tanya caught up to them. "Clean it up, you two. There are kids here," teased Billy.

"I told you before, we're not youngsters," chastised Melanie.

"I'm only kidding, Mel."

"I can see this isn't going to be easy with you."

Billy suddenly realized that Melanie had her sights on him and was determined to win him over. Maybe her youthful look and innocent appearance could change his attitude. After all, he had no one else, now that Penny was gone.

Randy reveled in his uneasiness. "Billy, are you giving the girls a hard time?" she chastised.

"Do I ever give anyone a hard time?"

Randy and Seamus laughed heartily while Tanya and Melanie smiled coyly. Billy rolled his eyes in disbelief and descended down the hill toward the lake alone.

"Don't worry, Mel. He's always been a slow starter," kidded Randy.

Melanie looked perturbed. "I might have to change that."

Randy and Seamus found Melanie's determination amusing. Melanie and Tanya pursued Billy down a jagged path toward the lake. Randy noticed a small ledge a short distance away, carved out of the rock. She and Seamus climbed out to the ledge and sat next to each other with their legs dangling over the side. "This ledge was man-made," Seamus mentioned as he studied it.

"How can you tell?" asked Randy.

Seamus pointed out the marks in the rock. "See these grooves. Someone chiseled them by hand."

"I wonder if they're still here."

Seamus looked below at the empty beach. "Doesn't look like it," he replied.

— ✗ —

Billy stepped onto the sandy beach ahead of the girls. "Can't you wait for us?" shouted Melanie, annoyed by his disregard for her.

"What's the matter? Can't keep up?" he teased.

Melanie rushed after Billy and tackled him in the sand. "I'll show you who can't keep up!" she exclaimed. They rolled back and forth until Melanie took a hand full of sand and dropped it into Billy's pants.

"Hey! That wasn't nice," complained Billy. He stood up and shook his pant legs as Melanie laughed at him. Meanwhile, Tanya took her jeans and T-shirt off. She basked in the sand in her bra and panties. Melanie glanced at Tanya and winked. She removed her T-shirt and jeans, revealing a thong and a slinky, lace bra. Billy became noticeably uncomfortable. "What are you doing, Mel?" he asked.

"I told you I didn't have a bathing suit."

Billy covered his eyes in embarrassment and thought regretfully, *I can see where this is going.*

— ✗ —

Randy and Seamus gazed down at the beach. They were entertained by Billy and the girls. "You know, Seamus, I think Billy's got a tiger by the tail."

"He just got rid of one tiger – Penny," joked Seamus.

"Billy can't help it. He's too nice a guy to stay out of trouble."

"I think he'll be strong."

"Wanna' bet?" challenged Randy.

"We'll just watch and see."

They were both surprised when Melanie took off her clothes. "Look, Melanie's pulling out all the stops!" exclaimed Randy.

Seamus was stunned. "Look at what she's wearing! That's not right."

"Why not?" questioned Randy giddily.

"How can a man refuse a vixen dressed like that?"

"What if I was dressed like that?"

"Oh, heaven help me!"

"Now we're getting somewhere." Randy removed her blouse. She wore a sports bra that accented her shape quite well.

"Whoa! I can't help noticing that your beauty is deeper than the deep blue sea."

"Why thank you, Seamus." Randy kissed his cheek in appreciation.

— ⧗ —

Melanie followed Billy across the beach. "Where are you going, now?" she questioned him, wondering what he had in mind.

Billy pointed to a series of flat rocks at the base of the waterfalls. "I'm gonna sit on those rocks over there and relax."

"Can I lay with you?"

"I guess so," he relented, knowing this could take an unexpected turn.

"Gee, you don't have to be so enthusiastic."

Billy cracked a smile as he pondered his predicament. He sat down on the rock and removed his shirt. After stowing his sword and scabbard nearby, he set his knapsack behind his head for a pillow.

Tanya watched them and decided the rocks were a better place to lie than the sand. She came over and joined them. Billy was uncomfortable with the girls being dressed so scantily. "Look, Mel, I had enough problems with Penny and meeting Faye didn't help either."

"You worry too much," Mel complained. "I can make you forget about both of them."

"We all live together now. It would be awkward if things didn't work out."

"But what if they did?" she pressed. "Suppose Penny already has another boyfriend. What would you do if you found out?"

"I don't know. I guess she wouldn't have to come back."

"Why don't I give you a little time to think about it?" She stood up seductively in front of Billy and displayed her shapely body through several sexy poses.

Billy admired her petite body. She was attractive but she still appeared younger than nineteen. "Thanks, Mel. You're all heart," he remarked cynically.

Melanie sauntered over to the falls and stood in the spray. Tanya got up and joined her. They pushed at each other playfully. Billy couldn't help watching them. *Damn, Sports Illustrated would kill for a picture of these girls for their swimsuit issue,* he thought .

Melanie fell backwards into the falls and disappeared. "Mel! Where are you?" called Tanya.

Melanie climbed onto the rocks inside a dark cavern. Eerie shadows of light reflected through the falls. "Wow, look at this place," she uttered in amazement and then returned to the daylight on the other side of the waterfalls.

"What happened to you?" asked Tanya anxiously.

"There's a big cavern back there."

Billy overheard and became interested. "What's this about a cavern?" he asked.

"Come on, Billy. You've got to see this." Billy reluctantly followed the girls.

— X —

Ronnie parked the Expedition next to the flatbed. "Now's the fun part – the climb," she kidded.

"A little exercise will never hurt us," remarked John.

"I doubt fitness will be a problem around here. It's not like we can eat too much and get out of shape."

"I don't know. Billy mentioned something about barbecuing nice, greasy dino-burgers on a grill."

"Don't listen to Billy," Ronnie cautioned him. "He'll corrupt you."

John chuckled as they climbed up the embankment together. "You still need stamina in this environment," he mentioned.

Ronnie was confused by his comment and asked, "What for?"

John pulled her close to him and said, "For this." He kissed her fervently.

"Then you'd better put me on a real good conditioning program," Ronnie teased.

"We'll see about that."

When they reached the top of the slope. Ronnie spotted Seamus and Randy on the ledge and then looked down at the empty beach. "Where are Billy and the girls?" she asked, concerned.

John scanned the beach but saw no sign of them. "I'm sure they couldn't have gone too far."

Ronnie took John by the hand and led him to the ledge. Randy and Seamus were in a serious discussion when Ronnie startled them. "Is this private or can anybody watch?"

"I didn't hear you coming," Randy said breathlessly.

"We can leave if you want," offered John.

"No, it's okay. Sit down and join us."

"Where are Billy and the teeny-boppers?" asked Ronnie.

Randy looked down at the beach. "Hey, they're gone!"

"When was the last time you saw them?" Ronnie questioned them, becoming more worried.

"Just a few minutes ago. The girls were doing a strip tease for Billy over by the falls," answered Seamus.

"Perhaps they're engaged in a little you know what," kidded Ronnie.

"No, I don't think so. At least not yet," replied Randy.

"Why don't the two of you stay here and keep an eye on things? Randy and I will see what's going on," suggested Seamus.

"I hope they're alright," Ronnie uttered nervously.

Seamus rephrased her words, "I hope Billy's alright."

"What do you mean by that?"

"It seems that those girls are no innocent angels," explained Randy.

"They undressed down there in front of Billy!" added Seamus excitedly.

"You mean like naked?" asked John.

"Well, Melanie wore a..."

Randy happily finished, "A thong. It's a narrow strip of material that barely covers a woman's pride. Come to think if it, she didn't have much covering her joy either."

"Things have changed quite a bit from our time, eh, Seamus?" remarked John humorously.

"That's for sure."

Randy and Seamus hiked down the embankment toward the beach.

"I swear, John, she's a piece of work," complained Ronnie.

"I think that's why the two of you are such good friends," John replied.

"Yeah, I guess you're right."

The two of them sat down on the ledge with their legs dangling.

— 𝕏 —

Billy reached inside his knapsack and took out a flashlight. He shined it around the cavern and spotted torches on the walls. "Hey, Mel, got a light?" he asked.

"Yes, I do."

"And what for?"

"Oh, I, um … I always carry a lighter."

"Smoking is bad for you. Would you mind lighting the torches?"

"I'll light them," Tanya offered and took the lighter from her.

As she lit the torches one by one, Billy was surprised to see primitive paintings on the wall.

"What is this place?" asked Melanie.

"Looks like a Jurassic art museum," quipped Billy.

Melanie ran her fingers over the painting. "This painting is fairly recent. Look at the clarity of the color," she noted.

"Do you think someone still lives here?" inquired Billy.

"How should I know?"

"Look. There are more pictures," said Tanya as she scanned the cavern walls.

Melanie put her arm around Billy's waist and nestled close to his body. "What are you doing, Mel?" asked Billy, suspicious of her motives.

"I'm chilly."

"Gee, I wonder why."

Tanya lit the last two torches and illuminated the perimeter of the cavern. The flames made an unusual pattern across the lagoon which Billy noticed immediately. "It looks like the shape of a five-pointed star," he remarked.

"Do you think that's by design?" Melanie questioned Billy.

"I don't know."

Tanya returned and commented, "There's nothing else around here to indicate they still live here."

"If someone did live here, why would they abandon it?" Billy pondered aloud. The girls looked clueless. Billy browsed at some of the paintings, while Melanie followed close behind with her hands in his back pockets.

Tanya found a sloped path that wound up the rear wall to a ledge high above. She climbed to the top and shouted. "Hey, you two! Up here." Her voice echoed around the cavern and startled Billy.

"Be careful that you don't fall off," he cautioned. Melanie left Billy's side and rushed up the path. She reached the ledge and sat next to Tanya.

Billy walked about the cavern, studying the paintings. Several depicted many warriors fighting a creature that looked like a snake or a dragon. *I wonder if giant snakes drove them out,* mused.

Randy and Seamus entered the cavern and saw Billy. "Nice of you to let us know where you went, Billy. I thought we talked about these disappearing acts," chided Randy.

"Sorry. This was a surprise."

"We were worried about you."

"Hi, Randy! We're up here," Melanie shouted as she stood up on the ledge. Randy waved to them.

Billy peered up at the girls briefly on the ledge and handed the flashlight to Randy. "What do you think about these paintings," he asked.

"They're pretty detailed if you ask me."

"I think they're telling a story," he surmised as he pointed to the first three.

As Seamus and Randy inspected each painting, Billy grew bored. "I'm going to see what the girls are doing up there."

"Behave yourself, Billy," teased Seamus.

"I'm trying, Seamus. Lord knows I'm trying." Seamus and Randy chuckled.

Billy climbed up the slope to the ledge. "Okay, girls, what kind of trouble are you getting into up here?"

Melanie pulled some furs out of a small cave behind the ledge. She wrapped herself in one of them. "This feels nice, Billy." She sat down on the ledge with her back against the wall.

"Are you really that cold?" asked Billy.

"Yes, I am! Can't you tell?"

Billy felt a light draft and relented, "I guess it is a bit chilly in here." He sat next to her. Against his better judgment, he put his arm around her for warmth.

Tanya's eyes were fixated on the lagoon and the beautiful shapes the flames made on the surface.

Melanie looked into Billy's eyes and moved her lips close to his. Billy became uneasy but kept his gaze upon her. Her eyes were deep blue and appeared so innocent but Billy sensed they were just a front for a tigress on the hunt. He recalled his initial feeling about Ronnie and Randy: maneaters – stay away from them.

Melanie noticed his apprehension. "We can stop anytime you like," she whispered.

Billy trembled and his will power failed him. He kissed Melanie briefly and paused. When he looked at her, there was something about her that appealed to him. Maybe her innocence, persistence or just the way she adored him. *Damn, this is hard*, he thought.

Tanya saw their brief kiss. She took the hint and went down to the edge of the lagoon. There she sat with her legs dangling in the water. The chilly air didn't bother her.

Billy took Melanie in his harms and kissed her passionately. "Now, is this so bad?" she asked playfully.

"Mel, I don't this is a good idea. You don't even know me that well."

"I told you before: I'm a big girl. Let me worry about that." Melanie rolled over on her back and pulled Billy on top of her. "Do I have to teach you everything?" she teased.

"Young lady, you'd best shut up before I change my mind." The two caressed each other as they kissed. Melanie brought out the beast in Billy and he loved it. She understood his needs and knew how to love him in a way that was satisfying.

— X —

As Ronnie and John conversed on the ledge, high above the lake, Ronnie noticed a long, dark shape gliding just beneath the surface of the water and became alarmed. "John, look at that!" she exclaimed.

John stared at the shape and recalled the giant sea snakes that he and his men encountered from time to time on the seas, but never on a lake. "It never fails. Wherever Billy goes, trouble follows," he complained.

"We'd better get down there and warn them." They scurried down the embankment as the snake swam directly for the waterfalls.

Seamus, Tanya and Randy browsed at the paintings along the back wall. Randy pointed to one that illustrated the mountains and a lake similar to the landscape outside the cavern. "This landscape looks awfully familiar," she commented.

"It looks like they moved up into the mountains on the other side of the lake," Seamus suggested.

"I don't understand why. This place is beautiful."

Tanya studied some of the paintings further down the wall. She noticed one particular painting. "Look at this picture! It shows snakes eating people."

Randy and John inspected the painting. "If these paintings are recent and five snakes attacked these people, then the snakes could still be around," Randy suggested with a note of concern in her voice. A dark shadow rose quietly behind them from the water and loomed near the edge of the lagoon.

"Sea snakes are very aggressive. I can only imagine what these snakes were like to drive a whole tribe out of here," remarked Seamus. Meanwhile, the snake crept toward them along the surface of the water.

On the ledge, Billy sat up next to Melanie and caressed her hair. They lay naked under a large fur pelt. "How was I?" asked Melanie coyly.

Billy kissed her nose and whispered, "You were great. Should I have thought anything less?"

Melanie looked relieved. "I just don't want to disappoint you. I'm trying to win your trust," she confessed humbly.

"Don't ever change, Mel," Billy said and he hugged her. Then he noticed something dark moving along the surface of the water.

Melanie attempted to kiss him but he pulled away. "What's the matter, Billy? Did I do something wrong?" she asked nervously.

Billy looked across the lagoon and saw the giant snake. "Holy shit! We've got problems." He looked down and saw his friends facing the wall. "Get out of there!" he shouted.

Randy, Seamus and Tanya turned around and were horrified. The giant snake hovered over them, hissing as it slithered out of the water. Tanya screamed and retreated to the wall. Randy and Seamus drew their swords.

Billy quickly dressed and warned Melanie, "Stay inside the cave until I tell you otherwise." He fired a rock and struck the snake's head. It turned toward him and coiled to strike. Melanie was terrified as she watched.

"Do something, Billy?" she pleaded.

"Like what, Mel?"

"I don't know."

Seamus lunged at the snake and pierced its thick skin with his sword. The snake spun and struck at him. Seamus dove to his left and the snake's head struck the wall just beyond him. It hissed and slithered toward the rear wall. Its body was nearly thirty feet long and stretched across the ground, cutting off any chance of escape.

"You and Tanya need to get out of here while you still have a chance," warned Seamus. "I'll keep it distracted."

"I'm not leaving you," replied Randy adamantly.

"Then let's do something about it."

Billy threw more rocks at the snake. It turned its attention back to him and crept toward the ledge with its dark, piercing eyes focused on him.

"Billy, that's not what I had in mind!" cried Melanie.

"Shut up and get inside the cave, Mel." Melanie scrambled into the cave and hid under the fur. She peeked out at Billy fearfully.

The snake struck at him, but he dove behind a rock. Again, the snake smashed its head into the wall. Ronnie and John rushed into the cavern. They were shocked by the snake's immense size.

Seamus and Randy rushed at the snake and hacked at its side about midway between the head and tail with their swords. The snake spun around and struck at them. Seamus pushed Randy into the water but he fell helplessly on the stone floor. When the snake struck at him, he dove out of the way and barely avoided it again. He scurried backwards as the snake poised to strike again.

Randy held on to the rocks at the side of the lagoon. "Seamus, get out of there!" she screamed.

Billy crouched over the ledge and tensed his body. "What are you doing?" Melanie asked frantically.

"I wish to hell I knew." Billy leaped off the ledge and landed on the snake's head. He drove his sword through the front of the snake's head and pinned its mouth shut. The snake shook crazily but Billy held on desperately to the sword's hilt. Melanie looked down from the ledge and sobbed as she watched in horror.

Billy dangled helplessly from the snake's head by his sword, but his weight hampered its movements significantly. Seamus hacked repeatedly at the snake's underbelly. It slapped at him with its tail and knocked him into the cavern wall. Randy crawled out of the water and struck just behind the snake's head. Billy hung on tightly as it jerked in a desperate attempt to throw him off.

Ronnie timed the snake's movements and shoved her sword into the bottom of its jaw and out through the side of its head. The sword exited the snake's head between Billy's legs as he lay draped down the side of the snake's head.

"Watch it, Ronnie!" he shouted, fearing an inadvertent sword to his body.

"Sorry, Billy," yelled Ronnie as she realized the proximity of her blade to him. She tugged on her sword's hilt but the snake jerked its head away before she could retrieve it. The snake quivered as it struggled to raise its head off the ground. It frantically tried to open its mouth and breath but the two swords held it shut.

"Jump, Billy!" shouted John, but Billy was too frightened to let go of the sword.

The snake fell backwards into the water and sank to the bottom with Billy pinned underneath its head. The impact of the water and the snake's weight stunned him and rendered him unconscious. The snake's corpse rested upside down at the bottom of the lagoon with Billy's legs underneath it.

Melanie rushed down from the ledge and leaned over the edge of the lagoon. "Someone help him!" she pleaded. Randy took off her shoes and her T-shirt.

"What do you think you're doing? You'll drown, too!" hollered Ronnie.

"I've got to try." Randy dove into the water and swam to the bottom.

"Damn it! I hate when this happens," muttered Ronnie. She took her clothes off, revealing only a black lace bra and a burgundy thong. The thong had a Tasmanian devil's face on the front and back. Without further hesitation, she dove in after Randy.

Randy swam twenty-five feet to the bottom of the lagoon. She immediately saw the snake resting on top of Billy's legs. Both swords were still embedded in an X-shape in its head. Billy was face down, which slowed the air exiting from his mouth. Randy grabbed the hilt of Billy's sword and pried up on it. Ronnie reached the bottom and helped push on the snake's head until it rolled slightly. She pointed to Billy and waved Randy away.

Randy grabbed Billy's arms and pulled him out from under the snake. As soon as his legs were clear, the sword broke loose from the snake's head and settled against the flat stone bottom of the lagoon. The girls dragged Billy toward the surface.

"They've been down there too long! They need help," John exclaimed. He took off his shirt and dove in. Seamus removed his shirt and waited for some indication from them whether or not they needed his help.

Randy lost consciousness about fifteen feet from the surface. She released her hold on Billy and drifted away from Ronnie. Ronnie panicked as she tried desperately to hold onto Billy and reach out to her. John saw them and took Billy by the arms from Ronnie. He rushed Billy to the surface where Seamus pulled him out of the water. Ronnie wrapped her arm around Randy and pulled her to the surface.

Melanie and Tanya helped pull Randy from the water. Melanie immediately started CPR on Billy while Ronnie did the same for Randy. John and Seamus didn't understand what they were doing and watched helplessly. Randy coughed and spit water on the ground. She rolled onto her stomach and groaned as Ronnie breathed a sigh of relief.

Melanie tried desperately to revive Billy but he didn't respond. "Come on, Billy! Don't leave me," she cried.

"Watch out, honey," Ronnie said as she pushed on Billy's chest repeatedly and blew into his mouth. After several tries, she became frustrated and teary-eyed. "Damn you, Billy! Don't do this to us!" she cried. Frantically Ronnie tried again to resuscitate Billy but to no avail.

John knelt next to her and put his arm around her. She lowered her head and cried. "There's nothing more you can do," he said sadly.

"We can't let him go!" blurted Ronnie.

Melanie cradled Billy's head against her chest and sobbed. Ronnie pushed her back and tried again to revive Billy. After four more attempts, she shouted, "Don't die on me, you son of a bitch!"

— ⧗ —

Ruger and Pirocles gazed expectantly at the smoke over the damaged silver chest. They saw the image of Billy lying on the ground next to the lagoon with his friends sadly looking on. Ruger howled with joy. "It's done! I knew I could count on the snakes to finish him off."

"What about the others?" asked Pirocles.

"Oh, they're dead too. Just wait and see." Ruger closed the chest and hurried to the stairwell.

"Where are you going?" asked Pirocles.

"To give the good news to Diomedes! Now I can focus on the battle at hand." Ruger laughed sadistically as he raced down the steps.

— ⧗ —

Billy felt as though he watched from someone else's body. He realized how much his friends cared for him and how much he meant to them.

But then, something strange happened. For the interval of time that Ruger watched him in the smoke, Billy could see into Ruger's mind as well.

Billy found himself inside Ruger's castle, observing. He witnessed Ruger's exuberance at his apparent death. Now he understood that a second person or creature named Diomedes had something to do with his misfortunes in addition to Ruger. There was much he didn't understand but he saw enough through Ruger's mind to realize they were behind everything that happened to him and his friends. Billy became excited when he realized he now had an edge on Ruger. He had to get back to his friends somehow.

Melanie's voice caught his attention and then Ronnie's desperate cries motivated him to return to consciousness. Melanie and Tanya stood by the wall and cried. Ronnie pounded Billy's chest with both her fists relentlessly. Suddenly, Billy coughed and startled them.

"He's alive! The son-of-a-bitch is alive!" Randy shouted ecstatically.

Billy rolled onto his side and spit up water. He gasped as he tried to breath.

"Breathe, Billy. Breathe," she urged him.

Billy crawled onto his knees and gasped. After several breaths he stood up. "What a rush!" he joked cynically. Ronnie, Randy and Melanie hugged him.

"How do you do that, Billy?" asked John, amazed once more by Billy's luck.

"I don't know and I don't care." He coughed again as he struggled to breath.

"I was beginning to think you were too soft," Ronnie mentioned, still shaken by his near death.

"Not me, but I hope I never have to do that again." Then Billy noticed Ronnie in her thong and lace bra. "Damn, Ronnie, look at you," he commented excitedly.

John was suddenly aware of Ronnie's bra and thong. "Oh, my!" he uttered.

Ronnie was terribly embarrassed. "You just shut your mouth, Billy, if you know what's good for you!" she warned as tears streamed down her cheeks.

John quickly gathered Ronnie's clothes and helped her dress.

"That wasn't nice," chided Melanie.

"Even after this, you still have your sense of humor," Seamus commented giddily

"That's all I've got," Billy replied weakly.

Melanie put her hands on her hips and complained, "What am I, chopped liver?"

"No, you're top choice. I heard your voice and that kept me fighting."

"I was so worried about you," she said and hugged him tightly.

"We thought you were gone for good," Tanya added.

Billy put his arms around the two girls. "So did I, girls. So did I."

"The paintings showed five snakes. There could be four more," warned Randy.

"We should get out of here immediately," John urged them.

Two smaller snakes, each about twelve feet long, approached the cavern underwater. One snake crossed the rocks at the entrance to the cavern while another entered underwater. Billy saw the shadows and looked ill.

"Now what's wrong?" queried Randy.

"Get up on the ledge now!"

The first snake rose out of the water. Randy saw it and groaned, "Not again!"

Billy trailed the others up the path to the ledge. Halfway up, he felt his scabbard and realized his sword was gone. He staggered back down the path and hid by the wall. The snake slithered past him and hovered below the ledge.

John, Seamus, Ronnie and Randy stood at the front of the ledge with their swords drawn while the younger girls huddled in the cave behind them.

"Where's Billy now?" asked Randy, worried once more over Billy's theatrics.

"He was right behind us," answered John.

Randy spotted him by the wall below them. "Billy, what are you doing?" she shouted. He hurried to the edge of the lagoon and slid into the water.

"That boy's out of his friggin' mind!" she hollered sarcastically.

The second snake slithered up the wall toward them. "There's another!" exclaimed John.

"Both of you should get inside the cave. We make too big a target like this," warned Seamus as he pushed the girls inside the cave. "Be prepared to join us when we call. We'll have to move fast." Ronnie and Randy reluctantly retreated to the rear of the cave with Melanie and Tanya.

Billy swam to the bottom of the lagoon and retrieved Ronnie's sword from the dead snake's head. He stowed it in his scabbard and searched through the clear water until he found his sword. He picked it off the lagoon floor and jammed it into the scabbard with the other sword.

As he swam swiftly to the surface, he became light-headed. Just when he thought his lungs would explode, he broke the surface of the water and desperately grabbed onto the rocks. He crawled out of the water and lay exhausted on the ground. The shouts of his friends alerted him and he saw two snakes extended upward near the ledge.

John and Seamus kept the snakes at bay. Each time one of the snakes got close, they struck at either side of its head and injured it. Billy regained his breath and crept up on one of the snakes with both swords drawn. He drove the swords into the snake's side as far as he could and then retreated. The snake hissed and turned toward him.

Billy taunted it by waving the swords at it and moving across the ground. It slithered to and fro, angling at him for an attack. As it struck, he dove aside and the snake struck the wall. He leaped on top of its head while it was dazed and plunged both swords through its jaws. The snake jerked sideways and struck the wall. The impact knocked Billy across the stone floor. The snake was stunned from the wounds and struggled to open its mouth.

Billy staggered to his feet and approached the snake. Blood seeped from his busted nose and from a wound on his forehead. The snake scraped its head against the ground in an attempt to rid itself of the swords. Billy jumped on the crippled snake's head and grabbed the hilts of the swords. He dangled helplessly as it slammed him against the wall of the cavern, but he refused to let go of the swords.

After several attempts to shake Billy off, the swords finally came loose and Billy crashed to the ground. The snake stared at Billy for what seemed like an eternity. It lowered its head and hissed as if it would strike one more time. Billy got up again and approached the snake. He lunged at it and drove the swords into each of its eyes. The snake quivered as Billy pulled the swords from its head. It slithered toward the lagoon but Billy raced after it and struck behind its head. The swords cut through three quarters of the snake. He backed away and let the snake die.

The second snake forced John and Seamus into the cave. Each time it poked its head inside, they repelled it with a series of jabs from their swords. Billy staggered up the path, wielding both swords. His arms ached from fatigue and he weakened further from exhaustion. The snake poked its head into the cave again as he reached the ledge.

Billy struck at the rear of the snake's head before it pulled out. The sword sliced into the snake, leaving a mortal wound. He struck with the second sword and cut further. He took two more strokes and the head was severed. The snake's body fell from the ledge to the ground.

Billy stowed his sword and dropped Ronnie's on the ground. He rolled the snake's head away from the cave and shoved it off the ledge. Randy and John exited the cave cautiously. They looked down at the dead snakes, still reeling from the attacks.

John patted him on the back. "Well done, Billy. Well done."

Melanie rushed out and hugged him. She wiped the blood from his face and kissed his cheek. "Thank goodness you're alright," she blurted, while in tears.

"Am I?" replied Billy coldly.

Melanie kissed him again and said, "Yes, you are."

"I think we should get the hell out of here before the other snakes show up."

"I couldn't agree more," replied John.

Ronnie placed her hands on Billy's shoulders. "It's my turn to thank you."

"So, you're not mad at me anymore?"

"Not right now, but that could change later."

Billy picked up Ronnie's sword and handed it to her. "You went back down there, huh?" Ronnie remarked sarcastically.

"Yeah, I needed my sword back. I figured I might as well grab yours, too."

"You are retarded, Billy. You really are, but thank you."

"Gee, Ronnie, that's one of the nicer things you've said to me lately."

"You're getting there, Billy. One day you'll be a man."

"Oh, he's already that. I made sure," said Melanie proudly.

Ronnie looked at Billy with a stunned expression. Billy was embarrassed and frowned at Melanie. "Mel, would you please shut up?" he requested.

"But, Billy..."

"Just shut up. You're not helping me here."

Ronnie shook her head at Billy in disbelief. "Billy she's a little young for you," she commented.

"We'll discuss it later." Billy followed Melanie and Tanya to avoid further humiliation. The others followed behind them.

"Did you hear what she said?" Ronnie whispered to Randy.

"I sure did. That little tramp!" blurted Randy.

"It's not Mel's fault."

"I know. I'm talking about Billy."

"Are you jealous, Randy?" kidded Seamus.

"Now why would I be jealous?"

"Well, you seem pretty upset about it."

"Seamus, look at her. She's young – real young."

"She says she's nineteen," commented John.

"I don't care. She's just a kid."

They exited the cavern through the waterfalls. Billy sat down on one of the flat rocks. The others stopped and waited for him.

"Keep going," he urged them. "I'll catch up."

"Don't be a jackass. What's wrong?" asked Ronnie.

"I have to sit." Billy took his shirt and wiped tears from his eyes.

Melanie was concerned about him. "Are you alright, Billy?"

Billy covered his face with the shirt. He trembled as he recalled his hallucinations and realized that he might have been dead at the bottom of the lagoon when he had them.

Ronnie saw that he was badly shaken and suggested, "Give him a few minutes, Mel. He just needs a breather." They watched the area for any sign of the remaining snakes.

Melanie put her arm around Billy and whispered, "I'm here for you, Billy. What can I do for you?"

Something struck Billy when he heard this. Here was a young woman who didn't know him that well and actually cared about him. He felt guilty about their affair on the ledge but realized that he meant more to Melanie than he first thought. To her, he wasn't just a commodity like he was to Penny and Charlene. Billy regained his composure. "I'm fine, Mel. Thanks for asking," he said appreciatively. Everyone looked concerned for Billy. He was in obvious pain.

"Let's go before mama and papa snake come looking for us," he suggested.

As they ascended the slope, Billy lagged behind, a result of recurring dizzy spells. Ronnie grew more concerned. "You look like shit, Billy, and you're wobbling."

"It's just a few cobwebs. I'll be alright."

When they reached the top of the slope, they paused and looked back. Two dark shapes glided across the lake toward the cavern. One shape appeared to be the size of the smaller snakes. The other was significantly larger.

"Will you look at the size of that? It must be over forty-five feet long," uttered Billy.

Seamus, Randy and the girls continued down the hill toward the vehicles. John and Ronnie waited with Billy. "I think it's going to hunt for us when it finds the other snakes are dead," John surmised pessimistically.

"Well, the bright side of it is that there are only two left," quipped Billy.

"Thanks, Billy. That helps a lot." They hurried down the hill after the others.

Seamus and the girls were obstructed by two Dimetrodons in their path about halfway down the mountainside. They ducked in the bushes and waited.

"Can't we just go around them?" asked Melanie, fearing another attack.

"No," answered Seamus. "This is the only way down."

"Well that sucks."

"Just relax and sit tight. I'm sure they'll move on soon."

Randy called to them from a bushy patch between two large trees, "Over here, you guys."

Seamus, Melanie and Tanya crept through the trees and joined her. When Billy, John and Ronnie arrived, Seamus whistled for their attention. They saw the Dimetrodons and skirted the clearing.

"What's this – the dino depot?" kidded Billy.

"I don't know if these things eat meat or plants. We figured we'd avoid them just in case," replied Randy.

They were startled when several trees snapped and crashed behind them. A twenty-foot snake darted into the clearing and attacked the Dimetrodons. "Damn, that didn't take long!" uttered Billy.

"Do we have a favorite in this battle?" inquired Randy.

"I think I'd root for the Dimetrodons. Besides, there's still the bigger snake out there," answered John.

The Dimetrodons bit the snake numerous times, but none were critical. The snake coiled around one of the creatures while the other bit into its tail. A loud snap of the first Dimetrodon's back ended any chance the two had to overpower the snake. The snake aggressively pursued the second Dimetrodon and coiled around its head and neck, applying incredible pressure to the helpless creature.

Billy rushed out of the trees and struck at the snake's head with four quick blows, but he was too late. The Dimetrodon's neck snapped like the other and the snake uncoiled. He savagely hacked at the neck until the head fell away from the body.

The snake's headless body wriggled for several minutes before it lay motionless. Billy gazed proudly at his conquest. Ronnie and Randy exited the bushes.

"What the hell were you thinking?" Ronnie shouted.

"You could have been killed – again!" Randy added.

"Well, great huntresses, did you have a better idea?"

"No, but that's beside the point."

"I'm starting to enjoy this hunting business," Billy admitted sadistically.

"We've created a monster," Ronnie complained to Randy.

"And a stupid one at that."

"Look, Billy, all we're saying is that we need to discuss things first," explained John.

"Sorry but I didn't think there was time to hold a congressional hearing about it."

"What's a congressional hearing?" John asked Ronnie.

"I'll tell you later. It's part of the democratic process of government."

"Uh, I think I see."

Trees snapped and crashed again, startling them. "Here comes mamma," replied Billy sarcastically.

"Shit! Where do we go now?" Ronnie fretted.

Billy looked at the dead snake and announced, "I've got an idea."

"Oh, great. I can hardly wait," uttered Randy.

Billy drew his sword and slit open the dead snake's body from end to end. "Now what, Einstein?" Ronnie asked cynically.

"Get in."

"I'm not hiding inside any stinkin' snake!" she muttered, disgusted by the idea.

Billy asked Melanie and Tanya, "Do the two of you want to live?"

The girls were terrified and shook their heads up and down in affirmation. Billy lifted the body apart and said, "Good. Get in and don't move." The girls promptly obeyed.

Billy looked at the others expectantly. "I hate you, Billy Brock," groaned Ronnie.

"No, you don't. You're just mad because you didn't think of it."

Ronnie glared at him as she and John climbed inside the tail section of the snake.

"If we make a run for the vehicle, you'll have a chance if it chases us," suggested Randy.

"And what if it catches you?" asked Billy.

"At least someone will get away."

"It's been fun," Billy replied, saddened by the thought of losing any of them.

"It's not over yet. Remember what you said: another time, another place," Randy reminded him.

"I hope so. Now get going."

Randy and Seamus raced for the flatbed truck that was parked a half mile away.

Billy crawled into the middle of the carcass next to Melanie and Tanya. He watched the clearing from between the folds of skin. Melanie ran her fingers across his stomach toward his belt.

"Mel, I'm going to break your fingers," warned Billy.

"If you don't leave him alone, I'll break them first," grumbled Tanya.

"It stinks in here," complained Melanie.

The snake slithered into the clearing and hovered over the carcass. "It's here," whispered Billy. "Now shut up."

The snake nudged the Dimetrodons several times before it was convinced that they were dead. It circled the clearing and paused over the snake's carcass.

Billy could see through a tiny gap that it was looking right at them. He broke a sweat as he wondered what it would do if it found them. The snake nudged the rear part of the carcass. Billy thought, *Please, don't anybody move back there.*

John wrapped his arms around Ronnie and pulled her close to him. "I love you," he whispered.

"Nice timing," she replied, annoyed. "I love you, too."

The snake slithered into the forest. Billy crawled out from the carcass and listened carefully. There was no sign of the snake. He pulled open the carcass and let the girls out.

"Is it safe?" asked Melanie.

"For now." Billy lifted the rear section of the snake. When Ronnie and John crawled out, Ronnie slapped John's arm and scolded him, "I can't believe it took something like this to make you to say that to me."

"What did you say to her?" asked Melanie, curious.

"It's personal, Mel," interjected Ronnie.

"In case that was going to be our last moment alive, I wanted you to know how I felt," explained John.

"Do you still feel that way, now that we're still alive?"

"Of course, I do."

"That snake's gonna come back real soon. How do we kill it?" Billy questioned the girls.

"Haven't you had enough?" bellowed Ronnie.

"I guess that means you're not helping."

Ronnie looked to John for support. "He's right. It won't go away on its own," answered John.

"I think you guys are both crazy."

"Ronnie, since you're the big weapons designer, what do you think about a slingshot spear?" Billy suggested as he studied the surrounding trees.

"What the hell are you talking about?"

"Can we make something that will launch a spear with a sword at the end of it?"

"You're serious."

"Deadly serious."

Ronnie looked at the trees around them and spotted one in particular that was tall and thin. "I've got a better idea." She pointed to the tree and said, "That one there."

"What do we do first?" asked Billy.

"Get some vines. We'll tie a sword perpendicularly where the branches split. After that, we'll pull the tree back until it's bent at a near ninety-degree angle and tie it off."

"That's clever but I have just one question," said John.

"What's that?"

"The sword will strike the snake about eighteen feet above the ground, right?"

"Yes, and your point is …?"

"How do we get the snake to raise its head into the sword's path?"

"Someone's gonna have to bait it."

"I'll do it," volunteered Billy.

"Why do you always have to do the dirty work, Billy?" asked Melanie, growing frustrated with Billy's risk-taking antics.

"Somebody has to or everybody dies. Now let's get to work." Melanie looked at him pitifully. Ronnie and Randy noticed and glanced at each other.

John grabbed a vine and climbed the tree with it. He wedged the sword into the split and tied it tightly. Melanie and Tanya stretched out several lengths of vines across the ground. Billy and Ronnie picked out the longest and strongest of the vines. After they twisted four lengths together, Billy followed John up the tree with one end. He passed it to John who climbed higher and tied the vines around the upper half of the tree.

Ronnie found a solid tree nearby to use for a pulley. "Run the vines around this tree and pull. We'll tie it off to the smaller tree behind it," she instructed the men.

Billy and John pulled from the front of the tree. The girls then pulled the vines after they passed around the tree. The thin tree bent easily at first but became very resistant soon after.

"Pull harder! We've got to get more bend," ordered Ronnie. The men strained as they pulled and the tree budged just a little more. "It's almost there. A little more," urged Ronnie.

Finally, the tree bent far enough backward. "That's it!" exclaimed Ronnie. She hurried over to help the girls tie the vines off to the last tree.

Sweating profusely, Billy and John were relieved to be finished. Their break was soon interrupted by the crashing of trees again. "Are you sure you're okay with this?" Ronnie questioned Billy.

"Only if you're sure this contraption will work?" She shrugged her shoulders and replied, "Who knows?"

"Then yeah, I'm fine with it."

Everyone but Billy hid in the trees. He waited, trembling in front of the tree. When the snake slithered into the clearing, Billy muttered, "Oh, man! What was I thinking?" He raised his sword defensively. The snake ignored him and nudged at the carcass several times. It looked at Billy with beady eyes. Suddenly, it bit into the carcass and swung it back and forth, smashing it against the trees. The carcass shredded into flying pieces of snake flesh. The snake slithered toward Billy and coiled to strike.

"It's not high enough! He'll be killed," fretted Ronnie.

"What can we do?" asked John.

"You watch the vines. When I holler, you cut them."

"Where are you going?"

"Don't worry about it." Ronnie climbed another tree nearby.

"Ronnie, come back!" shouted John frantically.

"She's so brave," cried Tanya.

"They all are but someone's going to get killed," Melanie muttered sadly.

Ronnie reached a practical height in the tree. She drew her pistol and fired three shots into the snake's head. It swung toward her and eyed her. "Come on, you chicken-shit coward!" yelled Ronnie.

"Get out of there!" ordered Billy.

The snake was reluctant to approach her. Ronnie fired three more shots into its head. The snake coiled but was too far from the tree.

"What's it waiting for?" shouted Billy.

"I don't understand it," replied Ronnie.

"It senses a trap. Get out of there!" warned John.

Billy attacked the snake and struck at it with his sword. He cut a chunk of flesh from its side and retreated back to the tree. The snake hissed and moved its head erratically back and forth. It raised its head and coiled to strike at Billy.

Ronnie screamed, "Now, John!"

John cut the vines. The tree whipped forward and struck the snake in the head, then flew back without the sword. The sword embedded itself firmly in its skull but the snake was still coiled to strike. It seemed immune to the sword's damage. Billy shuddered and wet himself.

"Don't move, Billy," cautioned Ronnie.

"I wouldn't think of it."

The snake wavered and crashed to the ground. Its head lay four feet from Billy. He became weak-kneed and fell backward against the tree. Tears formed in his eyes.

Ronnie hustled down from the tree. "It worked!" she shouted triumphantly.

"Yeah, it worked," said Billy, still shaking.

"Are you okay?" asked Ronnie.

"No." Billy stared at the snake with a distant look in his eyes.

Randy and Seamus emerged from the trees. "Thank goodness, you guys are all right," Randy hollered.

"Why'd you come back?" asked Ronnie.

"We had to because it cut us off. When it came back this way, we followed it."

John studied the precision that the sword struck the snake's head. He was awed by Ronnie's quick design and calculations. Melanie and Tanya huddled in the trees. Neither was anxious to come out of hiding yet.

When Randy and Seamus approached them, Randy complained, "Oh, gosh. What's that smell?"

"Snake guts. We're covered with it," John answered sheepishly.

"Guess what I'm going to do with those snakes?" she said excitedly as she eyed the dead snakes.

"I can hardly wait," replied Ronnie.

"I'm going to skin those SOBs and use their skins for furniture covers. In fact, I'm gonna make you some snakeskin seat covers, Ronnie."

"That's not necessary," she responded, fighting back tears.

"Sure, it is."

"Why don't we go back to the lake and wash up? This smell is nauseating me," suggested John.

"That's five that we killed. Maybe we're safe now," Randy commented.

Billy sat silently as he stared into the eyes of the snake. Melanie knelt by him and asked, "Are you okay?"

"No, I'm not."

"I don't know how you got the courage to stand in front of the snake like that," she commented. "You were so brave."

"Am I? Maybe I'm just that stupid."

Ronnie overheard Billy's words. She came over and offered him a hand to get to his feet. "You were brave," she affirmed. "If you weren't, we'd all be dead."

"You were brave, too, Ronnie."

"Yeah, I guess so."

"Don't you think about getting killed when you do this stuff?" asked Melanie.

"If you think about it, you will get killed," answered Ronnie.

John put his arm around her waist and said, "You were great, Honey, but I was worried to death about you."

Ronnie kissed his cheek. "Thanks, but so was I," she said. The two of them climbed the slope and left the lake.

Randy suggested to the two girls, "Why don't you get Billy back to the lake?"

"Why?" asked Billy, baffled by her suggestion.

"Because you smell! Get your ass down to the lake and wash."

Billy reluctantly got up. "You know, Randy, I'm not sure what's worse – you or that snake," he complained.

Randy pleaded to the girls, "Will you please do something with him?"

"I'll do my best," promised Melanie.

— X —

Ruger entered the chamber and sat down in front of the silver chest. He opened the lid and chanted a brief incantation. The white smoke formed and rose into the air. "Now we'll see if the rest of them are gone as well," he uttered confidently.

An image formed in the smoke and soon became clear. Billy sat on the ground and stared at Ruger through the dead snake's eyes. Ruger was enraged and threw the silver chest against the wall. The lid broke off and slid toward the stairwell. The chest bounced across the floor, spreading gray ashes all over the floor. Pirocles rushed in with a concerned expression on his face.

"He's still alive! They're all alive! What does it take to kill this pest?" screamed Ruger.

"Perhaps this is why Diomedes is concerned about him," suggested Pirocles.

"He must have magic of his own," declared Ruger. "That is the only explanation."

"In that case, we must be wary. He hasn't shown it, if he does have powers."

Ruger sneered and pondered. He raised his hands in the air and shouted several incantations. "I'll send the wolfen after them. I'll send the gryphons as well! He won't get away this time," he ranted.

CHAPTER 11

DARING ESCAPES

Billy, Melanie and Tanya returned to the lake together. "Billy, what do you think about when you face these creatures?" Melanie asked timidly.

"Surviving."

"What did you think about when you were with me on the ledge?"

"Why?"

"I want to know. Was it about surviving?"

"No, I thought about how good it felt to be held by someone who cared."

"That's it?"

"No. I wondered if there was an 'us' in the future."

"Really?"

"Yes, but I'm confused by so many things that I really don't know what to feel or who to feel it with. I don't want to hurt anybody but I need to belong to somebody."

"You can belong to me if you like."

"It doesn't work that way, Mel. I hardly know you."

"We can work at it."

"Yeah, but it takes time. Penny couldn't understand that and it caused lots of problems." They reached the top of the slope and looked down at the lake. "It's so peaceful right now, but I wonder what other horrors lurk nearby," said Billy sullenly.

"This is like living in a zoo without the cages. You know you're surrounded by dangerous creatures and it's just a matter of time before you encounter them," Tanya remarked.

"We've been very lucky so far," Billy reminded them. "It's inevitable, though, that someone will die soon."

"Would you risk your life for anyone or just certain friends?" asked Melanie.

"I would do it for anyone. That's the key to our survival."

"If you would be my protector, I'll promise to take care of you every day."

"Me, too. I don't want to die out here," added Tanya.

"I do my best to protect everyone."

"Please protect us. I'll do anything for you. I mean it," begged Melanie.

"I know you would, but the safest place is going to be inside the Post Office. I suggest you stay there in the future."

"If you get us back there in one piece, I'll stay there. I promise."

"Maybe I should heed my own advice," kidded Billy.

Ronnie and John washed up at the lake's edge. Ronnie noticed several gryphons swarming at the top of the ridge. "Oh, shit! Get to the cavern, John." John looked up in awe at the mythical creatures. They raced across the beach to the waterfalls.

Shadows flashed across the ground and startled Billy. He looked up at the sky and saw six dark objects descending out of the sunlight. "Now what?" Billy groaned.

"What are they?" asked Melanie.

"I can't tell yet but they see us and they're headed this way." Billy searched for a place to hide but they were on top of the embankment with no place to go. He spotted a man-sized hole in the ground and peered inside it. There was a ladder cut into the hard soil, which descended about ten feet into a small cave. Billy ordered the girls, "Get down in the hole, quickly."

Six large gryphons swooped in at them. Their white-feathered heads were beaked with large eyes and a white crest like an eagle. They had sharp talons on a brown lion's body with the wings of a condor. Billy dueled with them as they hovered around him. The gryphons grabbed at him and pecked at him repeatedly. He kept low to the ground and jabbed at them at every opportunity.

Melanie paused at the top of the ladder. "Come on, Billy!" she shouted.

"Get down there, now!" ordered Billy. Melanie dropped down into the hole.

One of the gryphons struck Bill from behind and knocked him over the edge of the embankment. He clung desperately to a root and held on. His sword tumbled down to the beach far below. The gryphon hovered close to Billy. It locked its claws around his arm and tugged at him. He held on to the root and kicked frantically at the gryphon but to no avail.

Suddenly, a volley of arrows filled the air. Four of them struck the gryphon in the back. It released its hold on Billy's arm and flew away, shrieking. The other gryphons fled from the barrage of arrows and disappeared into the mountains. Billy hung face first against the embankment, unaware of his mystery rescuers.

— ✕ —

Ronnie saw native women and children along the edge of the lagoon and was amazed. "Will you look at this?" she said. When the natives saw them, they circled and stared. Some of the children came up to them and touched their clothes.

"I think we freed their home from the snakes," commented Ronnie,

"Then they should be friendly, right?" John asked uneasily.

"I certainly hope so."

— ✕ —

Billy was startled when a native man grabbed his arm and pulled him up onto the ledge. The native wore a fur tunic and had long, scraggily hair with a necklace of teeth from various animals. Billy placed his hand on the native's shoulder and said, "Thank you."

The native smiled and motioned for Billy to follow. They descended into the hole and found the two girls huddled in the corner of the cave. The girls panicked and screamed when they saw the native. "Relax, already! He's a friend," replied Billy.

The girls watched nervously as Billy followed the native through the cave. "Are you coming or what?" Billy asked the girls.

"Yeah, but where did he come from?" inquired Melanie.

"I don't know but his timing was perfect." Billy and the native emerged onto the ledge inside the cavern.

"Well, it's nice of him to wait for us," complained Melanie.

"I think he expects us to stay with him," replied Tanya. The three of them followed the native down the path to the lagoon.

"They won't eat us, will they?" asked Tanya, fearing the worst.

Billy was amused by the question. "I don't think so."

"Are you sure? I mean they could be cannibals," mentioned Melanie.

"I don't know, Mel. If I think you look good enough to eat, I'm sure they do, too."

"You perv, Billy."

"Watch out for the kettle calling the pot black," warned Tanya.

Melanie smacked her arm and scolded her, "Don't be telling him my secrets."

"I'm sure he'll find out soon enough."

"Well, we'll just wait until then."

"Zip it, girls. I don't want to give our new friend a headache," said Billy sternly. The girls frowned at him.

The native pointed at the painting of the snakes and his people. Billy pointed to the picture of the man in front of the snake with a spear, and then he pointed to the native. "This, you?" he asked.

The native grunted twice. He pointed to the picture again and poked his own chest twice. "Teek!" he replied excitedly.

"You, Teek," responded Billy. The native smiled proudly.

Billy pointed to himself and said, "Billy. Bill-ee." The native repeated hoarsely, "Bi-wee."

"Yes. Billy." Billy pulled the two girls next to him and announced, "This is Mel. Mel." The native poked her chest and said, "Mel."

"Yes. Mel." Billy pointed to Tanya and said, "This is Tanya. Tan-ya."

"Ah. Tan-a."

"Close enough. Tan-ya."

"Tan-a-a."

"That'll do."

They heard a commotion at the entrance to the cavern by the falls. "Um, batta! Um, batta batta," hollered Teek. A native woman approached Teek and spoke in their language to him.

"What are they talking about?" asked Melanie.

"I think they're discussing your cleavage," joked Billy.

Melanie became self-conscious and pulled Tanya in front of her.

"What're you doing?" asked Tanya.

"Let them look at your cleavage."

"I don't have any."

Billy rolled his eyes at them. "Stop it, you two!"

"You started it," retorted Melanie.

"And I'm ending it!"

Teek noticed Billy's impatience with the girls and laughed. He pointed to his woman and uttered, "Mala." Teek put his arm around her and pulled her close to him. He repeated proudly, "Mala."

Billy explained to Melanie, "Mala is his girlfriend."

"No kidding."

"Maybe we can double date with them."

"Why would we do that?" Melanie asked.

"Maybe you can learn something from her."

"Brock, you're in for it now. That's the last straw."

"Promises. Promises."

Teek took Billy's arm and led him across the cavern with the girls behind them. When they passed through the crowd, Billy noticed John and Ronnie. They looked nervous standing among the natives. "Well, well, my friends. Welcome to my new kingdom," Billy orated playfully

John was stunned and asked, "How did you get here?"

"It's magic."

"What's going on here?" asked Ronnie.

"These are my friends," answered Billy as he pointed to Teek and Mala. "This is Teek. He's the chief of the tribe."

"And I guess this is Jane," said Ronnie mockingly.

"No. This is Mala. She's his queen."

"And I guess you know the whole family tree, too."

"I'm working on it."

Billy indicated to Teek as he pointed to John and Ronnie. "This is John."

Teek repeated, "John."

"Very good, Teek. This is grumpy. Grum-pee."

Ronnie grabbed Billy around the waist and shoved him toward the water. "That's it, smart-ass! Now you're going to get it."

"Go, Ronnie!" cheered Melanie.

Everyone was amused as Ronnie wrestled with Billy and shoved him into the water. She beamed with pride for her deed. Billy stayed underwater for a long period of time, holding his breath. Ronnie stopped smiling and grew concerned.

"Shouldn't he have come up by now?" asked Melanie.

"He's just looking for attention," replied Ronnie, fearing that something was wrong, leaned over the edge and looked down. Billy lunged out of the water and grabbed her around the waist. In a single motion, he pulled her in. They splashed at each other wildly. "Billy, you're such a jerk!" cried Ronnie.

"What's the matter? You can dish it out but you can't take it."

Billy climbed out of the water and offered Ronnie a hand. She glared at him before taking it. "You know, this is war!"

"Bring it on. I'm ready." He pulled her out of the water.

"This isn't over. You'll pay for this," Ronnie swore and walked away from them.

Melanie chastised him, "That was mean, Billy. Why do you embarrass her like that?"

"You're right, Mel. I shouldn't have done that to her."

Billy winked at Teek. "It should have been you!" He picked Melanie up over his shoulder and jumped into the water with her. They splashed each other playfully.

Enjoying their antics, the native males picked up their females and jumped into the water, too. Everyone splashed each other.

"See that, Mel, even the natives know how to have fun," ribbed Billy.

Tanya leaned over the edge of the lagoon. "See what you started, Billy," she mentioned giddily.

"Yeah, so why don't you..."

Billy leaped up and grabbed Tanya by the waist. He pulled her in the water, too. Tanya floated to the surface with a big smile. Billy finished, "… join the party."

Tanya splashed him daintily. "Now I'm all wet," she complained.

"So, you'll dry off."

Billy climbed out of the water first and helped the girls out. He eyed Melanie coyly. "You know, Mel, I think you look better than Ronnie in a wet shirt."

"Why thank you, Billy. I didn't think you'd notice."

Tanya looked forgotten and looked away from them. Billy noticed and pulled her over to him. "You look delicious, too, Tanya,"

"Thanks, Billy. It's nice to be noticed once in a while." Billy put his arm around her and gave her a friendly hug.

After Teek and Mala climbed out of the water, Teek led Billy out of the cavern and stood on the rocks outside. Many natives across the beach were cooking, fishing and performing other domestic activities. Teek pointed to the natives and said, "Guttoo nam sitaba." He moved his arm like a snake and slapped at it with the other hand. His arm went limp. "Daba sitaba." Teek pointed again to his people. He hugged Billy who then understood.

"What's he saying?" asked Melanie.

"He's thanking us for killing the snakes. His people were able to come home."

Teek and Mala lay down on the flat slabs of rock next to the falls. Billy saw his sword lying in the sand nearby and retrieved it. As he returned to the rock, Melanie emerged from behind the waterfalls and stood by him.

"Mind if I join you, Billy?"

"Not at all. It's a good day for a little sun tan action," he remarked as he looked up at the afternoon suns.

"I like to bask in the sun and read books," Mel mentioned, "but I'm sure I could settle for just lying in the sun right now."

"Bask, huh? That's a big word for you," he teased.

"I told you I'm nineteen. Haven't you ever dated a woman with an IQ before?"

Billy chuckled at her. "No, I usually like them dumb. They don't argue with me every time I say something."

"Keep it up, Billy. You're digging a hole for yourself."

Billy lay down near Teek and Mala. Melanie sat nearby and gazed at him.

"Is something wrong?" asked Billy.

"No. Just admiring you."

"Why would you do that?"

"You're amazing."

"No, I'm not. I'm insane. You don't know what goes on inside my head."

Melanie nestled playfully against Billy's chest. She ran her hands across Billy's stomach. Billy tried to ignore her but she was tough to resist.

Mala noticed and imitated Melanie. She ran her fingers across Teek's chest. Teek smiled at her. He and Mala left them and went behind the waterfalls. Melanie giggled at them.

"What's so funny?" inquired Billy.

"I think Mala just learned how to turn her man on."

"And how is that?"

"Women have magic fingers that make their men feel good."

"Yeah, right."

"It's so easy, even a caveman can do it, but not Billy," she teased.

"Mel, shut up."

Melanie lay back and closed her eyes. She enjoyed having Billy's attention. Billy studied her shapely body and thought about the possibilities they might have. He kissed her forehead and lay back, too.

— X —

Tanya sat with Ronnie and John inside the cavern. "Don't be mad at Billy. He doesn't mean to be a pain in the ass," said Tanya.

"I know. It just comes natural to him," replied Ronnie.

"I think he acts like that to hide his inner feelings," she suggested.

"Tanya, how close are Billy and Mel?" Ronnie inquired suspiciously.

"I think they're closer than they should be."

"Why's that?"

"Mel is only seventeen."

"What?" exclaimed Ronnie.

"Yeah, she told Billy that she's nineteen."

"Oh, dear. That's not good."

"How old are you, Tanya?" asked John.

"I'm really eighteen. I didn't lie."

"Have they indulged in things?"

"You mean like sex?" asked Tanya.

"Yeah."

"Knowing Mel, I'm pretty sure they did, up on the ledge earlier."

"We have to talk to Billy about this," said Ronnie with a concerned tone in her voice.

"Maybe you should stay out of it. Under the circumstances, it may be a reasonable relationship," suggested John.

"Reasonable! She's a kid for gosh sake!"

"This isn't the civilized world anymore."

"It's not like there's guys around here our age either," Tanya reminded them defensively.

"That's not the point. He needs to know."

"I'll take care of it if you want. Just don't be mad at them."

"I'm not mad. It's just that it could cause other problems."

"I get it." Tanya left them and exited the cavern. She saw Billy and Melanie lying on the rocks. Billy was asleep but Melanie was awake.

"Hi, Tanya. Where ya' been?"

"Talking with Ronnie and John."

"What about?"

"You and Billy."

"And, again, what about?"

"It's time you told him how old you really are."

Melanie grew concerned and sat up. "He'd never forgive me," she whispered.

"It'll only get worse by waiting."

In the distant sky, the gryphons approached again. The natives screamed and shouted warnings. Everyone evacuated the beach, dispersing into the trees.

Melanie shook Billy repeatedly. "Billy, the bird creatures are coming again!"

"What's wrong now, Mel?" grumbled Billy as he sat up.

"The bird creatures are coming!" Tanya cried and fled behind the falls to the cavern.

Billy stood up and strapped on the scabbard. He drew his sword and waited patiently. Several of the native men emerged from the trees with their bows and quivers of arrows. They fired volley after volley at the attacking gryphons. Two of the gryphons fell to the ground wounded mortally. Other natives speared them until they were dead.

One of the gryphons attacked Billy and Melanie from behind. It knocked Billy to the ground and grabbed Melanie in its talons. Flapping its wings vigorously, it lifted her off the ground. "Billy, help me!" cried Melanie.

Billy scrambled to his feet and instinctively leaped onto the gryphon's rear talon. He jabbed relentlessly at its underbelly. The gryphon flew into the sky toward its lair in the mountains with Melanie in its clutches and Billy desperately clinging to its talon. Ronnie and John exited the cavern and were horrified when they saw the gryphon flee with Billy and Melanie.

Teek, Mala and Tanya appeared from the cavern. "Gora! Be gora!" shouted Teek angrily. A large hunting party of natives gathered with spears and bows.

"Why do all these creatures hunt Billy?" asked Ronnie frantically.

"It's just coincidence," John assured her. "He's in the wrong place at the wrong time."

"No, it's not. I didn't believe his story before but this is too much."

"We have to find a way to rescue them first. Then we'll deal with whether or not it's a coincidence."

The natives chanted and jogged away from them along the lake. "The natives are hunting the gryphons, too. I think we'll be joining them. They know the area better than we do," remarked John.

"Go back to the trucks. Tell Randy and Seamus what happened," Ronnie instructed Tanya.

Tanya was visibly shaken and asked, "Where are you going?"

"We're going after them."

"Please get them back."

"We'll do our best." John and Ronnie pursued the natives into the mountains.

— X —

Melanie cried hysterically as the gryphon's talon cut into her side.

"Hold on, Mel. I'll take care of this," Billy assured her.

"Please, Billy. Don't let me down."

Billy climbed on top of the rear talon and grabbed the gryphon's leg. He buried his sword into the gryphon's side several times. It shrieked and spiraled toward the ground.

"Hold on, Mel! We're going down."

The gryphon leveled off close to the ground and released Melanie. She tumbled across the ground in a waist high grassy field. Billy leaped from the talon and fell awkwardly. He writhed on the ground in pain. The injured gryphon flew off, shrieking.

"Billy, where are you?" she called out frantically.

Billy sat up in the tall grass and grumbled, "I'm here. Mel."

She rushed to him and cried, "Oh, Billy, you saved me again."

"We're not safe yet."

"What do you mean?"

"It's late in the day. We have no shelter or food. We're sitting ducks out here."

Melanie looked around the field suspiciously. "Where do we go now?" she asked.

"I figure we have to cross the mountain to get back to the lake," Billy said as he surveyed the area around them.

"And how do we do that?"

"You have two legs, don't you?"

Melanie looked at the mountain and then at Billy. "You're serious."

"Uh-huh. You have a better idea."

"I guess not." Melanie noticed two shapes galloping toward them and grabbed Billy's arm. "What are those things?" she asked nervously.

Billy stood up and looked across the field. He saw two hairy creatures racing toward them. As they drew closer, he saw that they were large wolves. "You've got to be kidding me," he muttered.

"What are they?" asked Melanie.

"You don't want to know." He studied the creatures, as they closed on them. "Now I've seen everything," he groaned.

"Can you stop them?"

"I guess we'll find out, won't we?"

"I'm scared, Billy."

"Welcome to the club." Billy drew his sword and ordered, "Stay right here, Mel, and I mean right here."

Billy rushed at the creatures. The first creature lunged at him. He stepped to the side and buried his sword into its chest. The creature yelped and rolled over dead. The second creature leaped at Billy. He pointed his sword out in front of him but the creature's momentum knocked him on his back. He lay motionless with the creature on top of him. He knew his sword pierced the creature's chest but dared not move. The creature gasped and died; its fangs just inches from Billy's throat. Drool dribbled from its mouth onto Billy's face.

Billy was terrified and closed his eyes tightly. He blocked the creature out of his mind and thought about sitting at home in front of the TV. Ironically, he imagined watching a movie about people changing into werewolves. Melanie was horrified. She waited for several minutes but neither Billy nor the creature moved.

"Billy," she said shakily.

"What?" he answered coldly.

"Are you alright?"

"Mel, look at me. Do I look alright?"

She approached him and was even more frightened at the sight of the creature. "It looks like a werewolf, Billy."

"No friggin'shit!" He pushed the creature off of him and stared at it. It had all the characteristics of a wolf but was elongated like a man. "It's a good thing they don't walk like men or maybe they do."

"What do you mean by that?" Melanie fretted.

"Wolfen – half men, half wolves. I saw the movie." He covered his face with both hands.

Melanie felt pity for him. He was scraped up badly with two gashes on his back. His face was covered with the wolfen saliva. She removed her shirt and cleaned the blood and saliva from his face. When Billy broke down and cried, she hugged him tightly. "It's okay, Billy. You did good."

"I have nightmares when I sleep. There are dinosaurs, giant spiders, alien soldiers and now werewolves. I'm a freaking nutcase."

"It's not you, Billy. It's this world."

"It's breaking me, Mel. It's breaking me bad." Melanie felt good that he finally let her into his world. "You're different than the others, Mel."

"I hope that's a good thing."

"You'd better believe it. I think I'm falling in love with you."

"Well, you couldn't have picked a more romantic time to say it," she joked.

Billy looked into her eyes as tears streamed down his cheeks. "I never thought I needed anyone else. Today I did and you were there for me. I'll never forget that."

"I told you, I'll always take care of you, if you let me."

Billy wiped the tears from his eyes and face. "I have to take care of you now. We're in a lot of trouble."

Melanie kissed his cheek. "I believe in you, Billy. You always make things better."

Billy stood up and regained his composure. "We've got to get moving. Those things probably travel in packs."

"Then the others are sure to be nearby."

Billy pulled his sword out of the dead werewolf and uttered despondently, "I'm afraid so." He looked at Melanie for a brief moment. She was so attractive in jeans and a lace bra but she looked so young.

"What's wrong? Do you want me to put my shirt back on?" she asked innocently.

"Tell me the truth," he requested. "How old are you?"

Her heart broke as she realized this could be the end of her bliss. "Do you really want to talk about this now?"

"Yes, I do." Billy took her by the hand and they walked toward the forest.

"I'm seventeen," she said, her voice quivering.

"Seventeen, huh."

"Uh, yeah."

"Why did you lie to me?"

"I wanted you to like me," she answered sheepishly

"And you think that your age was the only thing that mattered?"

"I think so."

"That's pretty shallow, Mel."

"I never thought of it that way. I'm sorry."

"Mel, you're a good person. I like you for that."

Melanie poured her heart out to him and said, "I don't want to just be a good person. I want to be your girl."

"But Mel, I'm twenty-four. That's going to cause problems."

Melanie became frustrated. "Look around you, Billy. We're not at home. There aren't other boys around here my age. I'm growing up faster than I ever dreamed. I'm not at parties with my friends like a normal seventeen-year-old. I'm here with you, hoping to live to see the next day."

"It's not just that. There's going to be some flak from the others about this."

"The difference between me and you, Billy, is that you don't need anyone. You can defend yourself. I can't. I need you. So regardless of what everyone else thinks, I have feelings for you. I don't care about them."

Billy considered her words. "You're absolutely right. Part of my mind is still in our world and part of it is here. Sometimes I can't differentiate between the two. I'm sorry about that and I'm trying to come to terms with it."

"I'm trying, too, Billy. Give me a break."

"Mel."

"Yes."

"Shut up," said Billy playfully. He kissed her, slowly at first, then more passionately.

"Then you're not mad at me?" she asked, hopeful.

"No."

"Your friends are."

"Don't worry about them. They're always mad at me."

They held hands and walked to the edge of the forest. Billy looked back across the field and saw a pack of wolfen racing toward them. "Come on, Mel! We've got to run."

They hurried through the forest and up the side of the mountain. The slope became rockier and steeper as they climbed higher. They discovered a large cave near the top of the mountain. Loud shrieks filled the air.

"Guess what, Mel?"

"Don't tell me. We found the gryphons' lair."

"Yes, we did. I've got an idea, though."

Melanie was confused by Billy's upbeat attitude. When they reached the cave, they hid near the entrance. "Are you going to tell me your idea or what?" The snarling of the wolfen startled them.

"This should be close enough," he announced.

"For what?"

Billy picked up a rock and threw it into the cave. "Hey, gryphons! Come out and play," he taunted.

"I should have known he'd do something like this," Melanie muttered to herself.

Billy picked up two more stones and fired them into the cave. He pulled Melanie behind the rocks alongside the cave. "Billy, what the hell are you doing?"

"Just watch. This is going to be beautiful."

The wolfen approached the cave as the gryphons emerged. Billy and Melanie retreated away from the cave and watched. "See that. They'll kill each other."

"Billy, you're a genius!"

They climbed the rocks until they found a narrow crevice in the mountainside. "Maybe we can hide out in here for the night," he suggested.

"I hope you know what you're doing."

"Trust me, Mel."

They squeezed through the gap in the rocks and maneuvered through the darkness. The sound of running water caught Billy's attention. "Hear that, Mel?"

"Yeah, water."

"That could be our ticket out of here."

Several wolfen snarled from behind them. "Oh, shit! This just became a one-way trip," complained Billy.

"Keep moving, Billy! They're gonna get to me before they get to you."

Billy pulled her along hastily. They scraped against the sharp sides of rocks in the walls of the crevice and stumbled on the uneven floor. "I think we're close to the source! Stay with me, Mel."

They stepped out of the crevice into a large cave, littered with feathers across the floor. The air reeked with bird excrement. Billy realized they were in the gryphons' lair. "Uh-oh. This isn't where we want to be," he uttered.

"Billy, this isn't what I think it is, is it?"

"Yeah, it's the gryphons' cave."

"Now what do we do?"

"We keep going."

The rear area of the cave glowed with a dull light. "What's the light from?" Melanie asked.

"I'm not sure. Probably the minerals in the rock."

As they approached it, they noticed a dozen large eggs the size of beer kegs in the dim light. "I wonder if there's radium in the shells of the eggs that make them glow. The gryphons would have to ingest it somehow," Billy pondered aloud.

Melanie approached one of the eggs. "Whatever you do, Mel, don't disturb the eggs," he warned her.

"Don't worry. I won't."

They stepped around the eggs and discovered the stream passing through the rear of the cave. "There it is: our ticket out of here," said Billy confidently. Melanie was bewildered as to how the stream would benefit them.

One of the wolfen entered the cave from the crevice. It howled and alerted the others when it spotted them. Melanie looked back at the creature and panicked. She tripped and her arm smashed through the shell of an egg. "Oh, no! Help me, Billy!" she cried out.

Billy helped her up. Before she could pull her arm out, a baby gryphon inside the egg gripped her arm in its beak and squealed loudly. "Billy, it's got me!" screamed Melanie.

Billy kicked in the side of the shell and stomped on the baby gryphon until it was dead. "Damn it, Mel. I told you…"

"I know. I'm sorry."

Outside the cave, the fighting stopped and the gryphons returned to the cave. The wolfen entered the cave from the crevice and clumsily broke several eggs in their haste to reach Billy and Melanie.

Billy looked back and saw the wolfen walk upright toward them. "Holy shit!" he exclaimed. "They do walk like men."

A gryphon returned to the rear of the cave and snatched up the unsuspecting wolfen from behind, snapping its neck. It tossed the dead creature against the wall and pursued them. The remainder of the gryphons returned and stalked them, too.

When they reached the stream, Billy placed his arms around Melanie and jumped into the frigid water. When they surfaced, they waded downstream in a strong current. The stream ran through an underground cave in the mountain with only a foot of space between the surface of the water and the roof of the cave.

"I'm scared, Billy. Don't let me drown in here," sobbed Melanie.

"Just keep your head above water and don't lose your cool."

"I'm trying, Billy, but it's not easy."

The ceiling sloped lower until they could barely breathe. "Take a deep breath. We're going under," instructed Billy. Melanie breathed deeply and followed Billy underwater. Billy prayed that the stream took them someplace safe. He kept Melanie close to him and swam with the current. They were whisked from the stream into a larger underground river, which flowed significantly faster. When they surfaced, they found themselves in another cave.

Melanie choked as she struggled to catch her breath. Billy swam toward the rocky banks of the river with his arm wrapped tightly around her waist. She was limp in his arms and that worried him. "Come on, Mel. You have to try," he urged.

"I can't move, Billy. I'm so cold."

Billy felt a second wind as he realized at this point that they would either sink together or swim. He struggled with his left arm and his legs to push toward the bank. When he finally felt the bottom of the river with his feet, he pushed himself toward the rocks and shoved Melanie out of the water. He struggled to pull himself out with hands that were numb from the cold water. Every muscle in his body ached as he crawled onto the rocks. Melanie curled up like a child and shivered.

Billy looked downstream and saw a glimmer of light. He lifted Melanie up and carried her. As he staggered forward, his muscles cramped and felt like they would explode. He took a dozen steps and set her down. When he fell to his knees, he felt a warm breeze against his face. "Fresh air! We must be close to the entrance of the cave," he shouted excitedly and pulled Melanie to her feet. "We're almost there, Mel. Come on, Honey," he urged her.

When they emerged from the cave, they were on a ledge high above a valley. The river exited the mountain and became raging rapids. Further downstream, it became a magnificent waterfall to the bottom of the valley where it merged into a slow-moving river. Billy set Melanie down on the ledge. He collapsed on the ground next to her and passed out from sheer exhaustion.

Later that evening, he awoke and gazed out at the beautiful valley. Two moons shone brightly above them. Their rays illuminated the entire river valley below. Billy felt safe, at least for the night. He nestled against a broken log with Melanie tucked against his chest. He rubbed her back and arms gently to build up her body heat. Melanie awoke and gazed innocently into his eyes. "Are we still alive?" she asked.

"Of course, we are."

Mel looked up at the stars and the moon. "No, we're not. You're an angel."

"No," said Billy. "It's really me."

"I can't believe we made it out of there like that. How did you know?"

"Strangely enough, I think I'm destined for other things. I have to survive."

"Well, I'm becoming a believer. You keep surprising me with new and daring escapes."

"How do you feel now?"

"Much better. It's nice out here, even a little romantic."

Billy rolled on top of her and kissed her passionately. After everything they went through, Billy realized that Melanie was right. She wasn't a kid anymore. It was time he treated her like an adult. They made love until early in the morning and then slept for several hours.

— ⧖ —

John and Ronnie stood by the river, unaware they were across from the mountain where Billy and Melanie slept. Staring up at the night sky, John placed his arm around Ronnie. "Do you think there's a chance they're alive?" asked Ronnie.

"Honestly, no."

"I didn't think so," she responded sadly.

"However, Billy has an uncanny knack for survival," John pointed out. "I'd hate to underestimate him."

"But how could they possibly survive this?"

"I really don't know. I won't accept it until I see something to convince me otherwise."

"Thanks, John. I needed to hear that."

"Let's get some sleep. Tomorrow will hold the answer." They lay down among the native hunting party and slept.

— X —

Ruger watched the battle between his creatures and an army of warriors led by opposing wizards. "Time is running out. This stalemate does me no good. I must summon stronger forces," Ruger fretted. Suddenly, he felt distracted. He rubbed his eyes and walked away from the window. He picked the silver chest off of the floor and set it on the table. The battered chest billowed white smoke in the air and filled a larger portion of the chamber than normal. "What treachery is this? Pirocles, where are you?" There was no answer. Ruger observed the smoke and waited for images to form.

Billy awoke first and gazed out over the river valley. He could feel Ruger searching for him. There was a bond between them and he was learning to test it. He stood up and projected his thoughts over the valley. *Ruger, you've failed again. You and I have business to settle. I see I'll have to come to you since you won't come to me.*

Ruger became enraged by the image and Billy's words. He threw the chest at the stairwell. It clanked repeatedly as it tumbled down the stone steps. He raised his arms and shouted an incantation in anger. When he finished, he uttered sadistically, "You have not yet begun to feel my wrath, boy. You will not leave that mountain alive." His eyes were fixated on the remnants of the fading smoke.

Billy knew that Ruger was running out of tricks. He had the advantage and knew that he needed to hold out just a little longer. His thoughts were interrupted when he heard growling from down the mountainside. "Oh, not already!" he grumbled.

Billy shook Melanie calmly until she awoke. "You've got to get up, Mel. We have company."

Melanie's eyes opened wide. "Who?" she asked nervously.

"The wolfen are back."

She scurried to her feet in fear. "Where?"

"In the forest below."

"What are we going to do, Billy? We're trapped."

Billy massaged her shoulders and said confidently, "Don't worry, I'll figure something out."

Billy studied a fallen tree that stretched out over the rapids. He looked back at the cave and realized that route wasn't an option. Melanie noticed a group of people camping down on the far riverbank. "Billy, look at those people down there."

Billy saw the encampment but then looked upstream where a large pack of wolfen approached the group. "Damn, we have to warn them!" he exclaimed.

Billy jumped up and down and shouted, "Hey! Hey down there!"

Ronnie studied the mountainside across the river for any sign that the gryphons might nest up there. Teek stood next to her and pointed to the top. He was angry and hollered angrily, "Gora. Gora."

Ronnie understood that he was referring to the gryphons. "Yes, Teek. Gora." Then Ronnie noticed someone jumping up and down near the top of the mountain. "Look!" she exclaimed, pointing at Billy. Teek became excited and pointed as well.

John joined them and asked, "What's so interesting?"

"Someone's up there! Maybe it's Billy."

John stared at the figure on the mountain. His eyes widened with surprise. "If I didn't know better, I'd swear that is Billy." John waved back excitedly.

Billy pointed upstream frantically. The three of them looked in that direction but saw nothing. Teek sensed the danger, though, and yelled to his men, "Tonga! Snee tonga!" The natives grabbed their weapons and grouped together. They met with Teek privately.

Ronnie and John stared at Billy on the mountain in astonishment. "That lucky son-of-a-bitch! How does he keep doing that?" Ronnie uttered.

"I'd love to find out."

Six of Teek's archers disappeared in the forest. The others formed a line, armed with spears and axes.

Billy stepped onto the log and jumped up and down to test its strength. It teetered precariously. He pulled up a sizeable piece of bark from the log and held it like a shield. After he practiced deflecting an attacker, he gave up the idea and set the bark down on the log. Suddenly, a wolfen leaped out of the trees.

"Billy, look out!" screamed Melanie.

"I got him, Mel." Billy drew his sword and sparred with the wolfen. It stood up on its hind legs and swatted at him with its long arms. "Get on the log, Mel, and don't fall in," he ordered as he retreated toward her. Melanie promptly obeyed.

Billy backed onto the log, as the creature stalked him. The log teetered dangerously close to the water. Billy knelt down and jabbed at the creature's thigh. He pierced it and twisted the sword. The creature howled in pain and retreated. Billy then stepped forward and took a full stroke with his sword at its knee. He knocked the creature into the water with the sword's impact. The wolfen smashed against the first rock and was killed instantly.

Billy stepped off the log onto solid ground and surveyed the area. "Where are you going, Billy? They'll kill you."

"Stay put, Mel."

Billy studied the encampment down by the river. He recognized the natives by their dress. "Mel, that's Teek and his natives! I'll bet Ronnie and John are with them, too."

"A lot of good that does us up here."

"Just hang in there, Mel. We'll be out of here soon."

"Yeah, one way or another," she muttered, dejected.

They watched the wolfen charge at their friends on the banks of the river. "Looks like the battle's begun," said Billy.

— **X** —

John and Ronnie positioned themselves with their swords drawn. Teek's eight warriors held their spears up, poised for battle. Fourteen wolfen split into two groups and circled them.

"They can think!" exclaimed John.

"They can die, too. Let's get them," declared Ronnie confidently.

"Stay put. Teek has a plan."

Ronnie heeded his advice and watched as Teek organized his people into a circle. The wolfen tried to goad them out of the circle. "I can bait one of them closer," Ronnie suggested.

"Don't do anything stupid," warned John.

Ronnie stepped toward one of the creatures and shouted at it. She stomped her foot and spat at it. The creature was enraged but held its ground.

"Please be careful. I don't want you to get hurt," cautioned John.

"I know what I'm doing."

"You sound like Billy."

"That was uncalled for, John." She stuck her sword in the ground and held her arms out mockingly. The creature snarled and charged at her. Ronnie quickly grabbed the sword and stabbed the creature in the chest. She placed her foot against its body and pulled the sword from it. When the wolfen fell to its knees, she struck again and lopped off its head. The body and head fell at her feet. The other wolfen were infuriated.

"See that. They can be intimidated, John."

"You proved your point. Now stay put."

Ronnie picked up the head and spat on it. She threw it at the feet of another wolfen. The creature howled and rushed at Ronnie. She struck at it with her sword but it blocked her stroke with its arm. The sword snapped the arm in half but the creature's momentum carried it into her. The two tumbled to the ground.

"Oh, Lord!" bellowed John.

The wolfen snapped at Ronnie rabidly but she shoved the hilt of her sword in its mouth. John stabbed the wolfen from behind and resumed his position.

Ronnie pushed the dead wolfen off and scurried to her feet. "Thanks, John," she said appreciatively. "I didn't expect that."

"Don't do that again."

"Eleven against twelve. Those are better odds" remarked Ronnie.

"Forget odds. We have to survive."

The wolfen rushed the circle. Teek's men broke ranks and fought back. After intense fighting, most of the natives were slaughtered. Ronnie, John, Teek and one other native remained and were surrounded by eight wolfen.

"How do you like these odds?" asked John sarcastically.

"They suck."

Four arrows whizzed out of the forest and struck three of the wolfen with lethal accuracy. The remaining wolfen held their ground and searched for the source of the arrows.

"Outstanding marksmanship," commented Ronnie.

"Please stay put, otherwise you'll only get in the way."

Ronnie disregarded John's advice and took advantage of the distraction. She rushed at the nearest creature and sliced its throat. "No one listens around here," groaned John.

Ronnie charged at another wolfen and struck at its neck. The creature deflected her stroke and punched her in the face. She fell backward as blood streamed from her nose. She got up and felt the blood from her nose. "You rotten son-of-a-bitch!" she shouted.

Ronnie faked a stroke to the side of the torso and came up through the creature's chin with the blade. She punched it three times in the face and pulled the sword out of its head. In one smooth turn, she spun and decapitated the creature's head.

"Wouldn't it be easier if you just stayed put?" asked John.

Ronnie thought briefly and then replied, "Nah."

Teek battled one of the wolfen and was knocked to the ground. Three wolfen lunged at him but were sprayed with a volley of arrows before they reached him. Teek rolled out of the way as the creatures dropped to the ground dead. The archers marched out of the forest and cut down the last few wolfen with another volley.

Ronnie looked up on the mountain and saw ten wolfen stalking Billy. "John, look! They're in trouble," she said, panicked.

"I'm afraid there's nothing we can do about it from down here," he answered sadly.

Ronnie's eyes welled up with tears. "It's not fair. After all this, they can't die up there."

Teek joined them and pointed up at Billy. He said sadly, "Tonga. Biwee snee tonga."

"Yes, Teek. We hope Billy snees the tonga," John replied, hopeful.

— ⧗ —

Melanie waited nervously at the end of the log. She looked out over the water and cried, "We're trapped, Billy!"

"Nonsense! I have a plan." Billy retreated onto the log and sparred with one of the wolfen.

"I can hardly wait for this one," she groaned.

Two of the wolfen perched on the rocks near the water's edge and swiped at Billy.

"Billy, they're getting impatient," Melanie warned frantically.

"I see that, Mel. Pick up that piece of bark behind you."

Melanie looked at it and fretted. "For what?"

"Mel, pick up the damn bark! We need it."

"Don't holler at me."

"Then listen to me, damn it! You want to live, don't you?"

Melanie picked it up and held it like a shield. "Now what?"

"Face the water."

Melanie glanced at the water and back at Billy. She pleaded, "No, Billy. We're not going to..."

Billy stowed his sword and reached around Melanie. He grabbed both sides of the bark. The log teetered as the wolfen pursued them.

"I love you, Mel," blurted Billy as he pushed off the log into the water with Melanie and the bark beneath him. Melanie was terrified and screamed. She buried her head down against the bark and cried. They accelerated on the rapids and skipped off rocks.

Four wolfen fell from the log as it broke loose in the water. They were swept away by the fast-moving current and dashed against the rocks.

"Hold on, Mel! Here comes the big one," Billy warned as they approached the waterfalls.

"You asshole, Billy!" screamed Melanie.

The bark skipped off a rock and shot high into the air where the water dropped straight down into the river. They flipped over and separated while in freefall.

Everyone on the riverbank watched in awe as Billy and Melanie were airborne coming off the top of the falls. "Did you see what they just did, Ronnie?" exclaimed John in amazement.

"I sure as hell did! Let's go get them."

They watched eagerly for the location of the splashes while they removed their boots and clothes. Teek swam with Ronnie and John to rescue them.

Billy and Melanie hit the water with mammoth splashes and disappeared. Ronnie went underwater and found Melanie floating along the bottom unconscious. She quickly pulled her to the surface. "I got Mel," announced Ronnie.

"I can't find Billy," replied John.

"Keep looking."

Teek helped Ronnie pull Melanie to the bank of the river.

Billy popped up to the surface a short distance away, gasping heavily. "Whoa! What a rush?" he shouted.

John put his arm around Billy. "Hold on to me. I'll help you ashore."

"Thanks, John."

Ronnie and Teek pulled Melanie ashore and laid her down. Ronnie immediately gave her CPR. After three repetitions, Melanie coughed and burst into tears.

"You're safe now," Ronnie assured her.

"Ronnie, he's crazy!" cried Mel. "He's a friggin' nut!"

"I know, Mel. You'll get used to him."

"He has a death wish!"

Ronnie hugged her and consoled her. "No, he's just nuts," she explained.

John escorted Billy out of the water. Billy saw Melanie with Ronnie and hurried over to them. "Mel, wasn't that awesome?" he asked excitedly and extended his arms to hug her.

"Don't come near me, you maniac!" Mel cried. She stormed away and stood alone by the edge of the river.

Ronnie covered her mouth to hide her laughter. John chuckled and looked the other way as well. Billy put his hands on his hips and looked baffled. "I don't get it. This was like the greatest escape ever."

"Billy, she's only seventeen," chastised Ronnie.

"No kidding."

"You knew!"

"Yeah, she told me."

"And you were fine with that?"

"Well, yeah."

"That's sick."

Ronnie went to Melanie and comforted her.

John laughed harder. "Billy, you are a piece of work," he kidded.

"Thanks, John. Fortunately, I'm alive to laugh about it."

"Bi-wee snee Gora?" asked Teek.

Billy held up four fingers and explained, "Four Gora but twelve eggs."

Billy drew twelve lines in the sand and repeated, "Twelve eggs."

Teek understood. He pulled Billy by the arm and pointed in the direction of the lake.

"Teek wants to go home," explained John.

"I see you're learning his language well," replied Billy.

"It wasn't hard."

John put his hand on Billy's shoulder in friendship and they marched back to the lake with Teek and his remaining warriors. Ronnie and Melanie lagged behind the men and talked about Melanie's escapade with Billy. They arrived at the lake at nightfall and entered the quiet native camp. Randy and Seamus sat by a small fire on the beach. Tanya slept on a fur pelt nearby on the flat rock.

Ronnie and Melanie were the first to arrive. "Wake up, deadbeats! We're back," shouted Ronnie. Randy awoke and was relieved to see them.

Tanya saw Melanie and shouted excitedly, "Mel, you're alive!" She rushed to Mel and hugged her.

"Yeah, no thanks to that psycho, Billy."

The girls laughed hysterically. "What did he do this time?" asked Randy.

"He tried to kill me and not just once!"

"Come on," said Randy, surprised by Mel's emotional outburst. "He wouldn't do that."

"You wouldn't believe the stunt he pulled this time," said Ronnie giddily.

Teek's men emerged from the woods and the natives cheered them. Billy and John appeared behind them. Randy was elated when she saw Billy and rushed to him. "I am so glad to see you alive. What the hell did you do now?"

"You wouldn't believe it, Randy. I have you and Ronnie both beat in the stunt department."

"No way!"

John nodded his head and replied, "I'm afraid he did."

"This I've gotta' hear."

"Ask Mel. I think she has a better version of it than I do," Billy suggested proudly.

"Billy, she's gonna kill you. Whatever you did, she is hot about it."

"I know, but we really had no other choice." Billy walked away from them and entered the cavern alone. He went to a quiet corner in the back and settled down on the stone floor. It didn't matter how hard the ground was, he felt safe there.

Ronnie and Randy sat with Melanie by the fire and watched the natives celebrate. Everyone ate food prepared by the native women in celebration of their victories over the snakes, gryphons and wolfen as well as the safe return of Teek and his surviving warriors. Some women mourned the loss of their mates and sons but were honored by the other tribesmen for their sacrifice. Teek carried an animal skin sack around the group. Each of his people drank from it and cheered.

"Looks like they're getting loaded," commented Ronnie.

"Yeah, and it looks like fun," replied Randy.

Seamus called out, "Hey, Teek" and motioned to him for a drink. Teek joined them and handed Seamus the sack. He took a swig and passed it around to the others. Ronnie took a healthy swig and offered some of the concoction to Melanie and Tanya.

"No thanks," said Tanya. "I don't drink."

"I know, I'm too young," complained Melanie.

"After surviving that jump with Billy, you can drink as much as you like," declared Ronnie.

Melanie's eyes lit up with joy. She took a long swig. "Ooh, baby! I like it." She passed the sack back to Teek and said politely, "Thank you, Teek." Teek smiled and left them.

"So how high was this ledge? I don't believe it was near the top of a mountain," asked Randy.

"I kid you not. We were at least three hundred feet up," replied Melanie.

Ronnie affirmed, "It was at least that."

"Billy pushed me into the water on a big piece of bark. It was like riding a surfboard. We bounced off every stinking rock in the rapids."

"So, it wasn't a waterfall. It was rapids."

"No, there was a waterfall, too."

John acknowledged, "It was quite impressive."

Melanie felt tipsy but continued, "And we shot off the top of the waterfalls into the air. And we … And we … Oh, my head is spinning."

"Take your time, Mel. We're listening," said Ronnie calmly.

Melanie felt the effects of the drink and blurted, "And we made love under the moonlight. It was wonderful."

"Mel! Where the hell did that come from?" Randy exclaimed with a stunned expression.

"He's such a good lover. We made love in the cavern, too, that first day."

Randy looked at Ronnie in disbelief. "Does he know she's …?"

"Yeah, he does."

"That's just wrong."

"No Randy, it was good. Have you ever made love to Billy before?"

"What the hell, Mel? You've had enough for one night. Go get some sleep?"

"I miss Billy."

"I think you should stay away from Billy."

"I know but he's so warm and cuddly."

Ronnie whispered to Randy, "You didn't answer her question."

"Shut your yap and don't start any trouble."

"What's that?" asked Seamus.

"Nothing. Ronnie's just being a bitch."

"It doesn't take much to push Randy's buttons," said Ronnie playfully. She looked back and Melanie was gone. "Where's Mel? She sure disappeared in a hurry."

"We really ought to stop this," urged Randy.

"Why?" asked John.

Randy stood up and stammered, "Because I think …Wow, my head is spinning, too."

"Why don't you sit down? Everything's gonna be just fine," Seamus assured her.

— 𝕏 —

Melanie searched for Billy around the cavern. She picked up a fur pelt from a pile and carried it with her. When she found Billy, he was still awake. She covered him with the pelt and slid underneath. She felt good against his warm body. "Can I talk to you, Billy?"

"I guess so."

"Thanks for saving me."

"You're welcome."

"I'm sorry for getting mad at you. It's just that I was so frightened."

"I'm sorry for getting you into this mess."

"It's not your fault."

"Yes, it is. Maybe it would be better if you stayed away from me for your own safety, especially if you think I have a death wish."

"Honest, Billy, I didn't mean that. I told you that if you protect me, I'll take care of you. If that means staying at the Post Office, I'll do it."

Billy didn't respond. He turned away from her and went to sleep. Melanie became teary-eyed and cried herself to sleep.

— 𝕏 —

Ruger entered Diomedes' cavern and stood in front of her cauldron. He searched for her but didn't see her. "Diomedes, are you here?"

Her voice roared from the back of the cave. She stormed to the cauldron in front of him. "You failed again, you inferior, pathetic vermin!"

"I know you're upset, Diomedes, but this is no ordinary man."

"Why do you think he's coming to kill us, you fool?"

"I can take care of him, I swear."

Diomedes clapped her claws together and a bright flash blinded Ruger. Red smoke emerged from the cauldron and engulfed him.

"No, Diomedes! Give me another chance," pleaded Ruger.

"You had your chance. The next time it will be your life."

"But I sent the gryphons; the wolfen; the snakes; he's defeated every one of them." The smoke cleared and Ruger was grossly disfigured. "How could you do this to me?" he cried.

"I can do worse. Now get out of my sight!" Ruger cowered and left the cavern.

— X —

The next morning, Billy sat alone on the flat rock and stared out over the water. He felt as though he had an unholy bond with Ruger that started when their eyes met in the city and grew when he deflected the spell back at the two wizards. He now understood the link with him and Ruger was too obsessed to realize that. He knew something terrible happened to Ruger and it would be a while before Ruger could mount another attempt on his life.

Billy's friends emerged from behind the waterfalls and sat next to him. "Billy, we have to talk," Randy informed him.

"We do?"

"Yes, we do."

"I see. And what about?"

"We're concerned about the constant attacks from all these creatures."

"I can understand why."

"No, you can't. We think they're targeting you."

Billy continued to stare at the water, unmoved by their concerns. "And why would you think that?" he asked cynically.

"Remember when we defeated those creatures in the city?"

"Uh-huh."

"Remember what that cloaked weirdo said to you?"

"No. Refresh my memory," Billy humored her.

"Wherever you go on this planet, my creatures will be waiting to kill you."

Seamus added, "There's something else." Billy still acted disinterested as he looked out over the water. "Many of your actions, while brave, border suicide. We care about you and prefer that you stay alive."

Billy considered Seamus' words and responded, "In a strange sort of way, I feel as though dying would give me peace. However, I do plan on staying alive."

Randy became annoyed with him. "You had your heart broken and you still feel the pain. Imagine how that young girl, who worships you by the way, will feel if you get your ass killed."

"So, Randy, what should I do?" Billy inquired callously.

"For starters, don't be so damn impulsive. Ronnie tells me that you and Melanie could have died in that stunt you pulled coming over the falls."

Billy stood up and faced her. He noticed the others in the background and responded arrogantly, "What do you call your stunt on the spider or Ronnie's stunt on the dinosaur? Tell me that was rational."

"I call it saving a friend's life at a very high risk. Next time I won't bother."

"Well, I did it to save Melanie's life. If I was suicidal, I'd have fought those creatures to the end on the mountain."

Randy turned away but Billy grabbed her arm. "You all have different ways of dealing with pain. I've only had mine a short while and I haven't found a way to deal with it yet."

Melanie stepped forward and reminded him, "Yes, you have but you choose to ignore me."

"But, Mel, you don't know what love is. You're a kid."

Melanie grew angry with him. "You want to know about love! Love is about trusting your life in the hands of someone else at all costs even if it scares the crap out of you. It's about working with someone to minimize their pain, not increase it." Tears rolled down her cheeks as she stared sadly at him.

Billy looked at them and recalled each one's heroic deeds. "I'm sorry for all the grief I've caused everyone. I thought I was helping, not hurting everyone." He hugged Melanie and continued, "I never meant to hurt you. You're ..."

Melanie waited for him to finish but Billy couldn't say what he felt.

John broke the tension and asked, "How can we put an end to these attacks, Billy?"

"We don't have to. They're done for a while." They looked at him suspiciously.

"How do you know this?" asked Ronnie.

"Something happened in the city that day when I encountered the wizard. Somehow a connection formed between us. I know when he's up to something."

"So now it's a wizard," taunted Randy.

Billy replied straight-faced, "Yes and his name is Ruger. I'm destined to slay him and a cohort sometime in the future. Unfortunately, he is determined to kill me first."

"That sounds pretty amazing. It's also hard to believe," remarked John.

"You'll see. Things will be calm for a while. It seems that Ruger has bigger problems right now than me."

"What happens when they come after you again?" inquired Melanie.

"I guess we'll just have to wait and see." Billy looked at her and thought about what a beautiful person she is. "Mel."

She lowered her head and replied sadly, "I know, shut up."

"No, come here."

Melanie went to him. He put his arm around her waist and said, "Let's give it a try, for real this time."

"Do you really mean it?" she said excitedly.

"Yes. No duress. No chases. Just an honest to goodness relationship."

"You got it, Brock!" They left the beach holding hands and ascended the embankment together.

"I guess that solves everything," quipped Ronnie.

"Not quite everything," John said coyly. They followed Billy's lead.

"I guess that just leaves the three of us," commented Tanya.

"Maybe we can find someone for you, Tanya," said Seamus.

"I'm not worried about it."

"Smart girl. Men are way too much trouble," replied Randy resolutely.

Seamus looked surprised by her remark. Randy and Tanya high-fived each other over Randy's remark and laughed.

"Come on, you two," Randy ordered them. "Let's go find something to do before Billy gets us into any more trouble."

Seamus remarked giddily, "That won't take long."